A Secret Elixir

My Lady's Potions, Book 4

Katherine Lyons

ARE YOU SIGNED UP FOR DRAGONBLADE'S BLOG?

You'll get the latest news and information on exclusive giveaways, exclusive excerpts, coming releases, sales, free books, cover reveals and more.

Check out our complete list of authors, too!

No spam, no junk. That's a promise!

Sign Up Here

www.dragonbladepublishing.com

Dearest Reader;

Thank you for your support of a small press. At Dragonblade Publishing, we strive to bring you the highest quality Historical Romance from some of the best authors in the business. Without your support, there is no 'us', so we sincerely hope you adore these stories and find some new favorite authors along the way.

Happy Reading!

CEO, Dragonblade Publishing

Additional Dragonblade books by
Author Katherine Lyons

My Lady's Potions Series
The Love Potion (Book 1)
The Truth Serum (Book 2)
An Alluring Brew (Book 3)
A Secret Elixir (Book 4)

Rogues Gambit Series
Rules for a Fake Fiancé (Book 1)
Rules for a Bastard Lord (Book 2)
Rules for a Wicked Wager (Book 3)

Prologue

THE FIRST BABY Janelle Caddick helped birth was a calf in the field next to the witch woman's cottage. The woman's name was Mrs. Sundy, though no one knew of a Mr. Sundy, and Janelle was only there because she had a toothache. Janelle's father and brother might go to a doctor from London for such a thing, but Janelle was only ten and a girl, so Nanny took her to Mrs. Sundy. The tooth was pulled with the help of a string and a kitten, the feline being the distraction. But what really caught Janelle's attention was the mournful call of the cow that was Mrs. Sundy's only companion and source of income.

"Why does he sound so sad?" the young Janelle asked.

"*She* sounds sad," Mrs. Sundy said, "because she's bringing a baby into the world."

"But that's a happy thing," Janelle said.

"Yes," Mrs. Sundy agreed in a somber tone. "That's exactly what men say."

That was the first time she'd heard that what men say and what women say might be different. Even more, Mrs. Sundy's tone implied there was a vast difference between what men considered happy and what women did.

"Would you like to help?" Mrs. Sundy asked.

Nanny objected immediately. "She's the baron's daughter. She'll be a fine lady one day—"

"Then she'll need to know how things come into this world. It's a happy thing, after all."

At ten years old, she hadn't understood the undercurrents in the words between Nanny and Mrs. Sundy. She couldn't possibly comprehend that for many men, babies—be they human or cattle—were born in a different place. Out of sight, out of mind until someone informed them of the happy event.

"I want to see!" she declared, and at ten years old, she was stubborn enough to make it happen, at least with her nanny. No amount of stubbornness with her father made the least bit of difference.

Mrs. Sundy took her out back where the cow labored. There was no one else to help except herself and Nanny, and so Janelle brought linens, a bucket of water, and a sponge while Mrs. Sundy soothed her aging cow Hygieia. What followed took hours. It was backbreaking, sweaty work. Not for herself, of course, but for poor Hygieia because the baby did not want to come out. Worse, it was messy, smelled strange, and required physical strength from all three humans.

Mrs. Sundy needed to move the calf around inside Hygieia's body. Nanny had to hold down the cow while Mrs. Sundy worked. And Janelle ran back and forth, doing what she was told, when she was told, as if the world depended upon it.

And indeed, during that hour, three worlds did depend upon it. It was Hygieia and her calf's life. It was also Mrs. Sundy's livelihood. Three souls, three worlds, and one not yet born.

The calf took its time and Nanny wanted to leave, but Janelle refused to go. She would not abandon the task half done. And though she was the child and Nanny the adult, some things remained undeniable. She was the mistress, Nanny was the servant, and so they stayed while Janelle imagined her body compressed with every contraction in Hygieia's body.

And then it happened.

Forefeet first and head while Hygieia moaned a low cry of distress. In truth, once the calf was in the correct position, this was a relatively easy birth. Later, Janelle would learn about chains and handles and any of a dozen different ways to help a calf come into this world. But at that moment, all she knew was how it felt to measure time by contractions and the moan of a cow.

Once the calf's head appeared, Janelle wanted to rush to pull the calf out, but Mrs. Sundy stopped her.

"Everything in God's time," the woman said.

God's time took even longer. Hygieia was an old mother who tired easily. She needed rest before facing a newborn. It took another hour before all was said and done. When the calf finally greeted the afternoon sun, Janelle was ready with a sponge and bucket to wash the newborn off, but again she was held back. She watched in shock while Hygieia struggled to her feet and tended to her child with her large, rough tongue.

"It's important for mother and baby to do this," Mrs. Sundy said. "We are here to help only if needed."

Fifteen minutes later, the calf was up on all four feet and nursing. Then it was Janelle's turn to work. She cleaned the afterbirth and the straw. She washed Hygieia who didn't notice anything except her child. And she stood aside, flush with a new kind of happiness, one that mixed hard work with God's miracle.

"A job well done," Nanny said.

"Aye," agreed Mrs. Sundy.

It took a moment for Janelle to realize they didn't mean what they'd done, but referred to Hygieia and God. After all, it was the cow who had expelled the calf, and God who had created it in the first place. But it was they who stood by in joy, who helped where needed, and who felt the world settle into a new order once the full task—especially the clean-up—was complete.

"Would you like to name the calf?" Mrs. Sundy asked.

Janelle nodded, pleased with the honor. Lots of words floated through her mind. Indeed, she recognized the name Hygieia as the Greek goddess of health, and the calf should have something equally exalted. But the word that came out was nothing so elevated.

"Happy," she blurted. "The calf should be named Happy."

It was a simplistic word for what she meant. She now knew

that what men called "happy" was nothing like the complicated, difficult work of what women knew. Even in an easy birth, there had been sweat and labor. And so this calf was named Happy because she now understood that something so lighthearted still required effort.

"A good name," Mrs. Sundy said.

Nanny, however, didn't comment. Her attention was on the time, which was now well past tea, and on Janelle's dirty hands and face, not to mention the stains on her dress. "What will the master say?" she moaned as she pulled Janelle to the cart they'd used to travel here. They both knew that her father prized teatime with his children.

"It doesn't matter," Janelle said. "He'll spend most of the time quizzing Alex anyway." Alexander was Janelle's younger brother and her father's only heir. He carried the weight of her father's expectations which included mastery of several subjects of which the boy had absolutely no interest.

"It does matter," Nanny said as she whipped the old horse into motion. They jolted along the road at a bruising clip. Once home, they rushed inside to quickly change clothes, wipe off what dirt remained, and tie a ribbon around Janelle errant locks before dashing as fast as possible to the parlor. Just before entering, Nanny stopped her, they both took a breath to compose themselves, then they slipped into the room as if her father were too blind to see their entrance.

As expected, father was quizzing her brother on Latin declensions. At this point, Janelle knew them better than Alex did. But she didn't know the advanced mathematics that he'd been learning while she was helping Hygieia. She tried to slink into place beside her brother, but of course that wasn't possible. Eventually, her father turned his hard glare to her.

"Why were you tardy?" he asked, his tone heavy.

Unable to contain her excitement, she blurted out her answer. "I helped birth a baby calf! It was the most amazing thing. It took hours and hours, and Mrs. Sundy had to help. The calf was in the wrong position. Well, not exactly. The head was tilted back like this, but the rest was in the right place."

She was about to say more, but when she twisted her head to demonstrate, the butler's face came into view. He was a London butler brought down to Devon because of his advancing years. He was fond of saying that he was too old to manage an active London establishment, but here in the country, he brought much needed polish to the slower pace.

His name was Sambell, and he clearly didn't approve of what she was saying. Indeed, he seemed downright shocked by it. Her words slowed to a stop as she twisted back around to judge her father's expression.

Papa's brows were drawn down and his lower lip pursed. It was how he appeared when Alex failed the most basic Latin declensions.

Trying to recover, she stammered out something that wasn't at all important. "I...um...I was there because my tooth hurt." She pressed her hand to her cheek. "It's better now."

Her father's gaze leaped to Nanny's. "The birth of a cow?" he asked, his voice icy. "Is that an appropriate experience for the daughter of a baron?"

Oh dear. Her father only took that tone when he was very angry. It was another year before she understood exactly how much her education—or lack thereof—depended upon what he thought was appropriate knowledge for a baron's daughter.

"No, sir," Nanny replied, dropping into a quick curtsy. "It was simple happenstance—"

"It was my fault," Janelle rushed to explain. She liked this nanny. She was young and could keep up with her. She also had a kind heart that could be manipulated, as had happened this afternoon. Janelle hated the thought that Papa might sack the woman because of what she'd done. "My tooth hurt, Papa, but I wouldn't let Mrs. Sundy pull it. I was too afraid. And then Hygieia was in distress, and Mrs. Sundy needed to help. It took a long while—"

"Why didn't you return home?" her father asked, his hard gaze cutting back to her.

"B-because my tooth hurt. It needed to be pulled." Tears welled up. "Don't be angry, Papa. I was afraid, and I wouldn't let Mrs. Sundy help. But I knew I had to, so I screwed up my courage. I was brave and let her do it." She looked down at her hands. "But by then we were late for tea."

The lies rolled out as easy as the tears. It was bad acting, every bit of it, and yet it worked on her father. He didn't like it when she made a fuss, but he liked even less any perceived insult to his status.

"Janelle, listen to me and listen well. There are things a lady can and cannot do." He waited a moment, then snapped out her name. "Janelle! Look at me."

Her head jerked up.

"Are you a lady?"

"I will be," she said automatically.

"Yes, you will," he affirmed. "Which means you cannot attend animals. You must be brave immediately when having a tooth drawn and not belabor it with nonsense. And you must never be late for tea. Do I make myself clear?"

"Yes, Papa."

He glared at Nanny. "If you cannot see to the proper training of a young lady, then I will look elsewhere for her education."

"Yes, sir," Nanny said with a curtsey.

"Pour the tea, Janelle. Mine has gone cold."

Janelle rushed to do as she was ordered. Indeed, she served him a fresh cup perfectly, and Alex managed a perfect declension of the verb consequantur (which meant to attain or acquire). And then Alexander came up with a sentence about how his sister must attain the perfect countenance of a lady.

Annoying brother. Especially when he grinned at her as if he knew that her burden was just as difficult as his. Whereas he was forced to *learn* useless things, she was forced to *do* useless things.

It was a significant lesson for her, but one she took to heart.

Never again was she late to tea. She rarely appeared with a hair out of place, and she never, ever spoke about helping cattle again.

That was because she was fascinated about the birthing of all creatures, especially children. After that day, she devoted herself to learning everything she could from Mrs. Sundy and anyone else who knew how the young entered this world. Her nanny had to either join her in her secret activities or be fired because Janelle would not stop.

And because Mrs. Sundy was a passionate teacher, Janelle learned how men made a mess of all things female. They had command of everything including what a woman could say or think. A husband had dominion over his wife's body and her children. She could not have her own money, nor could she refuse to lie with him no matter his character. Whores got paid, but a wife was powerless against her husband. And so good women learned how to hide their business from all men. It was safer that way.

And very soon, Mrs. Sundy's passion became Janelle's as well. It wasn't a large leap, after all. After her brother's birth, her own mother had died of childbed fever, and that loss left her with an indifferent father and a younger brother who looked to her for the love neither of them could get from their remaining parent. If she could find a way to save women from the dangers of childbirth, then no child would ever lose a mother before knowing the shape of her face or the curve of her smile.

Which meant, she did everything to learn the business of women—specifically childbirth—while hiding it from every meddling, idiot man.

By the time Janelle was an adult, she was so well-versed in keeping her father ignorant that she was living two entirely different lives.

She was debutante Janelle Caddick, daughter of a wealthy baron, formerly from Devon but now residing in London. She danced at balls and slept in until tea, refusing callers because her constitution was so delicate.

Then while Janelle slept, Betty Gill appeared. She served as midwife to women who could not afford the lying in hospital (which was almost everyone). She studied where she could, learning medicine in the way Mrs. Sundy had—by reading medical books, asking questions, and experimenting where possible.

Indeed, her dual life was perfect so long as she never married anyone who would look into how she spent her time.

Chapter One

"**S**TOP! STOP PUSHING right now!"

Janelle used the back of her hand to wipe both sweat and a lock of hair out of her eyes. The room was beastly hot for all that it was early spring in London, but there was no window in this small airless room at the top of the Rose Garden. Though this was a notorious London whorehouse, it was not the worst place to deliver a baby. Even better, Janelle—or rather her alter ego Betty Gill—was the one catching the child and not the one trying to push it out feet first.

"I need to move the baby," she muttered.

"Move it? Where?" Madame Florina snapped. The woman wasn't usually this curt, but she'd been up all night keeping several overly enthusiastic customers from destroying her place of business. Spring in London often brought young men with more money than sense. As it was now well past tea on the next day, the madame was exceptionally tired.

But babies came on their own schedule.

"Have her pant," Janelle retorted. "Like a dog."

Madame Florina rolled her heavily painted eyes, but she obeyed. "Alright Holly, now you listen to the miss and stop working so hard. Stick yer tongue out like a dog and pant."

"Wot?" Holly gasped back. "W—ieeee!"

Bloody hell, Janelle hated first babes. Everything was small and tight. Give her a mother of six any day. Those ladies popped their children out like a greased pig. With new mothers, Janelle often felt like she was delivering a baby to a babe herself, and neither was ready for it.

"Show her!" she ordered as she pressed down hard on Holly's belly. The child had to turn. It was the only way.

The soon-to-be mother screamed. Of course, she did, but there was no help for it. Fortunately, it worked. The babe rolled, the contraction took hold furthering the adjustment, and the child finally settled into the place where it ought to be.

"There," she said with satisfaction as she rocked back on her heels. She really needed a chair or a stool for this kind of work. "Whenever you're ready, Holly, you give a big push."

"Wot?"

The girl was exhausted. Her labor had been going on for half a day before Janelle happened to hear Holly screaming. She'd been trying to buy possets from the madame because Betty Gill had heard rumors of the woman's magical brew to fight off infections. If it worked, she might be able to stave off childbed fever.

The whole purchase should have taken less than fifteen minutes. Plenty of time for her to get home and become Janelle. But then she'd heard Holly's scream.

Every midwife knew the cry of a laboring woman in distress. She'd heard and couldn't turn away for all that Janelle had an appointment elsewhere. But Betty was the best midwife in London. She knew how to deliver a footling breech. She also knew that the Rose Garden was much more than a whorehouse. It was actually a kind of information network that aided women in trouble. Women like poor Holly who needed a midwife like Betty.

"Push!"

Janelle did what she could to help. She pressed down on Holly's belly, she silently willed the babe to fight its way out, and she kept a hand ready to catch.

"Again!"

Twice more she commanded Holly. There was a special tone

she used when giving orders to a laboring woman. Calm but vehement. In control, and yet powerless to force the mother to obey. It worked about three quarters of the time. Fortunately, Holly was young enough to do exactly as she was told.

Very soon, a squalling, furious, and absolutely perfect baby girl slid into Janelle's hands.

"And here's a happy child," she said, as she always did.

Madame Florina grunted. "She's not wot I'd call happy." The child had a healthy set of lungs on her. Nevertheless, the madame took the babe and held it tight. She also pursed her lips and cooed, as so many did with a newborn. It would be a bit yet before Holly would be able to do the same, but the girl would get there.

Meanwhile, Janelle squatted down, prepared to do the rest of her work. From the doorway of the room, her maid hissed in a loud voice.

"Miss! Missssss! We must go."

Faye had one job as Janelle's maid. She had to keep her mistress on time. Indeed, Janelle had hired her specifically because she was older (almost forty) and could be more responsible than her mistress. But in this, she had no more authority than Janelle did over a laboring mother. She could beg, threaten, and command, but it was on Janelle to comply.

"Yes, Faye, I hear you," she said, her voice calm. "But I'm not done yet." Women had died when the afterbirth did not come out cleanly. It was Janelle's job now to see that the end was completed as well as the beginning.

It took another fifteen minutes, which was pretty good time for Holly, not so good for Janelle.

"I'm sorry, I have to go," she said to Madame Florina.

"You've done more than most. I'm grateful," said the madame. She pressed the babe into the arms of a nearby whore. Holly was too exhausted yet to greet her child.

"We never got a chance to speak about your recipe against fevers."

The woman nodded. "It's not mine. I get it from the apothecary nearby. It helps the ladies when they're cut or torn—"

"Misssss!" Faye called. "We must go."

"Yes, yes," Janelle said, frustration making her voice tight. "Please, can I come by tomorrow—"

"Tomorrow!" Faye squeaked.

"I'll check on Holly and the child—"

"Ack," Madame Florina grunted. "We know what to do fer her and the babe. But I'll be pleased to speak with you tomorrow." A gleam of avarice entered her eyes. "I've lots of possets and the like that'll cure what ails you, too. Some from next door. Some from the gypsies."

Of course, she did. Everyone in London had a tea or a posset or something else that would fix what ailed you. Janelle was here because one of the footmen claimed Madame Florina had the best potions in town. Since the cut on his hand had healed in a surprisingly short amount of time, Janelle had come in search of the recipe so she could experiment with it herself. Unfortunately, Holly and her babe had interrupted that discussion.

"Tomorrow, then," she said to Madame Florina. Then she pulled up her cloak to cover her head and face before heading outside. It would never do for a baron's daughter to be seen coming out of a whorehouse. Of course, it would never do for this baron's daughter to arrive very late to a ball thrown by her aunt, and she was definitely going to do that.

Faye breathed an audible sigh of relief as they headed down the back stairs. "I told you, miss," she grumbled, her feet tapping quickly down the stairs. "I told you not to come here."

She barely had the breath to respond, the woman was going so fast. "It would have taken...fifteen minutes."

"You didn't have fifteen minutes, and you took two hours."

Was it only two hours? It had felt like ten. "We'll get home in time," she lied. Fortunately, her father rarely cared what time they left for a ball. His interests put him in the card room which didn't get going until the second set.

"No, we won't!" Faye said as she threw open the back door. That took long enough for Janelle to jump down the last set of stairs, then together they rushed outside. "This ball is impor—umph!"

Faye collided body to body with a large man in a dark coat. That was all Janelle saw before she too stumbled directly into both him and her maid. A large hand came around her, steadying the three of them. Janelle bounced back quickly, gasping as she caught her breath. She could see that the gentleman was still bracing her maid and she categorized details of his appearance in a rapid scan.

He was a gentleman of some worth given the excellent state of his clothing. A large body with broad shoulders and strong arms as he kept Faye from toppling into the dirt. A grim cast to his rugged features. Plus a very nice scent.

Given that she often spent time in close rooms with laboring women, the clean scent of a well-groomed man pleased her. As did his close-cropped hair and clean-shaven face, not to mention the way the sun brightened his dark blue eyes.

She started to smile at him. It was what one did when one bumped into an intriguing man. But that only showed how far she'd forgotten herself. She was not dressed as Betty Gill, right then. She was Miss Janelle Caddick, and she absolutely was not supposed to be coming out of a notorious whorehouse.

Fortunately, Faye remembered.

"Gracious me!" she cried. "Let me go!"

The gentleman's eyes widened at her maid's sudden explosion of noise. He pulled back, frowning as Faye continued to thrash.

"Calm yourself," he commanded as he looked back at Janelle, probably wondering if she had an explanation for her maid's irrational behavior.

She did. It was a distraction because he could not, should not see her face. Janelle instinctively shrunk down into her cloak, but it was dusk, not night, and she'd just smiled at him!

"Wot are you doing? Unhand me!" Faye screeched, making as much of a commotion as possible.

Understandably, the gentleman took a further step backward at her maid's vehemence. Janelle knew that Faye was exaggerating her outrage, pushing the distraction so that Janelle could escape. There were hackneys nearby. All she need do was dash away and he would never know who the cloaked figure was exiting a notorious whorehouse. Or so she hoped.

But she was loathe to abandon her maid. Ridiculous, really, because they'd both agreed that this was the plan should she run into anyone who might know her. Indeed, Janelle made certain that the woman always carried cab fare for just this happenstance.

"Let go, you brute!" the maid cried even though the gentleman had his hands raised in the air.

Faye's screams were drawing attention, the exact thing that Janelle didn't need. Still, she didn't run yet. Not until Faye hissed, "Go, ya daft fool!"

Whenever Faye dropped into her Irish, Janelle knew it was time to obey. She ducked her head and dashed to the nearest hackney. She leaped inside and bellowed, "Go!" in a most unladylike manner. Thankfully, this was a hackney outside a whorehouse. The driver knew what was what and flicked his horses to a fast trot while Janelle peeked through the rips in the curtains to see if Faye would be all right.

What she saw reassured her. Faye was in rare form as she screamed and occasionally hit the gentleman on the chest as she punctuated her words. The man was fully absorbed in dealing with the "hysterical" woman while the crowd of onlookers grew. This had happened once before, and Faye had made it home within fifteen minutes of Janelle, and yet she still worried. A lot of bad things could happen to a lone woman in London, and this was not the best area of town.

Unfortunately, there was nothing to do but pray. Once she was away from the Rose Garden, she stuck her head out the window and gave specific directions to the cabbie. Then she did what she always did in a hackney. She pulled out a hand mirror from her bag and repaired the damage to her hair and face. No measly reticule for her. She carried a full carpetbag that included everything she needed to appear a well-pampered young lady of the *ton*.

Unfortunately, her efforts inside a bouncing carriage would not be effective for a ball. Certainly not one thrown by her aunt who would inspect every aspect of her body and attire.

The hackney stopped at the location she indicated. It was an alleyway a few houses down from her own. There, waiting for her, was Nanny who was much too old to be standing out in the cold waiting for her. Which was the first thing the woman said when Janelle exited the carriage.

"I'm too old for this," the woman muttered. "What were you thinking?" They rushed through the alleyway as Nanny wended a bright gold chain through Janelle's hair. She'd gotten very adept at dressing Janelle's hair on the fly.

"It's not my fault," Janelle answered, as she stripped off her gloves and shoved them into the carpet bag. "It was a footling breech—"

"I don't care," Nanny snapped. "Today of all days. Do you know you're three hours late? Three hours! You were supposed to be at dinner—"

"I told you what to say. I'm a delicate maiden overcome by—"

"I said it," Nanny snapped as she ducked in the back door of the house. "Nevertheless, your father is furious. Your aunt has sent missives from her home—"

"I know. I'll apologize."

"It won't work this time."

Janelle winced. "I'll do better."

"You won't be able to do anything at this rate. She'll never forgive you. You're supposed to open the ball!"

"Me? Whatever for?" That was her aunt and uncle's job.

"Does she tell me these things? She does not. You cannot keep being Betty in London! You're supposed to be a debutante."

"So I should let a laboring woman die so I can attend a party? It was a footling breech."

This was an old argument between them. It had been hard enough to keep her activities secret in Devon where the population was relatively sparse and nobody kept track of her comings and goings. No one cared that Janelle Caddick spent the day wandering alone or that Mrs. Sundy's niece Betty with the stooped shoulder and the perpetually dirty face had a busy day. Since her father spent the bulk of his time in London, she'd enjoyed near autonomy there.

It had been a surprise last Season to realize that London gave her even more anonymity. Most people didn't look beyond the dark cloak. So long as she paid well, the cabbies didn't care who was sneaking about or where she went.

That had worked well for her last Season, but this time things were different, or so Nanny said. Janelle acknowledged that her father did seem more interested in her activities this year. Also more determined than ever to share teatime. But that would pass. His interest in her was limited to making sure she upheld the appearance of being a proper young lady.

Unfortunately, today she was a proper young lady who had missed both teatime and dinner, so she rushed upstairs through the back servant's entrance. Hot water was waiting, but she didn't have time for a bath. Nevertheless, she stripped down and ran the sponge over herself as quickly as possible. Then it was into the gown while Faye—who had just returned—brushed a very modest amount of color into her cheeks and lips.

They were all very experienced in this task, and she soon descended the steps.

"Remember," Nanny hissed, "you've been overcome with a mild illness after visiting your friend. Stomach upset from the excitement of the new Season."

Parties were not something that caused her to be over-wrought. Having to deal with idiot midwives brought her fury up, but for tonight, she'd pretend to a tetchy stomach. Unfortunate, really, because she was starving.

Their butler nodded to her, his expression grave, then he threw open the parlor door. She entered with her customary, "Oh Papa, it's so good to see you," only to pull up short.

Papa was not alone in the parlor. Why hadn't anyone told her that? Right over his shoulder, standing at the mantle, was a tall man with an annoyed expression. He had been glaring at the ticking clock when she entered and now turned to her with brows arched over piercing hazel eyes. She knew this man or at least had been introduced to him. He was somebody important to her father, but she couldn't place him.

Two other people sat in the room as well. The man's parents? She would know if she placed the man by the mantle. Damn it, why couldn't she remember?

"You're late," her father said from his chair. He sat to her right, a few inches from her elbow, but his voice came to her from a distance.

"I know, Papa, and I'm so sorry," she said, the words tripping off her tongue because she'd said them a thousand times before. "The Season can be so overwhelming at times. The pace is so different from Devon."

Normally, he would respond with a grunt as he returned to whatever he was doing. Reading the paper. Drinking his tea. Readying to go to a ball so he could disappear into the card room. But this time, he simply leaned back in his chair.

"The pace isn't overwhelming, you just like wandering off. I've been much too lax with you, daughter, but that ends tonight."

That wasn't his normal response, and it was startling enough for her to pull attention away from the man by the mantle. "Papa, you needn't ever wait for me. You and your friends shouldn't be detained because of my thoughtlessness." She let her shoulders sag in a false sign of regret. "If I am forced to miss my entertainments, then it is my fault alone."

Her father grunted in his usual way, and then he waved to

the hazel-eyed gentleman behind him. "Go on. Get it over with. As she said, it's her own fault."

Alarm started to ring through her. She didn't even know who these people were. Her father hadn't bothered to introduce them. And here came the tall man with his expression tight and his lanky walk somehow regal. He was a titled gentleman, that was definite, but who was he? His age, which she guessed to be at most ten years her senior, put him in the most coveted group of aristocrats—old enough to be established, but young enough to still have all his teeth.

As was appropriate, she dropped down into a graceful curtsy. "My lord," she intoned.

"You don't know who I am, do you?" the man said. His voice had a smoothness to it that fit his refined exterior. And though she guessed he was impatient with her—she would be too if she were him—she detected irritation with the situation more than with her specifically.

She rose slowly, choosing her words with care. "I seem to be more ill than I thought. My mind is scattered."

"Not your mind," he said, a touch of humor entering his tone. "Your memory."

To the side, her father huffed out a breath. "I've spoken to you about him several times, Janelle. This is Lord Benedict, son to the Earl and Countess of Atterbury. If you'd been here for tea, I would have explained everything."

Doubtful. At the last three teatimes they'd shared, her father had approved of her attire, grunted his delight at the tea, and then informed her of the parties she would attend in her search for a husband. He and her aunt had regular discussions about that. She simply went where they told her to go.

Meanwhile, the earl and countess rose from their seats to greet her. To be excruciatingly correct, the earl would have already gained his feet when she entered, but he was very old and clearly unsteady as he gripped his cane in a shaking double fist.

"My lord," Janelle said. "Please do not trouble yourself—"

"Not going to trouble long," he said, his voice genial though somewhat weak. "Don't want to miss such a happy event."

What happy event? Meanwhile, she made her curtsey to the countess. If ever a woman was the opposite of her husband, that was Lady Atterbury. Where he was stooped and frail, she was tall and intimidating. Her brows were mostly painted on, but they arched in an imperious way such that her every expression appeared condescending. This look increased when added to her pointed nose and pinched lips.

"Tardiness is a thoughtless vice," the woman said by way of greeting.

"It is, my lady," Janelle said quickly. "I cannot express my regret strongly enough. If I had known you would be here, I would never have allowed the time to slip away so dreadfully."

"You were visiting an ill relation, I understand?"

Just what had Nanny told them? "Not technically true. The cousin of an old school friend. She's increasing, you see, and feeling poorly."

The lady sniffed. "And you caught her ailment somehow? Your stomach is that sympathetic?" Doubt laced her tone.

"It will never happen again, I assure you."

"See to it," the woman commanded, then she sat down as if she had given a royal decree and was now bored with the proceedings.

Meanwhile, still in his seat, her father clicked his pocket watch open. "We must go," he said. "We can get to know one another better in the carriage."

She gathered they were all travelling to the ball together. That would make it a tight squeeze in their carriage.

"Of course," she said, turning toward the door, but the sound of a throat clearing behind her stopped her movement.

"There is something to do be done first, I believe," said Lord Benedict.

"Right, right," her father grumbled as he pushed to his feet. "Get on with it."

A cold chill ran down her spine as Lord Benedict came to stand before her. All around her, the others held their breath with expectant impatience. As if they awaited a meal that they were barely interested in eating.

"My lord—" she began, but then she cut off her word with a squeak. The man dropped down to one knee before her and tried to possess her hand. Her instinct was to whip it behind her back, but she was too well trained for that. Such a thing would be inexplicably rude. And yet, she couldn't allow what was happening either. "Please," she whispered desperately, "we haven't even met before now."

"But we did," he said from his position on one knee. He didn't force her to give him her hand, but he stayed there, his head level with her chest, and his intelligent hazel eyes looking up at her. "I was arriving to see your father two days ago while you were preparing to leave. I heard you give several instructions to your housekeeper and butler."

Really? Nanny was their housekeeper, having graduated from simple nursemaid to household management when Janelle turned thirteen. As for the butler, he'd been devoted to her and her secrets from the moment she'd delivered his first grandchild last season.

"But that is nothing remarkable," she said.

"On the contrary, you were direct and succinct in your instructions. Not harsh, not cruel, and certainly not frivolous."

She had no idea why that was important. "I try to be kind," she said dully.

"They listened and, I assume, obeyed."

She nodded. "Generally."

"It was at that very moment that I realized you were the woman for me." To the side, his mother cleared her throat quite loudly. He glanced at her, annoyance on his face, but then he returned to gazing up at Janelle. "It was at that moment that I fell desperately in love with you."

He didn't sound like he was in love. Indeed, if she had to

guess, his mother had commanded him to pretend to that emotion. And yet, he did not seem like a man who lived under his mother's thumb. She was so confused!

"W-what?" she stammered.

Her father grunted. "Come on, girl. Say yes. We must be off."

Whyever would she do that?

In truth, she knew exactly why she would say yes. One part of her brain reminded her that her father had announced his intention to have her wed by the end of the season. She remembered now that he had never asked for her to beguile a man but had indicated that he would make the necessary arrangements for her. And clearly, he had.

A future earl was on his knee before her.

Lord Benedict grimaced. "Miss Caddick. Janelle. I realize this is happening very fast, and I would have preferred to discuss matters with you—"

"Yes," agreed her father, "but she wasn't here for that, was she? It's her own fault."

This *was* her own fault. She should have paid more attention to her father. Had he said anything about being in negotiation with a suitor? Could she possibly have missed that?

"Nevertheless," Lord Benedict continued. Then with an apologetic glance, he grasped her limp hand and pulled it forward. "Would you do me the greatest honor and become my wife?"

There was only one answer to give. Everyone expected her to say yes. Indeed, marriage to a future earl was perhaps the greatest alliance she could ever hope to achieve. All she need do was say, yes. But the word caught in her throat. She kept thinking, *who is he to me?* And the reverse, who was she to him?

"You are overcome," he said.

"I am…" Confused. Intimidated. Something. She didn't even know what, but he took it for agreement.

Then he held up a large ruby ring. "We need not be married immediately. There is plenty of time for us to get to know one another."

He touched the ring to the tip of her finger but did not put it on. To the side, her father grunted in annoyance. His mother took a breath, no doubt to say something, but Lord Benedict silenced her with a hard glare. Then he returned his attention to Janelle.

"Do you need more time?" he asked.

Of course, she did! Marriage was a serious business. It would determine whom she spent the rest of her life avoiding as she snuck out to tend to the women who needed her. But of course, she couldn't say that. What she could say was that he was an aristocrat of obviously good means. Her father would have seen to that. His appearance was neat, his manner refined, but she couldn't have him hanging around the house all day. He would know what she did.

"This has all been arranged," she realized. "Even down to my aunt's ball—"

"To which we are already tardy," her father said loudly.

Right. "My dowry and all matters are finalized?"

"Yes. This very afternoon."

"This afternoon." Goodness. "So there must be some urgency."

He nodded. "My work with Lord Castlereigh at the Foreign Office keeps me well occupied."

Her eyes widened. "You're political?"

"A diplomat," he said. "Or rather an aide to the Crown's foremost diplomat."

"You sound very important."

He smiled at her, and he squeezed her hand slightly where he still held it. "I'm afraid it means I shall not be home as often as one might like."

Excellent! If he was away from home, she could continue as Betty. Plus, as the wife of an earl, no one would question her comings and goings. If she had to have a husband—and her father was adamant that she did—then Lord Benedict seemed tailor made for her.

"You need not concern yourself about being away. I am used to amusing myself," she said.

"Enough," her father said as he thumped his hand down on the tea table. "She agrees with gratitude. Put the ring on her finger."

Lord Benedict did not comply though he did arch a wry brow at her. "This is rather hard on my knee," he drawled. "An answer would be welcome even if it is to delay—"

"Yes," she said, rushing the word to get it out. "Yes, Lord Benedict, I should be very happy to be your wife."

Chapter Two

WHO WAS SHE…EXACTLY?

That was Major Gabriel Vance's question as he watched Miss Janelle Caddick open the dance with her new fiancé, Lord Benedict. They'd announced their engagement not ten minutes ago, much to Gabe's frustration. And now they were opening the ball together.

Gabe glared at the couple, trying to ferret out the problem. Something about Miss Caddick felt *wrong*, and it was his job as Lord Benedict's aide-de-camp at the Foreign Office, to be sure that everything around his lordship was *right*. He was Benedict's attack dog. He smoothed his superior's way, he stopped problems before they arose, and he aided the man in every other way as he and Lord Castlereigh protected England from foreign threats, including the Corsican monster.

But what was the problem? Everything he saw now suggested Miss Caddick could not possibly be the woman he'd seen leaving the Rose Garden two hours ago.

Her face was sweet, her expression warm, and her posture proper. She seemed too fresh to be a common whore, even a pretty one. And the more he watched her, the more convinced he was that she was not a courtesan either. Thanks to his mother, he knew a great many of them, and every one had an innate sensuality that brought a man's mind down to its most primal place. Even when the women tried to hide it, there was always a shift to the hips, a way of smiling, or even a hand gesture that fogged a man's most elevated thoughts.

Miss Caddick had none of that. If anything, her gestures were efficient, not refined. Forthright, not subtle. Which made her appear like an excellent choice for Lord Benedict.

Except she had been at the Rose Garden. He was sure of it.

"Stop scowling. You're frightening the young ladies."

Gabe groaned internally. The last thing he wanted to do was banter vague things with Lord Nathaniel. The man was a ne'er-do-well who somehow, someway was perpetually underfoot. At least that was his public persona. Gabe knew him as a talented spy, recently married and blissfully happy, if his cheeky grin were to be believed.

"Ladies are too easily frightened," he said, refusing to look at Lord Nate.

"You underestimate your fierceness."

Gabe turned to the irritatingly perceptive Lord Nathaniel. Perhaps the secret to his survival in the *ton* was that the man was handsome and wickedly smart. Plus, he was the third son of an earl, which gave him a place at a society party. Gabe, on the other hand, was a bastard with no place whatsoever.

"What do you know of Miss Caddick?"

"That she's perfect for Lord Benedict."

That was interesting. "Really? How so?"

"In the perfect-for-him way." Then as Gabe deepened his scowl, Lord Nate elaborated. "Didn't you hear? They're madly in love."

"He hasn't met her before tonight."

"Love at first sight."

"From Lord Benedict? Never." Lord Benedict was a brilliant diplomat, an extraordinary tactician, and a noble man in all the ways the peerage was supposed to be but usually wasn't. Truth be told, Gabe saw him as King Arthur reborn without the weight of Guinivere, because the man *not* a romantic. He would never fall head over heels in love with anyone. Indeed, Gabe had expected a political marriage from his superior, but there was nothing politically advantageous about Miss Caddick. She was the daughter of a nobody baron. She didn't even have a huge dowry.

Meanwhile Nate was laughing at him. "You don't know what he does when he's away from the Foreign Office. They could have been carrying on a secret affair."

"He never leaves the Foreign Office, so that's not possible."

His companion blew out a frustrated breath. "Come with me," he said.

Gabe didn't move. "Where?"

"To meet a young lady who is perfect for *you*."

"Not possible." Gabe had come far from his bastard beginning, earning his rank and his position with Lord Benedict through hard work and a keen analytical mind. Finding the appropriate wife would help raise his status a notch higher. Unfortunately, all the appropriate women turned up their nose at his illegitimate birth.

"You haven't looked hard enough."

He'd barely looked at all. At least, not in the last couple years. His last relationship—all six nights of his last leave—had been with Spanish courtesan who was trying to get military information. He'd had fondness for her while they wandered the city eating until they nearly burst. Then he found her trying to go through Benedict's correspondence. It hadn't even broken his heart because he'd barely been surprised.

But perhaps London was different. Perhaps it was time to try again.

"Who is it?" he asked, falling into step beside Nate.

"Miss Elsie Hunter."

Gabe stopped moving. Now there was a woman he could believe frequented the Rose Garden. She likely preferred to watch rather than participate, but that did not make her the woman for him. "She's scandalous."

"Nothing of the sort!" Lord Nate protested. Then he winked. "But she is saucy and exactly the kind of woman to be intrigued by a bastard like you."

"I'm an *elevated* bastard," he corrected with a growl. The nature of his birth was well known. He was the illegitimate son of the Duke of Torbay who partially acknowledged his presence. His father had educated him, bought his commission, and occasionally shared a drink with him at his club. But that was the extent of their familial relationship. Still, that was enough to entice some women, and apparently Miss Hunter was one of them.

"Do be polite to her," Nate said. "I've been talking you up."

"Why would you do that?"

"Because Lord Benedict asked me to. If he is to take a wife, then he thinks you should, too."

Their situations were vastly different, but the pressures to wed were the same. Lord Benedict needed an heir and Gabe needed the appearance of legitimacy in any form he could find. That included matrimony. On the battlefield, no one cared about his parentage. As aide-de-camp to Lord Benedict, he needed to be competent, not legitimate. But now Lord Benedict was a rising star in the Foreign Office.

Those people cared. Those people wanted both Gabe to be deferential, charming, and have every appearance of a stable, moral life. If he didn't appear as such, then he couldn't advance alongside Lord Benedict. Indeed, he might hold the man back, and that was something he would not do.

He owed Benedict his career. On his own, he could not have advanced nearly so far. But Benedict had recognized his strengths and had not hesitated to utilize him in such a way that everyone understood his skills. Gabriel might have taught Benedict how to survive in a war zone, but Benedict had made sure that life had meaning. He'd made sure they'd risen together to an influential place in the military.

And then Benedict's brother, Anthony, had died, Benedict had become the sole heir to an earldom, and they'd both ended up in the diplomatic corps. A happy shift for Benedict. A difficult one for Gabe. But he could adjust, he reminded himself. He could at least try for a wife.

So with a curt nod, he allowed Lord Nate to introduce him to the saucy Miss Hunter.

It did not go well.

Miss Hunter was intrigued by his disreputable status. She also liked his medals and his muscles. And when he escorted her to the dance floor for the waltz she demanded they dance, she enjoyed herself too much. She laughed too loudly and cast several defiant gazes at her mother.

Women set on rebellion bored him.

He escorted her back to her mother, bowed over her hand, and left, making sure to glare at Nate along the way. Unfortunately, that simply prompted the man to make new introductions to every single female there, or at least those who would deign to dance with a bastard.

Those dances did not go much better. In fact, tonight reminded him why he had given up the social whirl. The eligible women of the *ton* fell into two camps: vapid or rebellious. And the *in*eligible women were a great deal worse.

There was only one woman who'd caught his attention this night, one woman he'd kept track of throughout the evening, one woman who'd danced perpetually at the edge of his awareness—Miss Janelle Caddick, his superior's fiancée. Throughout the evening, he'd watched as she'd interacted with every well-wisher or sycophant. Miss Caddick danced every dance, smiled with poise, and acted exactly as Lord Benedict's fiancée ought.

It was maddening.

He did not trust it. He was absolutely certain she'd been the woman rushing out of the Rose Garden this afternoon. He remembered the curve of her cheek, the flash of her eyes. He knew faces, and he'd caught sight of hers exiting London's most notorious bawdy house.

He wanted to know why.

So, rather than give Lord Nathaniel one more second of his time, he followed the urging of his gut and went in search of his superior's fiancée.

He found her in the room with the supper buffet eating what one could only call a generous amount of food. He didn't approach her at first but hung back to observe. The first thing to catch his attention was the healthy flush to her cheek and the impudent upturn of her nose. Her gestures might be restrained, but her exuberance was clear to anyone with eyes.

The woman clearly loved her food.

Each delicate bite was set to her mouth with precision, then she closed her eyes slightly as she appreciated the taste. She ate efficiently without stuffing her mouth. And if she were alone, he would bet she'd be ummming and ahhing at the delightful taste. He couldn't blame her. Her aunt set a divine table. Still, it was unfashionable for a lady to eat so enthusiastically and yet, he found the sight charming.

Every once in a while, she'd nod to her companion and say something mundane. "That is most fascinating, sir," was her most common phrase. "Do explain more. I vow I have never heard anything more interesting" came as a close second.

She was lying. Even he knew that Mr. Pena's fascination with carriage construction was tedious. A moment's more casual observation showed him that she'd used Mr. Pena's conversation as a cover while she consumed her food.

Gabe waited while she finished her plate, using the time to greet a few gentlemen known to him through Lord Benedict's work. Then when he judged she was done, he ended his conversation and introduced himself to her. It wasn't the correct protocol. He should have asked someone else to introduce him, but he didn't want to lose this opportunity. It was his intention to curb Miss Caddick's wayward ways now. No diplomat's wife could be seen near a whorehouse.

"Good evening, Miss Caddick. Might I have the pleasure of a word with you?"

She looked up with surprise and a grateful expression. No doubt, she was looking to escape a discussion of carriage springs.

"Major Vance, what a great pleasure to finally meet you."

He blinked, startled. "You know of me?"

She smiled. "Of course, I do. You're my fiancé's right-hand man. Those were his very words."

"He flatters me."

"I doubt it," she said dryly. "I don't think he's the type to flatter anyone."

How little she knew her fiancé. Lord Benedict was a deft hand at flattering those who were susceptible.

Meanwhile, she stood as she addressed him. "My lord pointed you out before he went to the card room. He said if I ever needed anything and could not find him, I was to contact you immediately."

"I stand ready to serve," he said in his most formal voice. Then he held out his hand. "Would you do me the honor of a promenade? At least until the dancing begins again?"

She smiled as she turned back to Mr. Pena, who had stood up rather awkwardly when the lady found her feet. "You don't mind, do you?" she asked. "I vow I have heard so much about carriage construction that I must think about it for a time. Any more information and I swear I shall burst from too much knowledge."

What could Mr. Pena do but acquiesce? Gabe extended his arm, and she touched her fingers to his forearm.

There was a back garden, and several groups were walking around its very small space. It wouldn't provide very much privacy, but at least they would get out of the overheated ballroom. They stepped outside and as the ashy London air hit her face, the lady exhaled a sigh.

"Is something wrong?" he asked.

"No, of course not," she said, but he could hear disappointment in her tone.

"I must insist that you be honest with me. We cannot work together otherwise."

She turned to him, her brow arched in surprise. "Are we to work together, Major?"

"Most certainly," he said. "Indeed, I believe it is both our jobs to see that Lord Benedict remains in the greatest state of mind. The responsibilities he shoulders affect not only England, but the entire world." Lord Benedict was the secret weapon of the Foreign Office. He was Lord Castlereigh's right hand man, using every advantage to not only defeat Napoleon but to ensure that no such monster appeared again to threaten world peace.

"Goodness," she said, her tone slightly amused. "That's quite an elevated depiction of my fiancé."

"It's a truthful one. Do you doubt it?"

She twisted her hands upward in a gesture of confusion. "Up until a few hours ago, I was not aware of Lord Benedict at all. Our engagement was arranged by my father, with no word to me whatsoever." Understandably, her tone was a bit peevish.

"And yet you agreed."

She said nothing for a moment, then she spoke in a tone so glib that he was sure she covered pain. "That is the truth of these things, is it not? Courtship is merely a pretense to the arrangement of property. I am honored that someone so exalted deemed me worthy of a place by his side."

"And yet you sigh, Miss Caddick. Are you upset by your coming nuptials?"

"Of course not," she said as she walked toward the edge of the property. He kept up with her easily. "I sighed because I had hoped for clearer air when we stepped outside. I cannot believe all the coal ash is good for the lungs."

"You prefer the country air, then."

"Doesn't everyone? But there are advantages in London. The society is much improved here, and Lord Benedict's work is here."

"So you intend to stay with your husband in London?"

"I intend to do as my husband wills. Naturally." Her tone was level, but he detected a note of annoyance in it. Interestingly, she didn't seem annoyed with him. It was as though she grew tired of rote responses to typical questions.

That was good, because they were finally out of anyone else's earshot. Assuming they both kept their voices low, he could say the words he'd been storing up.

"I doubt he wills you to visit the Rose Garden, Miss Caddick," he said. "We haven't much time, so let me be perfectly clear. Such activities are finished. If I find that you continue with them in any way, I will see that you never marry Lord Benedict. You will never be a countess. Fight me on this and you will be drummed from society as a slut." He took a deep breath, forcing himself to continue when he'd rather end the engagement now. "Find a way to become a model of propriety, Miss Caddick, because I am watching you. And I will not hesitate to destroy you." He lifted his chin. "That is my job as Lord Benedict's man, and I take it very seriously."

She gaped at him. Of course, she did. He'd just dumped a great deal of information on her—as well as a threat—and she was properly horrified to realize he'd discovered her perfidy.

Unsurprisingly, her expression changed from shock to fury. "Why you horrible—"

"Keep your voice low, Miss Caddick."

"How dare you!" she cried in a louder tone than he expected. Indeed, it was loud enough that she caught the attention of several people nearby. "I do not know what fever dream has caused such idiocy—"

"Have a care, Miss Caddick. You are drawing attention."

"And just what do you think you are doing?" she snapped. "Good God, how could you think such a thing of me?"

He kept his voice to a low growl. "I saw you, Miss Caddick. With my own eyes."

There was a flicker in her eyes. An acknowledgement, perhaps? Fear? It was gone too fast for him to tell. Instead, she sniffed loudly. "It baffles me, Major Vance, why you would threaten me within moments of our meeting. I am a young woman, newly engaged to your superior, and yet suddenly, you seek to be private with me? And to say such things!" She shuddered. "Good evening, Major."

She spun on her heels and stalked away. There was purpose in her step, a power to her retreat that he hadn't observed earlier. Indeed, it was a little surprising, and he couldn't stop himself from watching the way she stalked off.

Well done, he thought. There were several people staring at him, judging him to be the one at fault. That made Miss Caddick the winner in their exchange. In truth, it required little skill to turn the tide of opinion against a bastard, but she had managed it with the quick thinking of a veteran liar. That was impressive.

He could admire such skill, especially since she was set to become the wife of a diplomat. But first he had to make sure she set her talents to the *benefit* of Lord Benedict's ambitions, not their destruction.

This was the first skirmish between them. A testing volley, so to speak, before he won the day. Because she *had* been at the Rose Garden. Which meant she was a danger to Lord Benedict's political ambitions and, by extension, his own.

He crossed his arms and chuckled. That action was for the benefit of the people still staring at him. They needed to know he was not intimidated. But first he had to do the one thing he'd been trying to avoid.

He had to have a frank discussion with the owner of the Rose Garden.

His mother.

Chapter Three

NORMALLY GABE WOULD wait until the morrow to speak with his mother. As it was after midnight, there was an even chance she would be deep into her cups. But since Miss Caddick had made a scene, it was necessary to get as much information as possible, as soon as possible. If she truly were a political liability—and a woman who frequented whorehouses certainly was—then there was still time to end Benedict's engagement with minimal scandal. But they had to act decisively or risk everyone taking her side.

His plan was to tell Lord Benedict all the dirt he could uncover and dissuade the gentleman from his disastrous course. There were plenty of young ladies who would make a good political wife. A woman who dabbled at the Rose Garden was not one of them.

He knocked on his mother's door, noting that she had managed to keep the residence despite losing her latest paramour. The house was a neat little abode in a decent corner of London, unlike where the Rose Garden operated. His mother had not, however, managed to keep her butler. Her maid answered the door and, upon seeing him, curtseyed and gave him a sloe-eyed look that set his teeth on edge. Did every woman in his mother's world want to seduce him?

"Is she sober enough to speak to me?"

"Oh yes, sir," she answered. "She's entertaining in the parlor."

Was she? That did not bode well. Either she had found a new

admirer or she was spending her coin in the hopes of trapping one. Her parlor would be a busy place, and she would be loathe to leave it.

"Please sir," the maid purred, "let me help you undress."

"No, thank you," he said curtly as he set aside his hat and gloves, but kept the greasy package in his hands. It was a gift for his mother, and he would not surrender it to anyone else. He noted that his was not the only set of gentlemen's attire set there, nor was this maid the only one nearby with a low-cut gown and paint on her pouty lips.

They were trainees, girls who were being taught how to seduce any man, even those with unusual proclivities. Especially those, because they were the Rose Garden's stock and trade.

When he was young, he'd indulged in the offerings that constantly surrounded him whenever he was in London. But he was a man now, and he understood that he always felt vile after one of those encounters.

"I can show you the way," the woman said with a sultry smile.

He ignored her and went straight into the salon. Surprisingly, everyone was still dressed, and several were in different chairs.

"Gabriel!" his mother cried. "Did I not tell you that he would come here?" she said to the others in the room. "He always runs back to his mama at some point."

He ground his teeth. He came back here when common decency required it of him. And when he needed information that only she could provide. But since he was the petitioner tonight, he played along with her game.

"Good evening, Mother. You are looking beautiful as always." It wasn't a lie. She was a stunningly gorgeous woman with bright blue eyes and curling blond hair draped oh so casually across her bodice. She reclined on a settee, a glass of brandy dangling between her elegant fingertips. She wore jewelry, of course. Stones worth as much as he made in a year, or so it appeared. He had no idea how much of it was paste.

He pressed a kiss onto her powdered cheek, and she coiled an appreciative hand around his biceps.

"You're keeping fit."

How could she ooze seduction while fondling her own child? It made his back tense as he pulled away. "I should like a word, Mother," he said formally. "If we could take a moment in private?"

"Of course! But first tell me what you have brought for me. I do love your gifts."

He smiled and held up a greasy package. "Sausages, mother. Just as you love them."

"From Vienna!" she squealed in delight.

If she thought he could get sausages from Vienna before they grew rancid, she was much mistaken. But such was the nature of his mother's mind that logistical reality could find no purchase. "They are spiced just as you favor," he said.

"Well, it's not French brandy, but I shall love them nonetheless." She reached out to grab the package, but he held it aloft. He had been caught in this trap before.

"Come with me to the kitchen. Shall I cook them up for you?"

"Oh, you darling boy," she cooed. "You know just how to tempt me."

Indeed, he did. He'd learned, by the time he was six, that she would rather starve than figure out how to work a cookstove. Despite his powerful father, there had been lean times for himself and his mother. Times when no servant helped, and all their resources had gone to making his mother attractive enough to gain another protector. Indeed, it wasn't until she threw her lot in with Madame Florina that their finances stabilized. The fortunes of a single mistress might wax and wane, but a whorehouse always had customers.

Ignoring the mock outrage of the others in her parlor, Gabe left the front of the house and headed for the back kitchen. His mother was a few steps behind him after making sure that her guests were well entertained by her "students."

He stoked the fire on her stove and waited for her to join him. She plopped down on a stool with a grandiose sigh.

"I vow I am getting too old for these games."

"Which games, mother?" He was distracted with the setting the sausages in the pan or he would have realized that was the wrong question to ask. She was looking for him to decry her age, not ask for specifics.

"What a question to ask!" she snapped. "Do hurry with those. I'm quite famished."

"What happened with Mr. Alonso? Has he decamped back to Spain?"

"Oh, you know those foreigners," she said lightly. "They're here for a time to enjoy themselves, and then off they go to sunnier climes." She flicked her hands open as a performer might. "Poof and he no longer loves me."

Gabriel said nothing, his attention on cooking. Silence reigned until he heard the plaintive note in his mother's voice.

"But you still adore me, don't you?" she asked. "A son's love never ends."

"Of course, mother." A lie if there ever was one. His mother's need for adoration sapped every man's strength, including his.

"Of course, mother," she mocked. She knew when he was lying. "Very well. Out with it. What do you want?"

Tension eased out of his shoulders. For whatever reason, she had no interest in wheedling for more affection.

"What do you know of Miss Janelle Caddick?"

"Lord Benedict's new fiancée? I heard you upset the girl. Is it really wise to enrage your superior officer?"

His brows rose. Gossip flew fast in London. He'd only left the ball an hour ago. And they'd only announced the engagement a few hours before that. "Who told you about that?"

"Leo and Andre came from there." She grabbed a bottle of some kind of tincture from a nearby shelf, dabbed the liquid on her hands, then rubbed it into her throat. It was a lotion of some kind for fair skin, removal of wrinkles, or some other female nonsense. She always had something nearby. Her store of perfumes could keep a glass maker in business for a year. "The young bucks enjoy something fun after one of those tedious affairs."

Or they knew she would value gossip about her only son. "Not everything is as it seems."

"It seems you tried to scold a girl you'd just met and now are looking for dirt on her so as to defend yourself to Lord Benedict."

Very well. Things were exactly as they seemed. He turned with pan in hand, ready to serve a hot sausage to his mother. She had already grabbed a plate and was clearly happy for the treat, but he held back.

"I know she was at the Rose Garden this afternoon. What is her predilection? Does she watch or participate?"

His mother stared at him a moment, obviously startled. Then she abruptly laughed, a cascading sound that had mesmerized many a gentleman. "Don't be so dramatic, boy. Now give me those sausages!"

He used a fork to scoop one out, but he didn't give it to her. "What does she do there?"

"Nothing! Dear boy, what would a slip of a country girl do at the Rose Garden? I dare say she doesn't even know the place exists." She held up her plate, her eyes on the hovering sausage.

"I saw her there this afternoon."

Frustrated, his mother grabbed another fork and stabbed it into the pan before pulling out a fat prize. "What were you doing there?"

"You asked me to go, remember? To see if the roof truly needed repairs or if Madame Florina was being bamboozled."

She looked up with a hopeful expression. "And was she?"

"No."

"Well, that's disappointing. It's going to cost the earth to fix."

He set the pan back on the stove. "The building has been hard used and needs several repairs if you don't want it coming down on your customer's…ears." He purposely left the space before that last word, knowing she would appreciate the off-color joke.

She did, chuckling in that throaty way she used to captivate men.

It set his teeth on edge.

"Oh," she cooed, "if only the walls could talk, what tales they would tell."

"The walls do talk, and they sound like rats."

She shot him an annoyed look, then applied herself to her food. She used a knife to cut delicate slices, eating as neatly as if she were sitting with the king of England. His nose twitched at the excellent smell, but he knew better than to join her at table. She would eat every one of the sausages or share them with her guests. She knew the power of appearing to be generous with potential protectors.

Gabriel, however, was not a potential anything to her. He was her son, and she used her place as his mother as far as he would allow.

"Do you know someone," she asked shyly, "who could repair the roof without too much fuss?"

He knew several, but that's not what she meant. She wanted to know if he knew anyone who would do it for free as a favor to him.

"I do not."

"Gabriel—"

"And if I did, why would I extend myself to help you when you won't be honest about Miss Caddick?"

Her eyes widened. "What nonsense are you spouting?"

"I know she was there."

"You know no such thing. Gabriel Michael Vance, whatever has gotten into you? Miss Caddick has never been to the Rose Garden. On that you can be certain."

He nodded slowly. "The thing is, Mother, you told me that everyone has a scandalous side."

She took another bite, then grinned over her fork at him. "That's because they do."

"Indeed, you revel in leading the innocent down the path to debauchery."

"Even you, for a time," she said as if it were an achievement to introduce one's son to depravity.

"For a time," he agreed, working hard to keep disdain out of his voice.

She returned her attention to her sausage, cutting another slice before popping it into her rosebud mouth. "I do not force anyone," she said primly. "I merely—"

"Offer and entice. It's not your sin if they make the choice."

"Exactly."

"So why discard the idea that Miss Caddick had visited? Or that you could introduce her—"

"Introduce Lord Benedict's fiancée to the Rose Garden? Your superior's fiancée? As if I would!"

She would. She absolutely would. But she hadn't offered it, nor had she suggested that the lady might have been there or that Madame Florina might know more. His mother was a mistress of hooking a man and drawing him ever deeper into her clutches. But rather than entice him into further inquiry, she had tried to end the conversation.

"Mother," he said, using a tone she knew brooked no defiance. "Tell me what Miss Caddick was doing at the Rose Garden."

She threw up her hands in disgust. "Absolutely nothing, you stupid boy." Then she pushed up from the table and whirled away in a dramatic flounce. "Jonathan, darling," she called as she headed back to the parlor. "Do come into my kitchen for some of these fabulous sausages. They are simply divine." Her voice dropped to a seductive purr. "Shall I feed them to you? Bite by glorious bite?"

That was Gabe's cue to leave. He did not want to see his mother infantilize another man. He couldn't fathom why so very many gentlemen enjoyed it.

It was sheer peevishness that prompted him to grab one of the sausages out of the pan as he left. The thing was still hot and scalded his fingers, but it did taste wonderful. He ate quickly, and though he savored every bite, his mind was on something else.

His mother was an accomplished seductress who occasionally dipped into blackmail. She would likely take some secrets to her grave, but there were not many. At least not many that she could keep from her son. But she'd been uncharacteristically silent about Miss Caddick, and all his tricks to get a hint had failed.

Could he be completely wrong? He'd only seen the mysterious woman for a split second. But the more he chewed on it, the more he examined the lady's behavior and his mother's, the more certain he became.

Something about their reactions didn't feel right. Miss Caddick felt duplicitous. And now he was more determined than ever to ferret out her secret.

Chapter Four

MAJOR VANCE WAS not at the Foreign Office the next morning, and that worried Benedict. The man was as regular as the morning sun except after a visit with his mother. On those days, the major showed up with a scowl and Benedict's affairs would be in disarray for the rest of the day. Fortunately, Gabriel rarely visited his mother.

Today, however, the major showed up an hour late with a scowl that threatened to permanently distort his face.

"Didn't the sausages help?" he asked by way of greeting. That had been Benedict's suggestion on the best way to put Madame Sabate into a good mood. It usually worked.

"It did," the man growled. "But I didn't have enough to bring you some. I need you in a talkative mood." He stalked into the office with a stack of completed correspondence and dropped it neatly on Benedict's desk.

Major Vance might be in a foul mood, but that never prevented him from finishing his allotted tasks.

Benedict barely glanced at the stack of papers. He'd long since learned to trust the man's work. He took another long look at Gabriel's face, and then said, "Please shut the door and sit down."

The major nodded and then did as he was bid. It was the action of a subordinate, but the expression on his face made Benedict feel once again like a raw recruit. Though his title had given him the higher rank, the major far exceeded him in experience and on-the-ground wiliness. That was less useful here in London than it had been in Spain, but it was valuable, nonetheless. And besides, Benedict would never ignore the major no matter their ranks, occupation, or anything else. They were closer than brothers, had saved each other's lives, and relied on one other as critical pieces of a well-oiled machine.

And with the door shut, Gabriel might relax enough to share whatever was bothering him. So Benedict leaned back and smiled.

"Tell me," he said.

The major didn't hesitate, but he took his own sweet time coming to the point. "Three weeks ago, you told me you needed a wife."

"I did. I do." His older brother had died two years ago, making Benedict the sole heir to an earldom. His father was in precarious health, and his own was always suspect. It wasn't that he had a delicate constitution per se, only that he was finicky about his food. That had stood him in good stead against the odd poisoning since he rarely ate a hearty meal, but he sometimes wondered if he would have a more formidable physique if only he ate as other men did. In any event, he needed a wife and a son as soon as possible.

Gabriel nodded. "Three weeks ago, I compiled a list of eligible women who would serve you well in a diplomatic career, would likely give you strong heirs, and would seamlessly join her life to yours."

"I have it," Benedict said, pointing to a nearby stack of papers. In it was the major's list of eligible young ladies, complete with accompanying assets, virtues, and potential problems. The man had been impressively thorough.

"Miss Janelle Caddick was not on that list."

Benedict cocked a brow. The major hadn't asked a question, though he'd implied a dozen. Unfortunately for him, Benedict was not in a forthcoming mood.

Gabriel broke first. "Damn it, Benny, why her?"

"Why wasn't she on your list?" he countered.

"Because she's the nobody daughter of a baron without any useful connections. Why would she be on the list?"

"Because I like her." His response seemed to startle Gabriel, and no wonder. Benedict wasn't known for liking anything female. The business of nations centered around men, and he had no interest in being distracted from that.

"How did you even meet her?"

"Lord Nathaniel recommended her. He's much more into the social whirl than you are."

"A donkey is more in the social whirl than I am," the man grumbled.

"Which, incidentally, is part of the problem."

The major's expression turned thunderous. "What?"

Benedict ignored the warning. "You were brilliant in Spain. You took me from a raw recruit to the man I am now. You saved my life countless times, and I would not go to war without you by my side."

The major took the compliment with a steady expression. He was not a man to preen with praise nor crumple with criticism, but his head tilted as he tried to guess where Benedict was going.

Benedict sighed. "Gabriel, what do you want?"

"I don't understand."

Of course he didn't. "I wouldn't have survived Spain without you. You're the best aide-de-camp anywhere. But I'm in the Foreign Office now. I'm a diplomat, and you're not predisposed to playing the pretty with royalty or petty tyrants."

The man stiffened until Benedict feared he'd snap his spine. "Do you wish to end my service with you?"

"Good God, no!" Benedict sighed then abruptly pulled out a whiskey flask from his desk drawer. He offered some to Gabriel, but as expected, the man refused. He was not one to drink before noon. Benedict, on the other hand, felt the need. "If Anthony hadn't died, we'd be having a very different discussion. But he did, so I'm out of the line of fire and into the diplomatic corps."

"You're much better suited to diplomacy," the major said.

Yes, he was. But the major was not. "Do you want to go back to the front lines?"

Gabriel thought about that for a moment, but in the end, he shook his head. "Not unless you do."

An excellent answer. The major was still young, but he'd received enough wounds already. He didn't need to risk more.

"Do you want a wife? A family?"

There was a flash of hunger in the man's eyes. A need that burned hot enough that he couldn't suppress the desire. But then it was quickly shut down. "No, I don't."

"That's a damned lie," Benedict muttered. "And you know it."

He pushed the whiskey forward, and this time Gabriel did take a long pull. But then he set it down and his gaze never left the flask. "Even if I found a woman willing to marry a bastard—"

"There are many, I assure you."

"My children will still carry the taint."

True enough, but many bastards managed highly respectable lives. The major was a perfect example of that. "That can be overcome."

"My mother can't be. I'm a whoreson and she'll try to get her claws in them, too."

Benedict frowned. "What happened with her last night?"

Gabriel shrugged. "The usual. She wants me to repair the Rose Garden. The place needs a new roof and more. She wants…" He sighed as he lifted up his palms in defeat.

"Worship."

"Yes."

"Control over you."

"Over everything, but me especially." He shrugged. "I am not the child I once was, and she is determined to return me to infancy where I am dependent upon her whims."

Growing up as the son of a famous courtesan had marked the man. He could have become an immoral, self-indulgent hanger-on. Instead, he'd entered the military and become zealous in his moral core. He had some flexibility—no one could survive a war zone without it. But in his own actions, Gabriel was excruciatingly correct. It would become tiresome if Benedict didn't need the reminders while treading murky diplomatic waters.

"Does she hate you?"

"I don't know. She will be quiet for a time and then strike. I think she wants to break me."

"But why? You are her son."

"Any man who leaves her control must be forever despised. Even her own son."

Benedict shuddered. His own parents were prickly, set in their ways, and currently enfeebled. He catered to their whims only when it aligned with his own. He did not envy his friend a mother of influence who could damn his social standing merely by acting infamous. In London especially, Gabriel would always be Madame Sabate's son.

"You need to get married," he pressed. "It would give you an extra layer of respectability and it's a necessity in the diplomatic corps. Isn't there someone who interests you?"

The man sighed as if this were an old argument. This was, in fact, the first time they'd discussed it openly.

"I follow England's banner and you," Gabriel said. "I need nothing more."

"Every man needs more." Benedict capped the flask as he looked at his closest friend. "My banner is in diplomacy, in fighting Napoleon, in establishing a lasting peace once the Corsican is defeated." Something he hoped would happen any day now.

"I can help with that."

"You can. You are. But..." How could he phrase this delicately?

"You want a respectable aide-de-camp. One who is not a bastard."

Benedict put the flask away. "I don't care about your birth. Indeed, sometimes it's helpful when you get information from your mother, but I think *you* need more."

"I do not."

He ignored the response. "I think you need a new headwind, so to speak. You need to make the way smooth for someone who does not fritter away his time in ballrooms and palaces." Benedict did a great deal more than fritter away his time, but the social whirl was necessary in the diplomatic corps. And that was not the major's forte. "I don't want to lose you, but I think you would be happier in some other capacity. Possibly with another benefactor." One who could give Gabe a noble purpose that did not involve prancing around in ballrooms.

"I can be useful there!" There was a note of panic in the major's voice. A fear that echoed inside Benedict as well. He could not function half so well without Gabriel.

"You are immeasurably useful to me," he said, meaning every word.

"Then let us be done with this ridiculous conversation and focus on your ridiculousness." Gabriel leaned forward, pinning Benedict with a hard stare. "Why Miss Caddick?"

"Why not Miss Caddick?" He smiled. "I like her independence." And he absolutely needed a wife who could fill her own time without bothering him.

"Because we know nothing about her, and she is lying about something!" The major set his hands on Benedict's desk. "I saw her coming out of the Rose Garden. I am sure of it."

Benedict pursed his lips. He knew much more about Miss Caddick than Gabriel did. But that didn't mean he knew *everything*. "What was she doing there?"

"Most likely, she is a spoiled woman who likes to watch. The Rose Garden caters to all kinds, and you do not want a woman like that."

True. Such a wife could be disastrous. But Lord Nathaniel hadn't suggested anything like that. "Are you sure?"

"Of course not! You surprised me yesterday. I've done none of the research necessary."

"You've been too busy for something like this." He'd put Lord Nathaniel on the task because it involved moving through the *ton* so quietly that most people forgot he was there. That was Nate's strength, not Gabriel's.

"You cannot marry her until we know for sure."

"Very well," he said, his mind thinking through the possibilities. From what he understood, "watching" was the last thing on Miss Caddick's mind. But it never hurt to have a woman thoroughly vetted. She was going to be the mother of his children and a future countess. "Go ahead then. Find out everything you can about her. If she has no depravities, know that I will marry her. She is my choice."

Gabrial sighed. "But why? There are so many others—"

"Why are you so against her?"

The man frowned, clearly unsure of the reason himself. "There is something about her…" he said. "It doesn't sit right."

"Find out what it is," Benedict ordered. "Or make her fit because you will be the one to manage the details of her life."

Gabriel gaped at him. "You are joking."

"In Spain, you were my aide-de-camp. In the Foreign Office, you are my personal secretary. That includes making sure my wife functions exactly as she ought."

"Benny," Gabriel chided softly. "That should be handled by you."

"Until Napoleon is gone and a peace established, I have no time for other things."

"Siring a family is not something to delegate." Though his voice didn't raise, there was steel in his tone.

"Well," Benedict hedged, "some things I may wish to do by myself. But for all the practical things, I shall rely on you." Then he picked up the top letter on his correspondence pile and began to work. A moment later, Gabriel pushed to his feet.

"This is not a usual activity for a personal secretaries," he groused.

"Definitely not," Benedict quipped. "But then you are so

much more than that to me."

Gabriel huffed out a response. It was half grunt, half laugh and it meant that he had accepted his tasks. That was why they worked so well together. Benedict saw clearly what needed to be done, and Gabriel saw the things accomplished.

Even outrageous things, like the getting of a wife.

Chapter Five

"THANK YOU FOR meeting me before the fashionable hour." Benedict looked at the afternoon sun as it pushed weakly through the clouds. "I fear even an hour later would make it too cold for that dress." He glanced significantly down at his fiancée's cleavage.

She had lovely skin, lightly browned to a golden hue. He didn't hold with the fashionable idea of painting or bleaching one's face to a ghostly white. It made him think of death every time. Miss Caddick had a healthy pink to her flesh with a modest tan that he appreciated. Unfortunately, she also had full breasts and her ample cleavage detracted from her beauty, so he looked away rather than down.

Perhaps he should have selected a taller bride.

"I was pleased for the walk," she responded. "And you are correct, the weather is better now than it will be in a couple hours."

She spoke with a pleasant voice, calm and yet clear. She had no idea her voice was what first made her acceptable to him. She was one of a dozen possible brides, all based on her financial and social particulars. He'd wanted to delay matrimony as long as possible, but his time had run out. His parents were anxious that the title get an heir, and Lord Castlereigh had made it clear that his advancement at the Foreign Office required a useful wife. And so he had begun his search several weeks ago.

He'd been about to choose someone else when he'd heard

her speak that one time and had been delighted. Her voice did not grate, neither did it push. There was no nasal quality, which he abhorred, and he could well imagine his children being put to bed at night with her voice in their ears.

He'd decided upon her that very moment, though he naturally took pains to meet every woman on Major Vance's list before making his final offer to Miss Caddick's father. And now she walked beside him at a measured pace with a contained aspect. He could not be more satisfied.

"Are you recovered from last night's ball?" he inquired. "I apologize for leaving so abruptly."

"Of course, I understand. I hope all is well?"

"Missives arrived from the front. And yes, all is well. Napoleon is defeated and should abdicate very soon now. It is only a matter of time."

"That is great news," she said, and he could hear the relief in her tone. "But I expect you are very busy making sure he and his remaining army knows they are defeated."

He smiled. "That is the task of the military. My work is diplomatic in nature. My efforts are built upon their firm foundation. If they had not defeated the Corsican, then I would have little to do."

She slanted him an assessing look. "I believe you are being modest. But either way, I cannot expect you to dance attendance upon me when our nation is at stake."

It had hardly been the nation at stake. More his own sanity if he'd been forced to listen to more inane prattle at the ball. Nevertheless, he seized upon the excuse to make a point. "It is good that you realize I am not reliable at social events. I often need to leave early as I did last night, and that is if I attend at all. I enjoy a ball as much as any man—" A lie if ever there was one. "But my work requires me to miss too many of them."

"Do men enjoy them?" she wondered aloud. "It seems to me that unless a man is searching for a bride or launching a daughter, he is more interested in his own conversation over drinks at his club rather than in the heated space of a crowded ballroom."

He chuckled. "I do enjoy dancing with a good partner."

"Then you have selected the wrong bride, my lord. I am afraid I am barely adequate on the dance floor."

They were passing another couple strolling in the fitful sunlight, and he nodded to the pair as was appropriate. They responded in kind and would have stopped to converse (the gentleman had very specific political ambitions), but Benedict had no interest in a distraction. This time was carved out specifically to be with his future bride.

"You dance quite well," he said once they were far enough past the other pair.

"You flatter me."

He did, but she was by no means clumsy. "I am more concerned with your exchange with my aide-de-camp last night. I understand he upset you."

She tensed, but only by the most minute fraction. "It was nothing, my lord."

"It was enough that several people overheard and reported back to me about it. What did he say to you?"

"Truly, it was nothing. A minor bit of confusion. I have already forgotten it."

He waited a moment, as did she, to see if the topic was finished. He wouldn't allow it to drop, but he wanted to see if she was one of those women who claimed to forget something and yet chattered on incessantly about it anyway.

"Look how pretty that bird is," she exclaimed, pointing to a nearby tree. "A cardinal, I think, and so bright."

Good. She was not one to prattle on. "Major Vance has been my man for years. He served with me in the peninsula and came with me to the Foreign Office. He has my utmost confidence."

Her hand dropped back down to her side. Clearly the bird was forgotten, and then she spoke, her words filled with the flat notes of resignation. "Of course, my lord. I shall apologize to him when next we meet."

"You misunderstand me, Miss Caddick."

"My lord?"

"I would like to know how he insulted you."

She jolted, clearly shocked.

"Did you think I assumed you at fault?" He didn't need her to answer. "I have known Major Vance for many years. I know his value and his weaknesses. I doubt you are someone who causes scenes whereas he can be…"

"Irritatingly misguided?"

He chuckled. "The major is a passionate man. He is the most honest and trustworthy soul I know, but rigid ethics have caused him some pain."

"Oh?" she asked, a little too eagerly. "You find him rigid and uncompromising?"

Occasionally. "Do you know anything of his history?"

"Not even the tiniest."

"He is the by-blow of the Duke of Torbay and Madame Triana Sabate."

"He's a bastard?" She huffed. "One would think that a man with such parentage would be less inflexible in his thoughts."

"Then one would not know Major Vance. Because of his unfortunate birth, he must work harder and be smarter than any of his contemporaries. Worse, any deviation from the highest moral standard is seen as proof that he deserves every ill thing that has ever befallen him."

"All because he is illegitimate?"

"Yes."

He waited to see how judgmental she would be. Indeed, when he'd first heard of their disagreement, he'd thought she was reacting to the offense of his mere birth. But it would seem she had not known of it.

"Children do not choose their parents," she said. "His birth was their fault, not his."

"I am pleased to hear you say such."

She slanted a look up at him. "I am not a hard-hearted woman, my lord."

"Which is why I must ask you again, what did he do to upset you?"

She shook her head. "As I said, it was nothing."

Her hand was on his arm in the proper place at the proper weight. At her words, he grabbed her fingertips with his free hand and squeezed them tight enough to catch her attention.

"Honesty, Miss Caddick. Do not lie to me or our marriage will be very unhappy indeed." His voice held no censure, but she understood his message nonetheless.

"It was a simple misunderstanding, my lord. He thought he saw me someplace I was not. He was very insistent, but he was mistaken." There was force behind her words.

"Where?"

"It's not—" She cut off her words when his fingers tightened over hers again. "Someplace called the Rose Garden. Do you know it?"

"I do indeed." A great deal better than she did. "And he thought he saw you there? In what capacity?"

She snorted. "Not in any capacity that you can imagine." She took a steadying breath. "He was confused, my lord."

He stopped their walk near a tree. The park had several, and this one was mercifully deserted. He turned her to face him and stepped intimately close. To anyone observing, they would look like a newly engaged couple sharing a romantic moment. But when she faced him, he spoke with the full force of his personality.

"Think carefully before you answer my next question, Miss Caddick. We are to be together for the rest of our lives, and I cannot manage what I do not know. Sometimes the tiniest details can be the unravelling of the cleverest plots."

She pulled back, confusion on the delicate features of her face. "You are being disturbingly fierce."

He didn't soften any part of his stance or delivery. "Miss Caddick, were you then or have you ever been inside the Rose

Garden?"

She tilted her head back and stared hard at him. He noted every flicker of her eyes, every shift of her body. He was a man trained to spot lies, and he studied her for every possible tell.

"I have not," she said firmly. "And it does you no credit to suggest otherwise."

"Excellent," he said with a surge of joy. Then he pulled her gloved hand up to his mouth and pressed a kiss there. "You are a fantastic liar. That will serve me well."

Chapter Six

JANELLE'S HEART ABRUPTLY beat triple time. Had her fiancé just been happy to call her a liar? What exactly did he know? What did he *think* he knew? But she couldn't ask those things. Instead, she slowed her heart by using her best empty-headed miss expression. She lifted her chin and tilted her head, then capped it off with a narrowing of her brows.

"I'm sorry?" she said. "I don't understand."

He chuckled and it was a warm sound even as his eyes narrowed in a subtle kind of warning. "Perhaps we should discuss what I expect of my wife." He turned, holding out his arm to her so they could continue to stroll.

Part of her wanted to fight him. She wanted to demand exactly how he knew she was lying. She wanted to defend her actions. But that would be to admit she lied, and so she did what she always did when faced with her own deception. She smiled brilliantly and continued on as if the appearance of being an honest, honorable woman was enough to make it so.

"I am at your disposal," she said, hating the exact meaning of that phrase. It made her sound like a pile of old clothes that he could use or discard at his whim. Which, of course, was exactly true.

He spoke congenially as they continued their stroll. His tone was matter-of-fact and yet so cutting to her self-esteem that she found it hard to keep her composure.

"I am an important man in the government," he said without

hubris. "Several people will ask you questions, try to trap you into revealing my thoughts and plans. I expect you to be pleasant, charming, and completely blank, as if you haven't the slightest thought in your head. Exactly as you did just now." He tapped her arm. "But do try to control your breath better. Whatever happens, you should maintain an exactly even tempo. Should Lucifer himself appear before you, I expect your breath to remain at the same pace, as if you had just awoken from a pleasant sleep."

"That is a tall order, my lord," she said, working to keep her voice even.

"You can do it. I expect you've been practicing it since you were a young girl. Your father is not one to tolerate emotional displays, is he? Any type of independent thought or feeling had to be scrupulously hidden."

What to say to that? Her father cared only that she appear in every way a lady. That meant polite behavior in public and absolute silence in private. Anything else was punished ruthlessly. Indeed, that was why she got very good at entertaining herself far away from her father.

As for emotional displays, Mrs. Sundy had stressed remaining calm when everyone else panicked. Her aspect must always be one of gentle reassurance. Indeed, the woman had her practice by calming frightened animals. If Janelle could get a barking dog to settle, then she could quiet an anxious mother.

"A lady is always serene," she said softly, repeating a phrase written in a book about appropriate female behavior. It had been a gift from her aunt before her first season, and the basis on which she'd been judged since she was old enough to debut in society.

"My lady wife," continued Lord Benedict, "will also not question my activities, wonder about my whereabouts, nor respond to any queries about my person."

Gentleman always had a free hand with their lives. Unlike their wives. "I expect your work keeps you busy—"

"At all hours of the day and night."

"Of course."

"Similarly, I shall not question yours."

She jolted. That was absolutely not what most men required of their wives. And while she stared at him in surprise, he frowned down at her.

"Breath, Miss Caddick. Keep it steady."

She immediately inhaled and exhaled, smoothing her expression to one of bland happiness. "You…um…don't wish to know my whereabouts? Ever?"

"I require you to be safe, circumspect, and chaste."

She was mindful of her breath this time, for all that this was an extraordinary conversation. "My maidenhead is still intact, my lord, and I have never demonstrated loose morals."

"I assumed as much, otherwise I would never have offered for you. However, I must point out that if Major Vance discovers a secret interest, others may as well. Therefore, you have two choices. Either cease your unusual activities or have Major Vance accompany you on all your excursions."

It took a moment for his words to sink in, but when they did, she shook with outrage. "I will not!" she exclaimed. She would not have that disagreeable man dogging her every step.

"Breathing, my dear."

She was not "his dear" yet, and if he thought…

She steadied herself. Inhale. Exhale. "Just what kind of excursions do you think I engage in?"

He patted her hand. "The Foreign Offices has many contacts. I made inquiries about you."

"What?" she gasped, panic nearly choking off her word.

He patted her hand until her breath steadied.

"One of my contacts mentioned that you have a surprising education in medicine. Thanks to a Mrs. Sundy? Since women often do not get the best care, I find your childhood interest admirable. Provided that is all it is."

Oh hell. Just how much did he know? "You are…" *Aware?* "Um, you find it acceptable? And will allow me to continue?"

"Provided you are safe, circumspect, and chaste."

"I can be all of those things without Major Vance accompanying me."

He nodded. "Perhaps you can, but until I am sure of you, he will be by your side." He squeezed her fingers tightly. "Do not cross me on this. It will not end well for either of us."

They were nearing the edge of the park. Their time together was almost over.

"I have been all three of those things for my entire life. I shall continue as such without any—" *Interference.* "—assistance from your secretary. Who undoubtably has more important matters to attend."

"You have not been, Miss Caddick. A chaste woman does not go out alone at night. Nor is that safe or circumspect."

"I don't think you understand the nature of my actions."

"Let me emphasize that I determine the Major's priorities, and I have absolute faith in him to see you brought in line." Then he turned to her, his expression mollifying. "You have not wandered far, so it should not be difficult to rein in your intemperance."

Not chaste? Her intemperance? "My lord, you have a vast misperception about—"

"Purity is not just about one's actions, Miss Caddick, but also about one's thoughts. Your investigations into anatomy are hardly modest. Indeed, I believe your discussions with Madame Florina to be the exact opposite."

There hadn't been many discussions with Madame Florina. She'd learned last season by accident that the lady aided pregnant women—for a price—and Betty Gill had offered her services as midwife. Any other discussions had not happened yet. They'd been interrupted by Holly's labor. When they occurred, however, they would be about healing ointments and the exact location of the apothecary she trusted. But she couldn't say any of that without admitting she knew who Madame Florina was. So she raised her hands with a frustrated flick of her palms. "Who is

Madame Florina?"

He nodded as if very pleased with her. "You continue to impress, Miss Caddick."

"And you continue to insult me! I am no liar," she lied. "I am as circumspect and chaste as it is possible to be, and yet you accuse me of being a strumpet who—"

"I said no such thing." His tone was hard and flat, effectively cutting off her tirade. She knew that tone from her father, and it was one she defied at her own peril. She buttoned her lip though she was still burning with fury.

"For the life of me," she said through clenched teeth, "I do not understand you."

"Then let me be clear. Marriage to me will elevate you considerably in lifestyle and opportunities. Your children will be titled, and you will be treated with respect and honor wherever you go."

"I am well aware of your title, my lord, and the consequence you can bestow."

"Were you aware that I can also introduce you to Caroline Hershel, Lady Hester Stanhope, and Jane Austen?"

Janelle searched her memory. Everyone knew of Caroline Hershel, finder of comets. Her name had been on everyone's tongue when she'd received a pension from the king. People also talked when he'd bestowed a pension upon Lady Hester Stanhope, the woman who acted as the prime minster Pitt's hostess and private secretary until his death several years ago. "Who is Jane Austen?"

Lord Benedict leaned in close. "She is the author of *Sense and Sensibility* and *Pride and Prejudice*."

"Truly? But how do you know?" Everyone spoke about those novels, and many had speculated on who the author was. Her works were listed as written by *'A lady'*."

He smiled. "You will find I know a great many things, and I can share some of them with you."

"But at what cost, my lord? What do you think I'm doing?"

They were at the end of their walk, heading toward where his carriage awaited them. "That is why I have assigned the major to remain by your side." He paused as he looked directly at her. "Let me be clear."

"Yes, please!"

"I am marrying because Lord Castlereigh will not promote me unless I have wed. I also desperately need an heir. With Napoleon vanquished, there will be ample opportunities for advancement as new alliances are drawn throughout the continent. Therefore, I need a wife. But she must be above reproach and content to be left completely alone for months at a time."

"I am such a bride."

"So you appear to me after a cursory inquiry, but I need further assurance."

"Such as?"

"Such as Major Vance's approval. As I have said, his unfortunate birth has forced him to act at a level of morality that is unimpeachable. If you can assuage his concerns about you, then we can marry."

She stopped just short of her carriage door. "My lord, you have already proposed, and I have accepted. I am the only one who can cry off now."

He chuckled. "Then cry off, Miss Caddick. But you will never find another man who will allow you the freedoms I propose, nor give you the kind of life which I can provide."

"Assuming I prove myself to your aide-de-camp? Surely, I must prove myself to you."

His smile didn't change as he handed her into his carriage. "Major Vance has my utmost trust. He is driven to weed out the tiniest threats to my consequence. I have judged you worthy, but before we speak our vows, you must get his approval as well." He stepped back from the carriage. "Do try to be quick about it. I may need to leave for Vienna. There is talk of a congress there."

She frowned as he shut the carriage door behind her, while he remained on the street. "Aren't you riding with me?" she asked through the lowered window.

"I have a few things to accomplish nearby. I shall send Major Vance to you this evening. I believe you attend the theater?"

Yes, her aunt had accepted a seat at Lord Tomlin's box, but Janelle planned to suffer a migraine so that she could study Madame Florina's unguents. She wanted to see if she could figure out the recipe. "Er, yes, but—"

"He hates the theater, and so that should be an excellent time for you to get to know one another."

With a man in a grumpy mood? That sounded like the worst kind of hell to her. Nevertheless, her fiancé had spoken. Before she could find a way to get out of this ridiculous situation, the man doffed his hat and then spoke to the coachman. A moment later, he was lost from view, and she felt doomed to a miserable evening with Major Vance.

Chapter Seven

GABRIEL RELISHED THE idea of going to the theater tonight. He wasn't interested in the play—fiction rarely intrigued him—but the opportunity to study his quarry made it invaluable. Gathering intelligence was the first step in any endeavor, and tonight he was going to watch Miss Caddick interact with her friends, her former suitors, and any number of other interesting people. With all the possibilities, he'd be able to see a pattern in her lies.

Was she a twitcher? Or did she freeze her body instead? What was the woman's tell? If he couldn't figure it out by the end of the evening, then he was not the asset to Lord Benedict that a good aide-de-camp should be.

Diplomacy was about guessing people's intentions, recognizing their lies, and knowing when to trust that someone was telling the truth. If Gabriel intended to advance alongside Lord Benedict, then he needed to excel at these things. And if he couldn't figure out a debutante's lies, he'd be useless among the professional liars in international politics.

He stabled his horse nearby, leaving his evening clothes in a satchel there. What he wore now were the casual clothes of a laborer, complete with a dirty hat pulled down over his ears. He didn't bother with a gun, but he had his knives. No reason to keep them close except that it was crazy to walk around London unarmed, especially in the areas he sometimes wandered.

Miss Caddick lived in a respectable neighborhood. Nothing

like the exalted homes to which she no doubt aspired, but it probably served her purpose. The area was busy enough that a woman could slip in and out without anyone noticing. All sorts of mischief available to a curious miss.

He walked to the servants' entrance and saw exactly what he expected—something odd for a typical London household. There seemed to be several people loitering about the back door, more than should be expected for a household of two. Even with a large staff, what possible need could the baron and Miss Caddick have for a fruit seller, a couple laborers, and two footmen in the livery of Lord Gardner? Since they seemed to stand in a loose line, he slipped quietly in behind the footmen, listening for whatever he could hear.

It was all general talk, especially when people stood in a queue. The footmen griped about moving furniture around for the perpetually redecorating Lady Gardner who lived two blocks away. They'd both been injured while trying to maneuver a massive wardrobe. One had his hand sliced from an exposed nail. The other had been crushed—or so he claimed—when the wardrobe toppled onto him. There was much grumbling and teasing between the two, though the bloody gash did look deep.

Neither man said a thing when Gabe fell in behind them. They were more interested in making eyes at the young female fruit seller who was just now exiting the house. She was all smiles and saucy hips as she sauntered away, but nothing about her stood out.

What the hell was everyone doing here?

The first of the two laborers went in, pulling his hat off his greasy head in respect. It was only the luck of the light that Gabe saw that his hair wasn't dirty as much as bloody. Lord, what had sliced his head open? His friend followed, clearly there as support for the first man. Then the door closed leaving the two footmen still waiting and Gabe behind them.

What was going on in there?

Cleaning apparently, because ten minutes later, the housekeeper popped open the door. She had a bucket of bloody water to dump.

"Move aside or get yer boots wet."

The two footmen jumped sideways barely fast enough to avoid the splash. Luckily, Gabe wasn't in the line of fire, so he watched the woman's expression. It was bland despite her bloody work, as if she were accustomed to cleaning a man's head wound. He'd only seen the like on the faces of doctors on the battlefield. The housekeeper wasn't as world weary, of course, but she wasn't discomforted either.

Odd and odder, but he couldn't figure out a way to ask what was going on. She went back in and then a moment later, the two laborers came out, both nodding their thanks. The one with the head wound wasn't bandaged up, as Gabe expected, but cleaned such that a pink flush appeared on his cheeks. When he turned, Gabe saw that a thick unguent had been applied to his gash.

Medical care? Why were they coming here for that?

Meanwhile, the housekeeper came back out to address the two footmen. "It's you two again, is it? What now?"

The one with the cut hand held it up. The housekeeper scanned the wound, then stepped aside such that he could enter the kitchen. But when his companion stepped forward, the woman held out her hand to stop him.

"An' what of you?"

"I got crushed 'ard," he said. "My arm."

She frowned at him, then quick as a wink, punched his forearm. He pulled it back with a sharp cry, not of pain but surprise. That was enough for the housekeeper. "Off with you."

"But it's hurt!"

"What's hurt is your nether regions. Miss Betty's not got time for you."

"Are you sure?" The man pressed. "She can't work all the time."

"She can and she does. And if she didn't, she wouldn't be wasting time with you." She stepped closer, forcing him to retreat. Except the footman was determined. Rather than move backwards, he sidestepped and tried to sidle past.

He failed. The woman gripped the man's ear and hauled him away. Gabe winced in sympathy. There'd been a few good years during his childhood when he'd had a nanny of sorts. She was a retired whore who was quick with those pincher fingers, and his left ear was a quarter inch larger because of how many times she'd grabbed it.

The footman took his discipline with a good-natured shrug. "Just tell her Freddie Morgan was here. Just tell her—"

"Out!" the housekeeper ordered. "Or I'll be having a word with Mrs. Wallace about you."

Gabe guessed that Mrs. Wallace was the housekeeper at Lord and Lady Gardner's residence because Mr. Morgan ducked his head and rushed away.

"Impertinent dog," the woman muttered as she watched him run off. Then she focused hard eyes on Gabe. "And what about you? What ails you, an' who brought you?"

"Freddie said to come," he lied quickly.

"Freddie says a lot of things. So?" She looked him up and down. "You don't look hurt."

Good because he wasn't one to advertise his injuries. Fortunately for him, he had one that would likely get him inside. Three nights ago, he'd gone to help an old friend and gotten beaten with a poker for his troubles. Fortunately, he'd managed to dodge or blunt most of the impacts. All except the first which had landed hard on his ribs. He lifted his shirt and angled his torso so that the woman could see the mottled bruise.

She frowned, but didn't gasp at the sight, which was none too pretty. "Very well. Did Freddie tell you the rules?"

"Naw," he said. "Just that I should come."

"Course not," she said, rolling her eyes. "Not a word about this to anyone. If I find out you talked, Miss Betty can poison as well as heal, so keep that in mind. Now what exactly did Freddie say to you?"

He tucked his shirt back in place. "Nothing. I followed him. Wanted to see."

"Come to gawk at the witch woman?" He didn't think she could grow harder, but her temper showed in the low fury in her voice.

"No, ma'am. I just thought I could get help."

She frowned. "Does it pain you much?"

Nothing compared to some of his injuries. "Like the devil himself gripped me in his fist."

"Hm," she said, clearly not believing him. "Very well. You'll keep track of everything for a week. What you did, when, and how it looked. Everything, you understand? And ye'll come back to tell us."

"Yes, ma'am."

"Don't forget. And don't tell. She may not curse you, but I will." She shook her head. "And I'm going to start with Freddie Mason," she grumbled as she turned around and headed into the kitchen. "Stupid boy." Then she glanced back over her shoulder. "Well, come on then. She's got a minute for you now."

He followed obediently, pausing as the first footman waved his newly bandaged hand and headed out. Then Gabe was ushered to a small room originally meant for storage. It was a stillroom now with jars and bottles along the walls, a scarred wooden table in the middle, a basin of water, and a stoop-shouldered woman with a large bum. She had her back to him as she hunched over a ledger scribbling down something and muttering to herself.

Clearly Freddie was attracted to dowdy, maternal women because the dress and demeanor reminded him of the matron at Eaton. To his child's mind, she'd been a hundred years old as she talked about retiring to mind her garden and never seeing an impudent boy again.

"All right then," came a raspy voice. "Let's see it, hmmm?" The woman turned around and Gabe was shocked by her liquid brown eyes and the elegant sweep to her cheekbones.

Then he looked deeper.

It was a good disguise, he admitted. Her dress, her raspy voice, and the awkward way she moved would all lead him to think she was someone else. But those liquid brown eyes were hard to disguise, not to mention the overall bone structure beneath her dirty face. Miss Betty was none other than Miss Caddick indulging herself by playing doctor with the neighboring servants.

He knew the minute she recognized him. She jolted but then covered by setting aside her ledger. Would she accuse him right away? Or continue with her ruse? Clearly, she was a woman who enjoyed deception because she kept at her role of dowdy matron. She ducked her head to become more stooped than before, then squinted at him.

"What is it?" she rasped. "You look healthy enough."

She was brazening out her disguise in the hopes that he was as blind as she pretended to be. He could call her on the ruse, but why? He wanted to see just how far she would go until she cried uncle.

He used his regular voice, speaking slowly as he shrugged out of his coat. "I got kicked by a horse," he lied. "Two days ago. Knocked me clear across the stall."

She turned away from him to pick up one of the newly fashionable fountain pens. "Did you hear or feel anything break?"

"No mum."

"Can you take a deep breath without pain?"

"No mum." That was the truth. Though the injury was healing, he felt it every time he did anything, including sleep. The damned bruise was annoying as hell. Just not nearly as painful as he pretended.

"Let me see."

He pulled off his shirt, moving gingerly because of his injury, but also because he wanted to watch her while his chest was revealed. He knew he was a well-built man. Many women had praised his body, if not necessarily his face. He watched her eyes widen as the breadth of his body was revealed, but then they abruptly narrowed.

"This was not from a horse," she said, her voice tart. Then she folded her arms. "The truth now, Mr... Um, what is your name?"

"Gabriel Smith."

Her gaze flickered to his eyes at his lie but then snapped back to his torso. "Very well, Mr. Smith, tell me the truth of this injury or leave now."

"How do you know it wasn't done by a horse?"

"Because of the shape of it." She set her hand, palm flat, on the livid bruise. "It is not especially hot," she said, then she stroked the length of it. "That's a good sign, but the welt is pronounced. And the colors." She poked her fingers at the worst parts of the injury. "You have quite a painting here along your ribs."

Her tone was detached and professional, as if she truly were a doctor. Her hands, however, put the lie to her words. Her fingertips stroked across the length of his bruise, lingering on his abdomen before testing the swollen rise. Her eyes never left his body, and he felt the intense scrutiny of her gaze.

She pursed her lips as she drew a line across his ribs. "A block of wood, I think, but narrower." She snapped her fingers. "A poker, wasn't it? Swung lengthwise."

"Exactly right," he said, startled by the thickness of his own voice. What the hell? He was no green boy that sprung to attention at the mere touch of a woman. And yet he felt the familiar rush to his cock at her obvious joy. There was happiness in her voice at a puzzle solved. He, on the other hand, felt heat burn in his cheeks in embarrassment. "I had my hands full, and this was the thanks I got." He used his intonation carefully to suggest something lascivious. How a woman flirted back always told him something.

Except Miss Caddick didn't flirt back. Instead, she twisted her head as she looked closer at his bruise. "And why were you attacked by a poker?"

"Not by a poker. By the granny wielding it."

She twisted, her fingers flowing over his ribs with careful study. "Attacked by a grandmother. Did you deserve it?"

"Gad no. I stepped into her swing. Little thing, not tall enough to meet my shoulder, but she had strength in her arms."

She nodded. "Lie down on the table."

"What?"

She waved impatiently at the wooden table. "Lie down. You came here for medicine, didn't you? Unless you have another reason for coming to my door." She knew he was here to investigate her, but he wasn't ready to admit that yet.

"Will it fester?" he asked as he stretched out on the wood table.

"Did the skin break? Did you bleed?"

"No."

"Then you are likely fine. When did it happen?" She dipped her fountain pen in the ink, then brought it over to his side.

"Three nights ago. What are you doing?"

She didn't answer at first. Her attention was back on his body as she set her pen to his torso. With steady strokes, she outlined the edges of his bruise. She had one hand flat on his side while the other flowed in a smooth line across and around the discoloration.

"It's easiest," she said, "to remember an injury if I draw around it." Her tongue slipped out between her teeth as she worked. It was a tiny bit of red, pushed between her pink lips, but it hit his blood like a fire that burned all the way to his cock.

She stepped back to look at the outline she had drawn on his skin. It was such a simple thing, but damn it, he was sweating from the contact. "I thought you were going to give me medicine," he grumbled as he started to sit up.

"I am," she said as she pushed him back down. He could have bested her, but he liked the feel of her small hand on his chest too much to push her away. "Stay down. I'm not done yet."

Her fingertips were light as her fingers trembled across his bruise. She found the raised outlines of the welt and began to draw around that.

"Why was she attacking you?"

"What?" Good God, he had to focus on something other than her hands on her his body.

"The granny with the poker."

Oh. "She wanted to stop her son-in-law from taking his boy."

She twisted to dip her pen into the ink. "Well, that's hardly fair. If it's his son."

He shrugged.

"Don't move!"

He froze. He even kept his breath shallow. "He was out of his mind drunk. We were all trying to stop him." He winced as she pressed into a sensitive spot. "I had him, if the granny had just given me a moment."

"Grannies don't tend to be restrained when a child is threatened."

That was certainly true.

"So you were in the middle of a family fight as a drunk tried to take his child to…where?"

"I have no idea. I doubt he did, either."

"Why were you there?"

Because Rogers was one of his former company. He'd heard from someone else that the man was home and none too happy about it, so he'd gone to check. Some men didn't adjust to home life after the army, and Rogers was one of them. Gabe had gone to help and found a disaster instead.

"What did you do?" she asked. Her voice had lost its rough tone.

"Got him away. Sobered him up."

"Then what?"

"I'm trying to find him a job. He's a good man, but he's lost without a commander."

She set aside her pen and grabbed a jar off the shelf. "Sounds like this granny would make a good one."

Maybe. But Rodgers was not a man to listen to any woman. "What's that?" he asked as she scooped up something that looked like pig fat mixed with leaves.

"It's the medicine," she said as she began to work it into his body. Her fingers were strong as they kneaded it into his side. It was painful, of course, but there was something about her rough treatment that felt good. There was a brusqueness to her task, as if she knew it hurt but it had to be done. She worked efficiently and for some perverse reason, he enjoyed the ache even as he winced.

Whatever the ointment was, it heated under her fingers. His breath shortened as he alternately held or released it in a quick pant. It lasted more than a minute, or so it seemed. Her hands slowed and her fingers softened. Then she ran her thumb across an old scar along his side.

"What happened there?"

"Knife fight."

"Oh!" It wasn't a coo of admiration. More an embarrassed jolt that momentarily lifted her hand off his body. "Was it a terrible battle?"

"It was an amazing battle," he said, letting nostalgia color his voice. "I was six, he was eight. We were playing medieval knights. I thought a cleaver was the better weapon, being heavier. He picked a long cooking knife. We each held a pot as a shield."

"Good heavens. Who left you alone with knives?"

He was often unsupervised as a child, especially in the lean years. "Joey's mother found us, I believe, but not before I'd learned a valuable lesson."

"To not play with knives?"

"That longer reach is valuable in a knife fight. Joey was both taller and had the longer weapon. I never had a chance." He grinned. "Though I did whack him in the face with the pot. That's what brought his mother. He howled like I'd broken his jaw."

"Did you?"

"No. But thinking back, I could have easily done so."

She snorted, then rolled him forward so that he lay half on his side, and she could inspect his back. She even moved a lamp so she could see better as she stroked across his flesh. Her fingers heated his skin more than her ointment, and he closed his eyes to feel her touch better.

"What made these scars?" she asked. "This one looks terrible."

"Shrapnel," he said, remembering the pain as it had ripped through him.

"What's that?"

He smiled, though the expression was grim. "It's a who. Lieutenant Henry Shrapnel invented a hollow cannonball filled with shot. It explodes mid-air. I got hit by a piece of it."

She shuddered. He felt it all the way through her fingertips. "That sounds awful."

"Not if the cannonball goes where it's supposed to." He and his men had been squeezing the enemy's flank on the right side. If the cannonball had exploded over the French as intended, he wouldn't have a scar. Unfortunately, cannonballs don't always land where they're aimed. And if they explode mid-air, their radius of damage is a great deal larger than with normal balls.

"I expect it's awful, no matter whose side you're on." Her finger followed the jagged ridge again. "I'm sorry."

"I lived. As did many of my men." Unfortunately, surviving a battle wasn't enough anymore, as he was learning from Rogers. Bodies often healed faster than minds did, and no one came back from war a whole man. He flashed her a grin. "We won the battle."

She didn't return his smile. "As long as you're pleased with the result." The words were spoken with a dry disgust. As if the struggle of empires was folly to her.

"Would you rather Bonaparte won?"

She winced. "Of course not, but..." She cut off her words, and her expression closed down as she took a step back.

"But you think a monster can be fought without casualties. You want us to prattle and threaten but never carry through."

Her brows narrowed. "I never said anything like that."

She didn't need to. He heard the women in the street, wailing when the lists of dead came. He knew the politicians who wanted to hide on England's soil and never venture beyond. To hell with the continent, they said, as if Napoleon would stop before he conquered everywhere.

Gabriel understood the cost of war more than most, but he also knew the enemy they fought. "Napoleon had to be stopped, Miss Caddick. I am proud to have done my part."

She was silent a long moment as she stared at him, and then she gave a slow nod. "And so you should be, Major." She straightened up to her full height. "I apologize. I never meant to suggest otherwise."

He felt his expression settle into a satisfied smirk. She had revealed herself to him. She admitted that she knew his true name. He pushed upright, swinging his feet around such that he faced her bare-chested.

"So you admit your ruse."

Her brows shot up. "Hard to deny it when you call me by name."

"I—" He frowned. He hadn't done that, had he? And yet when he thought back over his words, he realized he was the one who had slipped first. He'd used her true name. Damn it! How had he gotten so sloppy?

"Why are you here, Major Vance? Ugly as that bruise is, I doubt you really needed my salve."

"Why are you playing at being a doctor, Miss Caddick? What is all this?" He gestured at her potions and unguents. He frowned at the ledger. "Just how long have you been doing this?"

Her brows shot up as she abruptly slammed her ledger closed. "Playacting? Good God, do you not see your own hypocrisy? I cannot so much as think about the cost of your war, and yet you dare question mine?"

He snorted. "Are you at war, Miss Caddick?"

"I am," she said stiffly. "Against disease and death. And it is a much nobler endeavor than finding new ways to kill a man. I would that Lieutenant Shrapnel had found a different use for his talents."

"And your fiancé wants you to find a new use for yours."

That was a bold statement. In truth, he often had no idea what Lord Benedict was thinking from one minute to the next. But on this, he had to be correct. What man wanted his wife to be fingering half naked men and playing at potions and possets? Certainly not an aristocrat. And definitely not a political one.

"Lord Benedict's fiancée must be the height of propriety. And this…" he said as he swept his sneering gaze about the room. "This is ridiculous."

"Get out," she said, her voice quivering with fury.

"Gladly," he said as he hopped off the table and pulled on his shirt. But lest she think she'd won this battle, he had one last thing to say. He waited until his shirt was back in place and his coat on. And then he picked up his hat and gave her his most elegant—and mocking—bow.

"I shall see you in an hour, Miss Caddick. I believe we are to go to the theater."

"If you think I will—"

"You will because Lord Benedict has ordered it."

She sputtered, but he didn't give her time to finish.

"And your father and aunt have been pleased to accept my escort." He chuckled. "I vow I cannot wait to see how you explain your kitchen activities to them. I doubt they will find it any more acceptable than I do."

Chapter Eight

OF ALL THE nerve! That arrogant man had sauntered into her kitchen as if she couldn't tell it was him. As if he deserved free medicine when he judged her at every turn. *Playacting at being a doctor!* Did he not understand the amount of quackery that assaulted every person in England? Cures for warts, putrid throats, or scabrous lumps. Almost none of them worked and many harmed the patient.

She could think of no better use of her time and energy than to sort through the idiocy and serve her people with medicine that helped. But to figure out what worked and what didn't took careful study and testing. It required intelligence and discretion. That Major Vance could believe she was *playacting* like a child with dolls was infuriating!

And that didn't even include the skills she'd gained in Devon. She was a trusted midwife there. Indeed, if only she could get some training at a lying-in hospital, then he wouldn't dare say such things about her. But such a thing would never be allowed by her father and likely not by Lord Benedict either.

It was maddening! Sometimes she dreamed about abandoning everything except the thirty-five pounds required to become a student at any of the lying-in hospitals. But if she did that, where would she live? How would she survive while she trained? And how ashamed would her family be if she threw away the benefits of her name to become someone significantly less exalted? She might not mind, but her aunt would suffer socially from the shame. And her father would be beyond furious. He put great store in his status as a baron. His daughter could not stoop so low as to work in a hospital.

So she learned as best she could. She kept scrupulous notes while testing every unguent and posset that offered a glimmer of hope. And now that idiot major wanted to ruin everything.

She locked up her stillroom and stormed upstairs. As usual, the servants had prepared a bath for her. It was part of her ritual as she changed from Betty into Janelle. One was a witch woman's apprentice. The other was the daughter of a baron and future wife to Lord Benedict. Back in Devon, she used a nearby stream as she made the switch. She washed away whatever she'd done in the freezing water. In London, the servants helped her. It was a terrible strain on them, but the dirt in this city got everywhere and she needed to be free of it as she became Janelle.

Unfortunately, bathing didn't clear the major from her thoughts. It wasn't just his attitude. She'd encountered plenty of men who thought women had nothing in their brains except sweets and hair ribbons. But none of them had power over her. None of them worked as her fiancé's right-hand man. And none of them had a body like a Greek statue that had been brutalized by God-only-knew what kind of battle.

She was a living, breathing woman, after all. She wasn't immune to a handsome man. And though she'd seen all sorts of injuries over the years, many on laboring men, none of them caught her fancy the way Major Vance had. Broad shoulders, powerful muscles, and a wicked smile as he threatened everything she valued in her life.

Too bad God had seen fit to give such a body to an idiot.

Enough! she commanded herself as she finished her toilette. She needed to decide how to handle the bastard tonight. She had to keep him from exposing her activities to her father and aunt. But how? Lying would not work. Not this time. Her aunt was prone to believe anything told to her by a man, whether it was that the sky was green or that flowers bloomed in winter. That was one way Janelle had gotten away with her activities for so long. She'd simply had her brother claim that whatever her aunt thought Janelle was doing was incorrect.

Damn Alex for being away at school right now and not here to help her. He was the only other soul to discover her activities on his own, but once he was over the shock, he'd joined in her conspiracy. After all, he loved duping their father even more than she did.

She spent the rest of her short dressing time mentally testing and discarding possible deceptions. None of them would work without her brother. In the end, she decided the best course would be to laugh off the major's ideas as a joke. How could she possibly run a hospital out of their kitchen? The very idea was ludicrous. Especially since she paid their servants very well to deny her activities. If anyone ratted her out, they would be dismissed without reference and (this was the real threat) none would get the benefit of her medical expertise. Every servant in London got hurt at some point. And those who didn't, knew someone who had. That made every one of their staff loyal to her.

It was the best plan she could think of, though it wasn't very good. But she'd survived for years living a double life. With luck, she could find a way through now. Meanwhile, she made her way downstairs and prayed the major got wretchedly ill and couldn't make it tonight.

"My goodness! Look who is here on time," her aunt exclaimed as Janelle walked into the front parlor. "And looking quite well, I should say. There's color in your cheeks that hasn't been there all week."

"Aunt!" Janelle exclaimed. "I didn't hear you come in. And look who else is here," she said with a sinking hole in her stomach. Major Vance stood up at her entrance. Good God, had he been sitting with her aunt this whole time? "Why didn't anyone tell me the major had arrived?" she asked her aunt.

"I told Parry not to bother you," her aunt said. "I knew you'd come down when you were ready. Besides," she said with a smile at the interloper, "I was having such a lovely time talking with the major. I vow I wanted to keep him all to myself."

Of course, she did. Aunt Esmee was a terrible flirt. Probably because Uncle Jonathan was a terrible bore.

"That sounds exciting." Or terrifying. "What are you two talking about?"

Major Vance caught her hand. "Nothing much," he said as he bent at the waist. He moved excruciatingly slow, his eyes steady upon hers as he lifted her hand. "She asked me what I'd done today."

His eyes were blue, but a changeable kind that could be dark or light or even gray. They seemed to change as he bowed, and she stood mesmerized by the color of them. Or perhaps it was the laughter in his gaze that matched the teasing note in his voice.

"You are making a game of it then," she said. "Hiding your conversation from me."

"Hiding!" her aunt cried. "What a thing to say!"

The major straightened to his full height. "But she is correct," he said, his lips curving in a devilish smile. "Can she guess what you and I discussed?"

"I wager I can," she said as she forced her gaze to focus on her aunt. The woman appeared slightly flushed, not with fury but the normal joy of talking to someone who wasn't a complete bore. That meant the topic had nothing to do with her illicit activities, but something much more mundane. "He must have asked you about your day," Janelle said as she walked the few steps to her aunt's side. "I bet you regaled him with a tale about how difficult it was to recover after last night's wonderful ball." She leaned down and bussed her aunt's cheek. "And that you are excited to watch tonight's plays from Lord Benedict's box."

Her aunt pursed her lips in a pretty pout. "You are too clever, my girl. You always have been."

"Me? Never!" she said as her breath eased out. He hadn't told on her yet.

"Oh," he said with a throaty drawl. "I bet your aunt can remember dozens of times you were mischievous. I'll bet Miss Caddick was prone to wandering off, wasn't she? Maybe to do something she wasn't supposed to?"

Janelle turned to glare at him, making sure her back was to her aunt. "What are you suggesting? I was a very obedient child."

"I suppose you became such after your mother died," her aunt mused. "But when you were little, your nanny had a terrible time keeping track of you. You were always off in the garden or the woods. Always wanted to play with the animals, even the disgusting ones." She laughed. "Your mother used to write me whole letters about how you wanted to touch the pigs or run about with the lambs."

"Really?" Janelle said. "I didn't know."

"Didn't you? Well, I suppose that's not something your father would remember. There was a great deal more important things for him to take care of than watching a little girl run after rabbits." Her aunt patted her hand. "Your mother used to run everywhere, too, but she especially liked disappearing into the woods. Our nanny had a terrible time keeping track of her, too."

Janelle dropped into the chair the major had vacated. The one right next to her aunt. "I have never heard this before," she said. "What did she do? In the woods, I mean."

"Well, I don't really know. Looked at insects. She had a great interest in mushrooms, probably from a fairy tale we once heard about magical ones."

The major appeared interested, too. "Did she eat any?"

"I don't think so. We learned from cook that most were deadly poisonous. She liked to make up stories though about bears and rabbits having tea parties in the woods. All nonsense, you realize, but we had such fun."

There was a wistfulness in her tone that echoed inside Janelle. She didn't remember her mother and there were no portraits to recall her face. "Do I look like her?" she asked. Pathetic that she pressed her aunt for even the smallest detail. Her father had never said anything and indeed had been annoyed whenever she asked, so she'd learned young to hide her curiosity. What did it matter anyway? And yet she hung on her aunt's answer as the woman frowned and inspected her from every side.

"Not much," she said, much to Janelle's disappointment. "She had lighter hair than you, and a longish nose. Her skin was fairer than yours." She wrinkled her nose. "I fear you've spent too much time in the sun without your bonnet. You should do something to cover your freckles."

Janelle put her hand up to her nose. It was true. She spent very little time caring about freckles when she went about Devon as Betty.

"But you have her intelligence," her aunt continued, her expression warm. "When she looked at something, she seemed to really look. She read everything Nanny allowed and a great many things that weren't."

The major chuckled. "Curiosity can be a dangerous thing for a girl."

"For boys, too," Janelle retorted. "But without it, we would never learn anything, never discover new ways to do things."

"Exactly right," her aunt said. "Indeed, I think your mother must have said something similar."

Janelle flushed, ashamed of how much she wished it was so. "You're just teasing me," she said. "Telling me what I want to hear. You cannot possibly remember my mother saying such things."

"Indeed, I can! But now I shall tell you how you most resemble your mother."

"Yes?" She leaned forward.

"It is in your smile." The lady tapped Janelle's lips. "You mother always smiled as if she knew things that no one else did and it made her confident. I vow it drew all the gentlemen to her. They wanted to know her secrets."

"Now that," said the major, "is something I can readily believe."

Janelle shot the man a dark look, but she was more interested in what her aunt was saying than in shooting daggers at the awful man. "What was her secret?"

"Your father, I think."

"What?" She couldn't imagine her dour, social-climbing father being anyone's secret. When he wasn't grilling her brother on who he knew and what favors could be had, he was at his club smoking cigars with rich and powerful men, all with the idea of becoming one of them.

"You didn't know your father back then. He was as smart as your mother, but she was his light. The only one who could make him laugh." Her eyes grew cloudy as she looked down at her lap. "Sometimes," she said softly, "I think it's awful of God to make the most glorious part of being a woman—the bringing of new life into the world—also the most dangerous. I have never cried harder than the day your mother died."

Janelle gripped her aunt's hand, squeezing it as she did whenever the topic of her mother came up. It was shared love between two women who knew the risks of getting pregnant. After all, her aunt had lost her sister at the same moment Janelle had lost her mother. And once again, as she did most days, Janelle vowed again to find a way to make childbirth safer. That was, after all, why she studied unguents and possets. There had to be one that held off childbed fever. Some secret elixir had to exist that would make it safe for a woman to bring a child into the world.

And nothing—including an arrogant major in a handsome coat—would keep her from that one mighty goal.

Chapter Nine

GABE INTENDED TO torture Miss Caddick for the entire evening.

He meant to hold the threat of exposure over her head long enough for her to realize that she was playing with fire. While he might admire a youthful interest in medicine—he now believed that she'd been at the Rose Garden to ferret out something medicinal—she had to understand that Lord Benedict's wife could not engage in such fancies. Politics was a dangerous business, and she had no restraint on the pursuit of her passion. Which meant she was not mature enough to handle it without a strong hand— his hand—showing her the way.

But then she'd started asking her aunt about her mother.

He did not want to feel sympathy for a girl who had lost her mother so young. It was clear she was embarrassed about her need to hear more about her parent. Indeed, he remembered feeling equally shy when he voiced the same questions about his father. But whereas her mother was gone, his father had been a few miles away, completely unknown to his bastard son.

Thankfully, Lady Boxval answered everything kindly. It was better done than his mother's responses. She'd filled his young ears with a casual dismissal of his father's sexual prowess. He hadn't understood half the words, but his mother's mocking laughter had been enough to keep him from ever asking again. Instead, he went directly to his father and demanded the man's attention.

It had been a bold act for an eight year old. But such boldness got him a place at Eton and later, another curt discussion bought his military commission. Unfortunately, Miss Caddick did not have that same kind of access to her parent, and so she hung on memories and casual comments. And how cruel it was that she had waited this many years to hear so little.

His estimation of her father dropped down several degrees. His evaluation of her, however, remained exactly where it was. She was too wild to be Lord Benedict's wife. And so he began a steady campaign to get her to cry off.

"I'm afraid that Lord Benedict will not be joining us tonight. He is with the Secretary of State tonight entertaining a few dignitaries. Boring stuff, I believe, as they discuss Malta." He smiled at Janelle. "As his wife, you will be expected to attend many of these affairs, even when they happen with little notice. That's why I keep track of the most important people in his life— every day, down to the minute—so you can join when called upon to attend." He paused to emphasize the most important part. "I must know every day, down to the minute, where you are."

"You must be very busy then," she responded as Parry called them in for supper. "We never know if Papa will join us either," she said gaily. "Every night, we hope he finds us, but more often than not, he remains with his own amusements."

"That won't work with Lord Benedict."

She laughed lightheartedly. "I believe it will because we were never introduced, never courted, never even spoke together before our engagement. I doubt he has a desperate need for my company."

He couldn't fault her for that. Even he thought Lord Benedict's method of obtaining a wife had been cold-blooded. "But a wife must attend to her husband's needs."

"Oh my!" she cried as she pressed her hands to her cheeks as if she were embarrassed. "I assure you, I shall handle my husband's needs without your help."

Well. The first round of banter went to her. Social conversation was not his forte, and he wasn't dismayed by his lack. Indeed, as the meal commenced, he noticed that she lost some animation. She appeared to grow thoughtful during the soup course. Could she be wondering what life would be like with him constantly dogging her footsteps?

His next conversational gambit was aided by her aunt, and it came at the end of the meal. "I've heard that Mrs. Belleford had to retire to the country," she said. "So sad. She always threw such lovely parties. Especially the masquerades."

"It was because of those parties that she retired," Gabe said. "Sadly, they were too enthusiastic for her husband's political leanings. Mr. Belleford decided that no hostess was better than a bad hostess who insulted the very people he needed to attract."

Miss Caddick looked up. "How did a party insult them? Did she leave them off the invitation list?"

"Oh no. That's the point. She invited too many people. For example, several of Lord Benedict's associates prefer quiet evenings with a specific guest list."

"They don't care for masquerades?" Janelle drawled. "How extraordinarily priggish of them."

"Don't be insulting," her aunt said returned. "A great many people find masquerades bad *ton*. You know they often get wild."

"And yet you just said you enjoyed them."

Lady Boxval admitted that with a coy shrug. "It is fun to see everyone's costumes." She turned back to him. "But I insist we leave early. Every time."

"Very wise," he agreed, though his attention was on Miss Caddick as he continued, "Lord Benedict will ask you to throw modest parties and attend only those appropriate to a circumspect wife."

Her lips curved. "I'll make sure to study the guest list carefully."

"Don't worry," he said with his most charming smile. "I supervise all of Lord Benedict's entertainments and will, of course, manage all of yours. It is an important part of being his private secretary. You can't be expected to know from one moment to the next which person is in or out of favor." He leaned forward. "That was Mrs. Belleford's error, you see. She was seen laughing with a gentleman who had just that afternoon insulted her husband in parliament."

"Oh heavens," Miss Caddick said. "Imagine laughing with someone. It's a wonder she wasn't tarred and feathered."

"You scoff, but it is a serious matter. Her husband sent her to the country because of it."

The lady dropped her napkin with an imperious wave. "Then I find both her and her husband complete idiots. Her for leaving, and him for demanding it. A husband and wife can have different friends and can be seen conversing—even laughing—with different people."

"That would be true with a normal husband," he said. "But politics is a small world, one that has consequences on the world stage. Lord Benedict will expect you to—"

"Rely on your guidance?" she interrupted before he could say it.

He held up his hands. "It is what I do."

It was decidedly not what he did. When they were in the Peninsular War, Gabe handled logistics, disputes between various underlings, and made sure the right communication got to the best person. In a war, everything hinged on correct, timely information. Several times, Gabe had risked life to hand deliver orders that could not go astray.

But here in London, he was reduced to investigating an impertinent slip of a girl and trading in gossip about that idiot Belleford and his wife.

"You must be very busy," Miss Caddick said as she pushed up from her seat. "You can be assured you need not supervise any aspect of my life. I am quite content managing it myself."

He rose to his feet as was proper. "And yet, my tasks are determined by Lord Benedict himself. Just as a wife's responsibilities are dictated by her husband."

She had no answer to that, and he took unnecessary satisfaction in seeing her lips press together in frustration. She knew as well as he did that a wife's life was structured by her husband's. And it was the sad truth that her life would be managed by himself, not her. Unless, of course, she cried off and married someone else.

Which meant he won that round, and they were now at a banter score of one to one. That made him excessively happy as they climbed into the carriage for the theater.

"Well, it seems it is just us," quipped Lady Boxval. "I knew Jonathan wouldn't join us. He hates the theater, but I had hoped to see your father, Janelle."

"You did? Why? He only goes when there's someone he can't find otherwise. He spends the whole evening looking about for whomever and then talking throughout the plays."

"Well," her aunt demurred, "he can be pleasant company nonetheless."

Apparently not in his daughter's estimation. "Do you enjoy the theater, Miss Caddick?" he asked.

"Not very much, to be honest. We don't have an annual box, so we attend in the middle gallery where there is a great deal of milling about and talking. It's difficult to follow what's happening on stage. I am excited to experience it from Lord Benedict's box. It was kind of him to offer it."

"What do you enjoy most? The company, the play, or the admiration of everyone looking up at you?" He smiled as he gestured to her gown. "You are very lovely this evening. Quite the change from the last time we met."

Indeed, he'd been shocked when she stepped into the parlor earlier. He'd been thinking of stoop-shouldered Betty in that dowdy gown when she'd appeared in a simple dress that emphasized her curves. Her lifted breasts would have been indecent except for the overdress of dusky rose that muted her carnal appeal. Indeed, she could have been seduction incarnate in that gown if she'd made the least attempt to be sensuous.

She had not. If anything, her carriage was proper and her movements efficient. And that, paradoxically, made her a thousand times more interesting to him. He even smiled when she drew herself up at his implied insult.

"Do you say I was ugly when last we met?"

"Of course not," he lied. "You were simply unprepared to greet me."

"Goodness," her aunt interjected. "How were you dressed, Janelle?"

"For housework," she said. "The major caught me unawares in the kitchen. He came to the servants' entrance to deliver a message from Lord Benedict."

Neatly done. She set the scene with him as a servant of no more account than the lowliest footman. "It was a private matter between the lady and her fiancé," he said. "I thought it best to deliver it as discreetly as possible."

"And yet you bring it up now in front of my aunt."

Of course, he did. He was reminding her that he could reveal her activities at any moment. "A mistake," he lied. "I simply meant to compliment your transformation. I stand amazed by your beauty." That was the truth.

He expected her to flush at that. What girl didn't like to be complimented? He intended to judge the depth of her vanity by her reaction, only to be amazed when she didn't appear to have any.

"My aunt chose my dress, and my maid does my hair. If any-one is to be complimented, it is they. Truth be told, I much prefer my working attire."

Her aunt was outraged. "What a thing to say, Janelle!" She shook her head. "I thought you had disposed of all those ugly clothes. It is one thing to assist with the kitchen work when you were a baron's daughter in Devon, but now you are Lord Benedict's fiancé. You must be appropriately attired at all times." She shook her head as she turned to Major Vance. "My brother-in-law appears to have missed some key aspects of Janelle's education, but I promise you that she will be ready by the time the banns are read."

"His lordship asked me to post the banns this week, my lady." He watched Miss Caddick's expression closely as he spoke those words. Her reaction would give him a good idea of how far he had to push her before she cried off.

Not far, apparently.

Her face paled and her hands tightened in her lap. "This week?" she squeaked.

"He did not tell you?" he asked. "Lord Benedict wishes to be married within a month. Indeed, we discussed a special license, but I thought it would look too hasty."

Lady Boxval pressed her hands to her cheeks in shock. "A month? But that is much too soon to plan a wedding."

Meanwhile, Miss Caddick was shaking her head. "He said nothing of the kind to me."

"Truly?" he pressed. "Did he mention a congress in Vienna, perhaps? That consumes his schedule as we discuss what is to be done when Napoleon surrenders."

Her chin jerked up. "But Napoleon has not surrendered. Indeed, who knows how long that will take."

"I believe we shall get notification of it this evening. That is the reason Lord Benedict is absent tonight. He is awaiting the news." Which is exactly where Gabe wanted to be as well. Unfortunately, there was nothing he could do to hasten the Corsican's surrender. But there was a great deal he could to do prevent Lord Benedict from saddling himself with a difficult wife.

And so he was here, poking a girl who clearly didn't want the life she would have with Lord Benedict.

"Was it not your choice to marry?" he asked.

"My choice?" the woman gasped. "I had never met Lord Benedict before he was down on one knee before me."

Her aunt reached out and patted her hand, as if to tamp down the coming flash of temper. "But that isn't why a woman of your station gets married."

"I know, aunt, but—"

"But nothing. Lord Benedict is clearly smitten with you."

That could not be true. And Miss Caddick shared his disbelief as she snorted her derision.

"It is an advantageous alliance for everyone," her aunt continued. "Good lord, Janelle, you will be a countess. Your children will be ladies and lords. Your father did very well to arrange this for you. I am sure you are very grateful." That last came out as a command. Miss Caddick would be grateful or she would answer to her aunt and father.

"Of course," the girl responded, her voice meek. "I shall be very pleased to marry Lord Benedict on whatever schedule."

Of course, nothing. Gabe did his best not to grin. A little more pressure and he would have the girl crying off before the last act.

Chapter Ten

THREE WEEKS? THREE weeks!

Janelle's head spun. She'd just started to grapple with the idea that she was engaged to a near stranger. This morning she'd looked at the ring on her finger and realized that she would get married someday. Some very distant day in the far-off future.

Until Major Vance started talking about special licenses. He said three weeks was the longest his lordship would wait. And suddenly, she was feeling sick to her stomach.

Thankfully, their carriage arrived at the theatre, and they were busy climbing out of the conveyance and heading toward their seat. People were still arriving. Indeed, they would be coming and going throughout the performances, but the flow was slow enough—and the major imposing enough—that they rapidly found themselves in Lord Benedict's private box.

How wonderful to be able to breathe with no one crowding around her. With only the three of them in the box, Janelle could not only see the performance but hear it as well. Or so she hoped. The tragedy had not yet begun, which gave the major a moment to lean forward and whisper into her ear.

"I did not mean to upset you, Miss Caddick. It seems you are apprehensive about your wedding coming so soon. If I may be so bold, exactly what frightens you?"

She turned to him. Indeed, how could she not? Just when she was feeling a stomach-churning tension, his soothing voice grounded her. Even better, he set his gloved hand upon hers. It was there only for a moment. It would not be appropriate for him to linger. But it was enough to draw her attention away from the sea of feelings in which she floundered.

"Major?" she rasped. Did he know that his title was like a lifeline cast outward? Apparently so, because he smiled at her. His blue eyes turned soft, his lips curved gently, and she noticed for the first time how full they were. His nose might be a blunt instrument on his face, but his lips were soft and tempting.

"Miss Caddick," he said, "it is my duty to see to your wellbeing. I have upset you, and so I must remedy it."

"You did not upset me," she said. "You merely surprised me, and that was my fault for not pressing Lord Benedict for details earlier."

"Ah. Well, Lord Benedict thinks at a different level than most of us. His thoughts are on affairs of state, not the mundane details of life. It is why he needs me."

"To inform his fiancée of their wedding date?"

"Exactly so." His expression deepened. "Do you wish to delay the wedding? I could broach the topic with Lord Benedict."

Yes, yes, yes!

But that was the reaction of a child, and so she lifted her chin and stood on her own two feet—metaphorically speaking. "I appreciate the offer, however any such discussions should be between myself and his lordship. Surely you can see how having a third person in my marriage bed is highly inappropriate."

He pulled back, obviously insulted. "That is not at all what I meant."

And now it was her turn to touch his arm in apology. "Forgive me. I spoke badly. I am unsettled."

"Then perhaps you can tell me—exactly—what disturbs you about your upcoming nuptials. Is it the timing? Do you fear you can't get the wedding plans in place by then? I assure you, I am a wizard at managing logistics. I coordinated an entire battle, I can handle a wedding."

"You coordinated battles?" For some reason, she thought he'd

be the one out front fighting them. Though by the looks of him—
and his scars—he'd probably done both.

"I was one of many. But yes, I became a trusted leader."

"A successful one, too," she said. "Napoleon was defeated in
Spain."

"He was indeed. Which leaves me free to arrange every detail
of your wedding."

She quickly shook her head. "Oh, don't do that. Aunt Esmee
would never forgive me." She looked over at her aunt who
turned at the sound of her name.

"Forgive what?"

"If the major handled the wedding logistics."

"No, no, no! I've been planning Janelle's wedding for years. I
had only sons, you know. This is my chance to really indulge."
She grinned at the major. "I had her wedding gown started the
minute I learned of the engagement. And our side of the guest list
is already complete. I will need to get with you to finalize Lord
Benedict's wishes."

The major nodded, his expression smoothing out into a polite
blandness. "I will be happy to. Indeed, if you give me your list, I
shall see the invitations printed immediately."

"Delightful!"

And so the conversation slid to her aunt and the major talking
about wedding details while Janelle looked toward the stage.
When would the tragedy start? Any minute now, if the movement behind the curtain was an indication. Or within three
weeks, if she were honest.

She was marrying a man she didn't know. Her life would be
forever tethered to him. He didn't seem cruel or violent, but how
would she know until she lived with him? That was the thing
about tending so many laboring women. They told her things in
the long hours as their bodies prepared to expel a child. She knew
men were rarely what they seemed in public.

Always, the women bore the brunt of their husband's perfidy.

"When will I see Lord Benedict again?" she abruptly asked.

"Is he at home tonight?"

The major turned from his discussion with her aunt to address her. "Should I arrange an appointment for you?"

She winced, hating the idea of going through another person to arrange for her to see her future husband. "Yes, please."

He nodded. "Shall we say another walk in the park tomorrow at the usual time? If he cannot make it, I will take his place and answer all your questions."

She tilted her head. "Major, I asked for a conversation with my fiancé, not a conversation with you about my fiancé."

His expression was sympathetic as he shrugged. "Unfortunately, that happens more often than not with Lord Benedict. It is the nature of his job, you know. Whereas most gentlemen of your status will be available to you with a modest amount of effort, I'm afraid Lord Benedict has a great many responsibilities more important than his fiancée. Or his wife." His expression grew rueful. "It is something you must accept now or be very unhappy in your marriage."

She looked at him hard. He didn't seem particularly regretful of the news, and her temper boiled over. "I think you enjoy Lord Benedict's status. I think you like being the only arbiter of access to him. Even to the point of inserting yourself between me and him. You want to plan my wedding. You want to tell me when I can and cannot see my husband. And you want to order the shape and details of my days." She shook her head. "I do not believe we suit, Major Vance."

He nodded gravely. "I agree, Miss Caddick. Unfortunately for you, Lord Benedict and I have been working together for a decade. We have waged war together, saved each other's lives, and now are poised to create a new world after Bonaparte. If you wish to marry Lord Benedict, then you must find a way to work with me." He leaned back in his chair. "Unless, of course, you want to cry off. There are dozens of gentlemen who would be grateful for your hand. Indeed, I might be able to steer a few very worthy men in your direction."

Good God, had she really thought him sympathetic? What an idiot she was. He was doing everything in his power to end her marriage before it even began. "Why?" she asked, her mind scrambling to understand. "Why are you threatened by someone as simple and unimportant as me?"

His brows rose. "A wife is no small thing, Miss Caddick. And you are far from simple. Indeed, I believe your intelligence is your problem. Boredom is the curse of a clever mind. And a bored wife is a dangerous one."

"And you stand to protect Lord Benedict. From me."

"I do."

"Because I'm so scandalous."

He arched his brows, and his gaze filled with double meaning. "Scandal is the plague of every politician. It is the one thing that can fell a great man. And I will not allow—"

"Enough!" Aunt Esmee all but shouted. Indeed, her outburst was loud enough to catch a few people's interest in neighboring boxes.

"Aunt Esmee!" Janelle hissed. "Lower your voice."

The lady did not. Indeed, she stood slowly, her chin raised and her body stiff. At that moment, the woman was every inch Lady Boxval.

"Walk with me, Major," the woman commanded, her body quivering with authority.

The major dipped in ghost of a bow, then he gestured with a casual wave to the back of the box. The lady proceeded him out the back, and he followed with a mocking kind of saunter. At least Janelle thought it mocking, but then she was not predisposed to think anything charitable about the man.

Fortunately for her own turbulent emotions, the orchestra announced the beginning of the tragedy with a loud flourish. The curtain opened and the play began. *Hamlet* was not a favorite play of hers. The prince dithered in a way that she thought showed the weak side of masculinity. A woman didn't have time to debate her actions, for better or ill. She either fought them immediately or accepted the status quo. Only men had the luxury of acting after thorough debate. If a man wanted to do something, he just did it. A woman had to plan and maneuver. She had to either hide her actions or surprise her opponents with the deed already done.

It was the nature of things.

And so as *Hamlet* began with all the moaning of the ghost nonsense, Janelle realized that now was her time to act. She had questions about her upcoming marriage, beginning with the major's exact role. And if she did not receive a satisfactory answer to that question, then she would indeed cry off and damn to the consequences. After all, what was the worst that could happen? She would be packed off to Devon where she could resume her life as Betty until Janelle ceased to exist all together.

With that happy possibility fixed in her mind, she pulled out her purse. It was much smaller than her usual bag, but it was large enough to contain a pencil and paper. On it, she wrote a simple excuse. One that her aunt had seen a dozen times.

I am feeling unwell. Don't let me spoil your fun. I shall return home immediately to sit in the dark. Migraines are terrible things.

She signed it and set it on her aunt's chair. Then she slipped out of the box using her cloak to cover her head as she left by the back stairs. She'd learned of them last season when she'd helped tend a prostitute who had been beaten and left there for dead. She wasn't the only one to know of these stairs. Indeed, there were at least two couples indulging together as she rushed past. Fortunately, they were too involved with each other to care about her.

Five minutes later, she made it outside to where a row of hackneys waited for people who wanted to escape.

"Take me to the Foreign Office," she ordered.

"Wot?"

She dug into her memory. The major had said that Lord Benedict was entertaining dignitaries tonight with the Secretary of State.

"Take me to Lord Castlereagh's home on Cleveland Row." At least she hoped that was where it was. She wasn't exactly sure. Either way, she was determined to find her fiancé tonight. She would have a discussion with him without Major Vance, even if she had to interrupt his superior at dinner to do it.

And if it forced Lord Benedict to request an end of their engagement, then she would make sure to gain a settlement from him that would make her father happy.

At least she hoped she could. And she prayed it was enough to prevent her father from killing her for the embarrassment.

Chapter Eleven

I T WAS ONE thing to sneak out of the theater in a fit of righteous indignation. It was another thing to bang on the door of the Secretary of State's home to find her errant fiancé.

Janelle had enough fury to sustain her through the cab ride, but two seconds after being deposited in front of Lord Castlereagh's front door, she abruptly reconsidered her actions. What would she to say to the butler? "I know I'm not invited and they're discussing matters of international importance, but I should like a word with my fiancé. No, nothing urgent. I'm just furious with his secretary. Major Vance and I do not suit at all."

She'd be lucky if he didn't slam the door in her face.

God, she was an idiot. Unfortunately, the hansom cab had already driven off and she was now a lone woman standing on a street corner. She was about to rush after the cab in the hopes of flagging it down when the front door opened. She looked up at the spill of light, praying that she would see Lord Benedict stepping out of the house.

She didn't. Worse, the gentleman just now putting on his hat saw her, and his eyes opened wide.

"Miss Caddick? Whatever are you doing here?"

Hell and damnation. What was she going to do now? It really would not do to be caught standing alone on a street corner by anyone but her fiancé. Why hadn't she thought this through?

Meanwhile the man rushed down the stairs. "Don't be frightened. It's me, Lord Nathaniel. We met the night you announced your engagement."

She nodded in a distracted kind of way. "Yes, my lord. I remember you, though I think we met long before then." She remembered him as someone perpetually around, always on the periphery of one event or another.

He frowned as he studied her face. "Is everything all right?"

She balled her fists in frustration. "I'm such an idiot. I came to see Lord Benedict, but I didn't think it through."

"Nonsense. I completely understand. The days before a wedding are particularly unsettling, and you want to see your fiancé. It's all perfectly natural." He turned to look back up the steps. The door had closed and suddenly it looked very uninviting. "The thing is, it's a delicate matter going on in there, and the French ambassador is getting unruly, if you know what I mean."

She didn't, not exactly. "The French ambassador is in there?"

"Several ambassadors, but he's the most cantankerous. He wants more land and more respect, which, in his case, means more wine and women."

"I thought wives were in there, too. At least that's what Major Vance implied. He said I didn't go because we weren't yet married."

"Oh well, that's partially true. The wives were there—mine included—but they know when to depart. We're in the middle of the Season too, so most went off to some other form of entertainment."

She frowned. "Is that typical?"

"Oh yes. Certainly, there are many events where women are required, but more often, it's a couple official functions a week, and then off they go to their own amusements."

So the major exaggerated her responsibilities to make it sound like her entire life would be wrapped up in her husband's. Her fury returned with a hot burn. "I really need to see Lord Benedict." She squared her shoulders. "I'll just have to knock—"

Lord Nathaniel grabbed her elbow. "You can't! If you present yourself now, the French ambassador will get the wrong idea."

Indeed, at that exact moment, a carriage pulled to a stop a few feet away and five women tumbled out. They were laughing gaily, dressed scandalously, and every one of them was a lady of easy virtue. Thanks to Janelle's extra activities, she knew how to recognize differing levels of prostitutes. These were of a higher class than the normal street walker, but not so elevated as to expect special courting. Indeed, if she didn't miss her guess, at least two of them worked at the Rose Garden. She remembered them from the night she'd delivered Holly's baby.

"Damnation, they're here," muttered Lord Nathaniel as he tugged her into the shadows. "Are you sure you want to speak to him tonight?"

"Is my fiancé likely to be…um…preoccupied now?" Many husbands tomcatted around on their wives. Indeed, it was so common as to be expected. Still, it turned her stomach that her future husband comported with these ladies and called it an affair of state. Especially when the Secretary of State pretended to be an upstanding, moral—

She was interrupted by Lord Nathaniel's chuckle. "I assure you, Lord Benedict is not participating in the revelries. At least not in the usual way."

"What other way is there?"

The man shrugged. "Have you ever heard the expression *In Vino Veritas*?"

"It means there is truth in wine. Or, I suppose, that drunks often say things they should not."

"Drunken lechers do it even more. And your fiancé is very skilled at manipulating such situations to England's advantage."

Oh. That sounded almost noble in a disgusting sort of way. Worse, she could not interrupt him during it. "I must learn to think things through before I act."

Lord Nathaniel chuckled. "It's something we all must learn, I'm afraid. Everyone except your fiancé. I swear he is playing chess when everyone else is just throwing dice."

"I wouldn't know," she said glumly. "Our engagement was

rather precipitous."

"And that, Miss Caddick, is where you are wrong. Lord Benedict does nothing in haste." He looked about him. "Come, I can see this is important to you."

"I cannot interrupt him now."

"Actually, you can if the timing is done correctly." He tugged her around the side of the house.

"Where are we going?"

"To the servant's entrance. I can stash you in the housekeeper's room while I find him for you."

"But what about the secrets he's gleaning?"

"Well, if it's something important, he won't come down to speak with you." The man winked at her. "Don't worry. I am very good at this."

"Do you often hide women in tiny rooms in the hope of interrupting state-sanctioned orgies?" She spoke lightly, her sense of the ridiculous coming to her rescue.

He glanced back at her, his eyes wide with surprise. "I do believe you find this funny."

It was either laugh or die of embarrassment. "There is too much tragedy in life to not take joy in the silly. And this is perhaps the silliest thing I have ever done."

"Then you are an excellent match for Lord Benedict. There is much in government work that is sublimely ridiculous. You should learn to embrace it, as Lord Benedict has."

They made it around the house, then waited in silence as a pair of maids left the house. They probably wanted to be far away from the entertainment above stairs.

"Cover your face," he whispered. Once she'd pulled the hood of her cloak down, he crossed to the back door. "Stay close and don't speak," he said, then he knocked three times in quick succession.

The door was opened by a man with a wizened face and eyes narrowed tight as he inspected both Lord Nathaniel and her. "I wasn't informed of another one tonight."

"Open up, Limpy." His voice had abruptly dropped to a coarse tone that perfectly matched the other man's accent. "They don't tell either of us everthing."

"Ain't that the truth. All right. I got room in the wine cellar if'n she don't drink."

"Not a drop. I swear it."

Limpy grunted as he swung the door wide. "We'll see about that."

A moment later, they were in the house and rushing down the stairs to a surprisingly large wine cellar, complete with a table, a cot, and several chairs. Good lord, did secret meetings happen down here, too? Was it a place to question prisoners or hide spies? It was large enough that she could comfortably use it to manage two women in labor at once.

"This'll do," Lord Nathaniel said. Then he grabbed Limpy's elbow as the man turned to depart. "Leave 'er alone down here. She's special, this one."

"Special, huh? Ain't everyone?" He didn't wait for a response. Instead, he frowned up the stairs. "Want me t' guard the door?"

"Be sure no one else goes down here."

"Do I tell anyone—"

"I'll manage it, thank you. It's not quite time."

Then all three of them fell silent as Limpy—who did not have a limp—climbed the stairs with a swiftness belied by his apparent age.

"You might as well sit down," Lord Nathaniel said as he dusted off the nearest chair for her. "This will take some time, but no one will bother you. Limpy's grumpy but he knows his job."

"I cannot thank you enough."

"Oh yes you can," he said with a sly smile. "If you marry Lord Benedict, you will have a chance to repay me. Of that you can be sure. Indeed, I think you and my wife will become good friends."

And didn't that make her pause? But she didn't have time to question it because he abruptly pulled out another chair for himself. "And since we have a moment while the gentlemen select their women, I should like to talk candidly with you, if I may."

"Of course." After all, they were in the Secretary of State's secret wine cellar meeting room. Why wouldn't they speak candidly?

"You came here in a high state of agitation. Who, exactly, upset you?"

She grimaced. Lord Nathaniel was turning out to be remarkably perceptive. "Lord Benedict has expressed his wish that I work closely with his aide-de-camp."

"Is Major Vance being prickly?"

"He's being impossible." She abruptly leaned forward. "He says he'll need to keep track of my every move once I marry Lord Benedict. He lied about tonight. And he…he pokes his nose into my business, as if it's his right."

Her companion shrugged. "He could hardly tell you the truth about tonight."

She frowned. "Does your wife know the truth?"

Warmth filled his expression. "She does. And she knows I will not indulge as the French ambassador does, but I might have to pretend here and there."

Warmth filled his expression, and she had no doubt that he was totally devoted to his new wife. "Lady Rebecca is a lucky woman," she said.

"It is I who am lucky, but never mind that. Tell me what Major Vance does to irritate you so."

"It's the way he talks to me. He doesn't want me to marry Lord Benedict and is doing everything he can to dissuade me."

"That makes sense."

"What?"

Lord Nathaniel's expression turned almost wistful. "Major Vance is a hopeless romantic."

She couldn't credit the thought.

"He believes in marriage in the original way. He believes in one woman and one man joined before God in love and devotion. He's incredibly moral about things like that. Indeed, if he weren't a bastard, I believe he would have gone into the clergy and been annoyingly priggish about how everyone ought to live." He leaned forward. "Believe me, Miss Caddick, it is God's own joke that he created the most godly man in the body of a bastard."

"Godly?" she said. "But he's… He…" She thought of all his scars and the warlike way he stood and moved. He was a fighter through and through. "He's violent."

"With you?"

"Goodness, no. But he seems like he could be."

"He can be. I have never seen him in battle, but I have heard. He is a fearsome soldier. He believes in his cause. He protected the Spaniards from being conquered and he protects Lord Benedict because he believes your fiancé will set the world to rights now that Bonaparte has surrendered." He shrugged. "That may be his biggest fault as well as his greatest strength."

"Being godly?"

"Being loyal. He knows the business of politics is not a moral endeavor, but he believes in Lord Benedict's vision. I don't think he trusts Castlereagh completely. But he will fiercely protect your fiancé in all things."

"Even to the point of driving a wedge between me and my husband?"

"Even so."

"And you think that is a good thing."

"I think that is a noble thing. Miss Caddick, is that not what we are all searching for? Something to believe in, someone to fight for?"

She tilted her head. "But isn't that dangerous? To put so much blind faith in one man."

"The major is not blind, and Lord Benedict has more than earned the respect we give him."

She considered his words, struggling to find her place in all this. "But what am I to do then? It seems you men have figured out all the pieces without telling me where I fit."

He chuckled. "I doubt that. If I might guess, I believe you are here because the major has told you where you should fit and you do not like the place he wants to put you."

She sighed, forced to admit the truth. "Perhaps that is true. Are my choices truly to do as the major wishes or cry off? Won't Lord Benedict fight for me?"

"Will you help bring peace to the continent? Will you ensure that we shall have peace for generations?"

She blinked, startled. "I cannot promise such a thing. No woman could."

"Then you are a lower priority for Lord Benedict. He and the major work well together for that one vision."

She threw up her hands. "You are telling me to cry off then."

"On the contrary, Miss Caddick. I am telling you to join their fight, in so much as you can. And where you cannot, show them that your passion, your priorities are equally worth defending."

She stilled. "What makes you think I have a passion the equal of world peace?"

"What makes you think you don't?"

Her thoughts skittered and scrambled like mice running in a dozen different directions. She was used to working in the places men did not go. She'd never had to defend her work because no one of importance ever saw it.

"I don't trust the major enough to show him my passions."

"If you don't, then you will never gain his trust, and he will fight you. Indeed, he will ruin any chance of peace between you and your husband."

"That's insane!"

"Would you risk world peace on the secret agenda of a wife? It is the truth that peace rests on the shoulders of Lord Castlereagh and Lord Benedict. They work day and night to settle things in the wake of the Corsican nightmare. Lord Benedict may have chosen you as wife, but you must gain the major's trust if you wish to have any kind of true relationship with your husband."

"Isn't that for me and Lord Benedict to figure out?"

"And has Lord Benedict shown any desire in doing that with you? I doubt it. I know how busy he is, and I think he handed the task to Major Vance. As odd as it seems, that is the way Lord Benedict works."

She didn't answer. How could she? Lord Nathaniel had hit the nail on the head. She'd expected to spend the next few weeks creating a relationship with her fiancé. Instead, she found herself constantly tripping over Major Vance.

Meanwhile, Lord Nathaniel slapped his hands on his knees then pushed upright. "Think on it, Miss Caddick. I do not know why Lord Benedict chose you as a wife, but I can tell you one thing for certain—his reasons will not be normal ones, for he does not think as normal people do."

"I am beginning to see that." Imagine setting your underling to figure out the details of one's own marriage.

"But he chose you. And now you must decide—as we all have—if supporting him is worth working with the major."

"You sound as if he is. As if Lord Benedict is a paragon of virtue—"

"I never said that!"

"That he is worth every devotion, even from the godliest man you know."

Lord Nathaniel smiled, his expression light despite his heavy words. "I believe he is. Else we will have another generation steeped in bloody war." His expression tightened. "And I am working in my own way to see that that doesn't happen."

And with that, he executed a respectful bow before leaping up the wine cellar stairs. A moment later, he was gone, leaving her to stare at wine bottles and dust while her thoughts scrambled around to no purpose.

How was she to make sense of this? And still preserve what she most wanted? And what did she most want? she wondered.

That answer came quickly. She wanted to make women's work easier so that great men of state like Lord Benedict didn't think about it—or her—at all. Hard thing to manage when she'd just stormed Lord Castlereagh's home to demand a reckoning with her fiancé.

She sighed as she slumped against the hard wooden chair. She really had to start thinking things through better.

Chapter Twelve

L ORD BENEDICT GAPED at Nate over the nauseating bulbous breasts of the woman on his lap. He was already physically ill from the charade he'd had to enact with the French king's ambassador. Any man with half a brain would realize he would be repulsed by the tawdry assets of this overly powdered woman. But that was the problem. LeFauvre had less than half a brain. He assumed that whatever he wanted would of course be the desires of every other man on the planet.

So it was that he greeted Lord Nathaniel with a sense of relief, though it was tinged with confusion. "I thought you were on the way to Carlton House." They needed Prinny to weigh in on some minor issues about Tobago.

"A problem with the wine," murmured Lord Nathaniel in his ear. "Of a personal nature to you."

Personal? He had no personal business that could be pressing. Unless something had happened to his parents. He twisted to see Lord Nate's face. "My father?" he whispered. Stupid that. It was a measure of his panic at the thought of his father's death that he did such a thing in full view of a half dozen dignitaries. Fortunately, the women were doing their job in distracting the men. Still, it was a mistake that warned him how much he was in his cups.

Nate shook his head. "Matrimonial," he mouthed back.

Matrimonial! That was when he forgot himself so much as to gape at the man. The word didn't even compute in his head. Maybe he misread the word off Nate's lips. He was overtired and a little bleary-eyed. Napoleon's abdication had transferred all the weight of the war from the military to the diplomatic corps. Every winning nation wanted to carve up the spoils for their own benefit. He and Castlereagh had been working day and night to ensure that Britain got her fair share and that the result didn't lead to another war out of disgruntled spite.

Meanwhile, Nate did him the amazing favor of extending a hand to the buxom woman on Benedict's lap. "Prinny is attending to other matters of state," he said loud enough for everyone to hear. "But he should be pleased to speak with you in the morning." It was a lie. Prinny was not a man to speak civilly to anyone in the morning, but it was a standard lie used to cover all manner of sins. Unfortunately, the French ambassador wasn't drunk enough to miss that.

"Ha," LaFauvre snorted as he flipped himself on top of his whore. "I know what *state* he is in."

The lady squealed in delight as the Frenchman loosened his breeches. Benedict tried not to vomit at the sight. Damnation, the night was rapidly spinning out and apparently there was something of vital importance still to be handled in the wine cellar.

Thankfully, Nate continued to tempt Benedict's woman away. "Pray allow me to entertain your companion while you attend to the prosaic matters of state."

The woman must have sensed that she was getting nowhere with Benedict, so she uncoiled out of his lap to wrap herself around Nate. "Coo, aren't you a muscular one," she said.

Nate responded with the natural ability of a born spy. He fondled the woman until she squealed. And while everyone's eyes were on his obvious hand movements, he caught and held Benedict's gaze.

"Malta," Benedict mouthed. They needed to know why the French king was suddenly so keen on acquiring the Mediterranean island. Louis XVIII was already getting his throne back. Why would he demand a tiny island as well?

Nate nodded, even as he neatly maneuvered himself and the woman to an advantageous position on the floor. LeFauvre was often loose-lipped right after he finished his business with a woman, and Nate knew how to take advantage of such a moment. Which meant that Benedict could spare himself the entire revolting scene. He stood up and straightened his clothing as if he hid an erection. He did not. Indeed, his privates had shriveled up into near non-existence. A few steps later and he was finally able to take his first full breath since the women had arrived. Whatever perfume the whores wore made him light-headed.

He saw Limpy standing by the wine cellar door. Fortunately, the clearer air allowed him to get his head together enough to ask a question without revealing his ignorance. "Everything quiet down there?"

"Aye, m'lord. Lord Nathaniel and her talked for a bit, then he went to get you."

"How does she look?" Limpy might be uneducated, but he had a keen eye for detail, and he'd been in this business for a long time. Benedict respected his acumen.

"Young, m'lord, but not dumb. She'll learn quick enough with the right guidance. She'll be an asset t' you."

So it was Miss Caddick. Damnation, what was the woman doing here? And on a night like this?

"Thank you. Please see that we're not disturbed." He paused a moment to consider his options. "And see that my carriage is readied. We'll be leaving soon."

"Aye, milord."

Then he opened the door and began his descent. He moved slowly, letting the weight of his step show his displeasure. And if she didn't catch the hint, he allowed his fatigue to show on his face.

"Miss Caddick," he drawled when he hit the bottom step. "To what do I owe this unexpected pleasure?" He let irony lace his tone.

Then he saw her face.

If ever a woman was tortured by her thoughts, it was her. There was frustration in her wide-eyed confusion, but whatever could be bothering her? As far as he knew, her life remained exactly as it had been before he proposed. Surely, she was not the kind of woman to fret over the details of the wedding breakfast. If so, then he had vastly misjudged her.

"I am so sorry to bother you, my lord. Indeed, if I had understood the importance of this evening, then I surely wouldn't have interrupted you."

The importance of this evening? "Tonight's work was awkward, but not any more important than any other night."

She frowned. "Awkward…because of those women?"

So she had seen them. Or heard them. Even down in the wine cellar, the irritating sound of giggles filtered through. "Diplomacy requires information. And sometimes the gathering of such knowledge happens in less than moral ways." He frowned at her. "Does this upset you?"

"What? No. Or rather only in the most general of ways. It is unfortunate that such tactics are required."

That was what he'd guessed, given that she treated all manner of patients without apparent prejudice. But that didn't explain why she was here now. With another person, he might have snapped at them, ordering them to get on with their issue while they had his attention. But she was not his subordinate in the typical sense. She was his future wife, and it was worth his time to understand her fears. So when she failed to speak—indeed she looked excruciatingly anxious about speaking—he did something rare.

He chose to make her more comfortable.

He turned to a cabinet hidden under the stairs. Opening it, he cleaned off a pair of wineglasses, then set them on the table. Fortunately, he knew exactly where the good wine was kept and quickly selected a bottle.

"Limpy said I shouldn't drink any," she said.

"Limpy knows I will." He opened the bottle and began to pour, too impatient to allow the liquid to breathe. He filled his glass to the brim, then paused over her glass. "You may do as you wish."

"By all means, fill it up," she said with a self-mocking snort. It was an indelicate sound that he appreciated. He hated simpering women. Truthfully, he hated most women, including his mother, so that hardly boded well for his future wife.

He gave her a full measure of drink, then set the bottle aside. Then he swirled the liquid in his glass as she did the same, though he could tell she was simply mimicking him. Ah well, she would learn. No person remained in his company for long without learning the finer points of wine.

"I've ordered my carriage brought around for you, so you don't have much time. Pray explain yourself." He tried to make his tone gentle, but he was tired, and she was nervous. He became very blunt in situations like this.

To her credit, she didn't flinch from him. Indeed, after a large gulp of wine, she squared her shoulders and faced him. "Actually, my lord, I'm here to ask you to explain yourself."

"I beg your pardon?"

Undaunted, she matched his cold tone with one of her own. "I am not a child who expects romantic gifts or poetic expressions of love."

He knew. That was one reason why he selected her.

"But if we are to build an amicable life together, then I require some clarity on your expectations of me."

He frowned. "I should think that was obvious."

She arched a brow as she stared at him. "What is obvious to you is perhaps less obvious than you think."

He felt his lips curve. "Major Vance often says that as well."

Her lips tightened and he could see that she did not favor the major. And that was going to make all of their lives difficult. He resolved to address that in a moment. For now, he answered her question.

"I require you to bear my children and raise them to meet or exceed the level of their station. Mine is an old name and an honored title that has served the Crown for generations. I will not have my children disgrace their heritage."

"I would like that as well," she said.

Good. But the very thought of procreating children sent him to his wine. He took his time with it, sipping slowly as he tried to order his thoughts. It wasn't easy, given that this was not his first bottle tonight.

"I should like you to attend various functions as my wife. The major will inform you of such events every Monday. They won't take more than a few hours of your time, though I should ask for your indulgence from time to time. My schedule can be unpredictable, however I shall make every effort to ensure that yours is not."

She frowned. "That sounds eminently reasonable except for one thing."

The dreaded "one more thing." Every diplomat despised those words. Rather than speak, he raised a single brow in query.

"Major Vance doesn't want us to wed."

It was unfortunate that Gabe had made his opinion clear to her, but then she was unusually perceptive. Or Gabe was unusually gauche. Whatever the case, Benedict had no intention of delaying their marriage. He needed an heir.

"Aren't you going to comment?" she pressed. "Do you allow your subordinate to have a say in your matrimonial affairs?"

"Unequivocally, no."

"But he is, my lord. He is being extraordinarily difficult."

Interesting. "How, exactly, is he being difficult?"

"He is..." She grimaced. "He questions everything, he tells me my responsibilities, and he phrases things such that no sane woman would choose to wed you. And he told me that we are to wed in three weeks!" She finished that off with another large gulp of wine.

"That is his job, Miss Caddick."

"To give me a disgust of our marriage before we have had more than one conversation?"

"To ensure the smooth execution of my professional life. Where my wife intersects with my profession, the major must be allowed to direct her actions."

She set her glass down. "He has made his disapproval of me abundantly clear."

Benedict shrugged. "That is between you and him. I have known Gabriel for many years, and have never known him to be difficult without reason." He took another sip of his wine. It really was an excellent vintage. "I suggest you have a frank conversation with him."

She huffed out a breath. "I am trying to have one with you! I thought I was marrying you, not him."

She had no idea how wrong she was. "That was your mistake. A wife must fold herself into her husband's household. Major Vance is the head of my household. I trust him with my life and my career."

"And your wife?"

"Yes." He arched a brow at her. "Is that a problem for you? You knew our marriage was a business arrangement. Your settlement was very generous and the requirements abundantly clear. I need children to carry on my name. You are the woman I selected who would most fit into my household—"

"Why?"

"What?"

"Why do you think I would fit with you?"

Because she had a secret he could exploit, one told to him by Lord Nate, but unsubstantiated by anyone else. Nate suspected she was midwife Betty Gill, though he had no proof. So Benedict had set Gabriel to investigate without mentioning the exact secret. He did not want to prejudice the man.

"Because you are levelheaded and uninterested in flattery. Because you understand the obligations of my name and you have very little attraction to me."

"What?"

Really? Did she truly not understand the basics of a successful partnership? He spread his arms wide, allowing her to see the lanky angles of his body and the harsh cut of his face. His was not a body women swooned over. And if they did, he spurned them.

"What could you possibly want with this?" She opened her mouth to say something complimentary, but he cut her off with a shake of his head. "I do not want attraction, Miss Caddick. A lovelorn miss sets my teeth on edge. I require breeding, and I have every expectation that you can do that to an exemplary degree."

She stared at him. "Let me guess," she said dryly. "You saw that there is no madness in my family. That my father—and his forebearers—have above average intelligence, exhibited good management of our land, and no tendency toward vice. My guess is that you realized my mother's untimely death was not because of an inability to breed but because of an unfortunate infection after my brother's birth. Excepting that, I come from good female stock."

"Exactly correct," he said. "But you forgot one important detail. It was, in fact, the primary reason I decided upon you."

"And what is that?"

He waited until she drained the last of her glass before answering. "You have an interest of your own that will keep you well occupied and out of my affairs."

"An interest of my own?"

"I am aware of your passion for medicine."

"That...that doesn't upset you?" The surprise in her tone made him smile.

"I applaud it." That was certainly true. "And I applaud the idea of a busy wife."

"One who won't interfere in your affairs," she said as her gaze drifted upward to the overly loud merriment upstairs.

"Not that kind of affair, I assure you," he said with a shudder. "Womanizing is not my vice. Neither is gambling nor excessive drink."

"Then what is your vice?"

That was not up for discussion, so he grabbed the easiest lie. "Peace, Miss Caddick. One that includes a strong England."

"Peace," she echoed. "And children." She picked up the wine bottle and refilled her glass. "I can fit my life to that goal."

"Then we are agreed," he said as she topped off his glass.

They clinked glasses and drank a full measure. Benedict was surprised to realize that it felt like a treaty between two great nations. Certainly, he had the superior power being the man. He was also aware of more about her than she realized. But that was how all his treaties were signed, and they tended to work out well.

"I hope you realize, Miss Caddick, that I hold you in great esteem."

She looked up from her glass. "No, my lord, I had not realized that."

"We have just this night shared two glasses of wine while my horses chill themselves on the street waiting for you."

She nodded as she looked back at her empty glass. "That is rare for you?"

"Extremely. Indeed, I can think of only one person I would happily do as much for."

"One person?"

"Yes." He waited while she appeared to think on that. A moment later, she proved how very clever she was.

"Oh my," she groaned. "You refer to Major Vance, don't you?"

"I do," he said with a smile.

"I have to find a way into his good graces, don't I?"

"You do. And I suggest you do it immediately. The wedding will be in two weeks' time."

"Two weeks!" she gasped. "I thought I had three!"

"I will need to depart for Vienna soon after our wedding. We may have a month's honeymoon—I am having my castle refurbished for our use since my parents reside in the manor house. But I cannot promise we shall have more than a week. Castlereagh would like me to arrange the details of a congress."

The lady shook her head. "I cannot possibly manage a wedding in that amount of time."

"Of course, you cannot. You must rely upon the major."

"But I told you," she huffed. "He disapproves."

He waited again and after as much wine as he had consumed, he knew his expression was becoming sloppy. She stared at him, trying to emphasize her point with a hard frown. He raised a brow in response. She glared. He smiled.

Quite a bit of discussion without any words.

Eventually, she gave in. She slumped back in her chair, and he chuckled, which was a surprise. He couldn't remember the last time he had laughed so easily.

"I'm not going to win in this, am I?" she asked. "You are going to force me to work with him."

"Unless you wish to cry off our wedding."

She swallowed as she stared into her last drops of wine. "I do not wish to cry off. I can be a good wife to you." She looked up. "I respect what you are doing. I respect you. And therefore, I will honor you as a good wife should."

Excellent.

"So you will negotiate a peace with the major?" he asked.

"You will allow me to wage my…uh…negotiations without interference?"

He snorted. Good God, what a sound! He was drunk. "Miss Caddick, the whole point of this conversation was so that I did not have to interfere in any way whatsoever."

"Then I shall see it done."

"And I will honor you as a good husband ought," he added.

She nodded once, as if she considered that a good bargain. He hoped it was.

"Salut," she said. Then she drained her glass.

"Salut," he echoed as he finished his glass. Then he smiled at his future wife. She had just risen to a challenge that no usual wife would know how to handle. And for certain, Gabriel had no idea what was coming.

By God, this was going to be fun to watch. And much more interesting that LeFauvre's sloppy interest in Malta.

Chapter Thirteen

From his earliest years, various people had tried to put Gabriel in his place. A bastard—even a duke's bastard—was a target for every social climbing, moralistic, or otherwise pompous ass on the planet. Fortunately, his mother had given him a weapon to deal with such people. It was, indeed, perhaps the best thing she had ever taught him.

"Choose your priority and your weapon," she said. "Ignore everything and everyone else."

Her priority was to be worshipped, and her weapons were her seductive talents. All else—including her own son—was classified as either useful or not depending upon how they served her priority.

It was a valuable lesson for him. It took him a long while to determine his priority. As a boy at Eton, his priority had echoed his mother's. He demanded respect from the other boys, and he enforced that with his fists or other devious means of punishment if he did not receive his due.

But then there came a girl. She was young by his standards now, but old for him back then. She was the wife of one of the instructors. A woman cursed (he later discovered) with an inability to bear children. But every year, she would pick a few to grace her table, to perform special tasks, and to receive motherly affection that had been so lacking in his life before then.

She did not select him.

He brought her gifts, he cleared her garden for her, he was

effusive with compliments. He did all the things that worked with his mother, but none of it worked with her. He knew he could not threaten her as he did with the other boys. No harsh treatment of her or her chosen favorites brought him the attention he craved, and he tried all of it.

Then one day he saw her reading a tale of King Arthur. The moment she set it down, he grabbed it—*Le Morte D'Arthur* in the original French—and read it from cover to cover, hiding it beneath his bed for fear that she would discover that he had stolen it. He cared little for the tragic love story. His imagination became riveted by the chivalric code which cared nothing for the circumstances of his birth. Indeed, Sir Galahad was Lancelot's bastard, and he was the only one pure enough to retrieve the holy grail.

He began reading everything he could about the Knights of the Round Table. He fashioned his own shield and began to learn the use of a sword. He memorized the ten commandments of chivalry, but focused most on the one that said, *Thou shalt be everywhere and always the champion of the Right and the Good against Injustice and Evil.*

That was a bitter pill for him to swallow because by every measure, he had been cruel to those weaker than him. Whenever he tried to cast himself as the hero in a tale, he saw himself acting more as the villain.

It was a cruel thing for a young boy to realize. He wasn't evil because he was a bastard. He was evil because he'd chosen to act that way. Fortunately, he was intelligent enough—and young enough—to change his behavior.

He never did gain the woman's attention, but he didn't need it. He looked to himself to earn his own respect. Might for Right became his creed. He defended the weak and lent his strength to the good. When he reached adulthood, he found his quest in the Peninsular War. Napoleon was bullying his way across the continent, expanding his empire by conquering weaker nations who could not defend themselves.

So he defended them. And during that time, he met Lord Benedict. Here indeed was his King Arthur, a man who strove tirelessly to repel the invader and to set out laws and alliances such that another bully could never rise again.

He was still serving Arthur in every way he knew how. And if that meant he used his might to make sure that Guinevere—Janelle, in this case—acted as an asset to Lord Benedict, then he would do so without hesitation.

So it was that when he returned to Benedict's box at the theater and found her hastily scrawled note about returning home, he had two conflicting thoughts. The first—and what he deemed most likely—was that she had run off to her own amusements. The second, which could not be completely discounted, was that Lord Benedict's enemies had taken her for their own evil purposes.

Whatever the case, his duty was clear. He had to find her immediately. What he did once he found her depended entirely upon whether she landed in the good or evil category.

He was nevertheless cognizant that he served as escort to her aunt. Fortunately, he had enough friends in the *ton* to find her a fresh companion. As she had just spent the last fifteen minutes disparaging his manners, his encroaching attitude, and his birth, she gave no objection to his departure. He did find it laughable when she declared that Janelle was of delicate health and often sought her bed when ill. Miss Caddick was the epitome of health and willful disobedience. That her caretakers thought her delicate was proof of their stupidity.

So it was that he found himself outside her home less than thirty minutes after discovering her note. He was about to climb the stairs when he saw a young messenger boy dash up the stairs and bang on the door. He wasn't sure of the boy's identity at first, though there was something about the child's uneven gait that triggered a memory. But when the boy banged on the knocker then handed a missive to the butler, Gabe quickly became certain. Especially when the child spoke.

"It's urgent, guv," the child said. "For Betty."

"She's not at home," the butler said.

"Madame Florina said to come right now."

The butler nodded. "I'll tell her as soon as I can, but she is not due home for hours."

Now he placed the boy. He was a messenger from the Rose Garden, asking for Janelle. And the butler was obviously in on the secret. Now he need only wait for the lady's return and follow her. Whatever her secret activity, he would have the truth of it tonight.

So he stayed in the shadows and waited. He was cold but not yet numb when she finally returned. But it was the manner in which she was delivered that shocked him to his core.

She arrived in Lord Benedict's carriage. He hastily reviewed all that he knew of His Lordship's activities. Lord Benedict meant to spend the entire evening entertaining LeFauvre in the crudest manner possible. He could not possibly have taken time away from that to attend to Miss Caddick. Neither would he have left the carriage for her use. Lord Benedict was fussy about that, and Gabriel would have known, were that the case. Such logistics were under his exclusive purview. And yet he could not deny the evidence of his eyes.

The coachman was quick to open the carriage door. It appeared that Miss Caddick was slightly drunk as she needed the man's help to disembark. She righted herself quickly as she thanked the man in very polite tones. Then she walked with great dignity up her front steps. Her butler opened the door before she was halfway up. He must have been watching for her. Then he slipped her the missive the moment she crossed the threshold. If a word was spoken, Gabriel didn't hear it over the sound of Lord Benedict's carriage pulling away.

But he did hear her soft curse a moment later. Whatever she was about this night, she was none too pleased with it.

"Five minutes," he heard her say. "Can you get me a hackney?"

"Yes, miss."

Gabe had already deduced that the servants were complicit with whatever was going on. Still, it was a bit of a shock to see the otherwise stiffly proper man help with her deception.

Miss Caddick was as good as her word. The butler hailed a hackney and within five minutes, "Betty" rushed out from the servant's door. She was covered in a dark cloak, complete with a stoop shouldered, slightly limping gait. The butler had gone back inside the home, so Gabe waited until the cab began to depart, then jumped onto the back. He was a good deal heavier than when he'd done this as a boy, but no one seemed to notice the added weight.

They drove for a bit and the cabbie must have been told to go fast because he pushed the horses on streets best taken slow. Gabe watched in alarm as the neighborhood turned from respectable to dark, from comfortable to wretched. Not the worst area, he realized as they finally slowed, but the rookeries weren't far away.

She climbed out of the carriage before it had fully stopped. But then she stood there in confusion. "Where am I going?" she asked the cabbie.

"That one, Oi think," he answered.

She nodded, then hefted a massive bag. It wasn't wise to carry such a large thing here. He scanned the surroundings, noting several people eyeing her with curiosity. Or perhaps something worse. And then he noticed it. There was a silence in the air completely uncommon in an area such as this. A kind of held breath as one waits for a scream or cannon shot.

Miss Caddick noticed it, too. She looked about and firmed her chin. "Right," she muttered to herself and then headed off in the direction the cabbie had pointed. She stopped once to speak to a girl too young to be sitting alone outside. He couldn't hear the words, but the child nodded and pointed into the building.

Gabe frowned as he slipped into the thick shadows. What the devil was she doing here? And in an area that she obviously didn't know. Whatever idiocy this was, he could not let her be harmed. He had to reveal himself, if only to make sure she wasn't accosted or worse.

He moved forward with purpose, stepping past the girl and into the dark interior of the rickety building. The halls were dark, the stairway tight, and the smell bad. Though he'd seen poverty in Spain, London had built its own kind of hell. He might have gotten lost. There were several rooms in this place, but he heard her call out as she knocked.

"It's Betty," she said clear as day. "The midwife."

Midwife! Of all the ridiculous things. She was a gently bred woman, sheltered from birth. Midwifery was a difficult and bloody proposition. It was one thing to play with potions and unguents, but to pretend to a skill that she couldn't possibly have was cruel. Laboring women needed a skilled hand, and he would not allow her to mislead these people.

He rushed upstairs, not bothering to hide his footsteps. But what he saw when he got to the top of the landing made him stop and gape. Her, too, since she'd stopped dead as she inspected the interior.

A very pregnant woman lay gray and barely breathing on the bed. A woman with dirty hands and a sour expression stood by the bed holding cupping implements as she steadily bled the lady's arm. A man, presumably the husband, stood shaking in the corner of the room. And a child—a thin girl of no more than ten years—stood on the opposite side of the bed as assistant. She held dirty rags and watched with a wide-eyed horror that Gabe felt echo through his own heart.

"Stop it!" Miss Caddick cried. "Stop that right now!"

"Git away you," the sour woman said. "I know wot I'm about." She was likely a real midwife and though he knew the sight of death, he was at least grateful that these poor people wouldn't be subjected to—

"The hell you do!" Miss Caddick snapped. "Look at her! She's too weak now!"

"She's swoll," the woman said back. "It's 'er only hope."

"Stop it, now!" Miss Caddick commanded, and everyone looked up in shock at the tone she used, himself included. He'd heard the like from old sergeants and some of the women who followed the drum. It was the sound of authority and supreme confidence in one's own knowledge. He knew it could be false confidence, but he responded as well as anyone to the tone.

The midwife frowned, then pulled off the cup, now more than half full of blood. "Was done anyway."

"Yes, you are," Miss Caddick snapped as she stomped into the room, supplanting the girl by the bedside. She touched the pregnant woman's cheek and neck, no doubt feeling for a pulse. If there was one, it had to be barely noticeable. "The babe's not yet ready," she said as she felt around the woman's belly. "Sir, what caused to you call a midwife?"

The man with hollowed eyes looked up. "She had a fit, she did. Fell down in the street. She's me sister and, well, what with the belly and all, I carried her upstairs. But I didn't know who to send fer."

"He sent for me," the midwife snapped. "And there's no need for you 'ere. The Lord'll take or not. It's in His hands."

"After you helped the devil with his work," Miss Caddick muttered. Whether or not the others heard it made no difference. The woman on the bed began to gasp and choke, her body shuddering with another fit.

"That there!" the man gasped. "That's wot 'appened."

Miss Caddick had been opening her bag when it began and she quickly pulled out a thick bite stick, but it was too late. The woman's mouth was clenched tight as she arched her back and began to thrash.

The girl jumped back with a gasp, her hands pressed to her mouth. The midwife too stepped away. "It's the devil come t' take wot's his."

"It's no such thing," Miss Caddick said as she pressed the woman's shoulders down. "Help me!" she ordered. "Keep her from hurting herself."

But sometimes even a commanding voice was not enough to overcome superstition. The other three in the room didn't move. Which left it up to him.

Gabriel was across the room in a moment, using his strength to pin down the woman's legs. It wasn't as hard as he feared. Though she shook with strain, she hadn't much power left in her. Her flesh compressed under his hands, the woman's swollen calves stretched taut despite the bloodletting.

Miss Caddick looked up when he appeared, but she gave no reaction beyond a curt nod. He saw clarity in her eyes despite the way she'd wobbled not twenty minutes before. Indeed, every aspect of her person was crisp and clear, as if she'd done this a thousand times before.

Well, hell. She really was a midwife.

He rocked back a bit on his heels, his mind reeling. She was a midwife, and he had no way to fit that into what he already knew about her. It simply could not be possible that a girl of the *ton* could have the years of experience required to be so competent now. And yet here she was, holding down the pregnant patient with the strength of a woman who had done it several times before.

It didn't take long for the fit to stop. The woman eased, the shaking stopped, and her breath escaped in a low exhale that he'd heard too many times on dying men.

"That's better," Miss Caddick said as if she were talking to a sensate woman. "What's her name, sir?"

No one answered, least of all the man in the corner who had folded in on himself.

"Sir!"

"It's Winnie Cook, mum," the girl said, proving that even little girls could have better presence of mind than grown men.

Miss Caddick pressed her hand low on Winnie's belly. "She's contracting. Has that been going on long?"

"Every four minutes, mum. But they ain't strong enough."

"And it's too soon," Miss Caddick said.

"Aye," the midwife said, her expression grim as she turned to the man. "They're gone, then. It'll take a day, mebbe. I'm right sorry, I am." She held out her hand for her payment. "You can call me if she lives fer longer, but I'd get the priest if I were you."

"Wot?" the man said, his swollen eyes on his sister. "Yer leavin'?"

"There's more babies in London. I can't wait fer every one."

"But the baby's in there. It's still got to come out, yes?"

The little girl stepped forward and touched the man's hand. "No, sir. It can't come out. It's too little and has no lungs."

"Wot?"

Damn it, the man simply couldn't understand. His sister and the babe were gone. It was just a matter of time. The only one who seemed to be fighting for their lives was Miss Caddick. She had settled on the bed and was filling a stopper with milk she pulled from a bottle. She carefully turned Winnie's mouth her way and gently dripped some into the woman's slack mouth, then she stroked the woman's neck.

"That's the way, Winnie," she cooed. "See if you can take a little in."

Did it get in? Did she swallow? It was hard to see, especially when the other midwife sighed.

"Waste of good milk," she said. "An' it makes the end drag on longer."

Gabe knew what she was saying. A slow death was no mercy, but Miss Caddick would not be stopped.

"It's my milk to waste," she said in a hard tone. Then she looked at the brother. "I'll stay and fight for her, sir. I'll stay until God comes, one way or the other."

The woman snorted. "Suit yerself." Then she turned to the man. "I'll need my payment. I know it's hard, sir, but Oi did what Oi could."

The brother was in no shape to respond. Neither was he likely to have much coin. "How much?" Gabe asked the little girl.

"A quid."

A quid to kill the man's sister with bloodletting. What a crazy thing. He pulled out a coin, but before he could press it into the girl's hand, Miss Caddick snatched it out of his palm.

"What's your name?" she asked the child.

"Polta."

"Do you know who I am, Polta?"

"You're the rich un Betty. They call you the death-wife."

Miss Caddick winced at that. "That's because they only call me on the hard cases. But I've saved plenty."

"'Ey now," the midwife said, her tone growing suspicious. "Don't be talking to me girl."

"You're a kind one, Polta, with a steady head. I could use one like you." She held out the coin and Polta took it with a canny look.

"Me, miss?"

"Do you know how to find me?"

"You truck with them whores. Down by the Rose Garden."

"I do. But there's no difference between women at this time, is there? Queen or whore, they all need a steady hand, yes?" She held the girl's gaze. "And kindness, yes?"

"Yes, mum."

"Then you think on it." She looked at the midwife. It seemed for a moment as if she would say something, but she didn't. Her lips pressed tight, and then she turned back to the patient. "Maybe a little more milk now, yes?"

The woman was unconscious. There would be no more yeses out of her ever. Meanwhile, Miss Caddick pressed a hand back to the belly.

"You rest a bit, Winne," she continued. "I'm right here with the milk when you're ready."

The midwife said nothing except to cluck at Polta. The child scrambled after her mistress, though her eyes lingered on Miss Caddick. Everyone's did, his included, as she sat at the edge of the pallet.

The midwife left with Polta trailing after her. The brother remained where he was, staring at the bed, and Gabe did the same. This was not a place for a man. No birthing chamber was. Though, he supposed, there wasn't going to be a birth, so he might as well remain. And he certainly wasn't going to abandon Miss Caddick now.

He waited beside her, and he passed the long hours by adjusting his thoughts. He'd believed Miss Caddick was a pampered debutant, a woman who played with potions and unguents. And now he saw she was also an accomplished midwife.

How in the hell did his mother and the Rose Garden fit into all that?

Chapter Fourteen

J ANELLE HOPED FOR miracles. She had seen a few. A mother who survived fever and blood loss. A father who fed a babe with a dropper without rest for a full week. And a child who grew, despite all odds. She'd seen these things and recalling them never failed to warm her heart.

But she never expected a miracle, and so tonight, she settled in for death.

She didn't expect that Major Vance would stay with her. She hadn't been surprised when he arrived. He had been plaguing her too much for him not to be here. But that he stayed was a miracle all its own. She didn't like waiting alone any more than the dying did.

"How did you become this?" he asked several hours into the vigil.

She looked up, startled by the sound in the otherwise silent room. Winnie's breath was too shallow to be heard. "What?"

He gestured vaguely to herself and the patient. "A midwife. One of some fame, it appears."

She frowned as she looked around. Her thoughts and her vision had been completely consumed with trying to drip milk into Winnie's mouth.

"Where's Winnie's brother?" She couldn't remember the man's name.

"He left an hour ago. Said he needed to go to work."

She looked out at the brightening sky. Hell, she'd have to

send a message to Nanny to cover for her this day. Fortunately, no one would expect her to be awake for several hours yet. It wouldn't be the first time she'd stayed up all night then made it home in time for tea.

She nodded as she looked back at the major. "Last Season, I visited one of the lying-in hospitals. The matron thought I was touring, but I wanted to learn."

"To train? In a hospital?" He sounded shocked by the idea.

She nodded. "But it turned out that I already knew more than most of the students. I knew how to read and had already studied all the texts. I didn't shy from the dirt. Once you've helped a sow in labor, a woman wealthy enough to afford a hospital is the height of luxury."

He blinked. "You've delivered pigs?"

"And cows and sheep. What do you think witchy women do in the country? It's not all chilblains and putrid throats."

He shook his head. "I cannot credit that you were allowed."

She shrugged. "I wasn't." Then she looked at him. "I expect there was a great deal you weren't allowed to do as a boy that you did anyway."

He didn't speak, but she could see his thoughts as if they were written bold across his forehead. She was a girl and the daughter of a baron. There were no more isolated women than the daughters of the aristocracy. And yet she had escaped into the world and was all the better for it.

"What do you think wealthy women do all day?" she asked.

He frowned. "I don't know. Shopping? Dressing and doing their hair?"

She gestured to her disheveled hair and the milk stains on her gown. "Do I seem like a woman who cares much for that?"

"No."

"What should a woman who doesn't care about fashion and hair do with her time?"

He clearly had no idea.

"I did as I pleased, Major. Since I was ten years old. And this is what I was pleased to learn. So long as I appeared dressed and happy for tea, no one noticed if I spent the morning helping a woman give birth."

He glanced at Winnie who was clearly not going to give birth today. Indeed, her belly had stopped contracting completely.

"How could your father not know?" he asked.

"Do you have sisters, Major?"

He shook his head.

"Think of your friends who do. Did they care what their sisters did? So long as it did not disturb their amusements."

"Young men have a singularly narrow focus on their own pleasures."

"My brother did as well."

He shifted his position to lean his other shoulder against the wall. She frowned. Had he been standing all night? His feet must ache abominably.

"Major, I did not ask you to stay. You need not remain. I assure you this is a task I am all too familiar with."

"You know how to handle bodies in London? I do not think her brother will return before nightfall."

Oh hell. She hadn't thought of that. This was the first time she'd been left alone to care for a forgotten woman. "Her brother went to work?"

"I don't think he could bear to see the end."

She should have realized that. Death was not a pretty process and, like birth, was often left to the women to manage. "I suppose I shall have to figure it out," she said.

He snorted. "I will handle it for you when the time comes."

She wanted to deny him out of pride. She wanted to inform him that she was well able to manage without his interference. But the truth was that she was at sea here. What she could manage easily in Devon was sometimes a mystery in London.

"Thank you, Major. I am very grateful for that." She took a breath. "If there is an expense for it—"

"I will handle it."

"I'm sure you could, but—"

"I do not need your money, Miss Caddick."

His tone was angry, and she knew better than challenge a man when he took that tone. So she looked back to her patient. The news there was even less appealing. Winnie would not last much longer. Then the Major surprised her.

"My apologies," he said. "I cannot find my footing with you, and that has made me short tempered."

"You mean you cannot figure out where I belong in your mind. I am neither a spoiled society girl nor a dedicated healer. You know how to treat Lord Benedict's fiancée, but only if she acts in a way you deem appropriate. Similarly, you know what to do with a London midwife, but not if she is engaged to someone you esteem. Major Vance, does it occur to you that your mind is too narrow to allow for my existence? And that the fault for that is entirely your own?"

"Of course, it does," he said, his words a low grumble. "Why do you think I'm short-tempered?"

She chuckled. How could she not? He sounded so put out to admit his own failing. "Don't feel bad. You are hardly alone in that sort of thinking."

"But I had prided myself on seeing things more clearly."

"Don't we all?" Unlike him, she was loath to admit that she might have misjudged him. After all, he was here helping when Winnie's own brother had left. He'd paid the midwife. And most important to her, he had not once chastised her for doing work normally reserved for family members or nuns, which is certainly what her aunt would have done. Her father would likely have dragged her out by her ears.

"What is your connection to the Rose Garden?" His voice was low, but it jolted her nonetheless.

"What makes you think I have one?"

He shot her a look that said he had no interest in playing games, but when he spoke, he kept his tone soft, likely out of respect for Winnie. "I saw you that first day leaving the building. I recognized the boy who brought the message to your butler."

He'd been watching her? Lord, he must have rushed back from the theater and stood outside lying in wait. "You were following me?"

"I was tasked with being your escort."

"You abandoned my aunt?"

He rolled his eyes. "I doubt she planned a run to the East End. Besides, I found her a suitable escort."

Of course, he did. The man was obviously conscientious about his responsibility. Still, his presence here showed a dedication that bordered on alarming. "Why are you so determined to chase me?"

"I should think that is obvious." He lifted his chin. "Enough deflection. What is your connection to the Rose Garden?"

"You are the one who recognized the boy. It would stand to reason that you have the untoward association with the place, not I."

"My mother owns it, in partnership with Madame Florina."

Oh. Well. That was not what she expected. "Who is your mother?" Lord Benedict had told her, but she'd forgotten the name. Or was too tired to recall it.

"She's part owner of the Rose Garden." Then before she could say something cutting back, he held up his hand as if in surrender. "We can argue back and forth with one another or we can make a bargain. I will tell you all about my mother if you would share exactly why you were sent here."

She remained silent for a moment, busying herself with checking on Winnie. There was no change, and she was merely delaying. She recognized Major Vance to be the proverbial dog with a bone. No matter how she deflected, denied, or deferred, he would still come at her for more information. He would show up unannounced, hide in shadows when she escaped, and then somehow follow her here when she thought herself free of him.

There was nothing left in her arsenal to defeat a man such as that. And no point anyway. Her reticence was simple habit. She did not like bringing any man into her business, but that was illogical now. So while she tried to drip a little more milk into Winnie's mouth, she explained what she had held secret for so long.

"I told you that I went to a lying-in hospital to learn. The matron was very clear that she would not allow me to help when I was available, even without pay. That is not how it works in a hospital."

"I imagine not," he said dryly.

"Well, it is how it works in Devon. One finds a teacher, and one learns." She took a breath. "Did you know that the hospital only accepts married patients who can afford to pay the fee?" She looked back to Winnie. "Who tends the other women, do you think? The unmarried and the poor?"

"Midwives who are not lucky enough to be hospital trained."

"Yes." She shrugged. "I became one of them."

"But what has this to do with the Rose Garden?"

"You don't know?" The ignorance of men boggled her mind sometimes. "The Rose Garden serves as a place where information comes and goes quietly, quickly, with none the wiser."

He snorted. "My mother has long since traded in information."

"Women's information, Major Vance. I care not for the secrets of men in power. I care for women like Winnie."

"I don't understand."

"You mean you cannot believe that there is a vast network of women who help each other. You cannot credit that the madame of a whorehouse might know the names and directions of talented midwives, kind apothecaries, and several helpful priests."

He shook his head, his expression incredulous. "Not my mother."

"Are you sure?"

He remained silent, his mind cracking open despite his unwillingness to believe. She remained silent, idly wondering if his male pride would win out over obvious truth. Would he deny everything she had just said—

"I cannot credit it," he said.

Male pride defeats all.

"But you are here and no dilletante," he continued. "At least not the kind I thought."

"Damned by faint praise."

He acknowledged the statement with a dip of his head. "Since the moment I went to war, I have lived almost exclusively in the world of men. It is only logical to believe that there is a great, vast world of women of which I am ignorant."

She smiled at him. "That is the truest thing you have ever said to me. I applaud you for opening your mind."

"And what of you, Miss Caddick?"

"What of me?"

"Will you open your mind? Will you see that you cannot continue this kind of work once you are wed to Lord Benedict?"

Back to this old argument? She could not express how very tired she was of it. "If I listened to every man who said a thing could not be done—"

"This is not safe. Not for the wife of a dignitary like Lord Benedict." He raised his hand before she could voice her objection. "As Lord Benedict's wife, you will be watched as never before, usually by unfriendly eyes. You cannot receive messages from a whorehouse. You cannot run off to the rookeries when a woman goes into labor. And you cannot be hurt by a footpad or worse, then left to rot in the most dangerous areas of London."

"Because it would damage His Lordship's standing?"

"Because you could be dead." He shook his head. "Do you not see the danger you are in just by coming to a place like this? A woman alone? Surely you must, for you are not that stupid."

She wasn't. She knew. In Devon, Betty was respected. And if not her, then certainly Mrs. Sundy. But London was a place of a great many dangers, and she had already had several close calls. This dual life of hers was already too stressful, and by all accounts it would get worse once she was married.

And yet the idea of giving up the work that she had chosen made her physically ill. She had studied hard, learned skills that were desperately needed in this world. It seemed criminal to stop doing something she loved just because it made some men uncomfortable.

"You are aware, are you not, that Lord Benedict knows of my activities and approves?"

Her tone implied that this was a foregone conclusion. It was not. Though Lord Benedict had implied he knew, the man had not exactly said the words aloud and she had been too afraid to push the point.

Either way, Major Vance showed he had a suspicious mind. "It does no good for you to lie to me."

"I'm not!" she cried. She gestured to the room at large. "He knows." Major Vance was quiet for a long moment. He looked at her, his brow furrowed, and his mouth pursed in discontent.

Her eyes widened. "He told you!"

"He said you were unusual and that I should determine your suitability as his bride."

Her lips curled, her first genuine smile in a long while. "He did not. Because he proposed to me without consulting you. And then we announced that proposal in a very public manner."

"You did," he groused. "He did." Then he dropped his hands onto his hips. "Then he told me to figure out how you would fit seamlessly into his life."

It would seem that Lord Benedict—a man who managed spies—was being cagey with his wife and his right-hand man. She saw the same realization dawn on Major Vance's face.

"What do you think he is up to?" she asked.

Major Vance shook his head. "I don't know. But then I rarely do, except in hindsight."

She nodded slowly. "Lord Benedict tells me that you are a man of extraordinary talent."

"He flatters me."

"I don't think so. He also says that I must work with you

instead of against you."

He dipped his chin. "That would be helpful."

"Then I think that you have the equal task of working with me. Major Vance, you must find a way for me to continue to be who I am. This is my work and I will do it as Lord Benedict's wife."

He shook his head. "It is too dangerous."

"Then make it safe."

"That is not possible."

"And yet, according to Lord Benedict, you do the impossible every day."

There. She had laid down the gauntlet. Would he accept her challenge? Or destroy what he could not control?

Chapter Fifteen

G ABE HAD A problem now. Several, if he were honest, but one leaped above the others as he watched Miss Caddick care for Winnie.

He found her worthy. Not just of respect, for every soul deserved that, but of loyalty.

Throughout his life, he had met a few men who had a fire within. People who worked for an ideal through muck and exhaustion, with their first breath of the day, and the last beat of their heart. They had God's call in their ears and rarely heard any sound except that. They could not be corrupted from their purpose nor swayed from their goals. Honest men with pure purpose.

Lord Benedict was one such man and Gabriel had dedicated his life to that man's righteous endeavors.

And now he had met a worthy woman.

Miss Caddick seemed tireless as night faded away and morning bled into the tiny room. When there was dirt, she cleaned. When there was rest, she watched. And when there was no more to do, she waited. If she dozed, he didn't see it, and he was watching her closely.

He helped when he could, and she didn't naysay him. There seemed to be little pride in her except in the steadiness of her work and the strength of her purpose. He found that worthy beyond the capacity of a normal person. Worse, he found it extraordinarily attractive.

Throughout his childhood, he had been surrounded by beautiful, sensuous women. There was a time he bedded them, exploring the limits of physical pleasure. It was a very short time because pleasure only lasted for a moment, but respect could last a lifetime.

He didn't respect his mother or her students. And he didn't respect himself when he availed himself of those women. But somehow a slip of a woman dripping milk into a dying woman's mouth had his staff rigid with desire in a most inappropriate place, and for the most inappropriate woman.

She was to be Lord Benedict's wife. And as the day wore on, he could think of no better equal to the man he served. Two souls, fired with purpose. They matched each other for ideological passion.

But two such souls were *not* practical companions. They might respect each other's fire, but neither would be willing to compromise in favor of each other's first love. Lord Benedict would be better served by a woman who denied everything else in favor of her husband's goals. Miss Caddick was not that kind of woman.

And yet he admired her all the more for it.

Certainly, he had felt this attraction to her before now. He had noticed the curve of her breasts, the lift of her cheeks, and of course the light in her eyes. She was a lovely woman who barely cared that her auburn hair had a glossy shine. She had succumbed to the paint pot, he knew, but only to cover the signs of exhaustion from working through the night. Good God, what must it take to serve a laboring woman through the night, and then attend a society party the next day? The mechanics of such a double life boggled his mind.

He had seen these things, felt the attraction to his superior's fiancée, and then buried it all under a tide of suspicion and contempt. The depth of his disrespect to her now shamed him. He had been unforgivably rude to her. But now, without any stop to his esteem, he suddenly felt all this lust for her body. And what the bloody hell was he to do about that?

It was nearly nine in the morning when a young boy knocked on the door. Gabe didn't recognize the child, but he understood the message well enough.

"Madame Florina asks after you and says there is another." He rattled off another address close by.

Miss Caddick looked up from where she pressed a hand to Winnie's neck. "I cannot leave until Father Harper comes. Will you get him for me?"

The boy nodded and dashed away.

"Last rights?"

She nodded. "Normally I would stay, but if there is another woman in trouble." She shook her head. "He can help Winnie more than I. And he will be better able to counsel her brother."

He heard no censure in her tone regarding the brother, but Gabe felt plenty of anger for the both of them. Imagine abandoning one's own sister to face death alone. It was the mark of a weak man, and he was ashamed of his own sex, even as he honored Miss Caddick for wanting to stay.

"If you would stay with her," she said gently. "I could see to the other woman."

He had already thought of that and discarded the idea. "I will not abandon you."

"It's hardly abandonment. It's daylight now, and I have travelled these streets by myself several times."

"More fool you." He shook his head. "Where you go, I go."

She sighed but agreed. "Then we wait."

Fortunately, Father Harper did not take long. And he came with a nun who embraced Miss Caddick with the warmth of a longtime campaigner.

"We're here now," the sister said.

"I've another nearby."

"Then you must go."

"There's a brother who went to work. Don't be too hard on him. He stayed with her all through the night."

"Likely needs the money to bury her." The nun's eyes narrowed. "Who bled her? I know it weren't you."

"Midwife Cooper."

"You mean Cupper. Does it for near everyone." The nun sighed. "Is that what killed her?"

Miss Caddick hesitated. "Probably not. She was already in labor too soon and swollen."

The nun nodded. "Then it's God's will."

For the first time since arriving, he saw Miss Caddick's expression harden. "I don't know about that," she said. "I do know we need to discover what helps and what doesn't in times like this. Some way to keep records."

Clearly the nun thought that was pie in the sky. "And while you are writing all that down, who will be birthing the babes of London?" The nun physically turned her around. "Go on now. There's a woman screaming that needs your help."

Miss Caddick started to gather her things. She stopped a moment to touch Winnie's face. "I'm leaving you now, Winne," she said as her hand trailed down to squeeze the woman's shoulder. "But Father Harper and Sister Julianne are here to help you. You're in good hands with them and God. And I'll come back if you need me. Don't you worry. You're in good hands."

She was saying that as if she needed to believe it herself. He could see the guilt on her face for leaving Winnie before the end. But there was another babe waiting to be born, and so Sister Julianne reminded her as she pushed them both out the door.

"Territorial little nun," Miss Caddick muttered as she hurried down the stairs. It didn't sound like a compliment.

"What?"

"Nothing," Miss Caddick said as she rubbed her eyes. "It just bothers me that she's right. There is naught but prayer left for Winnie, and that is Sister's Julianne's place. But I hate leaving a job undone."

"Your job was done," he reminded her.

"I know! But it…" She swallowed and looked away.

"It grieves you." He credited her for that. Most people would be grateful to leave the deathbed vigil.

"Come along. It's just a couple blocks away."

He knew better than to mention that she'd been up through the night. He could see her determination as she pushed her way through the rapidly clogging streets. It was full morning now with adults going about their work and children running everywhere making mischief. He grabbed an older one and gave him a penny to take a message to the Foreign Office. He had responsibilities beyond keeping Miss Caddick safe that someone needed to manage. Since he would not leave her, he must give word for someone else to handle his affairs.

Normally he would resent being pulled from Lord Benedict's tasks but today was different. He was beginning to see the value his lordship placed in the lady, and so he would serve her as faithfully as he served Lord Benedict.

Unfortunately, that delayed him a precious minute, and Miss Caddick was not one to wait. She rushed ahead until they could hear the screams of a laboring woman. It was hard to miss as children and adults alike stood round listening to the wails.

"Let me pass," Miss Caddick kept saying. "I'm the midwife."

They let her through, but only after grabbing her elbow to give her information they thought was helpful.

"It's her first, and she's tiny."

"Her mister is at war."

"She ain't got nobody."

Miss Caddick nodded, even as she rushed through. Then when she climbed the stairs, she grabbed one of the women waiting in the stairs. "Get me a basin of water," she commanded. "And towels."

"Wot?" the woman objected. "Why me? I got me own—"

Gabriel pulled her head around. "You have time to stand here, then you've time to help. Get her the water." Then he looked at another woman. "You get the towels."

Both responded to his commanding tone. They nodded and

scurried off. He rushed forward, trying to get ahead of Miss Caddick. He was her protector here, and yet she was leading the way. But with the tight corners of the stairs, there was little room to maneuver, much less get ahead of her.

He made it into the room a bare couple steps behind her, but she had already assessed the situation and taken command. There was a sweating woman on the bed, her legs spread and her face wretched with agony. Standing beside the bed was one of the whores in the Rose Garden. She was an older one, long past her prime, but the relief on her face returned some youth to her looks.

"Thank God. I been praying you got 'ere in time."

"Barely," Miss Caddick said as she squatted down to look into the wailing woman's face. "Hello there. I'm Midwife Betty. You look like you're doing just what God intended, but it's frightfully hard, I know."

The whore moved quickly to the opposite side of the pallet. "Her name's Mary. Husband's away at war. Left afore she knew she was in the family way. She's got neighbors who'll 'elp once the babe's here, but none what knew how to do this."

"Very good, then," said Miss Caddick. "Mary, I'm going to check on the babe now. Try to relax—"

There wasn't going to be any relaxing as another contraction contorted the laboring woman's face. Gabe had never seen this part. Never watched as a woman sweated and heaved, her entire body seemingly torn apart. The woman bringing the water had to kick him to get him to step aside, and he had the humbling urge to move all the way back out into the street. This was no place for a man. And yet, not twenty minutes before, he had sworn not to leave her.

If Miss Caddick could be here, then so could he. And if he wanted to be useful, then he would set the water and towels to hand and shoo everyone else out.

He watched as Miss Caddick gabbed a towel and wet it, using it to wipe off her own hands and face. Then she whispered a prayer of some sort before setting the rag aside.

"It's something I do," she said at his questioning look. "Helps me leave one woman behind as I turn to the next."

He had no response. She could jump up and down while screaming the Lord's Prayer and he wouldn't question her. She had the authority here. All others—including him—bowed to her directions.

What came next felt like an eternity though it was likely no more than fifteen minutes. A child was born—a little girl—who wailed and quivered as if she'd suffered the gravest insult a body could receive. And hadn't she though? She'd just been squeezed through a tiny passage amid heat and sweat with her mother screaming as if she were to die.

Miss Caddick eased the child onto a rag. She tied and cut the cord, then wrapped the wailing babe, all the while declaring that the bloody, squalling child was perfect in every way.

He thought that would be the end of it, but not so. While the mother sobbed with relief, there was more to come. The afterbirth seemed less dramatic. There certainly was less screaming. Miss Caddick handled it with steady confidence, and before long all was done.

"Do you need help with nursing?" she asked the mother. "Do you know what you're about now?"

"We'll teach her," said the woman who had brought towels.

Miss Caddick smiled. "Then I'll leave her to you. Mind she rests for at least a week." She looked around at the impoverished surroundings but didn't say a word. Instead, she expressed her gratitude to the women, refused payment, then gathered her things and left. This time he walked by her side, watching for a pickpocket among the gathered well-wishers. There weren't any, as all of them seemed to appreciate Midwife Betty.

The whore from the Rose Garden trailed in their wake. She was the one who shared the news with the onlookers. "The babe is a girl. Mother and child are well." She sent a child ahead to get a hackney, and soon all three of them climbed in to travel in silence back to the Rose Garden.

He wanted to argue that Miss Caddick had no business going there. She ought to go home because he could see the exhaustion weighing upon her, but she stopped him even before he spoke.

"This is the way it is done," she said. He heard finality in her tone the same as in the military. Every recruit was taught the Way Things were Done. And every commander reinforced it.

So he held his tongue while the hackney deposited them outside the Rose Garden. If Madame Florina was surprised by his presence, she didn't say anything except to inquire if he needed a bath.

He did, but he would not leave off his duty to do such a thing. Miss Caddick, however, said yes with clear gratitude. He stood outside her door while she bathed. He tried to ask Madame Florina or indeed any of the women who passed by for an explanation, a discussion, any detail he could glean about what he had witnessed. They said not a word to him. Even the talkative ones, girls he could usually charm for information, shook their head and walked away. And when he pressed Madame Florina, she too shook her head.

"This is for women. Mind your place."

Mind his place? Never before had a woman dared say such a thing to him, not even his mother. Especially not his mother! She had taught him that if he listened to the rules of the world, he would have no place at all. He was a bastard, after all. Instead, he created his place with persistence and intelligence. But apparently, that was among *men*, and this was for *women*.

"I will figure it out anyway," he said. He would learn every detail now because this was important to Miss Caddick, which meant it was vital for him to know as well.

"And what will you do with what you learn?" Madame Florina scoffed. "You will stop us? We are like rats in the sewers. If you stop us here, another place will hop up and you will be none the wiser."

"Why would I stop you?"

Madame didn't answer except for a soft snort and a raised brow. That said without words that she thought men stopped what they could not control. Or at least tried to.

"Maybe I can help," he said, though he had no earthly idea what he would do.

"Then you should have donned a cloth instead of a sword."

He shook his head. "I was never one for the clergy." Even if they would have a bastard like him, which was not at all certain.

Madame Florina frowned at him, then looked past his shoulder to where Miss Caddick bathed. "She will not be stopped. Not by you nor any man."

So he had guessed. "What she does is dangerous. Once she is married…"

His voice trailed away because Madame Florina was done listening to him. She waved a hand airily at him as she walked away. Apparently, what he thought was of no account. Especially since, as she said, if he put a stop to Miss Caddick's activities one way, then she would find another, and he would be none the wiser.

Before long, the maid from before knocked on the door. She was Miss Caddick's servant, the one who had screeched at him less than a week ago. Miss Caddick told her to enter, and she did without giving him a look or a word. It was as if he wasn't there.

A few minutes later, she and Miss Caddick exited looking for all the world like a woman and her maid out for a walk. He could hardly believe his eyes. Gone was stoop-shouldered Betty, and in her place stood Miss Caddick with a lifted chin and freshly scrubbed hair and face. Madame Florina returned as well carrying Miss Caddick's bag.

"Everything is cleaned for you."

"Thank you, Florina," she said as she dropped coins into the madame's hands. Then she paused, one last coin held suspended. "Where is the apothecary you use? I should like to discuss his elixirs."

The madame nodded her head. "My Lady's Apothecary, one

block east. But you'll not get in to see her. She's special." The woman's voice dropped. "She's Chinese and sorely pressed these days. She won't talk to any soul without a reference."

"You'll arrange for me to meet her then?" Janelle pulled out another coin.

Florina held up her hand to stop Janelle. "It's not for me to decide who talks to her and who doesn't. But I'll ask, and you'll hear if it's agreed."

"Thank you," Janelle answered as she gave Florina all the coins.

Finally, Gabriel understood the Rose Garden's place in all this. A secret paid for, as his mother would say. And given that Miss Caddick was a simple baron's daughter and debutante, one that could be easily kept. Of course, that would change the moment she became a countess.

And while he was sorting through the logistics of everything, they headed out the back and climbed into a waiting hackney. Miss Caddick tried to waive him off.

"I'm heading home, Major. And Faye is here for the proprieties. There is no need—"

"Where you go, I go." He settled on the squab opposite her then thumped upon the roof. "Besides," he added wryly, "until I see you inside the door, I will not believe that you actually mean to go there."

Her lips curved as she acknowledged the humor in his statement, but her expression quickly fell. They were only halfway to her home before she crumpled completely.

He had been looking out the carriage window, still marveling at the extent of her network. He heard the stifled gasp. And when he turned, he saw the way her face was averted.

"There, there," soothed the maid as she wrapped an arm around her mistress. "It were a bad one then?"

Miss Caddick said nothing. She was still working hard to stifle her sobs. So the maid looked to him.

"How bad?" she mouthed to him.

He thought back to the evening, to Mary and Winnie, to the night's work and how raw he felt. "Very bad," he answered.

"No," Miss Caddick said as she fought to gather her composure. "One lost, and one gained."

"An even trade then," said the woman. "And you to help with it all."

Miss Caddick said nothing, neither agreeing nor disagreeing. Instead, she curled her face into her maid's shoulders and let the tears flow. It was a release, he realized. A way to let go of the stress and emotions of the night.

"Does this happen often?" he asked.

"Oh aye," the woman replied. "It's all the feeling," she said. "It needs to come out somehow before she has to tuck it all away. Won't do, you know, for the baron to see her acting emotional. He'd ask questions then, wouldn't he?"

Wouldn't he indeed? So Miss Caddick held it all in while treating the women. She exuded confidence and steely-eyed command when they were at their most vulnerable. Then she hid everything she was doing, lest her father look too deeply into her life.

But in a life of deception, when could she be wholly herself?

Right here in the carriage. For the few minutes between the Rose Garden and her home. Here, she was allowed to feel everything in a rush of too much. And so she cried, and his arms ached to comfort her.

That was not his place. Indeed, this whole night he felt as if he were an interloper in a vast network of women's business. Someone who had forced his way in to see what should not be seen by a man. And this, right now, was something so private that he was ashamed of himself. He had accused Miss Caddick of horrible things, he had insulted her and met her with suspicion at every turn. And now, just when he was fully cognizant of how deeply he had misjudged her, he found himself seeing her at her most vulnerable.

She was crying. Her body shook and her breath came in gasps

violent enough that he imagined the carriage rocked with it. There was nothing to say. Even her maid was silent as she rocked her mistress gently in her arms. And all the while, Gabriel could do nothing but stew in his own incompetence.

He had not realized what she did. He had not understood. And now he was unable to do anything but bear witness to something he could barely comprehend.

How she humbled him!

Unable to watch so private a moment, he looked outside and worried that they would arrive at her home too soon. They were mere blocks away. The maid must have realized it, too, for she turned to her mistress.

"Do I tell him to go 'round again? Out to the park or something?"

An excellent idea. He was already rising to knock on the carriage roof when Miss Caddick straightened.

"No, no," she said, the words muffled by her handkerchief. "I'm better now. Truly."

She didn't look better. Her face was streaked with tears and her hair askew. Her breath was still stuttering and though her body didn't shake so much, her shoulders were high against her neck. But then he watched with amazement as she composed herself.

First her shoulders went down as she closed her eyes. Her breath smoothed and the last tear leaked away. Her maid was obviously used to repairing her mistress's looks. She patted Miss Caddick's face dry and quickly brushed out the hair that had fallen wrong. She had a paint pot, too, that she used to soften the dark circles under the eyes and to pat a bit of color into the cheeks. All of it came together in the short minute it took for the carriage to come to a stop in front of the lady's house.

Then Miss Caddick opened her eyes, narrowing them as she looked at him. "Can you straighten your cravat, Major? And pray, allow Faye to smooth down your hair."

He hastily complied, doing what he could in the small confines of the carriage, especially when her maid whacked him about the head with her brush. Then while he was still recovering from that, Miss Caddick instructed him as to their lie.

"If anyone asks, I took a morning walk to try to clear my migraine and you chanced to meet me along the way. Because I was feeling so poorly, you insisted that we take a carriage back, for which I am embarrassed but profoundly grateful. Do you understand, Major?"

"I do," he said, impressed anew by her forethought.

"I rely upon you," she said as she pushed the carriage door open.

She did not rely on him. Indeed, she was the most self-sufficient woman he had ever encountered. But still she sat in the carriage, her expression growing more blank as she ticked her head to the side.

Why?

Oh! He was supposed to disembark first. Scrambling to keep up, he nearly tripped as he stepped out of the carriage. Then he held out his hand to assist her, as if she were the frailest of women suffering from a brutal migraine. She acted the part beautifully, wincing at the light, and then smiling wanly at him.

Was she acting? Hard to tell. She had to be exhausted. He was aching with fatigue, and he hadn't done half the work she had. They made it up to the house where the butler opened the door with a formal greeting.

"Miss Caddick, did your walk help with the migraine?"

"A little, Parry. And look who I've found. Major Vance was out as well, and he insisted on calling a carriage for me."

"Janelle?" a voice called from the parlor. It was her aunt who wasted no time in joining them in the hallway. "Janelle! Did you forget that we are to shop today? There are any number of things to decide upon for your wedding. It's going to be an exhausting day, and here you are, starting us out late."

"I'm so sorry, aunt. I think it's my nerves. We can go immediately."

Go shopping now? After she'd been awake for more than a day already? "My lady," Gabriel said, interposing himself between Miss Caddick and her aunt. "She must rest. These migraines are terrible things. Lord Benedict himself has suffered from them."

"Oh, don't worry about Janelle," the lady said blithely. "She always manages to muster through." She glared at her niece. "We can't have Lord Benedict think he's marrying a sickly woman."

"Of course not," Miss Caddick said.

"He won't, I assure you," Gabe said forcefully. "However, I should note that Lord Benedict has ordered me to assist with his marriage. The devil is in the details, you know, and I am a fearsome devil."

Miss Caddick's aunt trilled a laugh at that. "A handsome one, at least. But Major—"

"I insist." He used his most authoritative voice. "I will go with you, my lady, and together we will guarantee that your niece and my superior have the most beautiful wedding ever."

The lady frowned. "But there are private things—female things—that must be seen to."

"And I am sure that you are very accomplished with those. If Miss Caddick trusts your choices—"

"Oh, I do!" Miss Caddick said. "I most certainly do."

"And Lord Benedict trusts mine," he continued. "Then together we shall get it all done in tip top time."

The lady frowned. "Are you sure, Major? Shopping can be such a tedious affair for men."

Yes, he knew. Indeed, he would rather face a firing squad that spend the day frittering about laces and ribbons with the Lady Boxval. But even so, he would not force Miss Caddick to do such a thing after a night such as she'd had.

"I will hear no more about it. Miss Caddick," he said as he bowed over her hand. "Pray get some rest while you can."

"Major, you are being very gracious. Are you sure—"

"And now," he held out his arm to her aunt, "let us be away."

He gave none of them a chance to argue. Within moments,

he had Lady Boxval out of the house and Miss Caddick, presumably, headed for bed. And all it took was a Herculean decision to delay his own bed in favor of a day of shopping.

He deserved a medal.

What he got instead was the shocking and wholly inappropriate realization that he'd fallen in love.

Chapter Sixteen

"She's a midwife, my lord. I've never seen anything like it. A complete double life."

Benedict stared at the one man he was closest to in his entire life. Gabriel Vance knew him better than anyone, and yet the man was still blissfully ignorant of the darkest shadows Benedict carried inside. It set a distance between them, of course, but it also allowed for surprise and growth. Something that was happening now because clearly, Gabriel had no understanding of why Benedict had chosen Miss Caddick for his wife.

"I know, Gabe. She's Betty Gill and has been, since she was a child."

The man blinked, but true to his nature, he covered his shock with a carefully blanked expression. "You are aware of her duplicity? You appreciate it?"

"She's highly skilled at it. I know of very few people—woman or man—who could do such a thing as well as she has."

"I cannot think of anyone."

Benedict heard admiration in Gabriel's tone. A kind of awe that he reserved for very few people. And that had him sitting up to take note. "You like her," he said. Though he suspected the term "like" was a tame word for the major's feelings.

"She has no artifice in her, yet she has successfully created two lives for herself. Her goals are to help—nothing more, nothing less—and she does it with such purity of purpose that I... I..." His words failed him.

"You thought it a complete lie."

"Yes."

"And now?"

The man lifted his hands in a gesture of helplessness. "I see why you want her," he said. "She is everything admirable in a woman, except…" The man winced as he struggled for words.

Now *this* was becoming a very interesting conversation. Lord Benedict set aside the papers in front of him. Indeed, he abandoned his desk altogether and took his glass of brandy to a chair by the fire. "Out with it, Gabe," he said as he poured a glass for his friend. It was late evening, and they both needed a break and casual conversation.

"She is a person of holy purpose," Gabriel said. "As are you. You are matched well in that, and likely there is no other woman that you admire more."

It was clear that was true for the major. "But?" he prompted.

"But it cannot be sustained. In a marriage, one of you must bow to the other's purpose. Husband and wife must be a unit working for the same goals."

"You don't find her goals worthy?"

"Of course, I do. But they are not yours. What happens when your needs conflict with hers?"

"When I require her presence at a party, and she needs to deliver a baby?"

Gabriel nodded. "Yes. Exactly that."

"What does she do now?"

"She claims an illness. The story is that she suffers terribly from migraines."

Benedict lingered over a sip of this excellent French brandy. "Then that will work for me as well." He chuckled at his friend's stupefied gaze. "You cannot think my vanity requires her to dance attendance upon me."

"No, of course not. But a diplomat's wife is an important partner to his ambitions."

Gabriel had the right of it, of course. A diplomat such as

himself gathered as many useful people around him as he could possibly manage, and a wife was a significant piece of a smart man's arsenal. Gabriel's problem, of course, was that he had been taught from his earliest days that birth—or the lack thereof—was a significant impediment to advancement. That was natural. He had suffered the consequences of his unfortunate birth from the very beginning. Were it not for his illegitimacy, he could have become a leader in any field of endeavor he chose.

Given Gabriel's predilections, Benedict guessed he would have gone into the law. If the man had any pure passion, it was for justice. It was to see that all men were treated fairly in a world that had mistreated so many.

And Miss Caddick, of course, sought the same for the women.

Benedict refilled his glass of brandy. It was one of the few pleasures he allowed himself, and he was not going to limit himself tonight. "Why do you think Napoleon was so successful?" he asked.

Gabriel frowned at the apparent non-sequitur. "There are any number of reasons. Brilliant military strategy in battle. The Russian campaign was a disaster, of course, but—"

"The common peasant cares nothing for military skill. And no matter how brilliant, a man cannot win a battle unless he first has men. How do you think Napoleon brought every able-bodied man in France clamoring to his banner?"

"He is a product of the French Revolution," Gabriel said, showing that he already understood where Benedict was headed. "Liberté, égalité, fraternité."

"Meaning every able-bodied man had an equal chance to be free, to advance, and to be treated as a brother by his compatriots. Bonaparte built schools, enforced fair laws. He gave the common Frenchman hope for better, even if—especially if—the man was not born a royal."

Gabriel nodded. "But what has that to do with Miss Caddick?"

"I do not need another political creature at my side. Those

that whisper into the ears of the powerful slither into my life like leeches. I do not need a wife who is privy to what I already can discover by other means." He arched his brows as he challenged his friend to follow the obvious line of inquiry. Gabriel did not disappoint.

"So the question is, What perspective does Miss Caddick bring you?" Gabriel sipped his drink as he finally sat down in the chair opposite Benedict. "She is connected to a vast network of common women. Not the ones who can afford lying in hospitals or have a doctor attend them for exorbitant cost."

"Exactly." Benedict smiled into his drink. "Women are the backbone of our world, Gabriel. Even Napoleon knew that the future destiny of a child is always the work of the mother."

His friend grimaced. "I hate it when you glorify that monster. Not everyone understands you are studying him, not supporting him."

"I only do it with you. Besides, only a fool disparages a powerful force. For better or worse, Napoleon trampled his way across the continent with the support of millions."

"But Miss Caddick—"

"Miss Caddick will let me know what the common woman thinks. Do you doubt that she talks to her patients in the interminable hours as they await a child's birth?"

"It's hardly a casual conversational time," Gabriel chided.

Benedict shrugged. "The process takes hours. Often more than a day. And in those hours, women talk. She hears what the peasant women think, she knows by extension what the men say."

"And you believe she will tell it to you."

"I am her husband. Of course, she will tell me, especially if I demonstrate my willingness to listen." He leaned forward, trying to impress upon Gabriel the strength of his conclusion. "If England wishes to avoid a rebellion of the lower classes, then England must hear the grumbles of her people. The only soul I know who is positioned exquisitely to provide me that information is Miss Caddick. And so I will wed her."

Gabriel said nothing at first, but Benedict could tell that he was thinking deeply. He could see, as well, the disapproval on the man's face. "But what of tender feeling? Do you not care for her in a personal way?"

Benedict sighed as he stared glumly into his drink. He blamed the brandy for what he was about to confess, but he could not bring himself to censor his words to his closest friend. "I do not have tender feelings for anyone, Gabe. God did not design me to be such a man."

"That is not true."

A simple statement, but it held a wealth of words unsaid. They both knew how he had cared for one man, now dead on the battlefield. They knew how he'd grown insane with worry when he could not find Michael after the Battle at Alcantara. And how, when the body was at last located, he had fought to suppress wails of grief at the sight. Michael had died alone in a trench, never knowing how deeply he was cherished.

"It *is* true," he said firmly. "I shall honor and respect Miss Caddick according to her place as my wife." Then he smiled in the sloppy way of all drunks. "Can you not see her with children? If the strength of the man comes from mother, think what steel will invigorate her sons."

"And if her daughters are equally independent?"

"Then England will be better for it." He chuckled. "If she can figure out how to serve her husband and her cause simultaneously, then she can teach such a thing to her children as well."

Gabriel shook his head. "But she has no idea the kind of scrutiny she will endure as your wife."

"But you do," Benedict said. "And that is why I have made her your highest priority."

"Benedict, no!"

"Gabriel, yes. Think! Who else do you know who has seen beneath her exterior?"

His friend sighed as if he took on a great weight. "How did

you find out about her life as Betty Gill?"

"Lord Nathaniel discovered it for me."

"Then let him—"

"No. Nate has a new wife. He cannot watch another woman right now. Not like I require." Benedict leaned back in his chair and studied his friend. He kept his tone casual, but he knew Gabriel was not fooled. This was an important moment, even though it was phrased as the random question of an inebriated man. "Is there a reason you find her objectionable?"

"Not in the least."

Benedict read his friend's face, seeing truth in the statement.

"Do you find it difficult to be in her close company?"

"Not at all."

That was a lie. Or at least not the full truth. Had his friend developed feelings for Miss Caddick? Benedict wasn't surprised by that. Indeed, he had always thought it was a possibility. But could those tender feelings have grown so quickly? He doubted even Gabe knew the extent it. The only reason Benedict guessed was because he knew Gabe so very well.

"You will figure out a way, won't you?" Benedict coaxed. "A way for her to be safe following her passion while still serving honorably as my wife."

The man winced. "She needs a location, Benedict. Right now, the Rose Garden serves as her waystation. People find her through that, and she returns there to transform back into Miss Caddick."

He frowned. "The Rose Garden is not the right place for that. Can another place be found? Or created?"

Gabriel shrugged. "With enough money, a building could be purchased." He caught Benedict's gaze, a great deal of information passing that went deeper than his next words. "It would tie her to London."

He meant she could not go to Vienna for his Congress. She would not be at his side for state visits to wherever the diplomatic life might take him. He meant that as a life companion, Miss

Caddick would not be around.

"I do not need her to tell me the minds of Vienna's peasants. Her use is in her knowledge of England's poor."

"Yes, but…" Gabe struggled with his words. Neither of them was prone to discussing feelings. It did not mean that they weren't aware of tender emotions. "Benedict, I know you are lonely. I thought you wanted a wife to address that."

How wrong his friend was. But perhaps the man was projecting his own lack onto Benedict.

"What about you, Gabe? Do you wish for a woman in your bed?"

"I serve you, my lord. I seek nothing more." The words were automatic and formal. Benedict scoffed.

"Don't start 'my lording' me. If I am lonely, you are ten times such. You work the long hours at my side, then spend even longer implementing my plans. There has been no time for any tenderness in your bed. Do you not wish for it?"

"I serve you," Gabriel repeated, his tone firm. And if will alone could deny the hungers of the heart, then he would believe Gabriel spoke the truth.

He did not.

"What if you were set here in London? If you were head of my household here, then you would have enough leisure to find the love you seek."

"I never spoke of love."

"Gabe, you don't need to. You have always sought someone who loved as purely as you do. But one cannot find that in a battlefield. Nor in the benighted evenings with the likes of LeFauvre." He topped off his friend's glass. "But you could find it in London. You could attend parties here, meet debutantes, and charm all the innocent girls of England."

"Those girls will not dance with a bastard."

"Some will. You might find one, if only you would look."

Gabriel set down his glass rather than drink it. "Is that what you want of me? Do you curse me to manage your errant wife so that I will dance with debutantes? Benedict, you are drunk."

"I want you to find love, Gabriel, because you want it. And if any man deserves it, it is you."

"Perhaps I will find it in Vienna."

"In that nest of vipers and villainesses? No, I want you to meet a good English girl. I want you to fall desperately in love and pop out a dozen worthy children. You must father England's next generation."

"And watch my mother poison anything I might create? No good woman will marry Madame Sabate's son. And no grandchild will escape her name."

"There is a way. If you fall in love, you will create an answer."

Gabriel openly scoffed. "When did you become such a romantic?"

Never. Always. "I am merely voicing what you will not. Tell me you don't wish for exactly what I describe. Tell me to my face. I know you will never lie to me. You have sworn it. Do it now and I will assign Nathaniel to watch over Miss Caddick. I will take you to Vienna where you can search among foreigners for whatever will slacken your lust."

Gabriel looked into his eyes. Indeed, Benedict had forced him to. And then he tried to lie. He formed the words, he moved his lips, but he could not bring himself to put breath to the words. In the end, because he was unfailingly honest, he confessed the truth.

"Sometimes, I long for a good wife. I wish for a woman in my bed and children at my feet."

"As all good men do."

"But I will not abandon you."

"Of course not!" Benedict snapped. "You will obey my order. And that is to find a solution for Miss Caddick and me. If it entails buying a building, then you have access to whatever funds you need. Create this future for her and me. And in the meantime, dance with some pretty girls. Kiss someone in the shadows. Open your heart to the future you so want."

Gabriel didn't answer except to abruptly slurp his brandy. From the looks of him, one would think he had been sentenced to the firing squad. But in this, Benedict knew the truth better than Gabriel. Some men—and Gabe was one of them—had been beaten away from their dreams so many times, it was easier to run from them than try again. But in this, he would not allow his dearest friend to fail.

"You will do this, Gabriel, or I will find a woman for you and force you to marry her."

Gabriel's eyes widened in alarm. "You will not!"

"I will, and you know it."

"Even you do not have that kind of power."

Benedict snorted. "Try me." And then he abruptly pushed out of his chair. "I shall demand an accounting of you when I return. See that you have something to report."

"What?" Gabe hastily rose to match Benedict. "Are you going somewhere? You did not tell me."

"I am telling you now. I am heading to Cornwall and my horrible castle. My father neglected everything while I was in Spain. Though his manor house is fine enough, he has left the castle in disrepair—"

"I should go with you. I can put things to rights"

Better than he could, truth be told. Gabriel was much better with that kind of detail than he was. "Not this time, Gabe. I need to face my family ghosts on my own."

Gabriel's eyes narrowed, no doubt understanding much more than Benedict was entirely comfortable with. His relationship with his family had never run smooth.

"When will you return?" Gabriel asked.

"In time for the wedding, but not much before."

"You will abandon your bride until the day you wed?" Though he clearly tried to keep his tone neutral, there was censure in Gabriel's voice.

"I am not abandoning her," he returned firmly. "I am leaving her to you. You will see that she has everything she wants."

"And what if she wants you?"

He shrugged. "She will have to accept you as my substitute. Indeed, that will be the tenor of our marriage, so I suggest you both get accustomed to it." There was no compromise in his tone, and being the seasoned military man that he was, Major Vance understood every word as a command.

Even so, the man reacted with laudable reluctance. "That is not how things are done, Benedict."

"And when have I ever looked to the world to teach me how to act?"

"Never." The word came out with a grumble.

Benedict softened his gaze. He went so far as to touch his friend's arm in a rare show of uncertainty. "I need this, Gabe. I know it's irregular. Please say that you will accomplish it for me."

It took a moment. Benedict could see the war in the man's eyes between what he considered moral actions and the gray area in which Benedict operated. But in this, Gabriel remained true to his loyalty.

"Whatever you need. You know I am your man."

He did know. But he doubted Gabriel knew to what extent that loyalty would be tested. Likely in the very near future.

"Good man," he said. And then he dismissed him, knowing that there was a strong possibility that he had just sent his best friend to seduce his future wife.

Chapter Seventeen

JANELLE ACCEPTED ANOTHER invitation to dance. Three balls in as many nights, and somehow she had become a popular dance partner. She was an engaged person and therefore off the marriage mart. And yet, she was abruptly popular with political gentlemen who wanted to know all sorts of details about her fiancé's work.

She had no answers for them. She didn't know anything. So she danced and smiled and tried to keep from worrying about the sudden absence of pregnant women in her...er, in Betty's life. Three nights and no messages from Madame Florina. Was there suddenly a dearth of expectant mothers in London? Or had Major Vance done something annoying?

Obviously, it was Major Vance, but what had he done? She'd been fretting about what he'd discovered about her—about Betty—for the last three days. He knew everything now, and she dreaded the angry discussion with her fiancé that was surely coming.

Except no such confrontation occurred. Indeed, she received a note telling her that Lord Benedict was to be absent for the next couple weeks but that she could put her every faith in the major.

Fat chance. And yet, she had no other recourse except to sit and wait for news.

She'd simply rested for the first day. With the lower population in Devon, she'd rarely needed to work the night through then appear bright-eyed before her father the next day. There had been a few times, naturally, but nothing like the fast pace of London when—up until now—Madame Florina had sent for her day and night.

Now she'd gone three days without a word. Something was up, but what? She'd already resolved to visit the madame in the morning and demand an explanation. But in the meantime, she danced, smiled idiotically, and fretted.

Then, at the exact moment she stopped thinking of him, what happened? He stood right beside her aunt, waiting for her to step off the dance floor. Damn irritating man. But her other choice was to remain with her current dance partner and that would be extremely tedious.

So with a stiffening in her spine, she left the floor and joined her aunt and her nemesis near the punch bowl.

"Good evening, Miss Caddick," he said bowing deeply before her.

"Major Vance—" she began, but her aunt interrupted her.

"You'll not believe the bother. There's something amiss with your wedding invitations and the major needs you to attend to it right now."

Janelle frowned. "Right now?" What could possibly be so vital—

"It's my fault, I'm afraid," the major said as he bowed again. "Matters of state have prevented me from attending to it before now, and I'm to send a missive to your fiancé by courier in an hour. There's also a letter from him." He held out his hand. "If you would accompany me, please."

"Where?" She wouldn't normally be so curt. Indeed, she was a woman who was polite by rote. And yet the minute the major showed up, her skin flushed, her tongue spouted all sorts of awkward things, and…well, and her body grew horribly, awfully *awake*. It was as if every aspect of her person was suddenly alerted her that *he* was here! As if that were of life and death importance when it absolutely was not.

And yet, here she was with her heart beating fast and her gaze noting that he looked especially handsome tonight. He was in his military uniform, and didn't that fit his broad shoulders exquisite-ly?

"I'm afraid I must take you to the Foreign Office for the let-ter," he said. "It's come in a diplomatic pouch and even something so mundane must not leave those premises."

She stared at him. Was he serious? He looked serious, but how could a letter from her fiancé be anything of national interest? Meanwhile, her aunt grew impatient at her standing there gaping at him.

"Don't just stand there. Go with the man."

"But aunt, you wanted to stay for the supper."

"I'm not going, you goose. The major has found a lovely young gent to serve as my escort tonight." She gestured behind her at a young lieutenant in full uniform. "He will see that I am returned home safely."

"But—"

The major interrupted. "I've a maid in the carriage, so you can be sure of the proprieties. I have taken every care."

Her aunt squeezed the man's biceps in admiration. "Of course, you have. My niece is being a ninny. Now go, Janelle. You must get used to this kind of thing now. Your fiancé is a very important man."

What could she say to that? She pressed a kiss to her aunt's cheek, then headed for the door. A footman already stood ready with her wrap, and another held the door open for her. She looked around as they headed out, but no one seemed to think the situation odd. In fact, when she stopped to take her leave of her hostess, Lady Leigh gripped her hands and said, "We are all slaves to our husband's careers. You'll get used to it."

"I suppose I'll have to," she said, then she allowed the major to whisk her away.

His carriage was parked a little way down the street, but that gave her time to talk to him. Or at least try.

"Major, as much as I appreciate—"

"Wait until we're inside the carriage." His words were curt, his tone low and…something. Did she hear anger? Annoyance? She had no idea and she despised speculating. She needed to understand exactly where she stood with a person. That way, she could play into their expectations and then fade completely away from their consciousness. Except with the major. She never knew what he thought of her, and that irritated her beyond belief.

"This is highly unusual," she said under her breath.

"Not for you," he retorted. Then before she could ask him what the devil he meant by that, he hauled open the hackney door. She was certainly accustomed to travelling in hackneys, but she had assumed they had Lord Benedict's carriage. And hadn't he claimed a maid would be with them? Because there wasn't.

She halted half in and half out of the conveyance.

"I don't understand—"

"Get in!" he huffed. Then he did something she never expected. He planted his very large hand flat on her backside and pushed.

She was neatly catapulted onto the seat. And while she settled on the squabs—her backside still tingling from the press of his hand—he leaped in, slammed the door, and bellowed, "Go!"

"What is the meaning of this?"

Rather than be intimidated by her tone, he relaxed back against the squabs. "The meaning, Miss Caddick, is that there is a woman in labor who needs your help. We are on our way there now." Then while she gaped at him, he frowned in consternation. "Sorry. I meant to call you Miss Betty."

She echoed his frown. "We're headed to a patient?"

"Yes."

"And you're taking me?"

"Yes."

"Of your own free will?"

"Obviously."

She snorted at his dry tone. Nothing was obvious with him. "Why?"

"Because you are good at it."

"Of course, I'm good at it," she snapped. "But that didn't make a difference three nights ago."

He crossed his arms as he met her hard stare with a casual air. "It made a great deal of difference." He sounded like those words choked him. "And because Lord Benedict ordered it. That and a great deal more."

Now that was news and not of a comforting sort. "So you told him."

"I did." Then he grimaced. "But he already knew."

She jolted. "Everything?"

"Everything," the major confirmed.

Of course, he knew everything. Hadn't she guessed as much? And yet the confirmation rattled her. "How?"

The major shrugged, a very distracting shift of muscular shoulders. "I do not know exactly, though I suspect Lord Nathaniel."

The kind gentleman who had helped her at the Foreign Office. The newlywed ne'er-do-well who was perpetually about. "How would he know?"

He stared at her as his tone became tiresome. "I told you," he emphasized, "you are now moving in a circle where such things are noticed. *You* are watched, tracked, and reported upon."

The idea made her shudder. With all the people in London, she'd felt so anonymous. "Lord Nathaniel was spying on me? But I'm nobody."

"You're Lord Benedict's future wife. That makes you important."

She was beginning to realize that. And yet, it still boggled her mind. "That is what you have been saying," she finally admitted. Then she looked out the window, her heart breaking with her next words. "Everything about my life really is going to change. You're going to make Betty a rarity, aren't you?" He might be taking her to a laboring woman now, but she could read between the lines. This would happen less and less after her wedding, until

Betty was no more.

Her eyes watered, and she pressed her hand to her mouth. What was she going to do? Her father, her aunt, and so many people told her she must marry. And indeed, she liked Lord Benedict, at least what she had seen of him. She thought they might get along well together. But if she had to give up being Betty…

She didn't know if she could do it.

"It would break you, wouldn't it?" he asked, his tone low.

She blinked back her tears. "What?"

"Not being Betty. Right now, you're wondering if you could manage giving it up. You're wondering if you could defy your aunt and your father, if you could give up everything to become Betty for the rest of your life. No more parties, no more nice clothes."

As if she cared for any of that. The real problem was much more basic. "My father doesn't realize it, but he pays for my medicines. My pin money gives me bandages and pays the cabbies who take me to the patients. I still want to study, and the cost of books alone is exorbitant."

"What would you eat? How would you live?"

All good questions. "Most midwives make a living." A poor one, but they survived.

"You don't ask for coins from the women themselves."

"But I would need to, wouldn't I? Or I wouldn't eat."

He nodded and she saw sympathy in his eyes. Damn it, it was an impossible choice. She needed support in order to do the work she loved. And that didn't even mention the other difficulty.

"If I'm always Betty, I'd have to give up my family, too. Father wouldn't stomach the embarrassment." He might be harsh, but he was her father. Her aunt had always been kind, and her brother was…well, he was her baby brother and she adored him. They had always helped one another. If he weren't right now at school, she'd be pouring her confusion into his ear.

"And yet, you are still thinking of it," he pressed. "What

would it cost you to give it all up to become Betty?"

It would turn her into Midwife Cooper. Not as stupid, of course. She wouldn't go about cupping everyone. But she'd have to be money-conscious, and she would hate it. And yet that was life, wasn't it? Her patients made such choices every day. Eat or pay rent. Hire a midwife or risk a neighbor's untrained hands. She—and her patients—had survived on the luxury of her father's money, but that would have to end.

"There has to be a way," she whispered, knowing that there wasn't. Even before having her first Season in London, she knew that her days as Betty were numbered. She would have to marry sometime. Her husband—whomever he was—would not allow his wife to go off delivering babies like a country witch woman.

"There is," he said, his voice grim.

It took a moment before she understood his words. And even so, she had to replay them in her mind three times before she stared at him. "What?"

"Did you wonder why I came for you? Why you haven't received a message from Madame Florina?'

"Yes, I did."

"It is because I have found a way—perhaps—for you to maintain this ruse even as Lord Benedict's wife.

"Truly?" The elation in her voice was hard to hide. "What have you discovered?"

"A possibility," he said, his voice hard. "But only if you will do exactly what I say, when I say it."

"Anything," she said, even knowing that that was a rash promise. And yet, the depth of her fears pushed her to confess the truth. "Whatever you need me to do," she said.

"You're going to regret saying that," he said grimly. "But it is exactly what is required of you now."

And so her bargain was set, though she had no idea what she'd just promised. Unfortunately, she didn't have time to argue. The hackney pulled to a stop.

"We're here," he said as he handed her a dark cloak. "Cover yourself and we'll see if you can do what needs to be done."

Chapter Eighteen

J ANELLE PULLED THE cloak up around her head and face, but she didn't exit the carriage. "My bag," she said with a grimace. "When Madame Florina contacts me, she sends a hackney with my bag."

"Yes," he said, as he stepped out of the carriage and scanned the surroundings. "I'm aware. She packed the satchel for me with clothes. Trust me. I have it all figured out."

A bold statement, especially from a man about childbirth, but she didn't have much choice. Typically, by the time she arrived at a laboring woman's side, the birth was very advanced. She was accustomed to rushing inside and evaluating the circumstances between contractions.

So she nodded and ducked out of the carriage. She grasped his fingers, reassured by the size and strength of his hand around hers. It was nice, she secretly admitted, to have a large presence beside her as she walked through the less proper areas of London. Except this location wasn't so bad. Indeed, it appeared on the poorer side of acceptable, which was a vast improvement from her usual locations.

"I am called to someone here?" she asked, relief in her voice. "This will be so much easier." A home with some wealth, even if it was that of a servant in a modest house, would make things better for the mother. There would be people to help and food for mother and child.

"I'm glad you think so," he said as he drew her to a large

building designed for several families to share.

Ah, so it was a woman in a flat, she reasoned. Not as good, but still, that spoke of neighbors who could assist. She paused as he directed her to the stairs. Normally this close, she could hear the woman screaming or see people waiting in taut anxiety in the street. Everything here was quiet.

"Where is she?" she asked.

"Upstairs," he answered, and he guided her up four flights of rickety stairs. She had climbed worse, of course, and she was grateful not to haul her heavy bag. It would be awkward carrying that while climbing the stairs in her ballgown.

She paused on the landing as he smiled at her. She recognized the gleam of triumph in a man's eyes, and immediately tensed with suspicion. What made men happy rarely translated to joy for a woman. At least in the general way of things. Still, she held her tongue and waited as he unlocked the flat with a key and threw open the door.

What she saw inside made her frown with confusion. There, in the middle of the room, was a large, beautiful birthing chair. It was well made as might be seen in a very wealthy nobleman's home. It had strong wooden bars to grip, supports for the thighs, and levers to widen or narrow the spread according to a woman's needs.

It was gorgeous, and she couldn't help but smile at the sight. "But what is it doing here?" she asked as she looked around the room. There was little else there. A couple rags, a single bucket, and a modesty screen.

"This is a safe place for you to work," he said. "The neighborhood is respectable, we are on the top floor for privacy, and there is a place for you to change your clothing as needed.

She glanced behind the screen. She saw her bag there and a stool for her use. Turning back, she gaped at the major. "You brought me from a ball with an elaborate ruse about some secret communication, all to show me a birthing chair?"

"No!" he said stiffly, as if insulted by the very idea. "There is a woman in labor. You are to help birth her child."

"Where?" The room was empty save for themselves.

"I sent the direction. She is coming."

"Here?"

He nodded. "It is much safer this way. A good neighborhood. You will not be robbed in the coming and going. And if someone sees you, you can claim to have a school companion here. No one will think the least thing about it."

"So it is safer for me."

"Yes." He seemed annoyed that she hadn't grasped the excellence of his thought process.

"And what about the women?"

He frowned. "What about them? They will come to you here. It's what happens at the hospitals."

"Lying In hospitals take women two weeks before their time." She looked around. There wasn't even a bed here.

He dropped his hands on his hips. "They will come to you here. If they want your help in their labor, then they will come to you. It is only right."

"Up four flights of stairs?"

"Yes!"

She arched a brow. He would catch onto the truth eventually. "Major, imagine you have a soldier who has taken a ball to his gut. Do you make him climb up four flights of stairs?"

He frowned, starting to get a glimmer. "He would be bleeding."

"And the woman will *laboring*." She rolled her eyes. "How will we get hot water up here?"

"I thought of that. There is a stream nearby for water. It will be an effort to bring it up the stairs, but I will help with that."

"With one bucket?"

He pursed his lips. "I will get another."

He would have to get several more. "And how will we make it hot?"

He shook his head. "We did not use hot water in Spain."

"I do."

"That might pose a problem."

Yes, she had guessed as much. "How close are we to the hospital?"

"What?"

"There are things that I cannot do. If there is time, I call for a medical student. I will need to send for one and have him arrive in a speedy manner."

He dropped his hands on his hips. "I thought you were capable of delivering a child."

She threw up her hands in frustration. "I cannot meet every possibility. How close are we to a priest?"

"What?"

Did he know nothing? "Not all of the babes survive, and they need to be baptized."

"The babes," he said, his voice low. "I hadn't thought about that."

No, he hadn't. The mothers, of course, already had their religious details handled, but sometimes there were scant minutes for a baptism before death. And only those who had been touched by a priest could be buried in hallowed ground.

He began to frown as he was thinking. In his defense, she could tell he wasn't the kind of man who argued when he knew he was wrong. So she threw him a bone.

"It's a lovely birthing chair. I can't imagine how you found it."

He grimaced. "Don't patronize me. I know I've erred." His tone wasn't surly so much as resigned.

She smiled at him. "Why didn't you ask me? I have often dreamed of a place like this. I have endlessly pictured what I want and what I need."

His eyes narrowed as he looked at her. She wondered if he would admit the truth. He was not a man who usually asked advice, probably because he could think circles around most everyone. Or maybe it was because intelligent women had been sorely lacking in his life.

"I should have asked," he said. "This was meant to be an enticement."

Her brows rose. "Into what?"

His expression was self-mocking. "Into a marriage I think you should refuse."

"Then you've done an excellent job of pretending to lure me in while actually discouraging me. You know this will not work."

He was about to answer, but he didn't get the chance. They both heard the building scream of a woman in labor. It started out low, but no one could mistake that distinctive wail. Janelle reacted immediately, rushing out the door to see. He held her back.

"No, no. Get changed. I'll bring her up here."

She tried to push past him, but he was adamant to the point that he picked her up and set her back into the room. "You cannot be seen in that gown! It would hurt Lord Benedict!"

She wanted to argue that Lord Benedict wasn't relevant at this moment, but that was short-sighted. The major knew her fiancé's world better than she did, and besides, arguing with him would take time. So she gave in with a frustrated grimace.

"Carry her if you have to. Betty will be there in a moment."

She didn't wait for him to respond but rushed behind the modesty screen. Pulling open the bag, she saw it was indeed Betty's massive satchel. It was stuffed full, but on top was an old gown and the leather apron she often used. It would take time to strip out of her dress, especially since the one she wore was buttoned in the back. Rather than rip the thing in her haste, she decided to keep it on. She used the leather belt to tie up her skirt before covering herself with the apron. Her hair went back into a messy bun, tied by another cord. And her jewelry—ear bobs and a necklace—were stuffed into a pouch.

Then she rushed to the door and down the stairs. As she suspected, the laboring woman had barely made it up the first flight of stairs. She was a teenager supported on one side by the major and the other by an even younger girl. All three looked terrified, and Janelle's heart melted. Three people determined to soldier on despite being completely out of their depth.

The pregnant one was gripping the major's arm as her body squeezed hard in a contraction. The man would have bruises as he kept the girl from falling. She'd seen lesser men faint at this point or babble uncontrollably. The major's response to stress was a calm demeanor that kept to the business at hand. That made him a good man to have around, and she smiled when he looked up at her.

She opened her mouth to say something encouraging, but he interrupted her. "Don't come down," he said firmly. "I've got her." And then in a stunning show of strength, he squatted down and scooped the laboring woman off the stairs.

It was a dangerous thing to do. Women in labor do not rest quietly in a man's arms. They writhe and moan while he thudded up the stairs. Fortunately, other people had come out to look and several held out a supporting hand. Janelle started to descend, but quickly saw she wasn't needed. The major was managing. He held the woman carefully, but another contraction was beginning.

"Hurry," she said as she held open the door.

Too late. The contraction was upon her. Worse, the woman was a biter. The pains took her, and she turned into the major's shoulder, biting down on his coat while he flinched in surprise. Then her water broke, and the gush of liquid darkened all the way down his leg. Those trousers would never be the same.

"Oh dear," she sighed, but he did not complain. Instead, he steadily, unerringly climbed the stairs with Janelle above him and the younger girl hovering behind.

Finally, he made it to the top landing, and she helped him gently set the woman on her feet. He was sweating as he did it, but his focus was on keeping everyone steady. "See," he murmured as he gave the terrified teenager a smile. "You're here, all right and tight."

Nothing during labor was ever right and tight, but she let him have that one.

"There now," Janelle said, pitching her voice into Betty's soothing tones. "Wot's your name?"

"I'm Suz, miss," she said, panting as she fought the pains.

"I'm Harriet," piped in her friend.

"Hello Suz, Harriet. I'm not a miss, I'm just Betty. And I'm gonna help get yer babe into yer arms all right and tight." They nodded, but both of them canted questioning glances at the major. "Don't mind him," she said. "He's just the m—an." She'd been about to say major, but realized too late that he would want to stay anonymous. He became the man. At his amused look, she shrugged. She could have called him Manfred. She knew a cantankerous old bastard by that name, but decided it was too much of a mouthful.

Another pain was coming, so Janelle set to business. She helped get Suz clean and into the chair. The major brought over rags and murmured, "I can get water or I can stay here and help."

"Water," she said, not even looking up. There was a lot to do at the beginning, and all her focus needed to be on Suz and the babe.

"Right away."

Amazing how she could be incredibly busy with her work, and yet still aware of when the major was nearby and when he was tromping up and down the stairs with water. More than aware, unfortunately, for she saw that he watched everything she did with a steady gaze. She knew when he was winded carrying two buckets of water (she had no idea where he got the second bucket) and noticed as well that he didn't flinch from the more gruesome aspects of labor.

He held Suz's hand when she needed it. He supported her back as she got tired. He breathed when Suz did and panted when instructed not to push. In truth, they all matched their breath to Suz, but he did it instinctively with a need to help rather than a wish to be far away from the business at hand.

All in all, an excellent help.

And when the babe finally emerged, he cheered with as much enthusiasm as everyone else. Indeed, he seemed a bit misty-eyed as he watched her cut the cord and pass the squalling boy into Suz's arms.

"He's a fine one, he is," she said as Suz half laughed, half sobbed against her son's bald head.

"Good set of lungs, I'd say," he added as he looked on. She thought he was fully absorbed in the sight of mother and child, but he also passed her a fresh set of rags as he spoke.

It was exactly what she needed for the afterbirth and Janelle was surprised that he knew what to do. Indeed, she had no idea how he'd gained the information, but they had been working in concert throughout Suz's labor as if they'd done it a dozen times before.

"You'd make a good nurse," she said as she prepared for the next bit.

"I've been a good nurse," he responded. "Not my favorite occupation."

In battle, he meant, and she shuddered to think what he had seen. "I hope this was a better experience."

"Decidedly so," he returned. And then he grinned at her. What a sight that was. There was the dazed, sloppy look in his eyes that all good fathers had, but also pride in what they'd accomplished together. There wasn't the usual dominance of a man quietly claiming victory, even in his own mind, but one of shared respect at a job well done.

It touched her, that way he smiled. Even more so when he wiped Suz's brow without being asked. And how he offered her a drink from his flask.

She opened her mouth to ask, and he answered before she could voice the question. "It's white soup," he said. "Nipped from Castlereagh's table an hour ago. I thought it might be good during a long night."

Veal stock, cream and almonds? "That's excellent food for a

new mother," she said as Suz tried to drink it all.

"Easy now," Janelle said as she eased the flask away. Too much cream could be a problem. "Not much more to do now," she said, "but I'll need your help for it."

The afterbirth came out easily and fully intact. This was a good birth, and Suz was quickly cleaned, but there was nowhere to settle her. No mattress, much less a bed, and the new mother was drooping with fatigue.

"Where do you live?" she asked Harriet, since Suz was three quarters asleep.

The girl's expression darkened. "It's not a good place for us, but we've nowhere else to go."

Not a surprise. They had the look of desperate children, now with another child to feed.

"Not to worry," the major said. "I've a name of a priest who will help. Maybe there's a better trade for you. And help with the babe." At Janelle's surprised look, he shrugged. "I knew who to ask. There's not a lot of help, but there is some."

"And how will they get there?"

He gestured behind her at a pair of women, both old enough to know how to handle a newborn. "This here is Bess and Ruth. They live downstairs and will help you, too. Come on, Suz. Not much further and you can sleep."

He waited for Janelle to nod her agreement, then helped the exhausted Suz to her feet. Harriet already had the child, and together they tromped down the stairs. Janelle remained behind, cleaning up what remained. She knew most considered her downright fussy in her needs, but she disliked the scent of blood clinging to her or anything near her. So she wiped down the beautiful birthing chair and sopped up the mess on the floor. The major joined her soon afterwards, doing the work with a quiet efficiency.

"Are there more women tonight?" she asked.

He shook his head. "I thought we would try one tonight to be sure my plan worked."

She arched a brow. "And what do you think?"

They were both on their knees scrubbing the floor like kitchen maids. She'd done it before, but it was a shock to see him so humble. He grew even more so as he dropped his rag into a bucket. "You know this is not the place. I should have asked you—"

"But you wanted to impress me."

"Yes."

"As a bribe into a marriage you don't want me to accept."

He shrugged, but his expression told her that she had it correct. Now she just needed to figure out why.

"Do you have other plans tonight, Major? Or shall we have a frank discussion now?"

His lips quirked. "I think it's well past time we spoke."

"I agree." Then because he looked so downcast. "You did very well with the birthing chair."

"Yes," he said with a grin. "That's me. The best purveyor of birthing equipment in London. I pride myself on that."

"I'm sure it will come in handy for your future diplomatic career."

He chuckled and stretched out his legs on the floor. With his free hand, he pulled over the stool for her. "Sit down, Miss Caddick. This discussion might take a while."

"Then don't give me that thing," she said in mock outrage. "That's the most uncomfortable stool it's ever been my misfortune to use." She pushed the thing aside then came to sit beside him, leaning back against the wall.

"That is not a dignified position. For either of us."

"It is perfectly acceptable for Betty and—"

"The man?"

"Yes." Betty and the man. She liked the sound of that. So did he, apparently, as he relaxed beside her.

"You are not going to like this conversation," he said.

She had guessed that. "I doubt you will either."

"Probably not, but I am used to difficult conversations."

"Do you honestly think a midwife has never heard nor spoken hard truths?"

He looked at her, his gaze assessing even as it steadily warmed. "No, I expect you have had your share of uncomfortable words."

"As have you."

"Buckets of them."

She touched the back of his hand, admiring the size and the width of it. In that single touch, she knew the sinews of his hand, and she remembered the strength in it as he'd lifted Suz. It was a handsome hand, and no less appealing than the rest of him. Indeed, settled as he was beside her against the wall of a nearly empty flat, she thought him akin to a knight of yore. An inexperienced one, at least in birthing matters, but one who was willing to learn. And that she found most appealing of all.

She felt her heart stir as she looked at him. More than that, her breasts grew heavy, and her belly heated. He was a powerful man, attractive in repose and formidable when he worked. And she was about to have a long, intimate discussion with him about her dreams for birthing quarters.

The idea was exciting, and she couldn't stop herself from scooting closer to him just to measure his size against hers. Goodness, she felt delicate and feminine here beside him. And he was her rugged and handsome knight errant.

She could hardly wait for what would happen next.

Chapter Nineteen

H E HADN'T REALIZED how beautiful she was.

Certainly, her face and form were pleasing. On a purely physical level, she was attractive. Her face was sweet, her skin clear. Her curves enticed him, including her full breasts and long legs. Many women seemed too delicate next to his huge body, but she had muscles to support her bones. It let him know she wouldn't break if he touched her.

And oh, how he wanted to touch her.

He distracted himself by paying a boy to get them dinner. Bread and cheese, plus a bottle of wine. Then he stretched out against the wall and listened to the dream she spun with her words. She'd thought about this a great deal. She loved the thought of a place for women. One room to deliver babies, one to care for them before and after. Another place to mix her potions. That was not her true passion, but one that aligned with the health of new mothers and their babes.

She was a healer through and through, and she dreamed of a place where life flourished when so much of the world beat it down.

"A simple room like this would be a miracle," she said. "But as soon as I had it, I would want more. You saw Suz. She was exhausted afterwards. If the babe was sickly, it would need care that she couldn't give it. A wetnurse would be the best choice, but so many of those ladies are malnourished and have their own babes to care for. It's an expanding circle of need."

She had started out leaning against the wall beside him, but once the wine arrived, she sat up as a proper lady would. Without glasses, they poured the drink into his flask, then shared equally from it. He became obsessed with watching her lips—so mobile as she talked—wrap around the top of his flask. Pursed tight, she drank, and he watched her throat work. She didn't take huge gulps but sipped as a lady would, and the sight had his cock pulsing in time with her drink.

He imagined her mouth wrapped around his organ. He thought of her drinking him, and he could barely hear for the roar in his ears.

She passed the flask back to him, and their fingers touched. He wasn't thirsty—not for wine—but he put his mouth where hers had been. He rolled his tongue around the opening, all the while knowing that her tongue had been there as well. He sipped from the flask as he would sip from her. And when her breath caught, as it did just before she took a bite of cheese, he would thrust into her with tongue or finger or cock, and the pleasure would be devastating.

"Oh, the things I could do with such a place," she said. "I wouldn't be able to manage it myself, but there's an apothecary associated with the Rose Garden. They say the owner is Chinese. She mixes teas that help with inflammation in the lungs."

Amazing that she hadn't heard of the new Chinese Countess of Artanges and her apothecary shop. That was the one she was referring to, he was sure, but that just showed how little she cared about society. Or perhaps how quickly society moved on from a sensational story of a future duke falling in love with a Chinese princess.

"If I had the time," Janelle continued, "I would study with her. If I had the money, I would set her up in a warm house with good food, and she would teach me everything!"

Her arms spread wide as she gestured. Her legs moved beneath her skirt as well. She had taken off her apron and now sat on the floor in her ballgown. He had no idea why she hadn't taken it off before, but now she sat in a pool of yellow silk. It was easy to liken her to a flower or canary. Indeed, it was like the yellow dress was the overflow from her light. When she spoke like this, the brightness of her being suffused her. Kissing her would be like kissing the sun. It would burn, but it would be worth it.

"Oh, how I go on," she said as she tore off a hunk of bread. "I believe, Major, that you have gotten me quite drunk."

He pointed at the bottle of wine. "We've barely had half," he said. "You are drunk on your own dreams."

"I am," she said as she tilted her head back. She braced her arms behind her, and her breasts moved enough to make his hands itch to shape them. "I have never told anyone what I just told you," she said. "I've sketched it on papers I burned. I've written my thoughts in a dairy that I've thrown away. But in my mind, it's so clear. If only I could."

"What if it could be?" he asked, the words choking him as he said them. He wanted to give her everything she desired. He wanted to be the one dripping in money who could see her desires fulfilled. But he was not that man. Certainly, he could find a way to match her dream with reality, but the money was not in his hands. Not directly.

She tilted her head to look at him. "Does Lord Benedict offer me so much?"

"Yes."

She laughed, the sound filled with frustration and hope. He knew it well for he had heard it from so many souls over the years. Disillusionment made that sound. When one has fought for years for something to no avail, laughter is the only recourse. And yet there is always a measure of hope, be it in a wish or a prayer. It usually sounded like God whispering, "Maybe. Someday."

But Janelle had more practicality in her than prayers. "No wife of his can do what I describe," she said. Then she straightened to look him in the eye. "Is that why you don't want me to marry him?"

She didn't mince words. He loved that about her. But he could hardly declare his own adoration. "Lord Benedict has tasked me with making your dream come true."

She giggled as she turned back to the ceiling. "Well, then, Major, you have been set a herculean task."

"Gabriel," he said, the wine making him impulsive. "If I am to be your magic genie, then you must call me by my real name."

"Gabriel," she said, rolling the word off her tongue, making him feel as if he'd been touched by it. "Gabriel, my angel, come to fulfill my every desire."

If only that were true.

She abruptly straightened, bracing herself when her head swam. He reached out a hand to steady her, but she batted it away in the expansive gesture of the inebriated. "God, I hate all these pins," she said as she began to pull them out of her hair.

Lock by lock, her hair tumbled down. He watched with rapt attention, as if she undressed completely before him. Her hairstyle was generally simple, but it had been knotted up tight when she worked as Betty. And now the brown tresses fell in untidy spills of mink and mahogany. They had two lamps here, enough light to make her appear as a fairy goddess before him.

And when she stopped, she looked at him with an unguarded smile. "I love the way you look at me," she said. "As if you would give me the moon and stars if I asked."

He would. "I would give you your birthing quarters," he said. "Indeed, I already have, though it was badly done. I will do better tomorrow."

"But why?" Her hands flopped into her lap as she regarded him. "Surely you know Lord Benedict will hate this."

"Lord Benedict knows you will not stop. And therefore, it is up to me to make it work so that you may have your dream while he focuses on his."

She stared at him, her mind working in ways he could not fathom. "And what of you, Gabrrrrriel?" The way she rolled his name in her mouth made a shiver roll down his spine. "What do you dream about?"

Her. Ever since he'd run into her outside the Rose Garden. "I am not a man with big dreams."

"Tut tut," she said as she leaned forward. The round tops of her breasts came into view, and he tightened his hands into fists rather than touch her. "You dream like everyone else. If you are so busy with my dream and Lord Benedict's plans, what room is there for yours?"

"You know I am a bastard, yes?"

"I do, but I never thought less of you for that. Even before my London season, I have met enough good people of unfortunate birth to know that parentage does not make the man." She chuckled. "And I've known several men with impeccable lineage that I would not trust to shine my shoes."

"You are unusually open-minded."

"That's not being open-minded. It's not being blind. And you still have not answered my question." She looked at him and he saw the misty beauty of her brown eyes. The light gave them a golden hue in flashes that mesmerized him. "What do you wish for?"

The opening was there. He had only to stroke her cheek and curve his fingers beneath her chin. She might come to him then. She was open and tipsy with wine. He could blame the drink for the inexcusable liberty, but he didn't do it. He was a man of honor, and he would not trespass upon another man's wife. Or future wife.

"I want children," he finally blurted. "Lord Benedict and I are the same in that. I want a boy and a girl to live in the sunshine. I want them to be strong and happy, to know they are loved, and that…" He could not voice the rest. His throat closed up at the image of giving his own children the life he had been denied.

"You want them to be legitimate," she said, reading his mind.

"Yes." How that word ached.

"How awful was it?"

He blinked to focus on her instead of a pair of children he

might never have. And yet, when he looked at her, he couldn't help but imagine a little girl with her eyes or a boy with her impudent determination.

"I grew. I learned. I have a good life."

"Serving Lord Benedict and me." She touched his hand. It was set by his hip, still balled into a fist. He was leaning on it and so could not twitch away. He felt her fingers settle upon the back of his hand and let her touch caress away his restraint.

"I was the child of a whore and a duke," he said. "He got me into the best schools. I learned how to fight. I learned that intelligence will beat brute force, if given enough time. So I became smart and brutal." He flashed her a wicked grin. "It was the perfect education for a military man."

"And did your mother give you something? Tenderness perhaps? Love?"

He shook his head, unable to voice even a glib lie. "I had a nurse who cared for me when I was young. What I know of love came from her."

"And your mother?"

"She taught me about sex. Not her specifically, but I was surrounded by it from my earliest days."

He expected her to recoil at that. Every modest virgin should be appalled. Instead, she tilted her head. "I learned from anatomy textbooks and from peppering my brother with questions." Her expression softened as she looked up at him. "I am not comparing yours and mine. I expect yours was a lot more…um…experiential than mine." She sighed. "And I doubt it was all pleasant."

How well she saw him. How wise to know that sex wasn't always good, even for a man. "You're a sheltered young woman," he said slowly. "How could you know about that?"

"I was sheltered, but Betty was not. And she was very curious."

She stretched out her legs in front of her, revealing trim ankles and slippered feet. He'd never thought those body parts particularly attractive, but any part of her drew his gaze. And his hunger.

"What have you seen?" he pressed.

"Not as much as you," she said. "But enough. Boys can be victims as easily as girls. And it might be more of a violation. Mrs. Sundy treated everyone, and she told me stories of things I could not imagine on my own."

He shook his head. "You should not have been exposed to those things."

"Why? Because they don't exist if I don't know? How can I help what I cannot even imagine?" Her head tilted back again, exposing her white neck. "Do you know that titled women were not so sheltered once upon a time? We were taught how to heal wounds, cook food, and manage entire castles. The lady of the manor knew how to fight with daggers, if not swords. Bows and arrows might be her skill. And she was in charge of everything while her lord was out fighting wars. And yet suddenly, it is 1814 and I'm not supposed to know anything but how to speak French, dance at a ball, and praise a man's horses. Or dogs. Or whatever it is he fancies. It's ridiculous."

"Indeed," he said as he looked at the curve of her cheek and the blush of skin at her bodice. How pure she was. How gloriously perfect. "You were born into the wrong time. You would make an excellent queen."

"Queen!" she exclaimed with a laugh. "I would hate that. All those people everywhere, having to wear so many layers of clothing, and listening to speech after boring speech about I don't know what. That would be like being at a ball every moment of my life. No, Gabrrriel, I much prefer this." She straightened with a smile. There was a surplus of energy in the woman as she shifted from one position to another. "A baby delivered, a full belly of simple food." She grabbed the wine flask and drained it. "And conversation." She looked to him. "I cannot say half my thoughts to anyone in my set. Nanny and Faye help, but even they maintain a distance because I am the mistress and they, the servants." She cast him a baleful look. "There is only you, and I didn't want to tell you anything. Yet you followed me, you poked at me, and now you know everything."

He watched the way her lips shaped the word *you*. If it were a hook, it embedded itself straight into his soul. He would kiss her, if given half a chance. He would devour her if he could. The only thing that held him back was his sense of honor. She was engaged to his superior officer. She was a noble woman in every sense of the word. And he was a bastard.

"Why don't you want me to marry Lord Benedict?" she said. "The truth this time."

Her gaze was level on his, her entire body held poised. He had a list of partial truths to say. Any number of them would have appeased her. Instead, honesty spilled from his lips.

"Because I want you for myself."

Her eyes widened. At first, she didn't say a word, but then she whispered her question. "Why?"

One word that revealed a kinship between them that he couldn't deny. It told him that she was as lonely as he was, buried beneath layers of duty and responsibility. He already knew that she valued her own skills, but now he knew that she didn't think anyone else recognized them. Not someone of her own set. Not even her own family, who knew so little of her.

"Because I know," he said. "I know your heart and your passion." He gestured at the birthing chair, but his gaze didn't leave her face. "Because a man such as me doesn't get to touch pure things, and yet we know them. And we prize them."

He touched her then, a slow caress of his hand down her cheek and to her mouth. He felt her breath heat his fingertips and he trembled with yearning.

"You are everything I want," he said.

"You are the only one who knows everything about me," she said. "I have held nothing back from you." She stretched forward. She came to him, her lips parted and her gaze liquid with desire.

"Have you ever kissed a man?" he asked. Why, why, why would he ask that? He did not want to know her as a sexual creature, and yet he had to know.

"Twice," she said. "Once as myself, once as Betty. I don't think they were good kisses. I never wanted more."

"Then they were terrible kisses." He curved his fingers beneath her chin then extended them to stroke her neck.

"You must know how to do it right," she said. "You must have kissed a thousand girls."

"Not so many as that."

"Make it a thousand and one," she whispered. "Please."

She was begging him to kiss her. Didn't she know how small a measure it was between a kiss and a babe in her belly? Clearly not, but he did. His blood pounded in his ears and his cock urged him to give her everything she wanted.

"You are engaged to Lord Benedict," he said.

She nodded, her expression sad. "I do not think he is a passionate man. Not in the way you are."

So she was perceptive in that way as well. "He is not," Gabriel rasped. "It doesn't change the fact that you are his."

She snorted. "I am not his yet. I am my own self and just once, I should like to experience a good kiss." She was up on her knees now, her hand stroking up his arm as she begged him. "Please Gabrrrriel. Please teach me. No one will know."

No one but himself, his honor, and her.

She flashed him an impish smile. "You are sworn to make my dream come true. You said so yourself."

"That is not what Lord Benedict meant." He kept saying the man's name as a way to cool his blood. It didn't work.

"It is my dream, Gabriel." She didn't purr his name this time. She wasn't trying to be seductive with her very limited skills in this arena. She was simply telling him the truth. She longed for someone in the way all women yearned. She wanted a man who could give her pleasure in the most carnal way.

"One kiss," he said. He could bend his honor that far. "And then I will take you home."

"One kiss," she agreed. "And then I will ask you questions."

Of course, she would. And of course, he didn't mind.

Chapter Twenty

J ANELLE HAD BEEN dying to kiss him. From the first moment he'd spoken to her, her irrational mind had insisted on bringing him up in the middle of the night. She'd lay in bed furious with him for one reason or another only to wonder what it would be like to kiss him. She set it down as a waking nightmare that she could not stop, regardless of how hard she tried.

Sometime around a week ago, she gave up fighting the urge. Rather than force herself to think of new diapering styles or some secret elixir, she allowed herself to indulge in fantasy. It was just a dream, right? No one had to know.

No one, that is, except her. She nightly tortured herself with fantasies of how he might touch her, of what his lips would feel like, of any of a million scandalous things. Then tonight, he had taken care of her, helped with Suz's delivery, and now shared wine and cheese as if they were old friends. She could hardly sit still for the desire burning inside her and so she twisted and fidgeted on the floor, when all she wanted to do was fling herself into his arms. What would it be like to be cherished by a man as sexy as him?

And now she had maneuvered herself into a kiss. Would he press his lips to her in a perfunctory manner or sweep her off her feet as he had done to Suz a few hours ago? She never thought she'd be jealous of a laboring woman, but at that moment, she'd seen his muscles bulge and felt her insides tremble.

His kiss came slowly, like a fine brandy when she should

absolutely not be tasting such a thing. The heat of his breath against her lips made her tremble. He held her chin where he wanted, pressuring slightly to get her to tilt, and then extending his fingers in a long caress of her neck. She ached to press her mouth to his, but she knew better than to rush. This was a kiss she wanted to savor.

That seemed to be his wish as well. He touched the barest outline of his lips to hers, moving slightly while her flesh swelled to meet his. She was on her knees, stretching forward toward him. He met her easily, opening his hand so that her head was cradled in his palm. And in this position, he began to tease her lips.

Tiny nips that made her smile. The slight scrape of teeth across her lower lip. And then he did something that made her gasp.

He sucked her bottom lip into his mouth. What a sensation! She gasped as she arched in reaction. He teased his tongue along the inner seam of her lip, and she met him then, tongue to tongue. Ah, the glory of touching him in such an intimate way. They stroked each other, twisted around, and then he won the battle. He thrust inside her mouth, and she stretched forward such that he could plunder her however he wanted.

He still cradled her head, but now she set her arm across his thigh before sliding her hand up his back. All too soon, she was stretched across his lap, still supported by his one hand, while she gloried in his kiss.

She knew the details of copulations. She knew that his tongue mimicked the thrust his organ would make between her thighs. And while he stroked every part of her mouth, she felt as if he were already delving below. Her belly heated, her inner core tightened with a wonderous kind of ache. The sensations were everywhere, and she wanted more.

She clutched at his back, trying to draw herself closer to him. He allowed it for mere moments before pulling back. It became a game of inching forward and back, of teasing thrust and parry.

His other hand crept up to her face, caressing her cheek and neck. She was in her ballgown with a bodice that she'd once thought indecently low. Now she was grateful for it.

He stroked down her neck and then caressed the tops of her breasts. Back and forth, back and forth, each time a bit lower. And then, his smallest finger pressed beneath the fabric. She wanted him to rip it. She wanted her dress gone. But she didn't want to interrupt the steady progress of whatever he planned.

He eased off his kiss while her breath caught and held. She was pressing her chest forward into his stroke. Would he go lower? Please, go lower!

He dropped his forehead to hers, speaking in a low rasp. "I said only one kiss."

"So don't kiss me again."

He chuckled but there was a groan in it as well. "How much do you know?"

"I deliver babies, Gabriel. I know." She did know the basics, but she had never experienced any of it. Nothing like this.

"Say my name again." He rolled his mouth to the shell of her ear. "Slowly."

"Gabrrrielll," she whispered. "Gabrrrriellll," she moaned.

He adjusted her in his arms, moving her head to his shoulder while supporting her from the back. Or not supporting her because his fingers eased the topmost buttons of her gown. Her bodice softened. And in front, he tugged at the ribbons that held her stays.

She breathed in, feeling the restraints fall away. She didn't care how scandalous this was. She wanted to feel it. And so she sat up, twisting her hands behind her back to pull open all the buttons on her gown. The action thrust her breasts forwards to his view, and she liked the way his gaze seemed to burn as he watched her movements.

She saw him swallow, knew he fought with his conscience, but she also knew he was weakening. Was it cruel of her to challenge his honor so? She didn't care. She wanted to see him overcome by the same kind of hunger that filled her.

Her gown opened down to her waist, then slipped the sleeves off her arms.

"Janelle," he groaned. "We cannot."

"We won't," she said as she pulled at the restriction of her stays.

Two sharp tugs later, she threw aside her stays. All that remained to cover her was a thin shift. It was nearly sheer. The dark shadows of her nipples were clear through the fabric.

"Wait," he said, and so she did. She sat there before him while he looked at her breasts. Then he groaned low and slow as he reached for her. She saw what he was doing, knew that he fought his desire, and nearly cried aloud when he held himself back.

"No man has ever touched me here," she said. "I want it to be you. Please be you."

"Why me?" His gaze broke from her breasts to search her face.

"Because you're you!" How did she express that her future was already determined? That Lord Benedict was never her choice nor whatever marriage he decreed. But at this moment now, she picked the man she wanted. "I dream at night about you," she confessed. "I touch myself and I think about you."

She blushed when she said those words. Heat suffused her, concentrating in her cheeks, and that seemed to change something in him. His lips curved and his eyes grew wicked. "Touch yourself how?" he asked. "I have been commanded to see to your desires fulfilled. Tell me, Janelle. Tell me what you have thought about."

Images flashed through her mind. Hungers that she never acknowledged, even as she fantasized them. The thoughts were in her mind, the words on her tongue, but how could she voice them?

"You must tell me," he commanded. "Else I am fulfilling my desires, not yours."

"Touch my nipples." The words fell out in a rush. She wanted his hands not just on her breasts, but on the hard points that ached for rough treatment.

He did exactly as she asked. He used both his hands to pinch her nipples. Just them through the fabric of her shift. He squeezed them and tugged while lightning burst through her body. She cried out. More importantly, she thrust her breasts forward.

"More."

He gave her what she demanded. He twisted her nipples, tugged at them with the nail of his thumb. And she grew more frustrated with the fabric of her shift.

So she pulled it off.

She had to straighten off her knees to do so. It was beneath her gown, held fast by her bottom, but she got it off and away. And when she faced him again, her gown was draped loosely around her hips. Indeed, she knew that if he looked just the right way, he would see her lower curls. He would know she was wet with desire. He would... He could...

He had no words. Never had she seen a man look with such hunger. Certainly not at her. It made her feel powerful. It made her feel feminine. And it made her feel as if she would never, ever regret what they were about to do.

"What do you want to do?" she asked.

He looked at her breasts then slowly raised his gaze. "We are playing with fire."

"I like this burn."

He chuckled, though the sound had a note of self-mockery in it. "Everyone does, Janelle, if they are introduced to it correctly."

"Teach me," she said.

"That is a husband's job."

It was and her promises to her fiancé made her pause. "Do you think he knows how to do it properly? Do you think he has the skill or the will to take the time? Because I don't."

"No," he admitted. "No, he will not. Not like you deserve."

"Then we are agreed." She took his hand in hers and pulled it to her right breast. She did not need to prompt him to lift or shape her. He did it exactly as she wanted, stroking her such that she sighed in delight. "Yes," she whispered.

His other hand joined the first, and soon she was arching back, her weight on the palms of her hands while she gloried in the feel of his on her skin.

"You know this pleasure," he said. "You touch yourself."

And she thought of him. "It's different with you." She opened her heavy eyelids to look at him. "It feels better with you."

He held her gaze and she saw a universe of thoughts whirling right behind his eyes. "You have never done this with another man?" he asked.

"Never." Then she smiled. "Just you. Late at night. In my dreams."

His hands twitched when they were pressed against her, tightening as if to hold her forever, before relaxing. Then he opened his palm and caressed her in ways she'd never done to herself. Large flat palms, strong hands, and a twisting motion between his fingers. She writhed, loving every moment of what he did.

"I will show you," he said as he leaned forward to kiss her neck. "I will teach you how to touch yourself."

"I want you," she said.

"Then you must remember everything I do."

He lay her back against the floor. Her dress lay pooled about her, and he folded up his jacket to set beneath her head. She stroked his chest as he put her in place. She tried to worm her fingers beneath the fabric, but he stopped her.

"Why?" she asked. "I have seen you before. Back in the still-room of my house. I touched you then."

"Not now," he said. "Not like this. It will tempt me too much."

She knew what he meant, and yet she regretted his answer. "I trust your control."

"Then you are an innocent."

She wasn't truly innocent. She knew that madness had gripped her. She should not do any of this, but she trusted him. She would never allow herself to be alone with any other man, but he was an angel. After all, it was his name. "Gabrrrriel. I trust you."

"Then obey me."

Her arousal was undercut by his words. They were part of her wedding vows, and she should be uttering them to Lord Benedict. But her fiancé did not look at her the way Gabriel did. And if she ever wanted to experience pleasure, then Gabriel was the man to teach her. "I do," she whispered, thinking that this too was akin to a wedding vow. She would allow no other man to do what they were about to. Tonight, she was giving herself into his hands.

Thankfully, he did not give her time to work through her tortured thoughts. If she thought much longer, she would have to face how far she'd fallen. Instead, she threw herself into his kiss. She dueled with him, tongue to tongue, and when he allowed her, she nibbled at his mouth and sucked upon his lips.

"You're a fast learner," he murmured as he kissed her jaw.

"You're a good teacher."

He kissed down her neck, across her chest, and then between her breasts. His hands molded her, his teeth aroused her, and his tongue wet her. "Remember this," he commanded before he caught her nipple between his teeth.

As if she could forget it!

The way he worked her nipples had her shuddering with pleasure, but this time it wasn't enough. Her legs twisted restlessly, her hands gripped his shoulders, and she could not stop whispering that she wanted more, always more.

He lifted his head. "How do you touch yourself? Do you know about a quickening?"

"Yes," she gasped. "Mrs. Sundy told me about it before my first Season." Her lips quirked in a half smile. "She said to learn it early on, for my husband would not know how to do it."

He ran his knuckles down the side of her breast, his expression so tender. "That is true."

"Do it for me, please."

"I promised to teach you something new."

Something new? What could be newer than a quickening? She didn't ask. She was too absorbed in feeling his hand slide down her belly. Such a difference from her own. He was large, his fingers had callouses, and when he slid inexorably through her curls, she spread her legs to feel it all.

"Is this what you do?" he asked as his fingers stroked and swirled through her folds.

Not like that. Not with surprising pressure and...oh! He pushed a finger inside her. So large, so masculine.

Her belly tightened, her hips lifted. Her legs were restricted by the fabric of her gown, but he had room. He cupped her, his palm pressing down against her mons. She'd never felt that before. It was ever so nice. Then he pulled his hand upward, his fingers dragging through her folds.

He found it! He was stroking her place where sensation gathered. Where everything thrummed and his every press made her undulate with excitement.

"Touch your breasts," he said. "The way you like it."

She did it. She gathered her breasts in her hands and kneaded them. She pinched her nipples the way he had. She felt wanton and was not ashamed. It felt so good.

He built her pleasure quickly. She didn't want it to go so fast, but she'd been imagining this for so long. And here he was, rubbing between her thighs, opening her with his fingers, and...

"Yes!"

He plunged inside her. More than one finger, she was sure. She felt the stretch and wanted more. And still he pleasured her nub. Her heels ground down onto the floor, her knees were as wide apart as she could get them, and he played her flesh like a maestro.

Her belly tightened, her back arched. Too fast! Not yet! But it was too late. She couldn't stop the explosion of sensation. She cried out in joy, she rode the pleasure of her inner muscles contracting around his fingers. And still he plunged in and out while she gripped him.

Bliss!

She rode it as long as she could. She felt the waves soften. She murmured as they rolled through her. And she smiled because she was so happy.

"Yes," she finally whispered. "Thank you."

She felt his hand on her belly, a warm heat where it lay. His other fingers were still inside her, and that realization startled her. He was still embedded there, a grin on his face as he felt her quiver around him. A tiny contraction. A final pulse.

"You have felt that before?" he asked.

"Not one so lovely as that."

"I am happy to hear it."

"I am happy to experience it."

He grinned, a boyish look that made his entire body light up. "But I promised to teach you something new."

She frowned, not understanding what he meant. What more could there be except the penetrative act? The one they would not do.

"There is more," he said with a smile. "Do you trust me?"

"Obviously."

"Then let me do this."

She looked at him. "I will keep my virginity?"

"I swear it."

In for a penny, in for a pound. She laughed at the silly phrase. It should not apply to what they had just done, but why would she stop him?

"Yes. Definitely yes."

"Lie back," he instructed. "I am going to take my time with this."

Chapter Twenty-One

ONE OF THE benefits of growing up around women was that Gabriel learned early how to view things from their perspective. He knew how to give a woman pleasure in a myriad of ways, no matter who the "her" was. It was on his sixteenth birthday that he discovered how much he adored hearing a woman's sounds as he feasted between her thighs.

Janelle didn't understand what he was about to do. She clearly had never imagined such a thing, and so he eased her into it by rubbing her feet, teasing the back of her knee with his tongue, and then easing her thighs open as he kissed his way to her core. By the time her modesty tried to protest, his fingers were already spreading her open, her breath came too quickly for her to protest, and his tongue was already tasting the juice of her body.

He settled in to enjoy her, taking his time as he tongued her. He learned her sounds and the way she writhed beneath him. He teased her to the peak, then brought her back down as he plunged fingers and tongue into her. He could only take her to the verge so many times before she gripped his ears and demanded he take her the rest of the way.

He did. Eventually. And then he made a game of keeping her climax going while he explored her every sound and whimper.

He was grinding his own cock into the floor while he pleasured her. The need to release darkened his vision while his back burned from the restraint. But he had justified this action by telling himself he was teaching her how to enjoy life in a loveless marriage. His reward was the knowledge that she would remember him as her first. He was the one who took her to the height of ecstasy. Indulging himself was not an option.

He took her to heaven in the only way he knew how, and he kept himself…well, not pure so much as restrained.

Until she said, "Stop."

She didn't cry it aloud. She didn't have the breath. But he heard her whisper it even as her body pulsed around his tongue.

"One mmmmmore," he hummed against her clit. Then he licked her slowly, knowing it took very little to keep her aloft. She whimpered her surrender, so he let her fall boneless back to earth. He watched her face, her breasts, and her whole being flush rosy gold amid the yellow silk of her dress. He stretched forward to lave her nipples again. Such hard points of sensation, so sweet on his tongue.

He kissed her neck, her jaw, and then teased her mouth. She met him with what strength she had left, and he fought the urge to lower his falls and drive into her. She would take him easily now. She was stretched open, relaxed enough to enjoy the slide of his cock, and he would surrender the last of his honor in the act.

So he kept himself back. But he still had to stake his claim.

"You will remember me forever," he said against her ear.

"Longer than that," she said with a low chuckle.

"And every time you pleasure yourself, you will know that I was the one who showed you this. You will think of this and remember me."

She was silent after he spoke, her body stilling until she rolled her head to look straight at him. "This is how you want to be remembered? This is your legacy?"

He smiled. "What else is there for me?"

"Your work. Your children. I can think of a thousand other things, but you have chosen this." She languidly stroked her fingers across his cheek, threading them into his hair as she continued to study his face. "Don't misunderstand. It was wonderful."

He brushed his fingertips across her belly, a mimicry of how she stroked through his hair. She gasped in reaction, arching her back as a purr rumbled in the back of her throat. God, he loved the sight of a well-pleasured woman.

She must have seen his smirk because she rolled her eyes. "Yes, Gabriel, it's still wonderful." Then her expression turned serious. "But I cannot imagine you believe this is all you have to offer the world."

"I offer my service to you and Lord Benedict."

"Well, I certainly hope you haven't done this for him," she said with a laugh.

A frisson of worry burned down his back. What did she know? "I have not," he said firmly. "This was for you alone."

"Liar," she chuckled. "If you truly think this is your legacy, then there are a string of women in your past, all aching for your return."

"There are a few," he admitted. "But it has been years since I have done something so…" dishonorable. "So sweet a service."

"I shall grow cross with you if you continue to view me as your duty."

What else could she be? She was engaged to Lord Benedict. "You are more than a service, Janelle." Daring of him to use her first name, but he would say it out loud now and every time in his thoughts. "But to wish for more would be—"

She stopped him quickly, pressing her fingers to his mouth. He held himself still, but in his mind, he was curling his tongue around her fingers, pulling them into his mouth, and nibbling at the tips.

"You are my choice," she whispered. "I want to be yours, too."

"You are too innocent to know—"

"Do you think I haven't had choices? Either as Betty or Janelle, there have been men. I wanted none of them. Only you."

Now he did kiss her fingers. And then he pulled them away and pressed his mouth to hers. It was by no means a chaste kiss, but it was restrained. And when he pulled back, he looked her in the eyes. "You are my choice as well," he confessed. "But I was bound to Lord Benedict first."

"Me, too."

"He is a great man, and he will keep the war from coming back. He will see peace in our country and on the continent."

"I know," she said. Then she sighed. "I cannot understand why he picked me."

How much could he tell her? "He wants a wife with her own interests. Your hobby is one that he respects. Better yet, it gives you access to the peasants and the laborers."

She pulled back from him, her face tightened with confusion. "I deliver their babies," she said.

"And you would know if they speak of violent rebellion."

"Like the mad French? They don't. Not really."

So some did. "You would know if they grew serious, and you would tell him."

"That cannot be the whole of my appeal."

"Of course not. You have all the accomplishments of a well-bred young lady and none of the vices."

She sighed. "Damned by faint praise."

"Did you want him to love you?" The words cut as he uttered them. Did she long for love? Of course, she did. All souls did.

"I had hoped for a little."

"He gives you what he can."

She turned back to him. "And I give you what I can."

He smiled, though the expression hurt. "And I am pleased by your gift."

She touched his face again, tender across his cheeks and lips. "Of the three of us, you are the one who can choose better. Find a wife whom you love. Have children of your own. Ones that will not be tainted as a bastard."

"Every child of mine will be tainted by my parentage. Not as badly as I am, but their options will be limited."

She knew it was true. He could see the acknowledgement in

her eyes. "So you spend your time giving quickenings to lonely women? Instead of finding a wife?"

"Just you," he said. "And just this once."

"And another heart breaks in your wake."

Yes. It was his own. "You do not love me," he chided.

"Are you sure? Because I am not." She took a breath. "I have all the symptoms, you know. I have thought of little more than you."

"You have been cursing my name."

"That, too. And then the first time you touch me…" She bit her lip, but the rest of her statement was clear. One kiss, and now she lay sprawled before him in naked abandon.

"This was pleasure, Janelle. It is different than love."

"Maybe. But I would not do this with anyone else."

A surge of pride hit him, swelling every part of him including that part that had just started to ease.

"I must take you home now," he said.

"I know."

"And I will look for a better place for your work. This room will not do."

"It will not." She flashed him a mischievous smile. "But I love it nonetheless."

He would certainly never forget it.

Moving slowly, he pushed up from her side. The brush of his clothing sent the fires of hell across his flesh. He counted her worth every agony. He helped her stand, and he groaned at the sight of her rising naked from the pool of yellow silk. She blushed as she made it to her feet, her hands shaking a bit as she ducked her head.

"What you must think of me."

"That you are beautiful. And I am very lucky to see such a sight once in my lifetime." And that he had never hated Lord Benedict more.

Because she was skittish, he held out her shift. She took it but didn't release his hands. "I would have touched you. I—" She swallowed. "I would like to touch you."

To do such a thing would kill him. His heart would not be able to withstand the pleasure. "No, Janelle. Leave me some tiny bit of honor."

She nodded, pulling back and quickly donning her shift. When her head emerged from the fabric, she slanted him a quixotic look. "Men's honor is very changeable concept."

He could not deny it. "We rarely understand it ourselves."

"And yet so much is done in its name." She said no more as she gathered her dress and shook it out. The thing was crushed, and yet she shrugged. "No blood." She chuckled. "All in all, that makes this a good night clothing-wise."

Good lord, what must her clothes look like regularly? "I hope this was a good night for other reasons as well."

"Fishing for compliments, Major?"

He winced at her more formal tone, but then again, she was pulling the ribbons of her stays tight and so the changed tone was appropriate.

"Maybe." He stopped her hands as she finished tying the bow. "Or maybe I hope we both don't come to regret it."

"Never," she said, the word surprisingly sharp. And at his look, she lifted up her chin and dared him to deny her. "And if you ever do, I command you to never tell me. This was wonderful. I don't regret it."

Her eyes had gone wet with her vehemence, and if she weren't speaking so forcefully, he would think that she was steeped in regret. Instead, he thought perhaps she was feeling the same melancholy that gripped him. They might have been more to one another, if only they had met at a different time in a different way.

"I could not regret this either," he said as he cupped her face. "I feel too lucky to have experienced it to ever regret—"

"Oh, stop it!" she said with a huff. "Kiss me already."

He did. And since they both knew it was their last, they lingered at it, lip to lip, tongue to tongue. And when he deepened it, she opened willingly. His lust drove through him, demanding more, always more, but he kept it back with an act of will. He would not taint this moment of tenderness with any baser needs. Not when she was so sweet in his arms.

But even that had to end. He broke off the kiss and watched while she pulled on her gown. He helped button the back while he fought the urge to caress her skin. Then he gathered Betty's huge bag and held out his arm to her.

"What about the other things?" she asked.

"I have a lady coming to clean in the morning. Then once I find a new place, I'll move—"

"The birthing chair."

He smiled. "Yes, the birthing chair. I will not forget the one thing I did right when finding this place."

"We will do better if we work together."

More time in her presence? More moments when they could banter with ease while he watched the light on her skin or the blush on her cheeks?

"I will consult you every step of the way," he promised.

"I will hold you to that."

And what sweet torture that will be.

Chapter Twenty-Two

HE DIDN'T KISS her again, though he held her hand while the hackney travelled across the city. Janelle sat as close as she could, brushing his shoulder with hers and pressing her thigh against his. He intertwined their fingers, his grip strong. How ridiculous that she was falling in love with the strength and size of his hand. She knew that the hard bones supported strong muscles, but he also could be extraordinarily gentle. And right then, he was surrounding her tinier hand with his, and she had never felt more cherished or protected.

He walked her to the servant entrance of her home. She always carried the key, as she was well used to slipping inside in the early morning hours. Nanny kept a candle burning for her there. She tried to pull him inside, but he refused. He was Major Vance again, and nothing would sway him from acting in the most formal manner. He was an aide-de-camp assuring his superior officer's fiancée remained safe.

Since she could not kiss him, she gave him the only thing he would accept. She lifted her chin, squared her shoulders, and then she dropped into the most formal of curtsies she'd ever made. Indeed, she would not drop so low before the king himself. And when she straightened, he looked at her with a half-quirked smile. Did he think she was mocking him? She was not.

"Gabriel," she began, but he cut her off.

"Thank you for the most glorious of evenings, Miss Caddick."

"When will I see you again?"

He answered with a shrug as he turned away, carefully shutting the door lest it make an untoward sound. He needn't have worried. She made sure the hinges were well oiled.

She listened for his footstep, but she couldn't hear anything through the door. Which meant that her evening was over. Her magical night was at an end, and she must rest now. She never knew from one night to the next if she'd be up all night with a patient or dancing until dawn. How wonderful it would be to finally have a home of her own, one where she need not hide what she did. At least not from her family.

She wondered for a moment if that were possible with Lord Benedict, but her entire body recoiled at having to think about her future with anyone who was not Gabriel. She would much rather wander through memories of what she'd done this night. Of what he'd looked like just before he kissed her. Of how he'd touched her and how she had given herself over to him in all ways but one.

She was a wanton now because she longed to do everything again as often as possible. Especially if she could explore his body as he had done hers.

There was a cooled basin of water in her room, left so she could sponge away the detritus of Betty's work. For the first time in years, she ignored it. She had no desire to wash away his scent on her skin. She set her large bag in its place along with her attire. Nanny would see her things cleaned. Then she climbed into bed, hating the coarse brush of her nightrail. She wanted Gabriel holding her this night. She wrapped herself in memories instead and pretended the sheets were his body.

Then she slept deeply the whole night through. The whole night and the morning, too. She woke after noon when Nanny brought her strong tea and a letter.

"It must have been a terribly late night," the woman said, "but this just arrived in the post. You cannot neglect it."

Janelle yawned and stretched, feeling the pull of muscles that she'd rarely used before last night. She was a fit woman, well used to overtired muscles, but this ache was new. The sensation was deep in her belly, and she smiled against her pillow.

"A good birth then?" Nanny asked. "Something special?"

"Very," she said, mentally chastising herself for being so open with her thoughts. Some secrets should be kept from even her beloved Nanny. "It took much longer than expected but was very happy in the end." What a lie that was. Already her mind was turning toward last night's ending. She had made her choice and, she hoped, so had Gabriel. But that path could only lead to heartbreak. Unless she found a way out.

"Nanny," she said as she pushed herself upright. "Is Papa awake?"

"He is just now rising, which is why I came to wake you. He'll want teatime with you, you know."

She did. "Is it as late as that?"

"You've a couple hours. Read your letter, then you'll be able to plan your day."

She didn't want to read her letter. She'd seen out of the corner of her eye who it was from, and had no desire to touch anything from Lord Benedict just yet. But she couldn't avoid it. Not with Nanny watching her with a too-discerning gaze.

She picked up the fine linen, noted the elegant stretch and curve of his letters, and forced herself to touch the hard wax cast of his seal on the back. It was done with his heavy signet ring, the mark of the earldom. If she stayed the course, she would have a similar ring, one that was slender enough for a woman's hand but still forming the bear and bell of his crest.

"Nanny," she began, "what do you think Papa would say if I cried off?"

"Cried off of what? Never say you're rethinking Lord Benedict!"

Janelle winced at the woman's outraged tone. The woman was her co-conspirator in more than just her work as Betty. She managed the staff with a discerning eye, she set it such that Betty could test potions in the stillroom, and she had acted as confidante and best friend from the beginning. After all, she'd come to the household when Janelle was a lonely, neglected little girl.

"I don't even know Lord Benedict." It was the plaintive cry of a child, and she knew it. Her father had made it clear from her earliest days that she would marry the man he picked for her. She might be a lowly baron's daughter, but she would marry into the aristocracy by hook or crook. And now that he had an earl caught, he would not let her cry off without consequence.

"Janelle!" Nanny snapped as she sat down on the bed. "Your father will disown you for sure."

"Then I'll go out as Betty and be done with it."

"And how will you eat? Where will you sleep?"

"Midwives make enough to live on—"

"Some."

"And I can apprentice at the hospital. I've saved the money to do it."

Nanny sighed as she studied her charge. Janelle had long since grown into a woman, but that hard stare never failed to make her fidget.

"Out with it," Nanny ordered. Goodness, she hadn't used that tone of voice since Janelle had been sixteen and keen on a farm boy she'd met as Betty. And how embarrassing that she found herself in the exact same situation nearly a decade later.

"I've met a man," she finally confessed. "A good one who cares for me as well."

"Does he know what you do? Who you are?"

She nodded. "He knows all of it."

"Ack, child," Nanny cried. "And who are you to tell anyone such things? Don't you see how it will bring all of it down around our ears?"

"He won't tell. And he values me for the work I do."

Nanny didn't argue, but her tight lips expressed her feelings clearly.

"You needn't worry about your job," she said. "I would bring you with me. You can set up my home and manage—"

"With what money? Does this man, this paragon of virtue who would keep you from being a countess—does he have enough money to keep you in half of what you're used to?"

She didn't answer. Truthfully, she didn't know how much money the major had.

"Does this man work?" Nanny pressed.

"He does, but…" She sighed. "He would have to leave it."

"And what sort of honest labor does he do that he would leave it when he gains a wife? It's for certain that he's thinking of the money you'll make as a midwife, then, but I tell you, it's not enough. You won't even charge the people you help—"

"I would start—"

"And what will you do when your own babes come? You can't help someone else deliver a baby when you're thick with child yourself. I might be there to help you rear them, but it takes money to feed and house them. Think of your own childhood. Your father's a hard man, I won't argue that, but you had food, clothing, and a lady's education. Respect, too. Everyone you met tipped their caps to you and treated you fair. Betty won't have that, any more than Mrs. Sundy did."

"Mrs. Sundy has a good life!" she cried.

"Aye, she does because you protected her. You, the baron's daughter, sang her praises and gave the cold shoulder to any who would treat her ill. That kept the nasties away, and a hard time she's having now with you away."

Janelle's head snapped up. "What? What do you mean?"

Nanny waved the question away. "Only that Mrs. Sundy is not as young as she once was and it's a hard life she has."

"I'll send her money," she said. Indeed, she had planned to set the woman up more comfortably once she had more money of her own. But that couldn't happen, could it, if she cried off from Lord Benedict.

Nanny could see the thoughts cross her face, but rather than become more sympathetic, she pushed her point. "You won't have the money to help yourself, much less her. And without money and status, you won't have protection either. Will this man without work shield you?"

"Yes, he will." She knew that for certain. "He is honorable, through and through."

Nanny's eyes narrowed. "And has he spoken of marriage to you? If he knows who you are to wed, would he still take you away from all that?"

She sniffed, setting aside Lord Benedict's letter so that she could not see it. "He might," she said quietly. "If he knew I was no longer bound to Lord Benedict."

"*Might?*" Nanny scoffed. Then she stood up, dropping her fists on her hips. "Always, miss, you have been the practical one. You have seen what happens to foolish girls. You have seen your father with a clear-eyed gaze knowing what he wants and what he will ignore. What did you tell me when you were a child and wanted to become Betty? What did you say to me?"

Janelle turned away, the words stuck in her throat. She knew exactly what Nanny was driving at, but she didn't want to admit it. The words had been bouncing around her brain ever since her first nighttime fantasy of Gabriel. They were what kept her from ending her engagement before. They stayed her hand right now. But what if all it took was for her to be bold, to face the worst and still carry on? What if all she needed to do was be brave and she could have everything she wanted?

"What did you say to me?" Nanny pressed.

"That Papa looked for advancement. So long as I acted the proper miss and married who he declared, then he would see nothing else. He cared for nothing else."

"There's more," Nanny said. Her tone had gentled, but there was still steel behind her words. "Say it all."

Janelle looked into the eyes of her closest friend and companion. She studied the woman's long nose and clear eyes. She knew there had been men looking at Nanny some years ago. She might have married one of them and gone off to a new life free of deception. She hadn't. And maybe that was because she had dedicated herself to helping Janelle gain her dreams.

"I told you he cared for nothing else than advancement. His love was for that, not for me. He might care for a girl in a distant kind of fondness, but only if I did not challenge that."

"And in all this time, has he given any indication of a change? That his feelings are more tender toward you than you thought?"

Janelle's eyes watered, but she did not shed the tears. She had spent too long crying as a child as she tried to gain tenderness from her only surviving parent. "No," she whispered.

"No," Nanny repeated. "Indeed, I have heard nothing from him except delight at your upcoming nuptials. He has crowed to friend and foe alike. My grandson will be an earl. That's what he says from the moment he wakes until he stumbles drunken back into his bed. I will be the grandfather of an earl."

Janelle knew it was true, and she hated it with a blistering fury. She wasn't the first girl to be nothing more than a token to be traded for social advancement. Indeed, that was her sole purpose, according to her father. If only he would see her as Betty. If only he valued the things that she did, as Gabriel did, as even Lord Benedict seemed to.

"I have been so lucky," she said. "I have found a life I love, and a man who values that I do it."

"Can he support you as you have been here? Can he give your children the life you'd have with Lord Benedict?"

Of course not. Few men in the world were as wealthy as Lord Benedict. His children would be educated in the best schools, would have royals as their playmates, and she would see that they pursued their passions, whatever stirred them. The girls as well as the boys. It was possible if one could pay for the right tutors.

"What if I love someone else?"

"Then you do what every other woman of your set does. You take him as a lover. You keep chaste until the children come, and then you—"

"He won't do that. He has already said so. He is too honorable." She nearly spit out that last word.

"Then he is too good a man to take you away from Lord Benedict even if he does love you. Especially if he loves you." Nanny leaned over and picked up Lord Benedict's letter. She forcibly opened Janelle's hand and set the missive there. "You'll find a way to get what you want," she said. "You always do. But you can't do it in the open. I thought you knew that."

She did. But just once she wanted to step into the sunlight and declare her future as only a man could. She would be Betty and damned to all the things that had stopped her from doing it before. Forget her comfortable life, ignore a wealthy, respectable future. She could scrabble for coin. Midwives made enough.

But could she do it to her children, too? Could she damn them to a peasant's life when they could be born into privilege? What kind of mother did that to her children? Especially when it was perfectly normal for a woman of her set to marry wealth then take a lover.

Damn it, why had she fallen for a man of honor?

"Is it settled then?" Nanny pressed. "Do I need to talk more reason to you?"

"No, Nanny," she said, her words slow as she thumbed open Lord Benedict's letter. "I am rational again."

Rational, yes. But stubborn, too. As soon as Nanny left her room, she set the letter aside and dressed as quickly as she could. Then taking her heart and her determination in hand, she knocked lightly on her father's bedroom door.

He was awake, shaved, and in his dressing gown as he sat by the fire. He greeted her in the usual way, not even looking up from the racing sheets. "Why are you interrupting me? It's hours before teatime."

"Father," she began, "what if I fancied a man different than Lord Benedict?"

He looked at her, his expression flat. There was no interest in his gaze, no curiosity in his expression. Then he answered her with the hard end of a cane. She hadn't seen it near his hand or she would have been more careful. But it had been on the other side of chair, and he could be fast when he chose.

He hit her with stunning force, knocking her to the floor and cutting off her breath.

He knew not to beat her face, but he could crack a rib or two without killing her. Especially when he dropped the cane to use heavy fists.

No soul came to save her, and she had nowhere to run in this house. The servants supported her silently, keeping her secrets and filling her bath. But when it came to a choice between herself and her father, their allegiance was clear.

Her father's valet held the bedroom door closed so she could not escape.

And in this way, she knew that any attempt to change her wedding plans would have to be a complete break. Her father would give her no quarter, no forgiveness, and no choice whatsoever.

Chapter Twenty-Three

Dear Janelle,

I hope you are not startled by the use of your Christian name. I confess it gives me a jolt to see it there, written so boldly. Even I, who thought long and hard about our nuptials, am unnerved by the speed at which our marriage will begin. Still, plans must continue apace. The intention for a congress in Vienna grows more urgent, and if we are to have any time together before I leave England, then we must marry in proper haste.

Do you note that I said "I" would leave for Vienna and not "we"? I foresee that I shall be occupied so dreadfully in Vienna that I will be in a cursed mood much of the time, and that is only when I am free at all. Such is not the frame of mind to entertain a new wife. I hope you understand that I am thinking of your comfort.

To that end, I have instructed Major Vance to establish your situation in London. I believe that you shall be happiest there among your friends rather than isolated in Vienna or holed up in my ramshackle castle in Cornwall. Even my parents have found it uninhabitable. I am surviving now only because I am used to rough quarters, thanks to my time on the Peninsula. I would not dream of subjecting you to such difficult environs.

Please do discuss your needs with the major. I am fully cognizant of your delightful hobbies, and he knows my requirements better than I do. That makes him the one soul who can best provide for our mutual comfort, but only if you are honest when speaking with him. I assure you, there is nothing that he cannot manage. If that were not true, I would not be alive today.

Have I ever spoken of how he and I met? I was a green boy, I am ashamed to say, set upon a military career by virtue of being a second son. My older brother, you understand, had not yet contracted the disease which took his life so prematurely. I was sent to Spain to take command of a regiment sorely reduced in numbers. Though Gabriel and I are of an age together, he had been at war far longer than I and therefore seemed a great deal older. (Do not wonder that I use his given name. Such is the nature of bonds forged in war. I sometimes believe they are closer than that of man and wife.)

He seemed quite arrogant to my young eyes. He had already proven himself, you see, and commanded a small group of elite men. He had little patience for an earl's son steeped in pride. The harsh truth is that I was the arrogant one with no experience of anything beyond my books. Yet because of the fortune of my birth, I was given command, and he was ordered to escort me to the first test of my young life. If only I'd realized the depth of my ignorance, things might have gone very differently.

We travelled in unaccustomed luxury, though I did not realize it at the time. I was unhappy with the rickety carriage and complained that my delicate digestion would suffer irreparable harm. Am I giving you a disgust of me? I was a mere boy, and it is thanks to Gabriel that I ever had a chance to grow into the man I am now.

We stopped for the night at a village near an abandoned convent. By chance, I began conversing with a pair of nuns who had tarried in the area despite the loss of their home. Gabriel took pains to point out the errors in the ladies' stories, but I had grown weary of his harsh attitude. I would not hear that women with such sweet faces could be something nefarious. They knew the words of their prayers, they had fashioned crude rosaries with the correct number of beads. Ergo, they must be honest, holy women.

To this day, I believe they were nuns or at least taught by such noble women. Their education was clear, though Catholic in nature, not Anglican. When they begged to sleep for the night inside our crude camp—for protection, they said—I happily agreed. I thought them a welcome relief from the company of brusque, unwashed men.

What an idiot I was.

They poisoned us that night. I do not know when. I thought I was being careful. I know Gabriel was on guard, but skilled killers are able to distract and attack even while saying their prayers. I survived because I ate sparingly and because it was easy for Gabriel to force me to cast up everything I had consumed. The others were not so lucky. I am amazed that he tended to me first and not any of the other men who were so much worthier than I, but such is his nature. Loyalty to the Crown dictated that he defend me over his weakened men who were then set upon by the murderesses. Murderesses that I had forced him to admit into our camp.

He defended me. He killed the women who were using barbs set in their rosaries to slice men's throats in case the poison failed. And he tended his dying men while half dead himself from the poison. I helped as best as I could, which is to say I was all but useless. We survived because I obeyed his every command like the raw recruit I was.

He became my mentor, my protector, and my most trusted ally. Aide-de-camp is so small a term for what he was to me. Indeed, I fought daily to gain his respect and am proud to say I earned it, though it took years.

Do you wonder why I tell you this gruesome story of war? It is so you will look beneath Gabriel's rough exterior and see the sterling man beneath. You must know I trust him with my most valuable treasure—you, my future wife. You may tell him anything, and he will see the right path ahead for us both. He knows our secrets, you see, and will spare no effort to see both our lives fulfilled.

Trust him, I beg you. He is my proxy when it comes to do-

mestic matters. As I stand for England in Vienna, he stands for me in London.

Signed, your faithful fiancé,
Benedict

"Well," Nanny said as she set down the letter. She had been reading it aloud to Janelle, her tone brusque. "That's a delightful thing. Explains it all, doesn't he?"

Janelle didn't even open her eyes. Though her face remained untouched, the rest of her body was in agony. She rasped one word and prayed it would be understood.

"Laudanum."

Chapter Twenty-Four

GABRIEL DID NOT see Janelle for a week. She did not attend any of the parties that her aunt accepted on her behalf. Nor did Betty administer to any of the servants in the kitchen stillroom. Normally, Gabriel would have investigated this change in activity, but he guessed that their illicit kisses had upset her. He understood that some women—moral woman like her—did not feel the constant state of arousal that tormented adolescent boys. Therefore, when they experienced true attraction, it overwhelmed their systems. Some women would then withdraw as they fought a desire that they could not manage for a man they could not have.

That reasoning sounded completely plausible for five days and nights. Days when he was abruptly busy with work left for him by Lord Benedict, things that could not be delegated to another. And nights where he relived every moment spent with Janelle. Every shared looked, heated exchange, or lustful action. He stroked himself often while imagining her hands, her mouth, her body pleasuring him as he ached to do with her.

He had just finished one of his favorite fantasies when it occurred to him how ridiculous his conclusions about her were. Their one night together showed Janelle to be a woman bold in her desires. She was certainly inexperienced, but in every aspect, Janelle did not shy from exploration. Indeed, if anyone hid away from uncomfortable desires, it was himself.

That was the truth of why he had not sought her out. Certainly, he'd been working hard on Lord Benedict's list of tasks and had been too weary to dress for an evening's entertainment. He'd also been leery of what he would say in her presence, of how he would hold himself apart from her, and questioned how he could maintain his honor while standing near enough to smell her scent, see her delight, and not touch her.

He feared what he might do if tempted again, so he stayed away, only belatedly discovering that she had not attended the amusements that had been on her schedule.

That wasn't worrisome, he'd told himself. He could visit Betty at her stillroom the next day. But then he thought of being in an enclosed space with her, of taking off his shirt and letting her hands touch his scars. That would be too much for his control. He was sure of it. And the risk of discovery was too great inside her own home with the servants right there. Indeed, he wasn't sure how he'd kept himself apart from her the first time.

So he'd sent a subordinate who'd cut his hand to see Betty. Better that than risk exposing how much he wanted her. And to keep himself away, he went off on an exploration of London in the hopes of finding a new location for her to work. It wasn't until the next day that his subordinate informed him that Betty wasn't seeing anyone.

That was disturbing, and he sent around a letter that very day. He inquired after her health and asked if he could escort her about Hyde Park that afternoon. She wrote back that she would be pleased to do such a thing, but she was otherwise occupied this day. Perhaps he was available later in the week.

The letter was polite, the handwriting somewhat scrawled, as if she had dashed the note out in haste. Could she be working? Of course, she was!

It mattered not a whit that he had commanded Madame Florina to cease sending her midwifery messages. He'd paid the woman an exorbitant amount to remove Janelle from her thoughts until after he established a safe location for Betty to work.

How perfectly Janelle-like to find a way to subvert his orders. And how stupid that he thought he could command women to do as he wanted and not exactly as they pleased.

Unfortunately, his work at the Foreign Office required his attention and he was unable to interrogate Madame Florina until the early hours of the next morning when they were both irritable and uninterested in difficult conversations. He tried every manner of persuasion he had at his disposal, but she would not be intimidated or coerced. She swore she had not sent for Betty and threatened to have her bouncers cast him out. He had no choice but to leave.

He presented himself at Miss Caddick's home the very next day. He intended to wait until he could see her for himself. He was forestalled by the butler and then her aunt who was anxious to settle several details about the wedding. He could not storm her bedroom—that would be highly inappropriate. Nor could he put off the wedding discussion with Lady Boxval. The guest list and seating arrangements were important. They were always important at diplomatic affairs.

And so he lost another day in fruitless speculation and endless work.

He spoke to his mother next. He hoped to gain insight into the informal network of communication that seemed to go through the whorehouse via Madame Florina. He learned instead of a myriad of damages to the building, structural weaknesses, and roof decay. He thought if he spent his time listening to the woman's full list of complaints, he would find some way to bargain for information. After all, with a simple word, he could have an army of repairmen at the Rose Garden. But again, his mother remained completely intractable. He didn't understand it. If she wanted a roof repaired, then all she had to do was tell him how Betty came to work for her, and how information was passed. And most important, *where* Janelle was at that very moment.

He garnered no information at all, most likely because his

mother knew very little about Madame Florina's midwifery network. She had no idea how Janelle had come to Florina's attention and likely knew equally little about the day-to-day operations of the whorehouse.

Which left him at a complete loss. In desperation, he resorted to the one person he never expected to be lounging in his mother's parlor: Lord Nathaniel.

The man lay sprawled negligently beneath a window. A new girl petted his chest, but he appeared less interested in her than he did the comings and goings around him. And when he caught Gabriel's tight expression, his brow rose in query.

"I see she has forgotten your birthday again," Lord Nate drawled.

His birthday wasn't for another month. The only reason he knew that was because it was near to his mother's and that was something never forgotten. He'd ceased thinking about it the day he entered the military and was finally free of her control.

"Let me buy you a drink to celebrate," Lord Nathaniel said as he disentangled himself from the girl. "You can tell me what special treat you have in store."

"My treats are my own," Gabriel grumbled under his breath. It was a sour comment after a frustrating time with his mother, and he usually had better control of himself.

It would seem Lord Nathaniel agreed as his brows rose in surprise. "At least accompany me to the Barringrey ball. My lady wife is there tonight, and I am desperate to dance with her."

Good God, the man wore his love for his wife right out in the open. Gabriel felt a flash of envy at such a thing. Then, when he said nothing, Nate continued, "I believe several of the government set were invited, including Miss Caddick. It must be terribly difficult for her with Lord Benedict out of town. Do the plans for their nuptials proceed apace?"

The mention of Janelle caught his attention. The reference to her wedding cut at his already soured gut. But since Lord Nate appeared to know more than Gabriel did about Janelle's invitations, he slowed his steps enough for the man to accompany him out the door. But he didn't give much grace beyond that.

"Was she truly supposed to go to the Barringrey ball?" he demanded. "Or was that an excuse?"

"She was, but I hear she has a hideous migraine." He shot a wry look at Gabriel. "It seems to be catching."

His head did pound, but that always happened after he spoke with his mother. "Do you know where she is?"

"I assumed you did. Indeed, I was giving you the opportunity to increase the mirage that she is safely tucked in bed with a throbbing temple."

Damn it. He should have realized that. Instead, he slowed his steps even further. "So you know she's a midwife."

"I suspected, and you have now confirmed." Lord Nathaniel smiled. "I find it admirable."

"I find it dangerous."

"But surely that is manageable." He turned so that he studied the Gabriel's face closely. "You hate the very idea, don't you?"

"Don't be ridiculous. She births babies. That is to her credit. And it's bloody hard work."

"Then it is the wedding you object to. Surely you can see that Lord Benedict is the perfect solution for her. He approves of her actions, provided it is done safely. There is wealth enough to create an establishment for her. It is only the details that need arrangement, and you are unmatched in your ability to settle details."

He was usually, but in this, she had stymied him. "She runs off on her own. Has done, apparently, since she was young. She says she will allow me to manage things, but then disappears completely, no doubt delivering triplets to someone in the rookeries." They turned the corner enough that he could gesture back at his mother's home. "And my blasted parent knows something but will not share it! Not even if I promise to fix her blasted roof."

"Well as to that, your mother knows what all women know.

Childbirth is the one place where a man can do nothing. He has no influence, no sway, and no female has the least interest in obliging him."

"I am trying to help!"

"No, Gabriel. You are trying to manage. It's what you always do, and Lord Benedict found it incredibly useful during war. But London requires different skills."

"Logistics are the same the world over. Someone wants something, someone sells it. I'll find her a place to work, she'll obey or find herself restricted. Indeed, she has already agreed to it."

"Then why do you storm your mother's house and leave angry? She does not know where Miss Caddick is. She would have said. Madame Florina as well." He gripped Gabriel's arm and tugged him around. Gabe could have fought the motions, but he was at the end of his rope and would love an excuse to hit something, even Lord Nathaniel. "What is it you fear? Is she truly missing?"

"Her servants were much too casual for her to have disappeared. Things are running as usual for her which means she is off being a midwife somewhere."

"Then you do not fear for her safety."

"No more than usual."

"And yet you are as unmoored as I have ever seen you."

The man was much too perceptive. That was a good quality for a spy, but an incredibly useless one right now. "Point your nose somewhere else," he growled.

The man obliged. He held up his hands, turned to face ahead, and matched his pace with Gabriel's. Then he did what he did best. He remained silent while his prodigious brain worked through the possibilities. It wouldn't take him long to ferret out the truth—that Gabriel spent his nights dreaming about Janelle— and that was something he couldn't allow.

"I am frustrated with being kept out of the action," he lied. "Lord Benedict has made it clear that I am to remain here arranging the wedding and dancing attendance upon his future wife. I am a military man most comfortable in a war." He gestured vaguely to the city. "London life is not for me."

"The military has done a great deal for you. It gave you purpose, time to mature, and an obvious enemy. But we are no longer at war, Major."

"Napoleon will not go away so easily. And the diplomat's game is a good one."

"No, it's not. Not for you. You're an abysmal liar."

Gabriel snorted. "That is not true."

"You're an abysmal liar to one who knows how to see." He shook his head. "You're straightforward, loyal to a fault, and wouldn't dishonor yourself or anyone else without first slitting your own wrists." His steps slowed as he turned again to face Gabriel. "And you have the look of someone whose honor is strained to breaking."

"Don't be ridiculous. My duty has never been clearer."

"And that's the problem, isn't it? Oh Gabriel, there's only one thing that trumps your honor. It's love, isn't it? You're in love with someone you shouldn't be."

Gabriel tightened his stance until his back creaked from the effort. "This conversation is concluded," he snapped.

Lord Nathaniel snorted. "As if that makes the least bit of difference. I've called out the truth now. You won't hide from it because that's not in your nature. The question now is, which will win? Love or honor? With anybody else, I'd put my money on love. We all have stiff upper lips until our heart truly engages. Once that happens, we're lost." He grinned. "I should know. That was exactly the way with me."

"I do not care for one of your silly romantic tales."

He shook his head, blithely continuing as if Gabriel hadn't spoken. "But you, Major, are cut from a different cloth. You've learned, thanks to your dear old mum, that loving the wrong woman or the wrong way is a waste of time. So you gave your heart to the Crown and that was that. Until now."

"My heart is exactly where it's always been."

The man chuckled. "Abysmal liar." Then he held up his hands in surrender. "I'll stop pestering you. Sounds like you have a difficult choice ahead, and you're not one to sort it out with a friend."

No, he absolutely was not. But that didn't stop him from asking a question. "I think, mayhaps, you're talking more about yourself than me. I've never seen you lounge in my mother's drawing room before and certainly not with a ginger-haired girl more stupid than a lump of coal."

"I was waiting for you."

"No, you weren't. What ginger girl has you questioning your loyalties?" If their best spy among the upper crust had just adjusted his loyalties, then Lord Benedict needed to know. But in this, Nathaniel proved wilier than Gabriel. His smile was slow as his body shifted into a more predatory lean.

"Not a change in loyalties, my friend. Merely a very interesting little game. My wife wants to join me in this work, so we have set each other a task."

Gabriel grimaced. He knew Lady Rebecca had talent—she'd already proved as much—but he was always against putting women in danger. "What task? And is it connected to my mother?"

Nathaniel jolted. "What? No. At least not in the usual way." Then he grinned. "Never fear, Lord Benedict was the one who suggested the wager. We have his complete approval."

"That's not as reassuring as you think."

His friend's expression tightened. "I assure you, Rebecca is not at risk."

Which meant that Nate was. Two spies in one couple could be an enormous asset, but it also split loyalties. Did one serve the Crown? Or one's lady wife? It was clear that Nate had chosen his wife. But it was equally clear that Benedict wanted to use Lady Rebecca anyway.

And what could Gabriel say to that? Nothing except, "Be

careful. London can be a dangerous playground."

Nate's expression softened. "It's what she wants. And so I will do what I can to support her." Then he winked. "At least until she's pregnant. Then I shall do everything in my power to make her and my child happy safe at home."

That was the truest thing he'd ever heard the man say. And so he wished him well. "Go find your lady at the ball. And then—"

"I shall whisk her away to work on that babe." He lifted up his hand in a jaunty wave. "Good evening, Major."

The man didn't wait for a response but melted into the surrounding darkness as if he truly was a jaguar hunting through the urban jungle. Not for the first time, Gabriel wondered what would push an aristocratic man into the spy game. Something drove the man, and it was more than boredom and deeper than simple patriotism.

It was a puzzle for sure, but not one that Gabriel could solve tonight. He gave it a good try, though, because it kept him from facing his own problem. Unfortunately, Lord Nathaniel was correct. He'd named the question exactly, and once voiced, Gabriel had to answer.

Honor or love?

When faced with that choice, honor must always win. No one could truly love the dishonorable, so the question was moot. There was no way to choose love.

Right?

Right.

He shoved his hands in his pockets and trudged his way home.

Chapter Twenty-Five

I T WAS NEARLY a week before Janelle was strong enough to leave the house. Aside from needing to escape her bedroom, her aunt had become more insistent that they discuss wedding plans. The banns had been read once already. Two more weeks until the wedding and there was still a great deal to do.

Unfortunately, the first task was a fitting and there was no way to hide the bruises during that. She made sure they were in the back room of the dress shop, but she had to disrobe completely. The girl apprentice saw them first, then the seamstress. Their eyes darkened with pity and their mouths compressed into tight lines. Janelle knew this was coming. This wasn't the first time a servant of some kind had seen the blackish-green welts on her body. But it had been a while, and the shame hit her anew.

Especially when her aunt finally saw.

"Oh Janelle," Aunt Esmee moaned. "What did you do?"

What had she done? "I asked Papa about the details of the marriage settlement." She flinched as she straightened her shoulders, trying to force herself to be brave. This wasn't her shame. It was her father's.

"But why would you do that? That's not your concern."

The details of her own marriage weren't important? How was it that something so massive in her life was not her concern?

Her aunt stepped up to her. She held up a hand, nearly touching Janelle's back, but the mottled skin would not bear more weight and she flinched away. So Aunt Esmee touched her cheek instead. "It's best that you get out of the house. Your marriage can't come too soon."

"I've met someone else," Janelle blurted. She blinked as tears flooded her vision. "I love him."

"You can't love him. You've just met him."

"Don't tell me what I feel!" she snapped. It was all she'd been doing for the last week. So many feelings! Pain and rage were the least of it. She also felt powerless, vulnerable, and completely unequal to manage anything. She, who had the skills to bring life into the world, felt so inept that she lost herself to laudanum for nearly a week. She'd only come out now because her aunt had threatened to storm her bedroom and Nanny couldn't keep the woman away.

So she was here now with her mottled body covered in welts. And her aunt would not hear what she wanted to say.

"I. Love. Him." It was an act of defiance to say it aloud. It was also completely futile.

"Does he have a title? Money?"

"He is my choice."

"And you know exactly how much choice you have, which is to say none." With a sigh, her aunt gestured the modiste and girl away. "Bring us some tea and biscuits," she ordered. Then she gently helped Janelle pull on a silk chemise. "This is the cause of your migraines?"

Janelle stepped gingerly over to a chair and sat down. It hurt too much to lean back, but it was a relief to get off her feet. Her father had not broken any of her bones, and she was grateful. Not to him, of course, but to Mrs. Sundy who had helped her study the body and learn how to protect what was vital to defend during a beating.

Meanwhile, Aunt Esmee looked at her gently. "Tell me about this man. Does he have anything to recommend him over Lord Benedict?"

She noted that her aunt didn't ask the most important question. Did Major Vance love her? Her dreams of escape meant nothing if he would not have her. "He does not." Nothing except that she wanted him.

"Will you tell me his name?"

Janelle shook her head. There was no point in tarnishing his reputation. Not unless there was some hope of a solution.

"Oh Janelle, you know there is no possibility of changing course. Has Lord Benedict done something to give you a distaste of him?"

"Nothing except disappear." She looked up at her aunt. "Do you think I wanted to fall in love? Lord Benedict is kind and will give me everything I thought I wanted."

"Except now your heart has suddenly attached to something else, someone else."

"Yes."

"Do you not see how ridiculous that is? You are afraid of marriage, and well you should be. It's a mysterious future with a man who will control every aspect of your life. So you latch onto the nearest man and fall desperately in love. You know that is not how it works. Love takes time. It needs respect and space to grow." She paused as the modiste brought in the tea. Aunt Esmee poured it, then urged Janelle to take a sweet biscuit. "This panic has nothing to do with falling in love. It is about fearing the married state and that is something I completely understand."

Was that what she was doing? What she felt for Major Vance was so deep, so urgent. It overwhelmed her, and that was completely unlike her. She was never rash. She couldn't afford to be. And yet she had tumbled headlong into love barely two weeks after her engagement. That wasn't normal.

She sipped her tea and chewed at the edge of the sweet, her thoughts in turmoil.

"I was terrified of your uncle, you know," Aunt Esmee said, her voice and attitude casual. "The idea of the wedding night filled me with terror. I had heard such things. So many *unpleasant* things."

"I'm not afraid of that."

Her aunt's brows rose. "Really? That would be most unusual."

"Well," she hedged. "Maybe a little apprehensive." Her night with Gabriel had showed her that the experience could be pleasurable. That night, she had wanted all the things that a man does with a woman. But with Gabriel. It wouldn't be that way with Lord Benedict. Indeed, Gabriel had said exactly that.

"I was terrified," Aunt Esmee continued. "The week before my wedding, I imagined all sorts of ridiculous things. One day I thought I was dying of a fever. The next day, the butcher's boy smiled at me, and I thought he was my true love. You can't imagine the things that were rushing through my head all the time." Then her expression softened as she looked at Janelle. "Or maybe you can."

"I don't know," she said. Aunt Esmee had been a very silly girl, or so the family stories went. Marrying Uncle Jonathan had been the making of her. She'd settled down and grown into a very kind and capable lady of the *ton*. Janelle, on the other hand, had never been thought silly by anyone.

"Of course, you don't know. You're just a child. That's why you need to trust me. Now eat that sweet or I shall be tempted to steal it from you."

Janelle did as she was commanded. She even finished her tea which went down better than most of the food she'd managed this past week. Then she came to a decision.

"I shall write to Major Vance and see if he is available to walk with me tomorrow afternoon." She had to know if he felt the same as she did. If he didn't, then it was done, wasn't it? She would marry Lord Benedict knowing that she had tested the other path and found it blocked.

"That sounds like an excellent idea," her aunt said. "I've found him to be very level-headed. He will be able to reassure you as to Lord Benedict's true nature."

"The major has already been clear on that point. He has enormous respect for the man, and Lord Benedict clearly returns that esteem."

"Then it sounds as if you should spend more time with the major." Her aunt stood up. "But first, let's finish fitting your gown. You are going to be the most beautiful bride."

Janelle smiled and pushed up from her seat. But her aunt distracted her, and she forgot to moderate her movement. She twisted as she stood, and a shooting pain gripped her side. She gasped in reaction, the pain all that much worse. Had she broken a rib? Or was this the normal reaction to moving too fast? She pressed a hand to her side, trying to stem the tide of pain.

"Janelle!" Her aunt gripped her arm, holding her upright. "Should I call a doctor?"

What a question. There had been no doctor after she'd been beaten until her father couldn't raise his arms anymore. The secrecy was too important to him. If she'd died that night, it would've been named a mysterious ailment.

"Who would you call?" she said, her breath shallow.

Her aunt winced. "Well, there are discreet ones, I'm sure. But you probably don't want a man poking at you right now. Maybe what you really need is some laudanum."

Janelle waved that away. "I have had too much of that lately." She straightened slowly, holding her hand lightly to her side. It was easy because she was in her shift. "The swelling is down, the heat is lessened, and the pain is reduced. I am on the mend."

Her aunt smiled at her. "You have a gift for healing, Janelle. What a blessing."

Any other time she would have smiled and let it go, but she was in pain, and she was very tired of being dismissed like that. "It's not a gift, it's learning. I got books and studied them. Back in the country, I've set bones, treated fevers, and—"

"Stop! Stop!" Her aunt took a deep breath. "All of this is to your credit, of course, but you are a diplomat's fiancée now. You cannot talk about that anymore."

"Why not?" She forced herself to her full height. "Wealthy women don't need to be stupid."

"No, they need to be elegant and smart. An example of all that is refined. They can't be squatting in a pig farm tending some peasant with scurvy."

Scurvy was a sailor's affliction, not a farmer's, but she knew better than argue that point. "There needs to be a place where women can help each other," she said firmly. "A place for us to support one another, away from men. A way to get more than platitudes and laudanum."

"Well, maybe you can do that," her aunt said as she waved the modiste back into the room. "After you get married and have all Lord Benedict's money at your disposal."

Janelle nodded, already thinking through some of the particulars. It would take a great deal of money to do what she envisioned. A very great deal. She'd never have access to that if she married Major Vance. Even Lord Benedict's coffers might not be up to the task. But the idea had taken root, and she focused on it as much as possible while being poked with pins. It was a more productive use of her energy than pining for another night with Gabriel.

Indeed, it was in the forefront of her mind when she wrote to the major suggesting she was available tomorrow for a promenade in Hyde Park. She wanted to discuss the specifics of what Lord Benedict might allow her to spend and on what. It helped that her aunt suggested she rest this evening. No need to dance all night, Aunt Esmee said, when Janelle was already engaged.

Unable to stop from herself from exploring the idea, the question became part of her missive to Madame Florina. She told the woman that Betty was once again available to work and inquired after a shop location near the Rose Garden that had recently closed its doors.

And when her ideas became too grandiose, she was effectively distracted by a response from Madame Florina. The new apothecary would be pleased to meet her at My Lady's Apothecary. Could she come immediately?

Janelle read the missive with a sigh of relief. Work was the antidote to feeling lovelorn. A fruitful conversation with a good chemist was exactly what she needed to set her thoughts in order. It would be like having Mrs. Sundy back in her life.

Chapter Twenty-Six

THE OUTSIDE OF My Lady's Apothecary was simple wood. The only grandiose thing about it was the elaborate lettering of the name on the placard above the door. The hinges squeaked when she stepped in and a bell tinkled above her head. There was a table to her right with sparse wares, and a chair to her left that resembled something akin to a throne.

On it reclined an older woman in exquisite clothing whose face was all the more beautiful because of her icy disdain. She was not warm or welcoming, but her attitude made Janelle want to duck her head in deference to the higher title. Such had been ingrained in her from the beginning.

"My lady?" she inquired, wondering if this might indeed be the "lady" of My Lady's Apothecary.

The woman smiled by slow degrees, her teeth revealed in tiny bits while triumph burned in her expression.

Ah. She was not a titled lady. Only the social climbers showed such delight when someone mistakenly used the honorific. Janelle lifted her chin and straightened her knees. She need not bow before this woman.

The woman's eyes cooled, seeing the change. "So you don't know who I am." A statement, not a question.

"I was sent to speak with the Chinese chemist." She'd learned that much at least. Gossip that had finally filtered to her ears from Nanny as Janelle had laid in a laudanum daze. The owner of the apothecary was none other than the Chinese princess Yihui, now engaged to the future Duke of Fernbury.

"And so you shall. If I allow it." She regally inclined her head. "You may call me *The* Lady."

Well, that was certainly grandiose. Janelle reframed from rolling her eyes. It was clear if she wanted to talk to the Chinese princess, she had to go through this woman. So she spread her hands and smiled.

"What do you want?"

"So much," The Lady responded. "But let us begin with what you want." She rose slowly from her chair, every moment graceful in the most sensuous way. She was a seducer of men, that was for sure, but what did she want from Janelle? "You are a midwife, but what do you know of potions?"

"Enough to say that none help against childbed fever."

The Lady arched her brow, as if that were of little interest to her. "Anything else?"

"Like what?"

She waved her hand. "Love potions, creams to make the skin glow, sleeping draughts, poisons."

"Is that what is sold here?"

"Of course. And any other posset you might desire." She leaned forward until Janelle could smell the spice of her perfume. "So why does she need you?"

Another time, Janelle would have listed her skills. If she weren't still in pain, she might have offered to create a draught to prove she had some knowledge. Today was not that day.

"I can see that this will not work." She sketched the barest of curtsys. "I bid you good day."

"Truly? You want to leave this?" the woman said.

She pushed open a door in a wall that Janelle had thought was hard wood. Beyond it was a stillroom that caught her breath. Shelves were full of ingredients, all labeled in a shaky hand. There was dust on the top jars, cobwebs in the corners, but nothing could diminish the sheer possibility in the room. And better yet, there were two books, one left open to a recipe.

Janelle moved forward slowly. She wanted to inspect every aspect of the room, but the books were what drew her the most. She touched the heavy tomes, seeing that they were generations old, handed down from mother to daughter, healer to apprentice. She had seen other such books, none this old. Mrs. Sundy had one that recorded all her recipes for healing draughts. Janelle had one as well, much smaller than these, and every page was copied from Mrs. Sundy. None of her experiments had yielded steady results.

But these books would give her a place to start. They would show her things that others had tried before her. Her hands were shaking as she turned page after page. It would take time for her to decipher the words. The language appeared to be French or Italian, perhaps. Janelle had never been good with languages. But the newest pages had scribbles in English and in Chinese.

She was on her fifth page, her breath suspended as she tried to understand, when the woman slammed the book closed fast enough to catch Janelle's fingers. Janelle cried out, not from the pain, but from the possible harm to the book. Didn't this "lady" know how fragile some of the pages were?

"Be careful!" Janelle snapped. "They could tear!"

"Would you like to know what they say? In English?"

No point in denying it. "Yes."

"Would you like to study here? Learn from the woman who wrote them?" She leaned forward, her voice dropped to a throaty purr. "Learn the secrets from the Orient, perhaps?"

"Yes!"

"And what would you give up to remain here and learn?"

Everything, but she knew better than to say it. Instead, she looked pointedly about the room. It was clean with a decent amount of jars and the scent of strong tea, but there weren't any customers out front. It was hard to believe that the sensation of the Chinese princess had already faded. More likely, the lady had lost interest or was occupied with wedding plans. Either way, there was no one here who could teach her. At least not right now.

"The owner of the apothecary is not here," she said. "You have nothing to offer me."

The lady sniffed. "Madame Illie is here."

"Who is Madame Illie?" She'd heard the name before, perhaps. An old woman who hid in the back of a different apothecary shop. One run by a patronizing man. What was she doing here?

"She is right through there."

Janelle turned, annoyed with herself for not seeing the doorknob before now. It was on the far side of the room, and she quickly turned the handle only to gasp in surprise. She had expected a dark room on the opposite side. Perhaps a dimly lit fire with an old woman shivering next to the coals. Instead, she walked out into what was supposed to be an open courtyard. Instead, it was a massive garden—at least massive for London— complete with a narrow stone path that led to a central bench where an old woman sat with her face lifted to the sun.

She wasn't asleep because she turned the moment Janelle stepped through. Her hands and dress were dirty from working the garden, though it was hard to tell on a black gown. And her smile was warm beneath her bright brown eyes. Only the streak of gray from her left temple betrayed her age and the tremors as her head bobbed in an uneven tempo.

Janelle wasted no time as she moved along the path to greet the woman. "Madame Illie? I am Janelle Caddick, a midwife. I should very much like to speak with you."

Madame Ille smiled, nodding her head in acknowledgement. "Will you tend while we speak?" she asked, her voice strong enough to hear, but long since its prime.

"I will happily do as you instruct," she answered as she looked about her. "I have little knowledge of my own on how to tend a garden as magnificent as this."

The woman shrugged then waved Janelle off. "There are others who will be my hands here, then."

Janelle looked around. There was a slender woman in the shadows carrying a bucket of water. She carefully scooped water and dripped it along the farthest edge of the garden. Janelle narrowed her eyes to look closer. Perhaps the woman was Chinese, but she couldn't really tell.

"Is that Miss Wong? The Chinese princess?"

Madame Illie chuckled. "Yihui has been called away. Preparations for her wedding occupy her time. But she will be back soon. Wild horses would not keep that woman away."

A moment later, the unknown woman disappeared. That left them alone except for The Lady who watched from the doorway and Madame Illie who ambled slowly along the path, keeping her skirts from damaging young shoots. And when Janelle looked at her, Mme Illie spread her arms and lifted her powdered face to the sun.

"The Lady owns all of this," she said. "We rent this space, and Yihui brought me here to tend it." She waved absently at tiny windows above the store that indicated rooms. A few looked lived in, some were obviously empty. "We have rooms above for those who need it."

"Patients?" Janelle asked.

"Sometimes," The Lady answered as she stepped into the garden. "Mostly ladies from the Rose Garden who need a rest. They come here and garden for Madame Illie. They mix her potions too because her hands are so unsteady."

So that was the problem. Madam Illie needed help to set all that was possible here to rights. And The Lady needed someone—a young someone—to create inventory. And maybe bring in customers. It was likely that the Chinese princess brought in attention and possible customers, but she had other duties. No person had enough time to be a duchess and an effective apothecary. There weren't enough hours in a day.

"You could have a room upstairs," The Lady continued. "One for you, another for deliveries."

It took her a moment to realize she meant delivering babies, not packages of linens or the like.

The Lady smiled at her, the expression oily. "Think of things you could learn here. Think of women who could deliver safely thanks to your able hands."

She didn't want to consider it. This woman, whomever she was, likely took her due in all sorts of uncomfortable ways. If Janelle had to guess, The Lady would expect free services, a portion of all sales, and a bit of worship every time she wandered through, disrupting things. And yet, the possibilities were hard to deny.

There was unused space here. Such space! "What is done here now?"

"Not enough," The Lady huffed, then her words turned sweet again. "You could learn how to make potions, find a girl who will learn beside you and can sell things for a pretty penny."

"Why don't you have one now?"

"Because she will not train them. She finds them too stupid." There was anger in The Lady's voice.

"I have just escaped one stupid son-in-law. I will not trade him for stupid apprentices," Madame Illie said. Then she trained her attention back on Janelle. "I have heard much of Betty Gill. Nothing of you."

"That will take some explaining," Janelle said as she settled onto the bench beside the older woman. "Will you listen?"

"I will," the woman answered. And so began the most casual of conversations, as if over a pot of tea. Janelle hadn't spent so pleasant at time since she'd been back in Mrs. Sundy's home on a cold winter evening. Janelle told stories of what she'd done and answered when Madame Illie asked about her recipes, her mixtures, and her choices in one tale or another.

She was being tested, but in this, she had no fear. She knew what she was about, and so too did Madame Illie. Before long, they were discussing ingredient mixtures, the benefits of boiling against a low simmer, and the herbs that make the worst medicines taste less vile. Janelle could have sat there for hours, but her body ached and The Lady grew irritable. Indeed, Janelle could not believe the woman had been patient enough to wait for an hour, much less close to three.

But in this she erred. It appeared "The Lady" had the patience of a saint when she was baiting the hook. Madame Illie had just invited Janelle to discuss the books and her best recipes when The Lady pounced. She was reclining negligently against the wall, her gaze languid as she sipped from a glass of wine she'd found somewhere. But when Madame Illie rose, so did The Lady.

She smiled, straightened, then neatly blocked the path to the stillroom.

"Betty Gill could make a good life here. She could train others to do as she does. She could learn and help countless women in London. There's room here to grow. It only takes strong arms and a willing heart."

"How many free rooms after you, me, and Madame Illie?"

The lady didn't answer, but Madame did. "Two."

"Who works the gardens? Who minds the till?"

"Hire whomever you like."

And pay for it from her till, no doubt. "What is your part in this?" she asked The Lady.

"My usual fee."

Madame Ilie answered. "Free potions—"

"Ones that work," the lady groused.

Madame Illie shrugged. "They work as they are meant to. I cannot help it if you want the Fountain of Youth."

"And half the profits," The Lady added. "It's that or rent. I am being extraordinarily generous."

That might be true. Janelle didn't know anything about the costs of living in London. But she did know potential. She knew there was a great deal that she could do here. More than ever before.

"What is the price?" she said, her voice hard.

"I have already told you," the lady answered.

"No, you haven't." She returned to her first question. "What do you want?"

The woman folded her arms across her chest. "Never speak

again to my son."

Janelle threw up her hands. "Who is your son?"

The woman's mouth compressed tight, but she still forced out the words as if she were spitting poison. "Major Gabriel Vance."

The words hit Janelle like a blow. She should have expected it. An offer like this—coming out of the blue—had to be tied to him somehow. But she hadn't expected it to be at the cost of her relationship with him.

"So you are Triana Sabate," she said. Former mistress to the Duke of Torbay, courtesan, demi-rep, and all sorts of scandalous labels, wrapped up in a beautiful package. Janelle cared nothing for the wrapping, but clearly the woman did, even to the point of naming this place she owned *My Lady's Apothecary*. "Why would you want me to stay away from your son? I am no threat to him."

"He has no need to poke his nose into my business," she stated. Then she waved at the entire building and courtyard garden. "This is my business."

One of them at least. Janelle rocked back on her heels, her gaze taking in the environment, seeing what existed now and what she could do with it. Still, she kept her voice hard as she spoke. "I am to marry Lord Benedict. The major is his primary secretary, his aide-de-camp, and I don't know what else. I will see Major Vance whenever my husband deems it appropriate."

"Cry off. Leave your horrible father. Come here. Live and study *here*." The woman's expression turned almost ecstatic. "Serve the people who need you and forget the men who abuse you."

One week ago, she would have said yes without hesitation. She knew some of the worst that men could do. Why should she help them when they thwarted her at every turn? But Lord Benedict sought to do good in this world. Gabriel, too, since he was working night and day to find her a location just like this.

"Sell this to me," she said. "Let me make it what it should be.

"Why would I?" the lady scoffed. "This is my retirement. I

don't want to go off to Italy or some foreign clime. This is my home when I no longer care to please a man."

When she couldn't entice a man to support her. Still, it wasn't a bad choice. Indeed, it was forward thinking of her to plan for it. Janelle stepped around the garden, picking her way to the opposite side building, seeing the small gate that led out to…was that the Rose Garden?

"How much of this area do you own?"

The lady grinned. "More every day."

So she was one to acquire, not sell. Janelle turned back to her. "I will work with Madame Illie. I will manage the shop and see to the hiring of workers." It shouldn't be much different than managing a household, or so she hoped. "But you will not dictate to me the details of my marriage." She shrugged. "And why would you want to? I would think your son would want to know that you have attended to your future."

"My son prays for the day I die!" she abruptly bellowed. It was a dramatic statement, but one that did not find its mark in either Janelle or Madame Illie.

The old lady dropped back onto the bench with a sigh. Apparently, this was a tirade she was used to. And Janelle was well used to the explosions of overwrought men and women. She took them in stride, merely arching her brow at the courtesan.

"Do you think I don't know?" Triana continued, stepping closer and closer as if stalking Janelle. "I see the way he sneers at me. I know what he thinks of me and my business. He only comes around when he needs something from me. I should have smothered him the day he was born."

That was quite a lot of venom from a mother to her child. Poor Gabe. How did he stand it? "What have I to do with that?"

"You cannot be part of them if you want part of this. I have straddled that line for years, and I tell you, it kills your heart and your mind. This is where we thrive, away from their greedy fingers and casual brutality. This place is for us. Let the world of men burn."

She meant this place was for her, free of all the men she had used and abused. But also free of their crimes.

Janelle acknowledged the appeal. How many times had she wanted a place just like this, free of her father and the restraints he put upon her? Her body still ached from his beating. But she couldn't lump Lord Benedict or Gabriel in their mix. Nor could she abandon them. Her desire to continue with her marriage was so that she could be with Gabriel, not leave him entirely.

So she turned and pressed a kiss to Madame Illie's hands. "I hope I can see you again. I would very much like to speak more with you. And the duchess."

The lady patted her cheek and smiled. She didn't speak. They both knew Triana ordered the details of her life.

"You are giving this up?" Triana gasped. "Everything you dreamed, everything you've ever wanted?"

"Yes," she said firmly. "Because it's not quite *everything*." And that was a surprise. She would not give up love, even at the price of her dreams. Never would she have expected that. She had spent so long dreaming of a location such as this, but one threat to Gabriel and she walked away with her head held high.

Now she had to see if Gabriel would risk it all for her.

Chapter Twenty-Seven

THAT NIGHT, JANELLE made a thousand plans—one might also say "fantasies"—on how to bring Gabriel around to her way of thinking. In the end, she decided to simply be honest with him. Unfortunately, someone else needed to see her first.

Madame Florina sent a message requesting Betty's help immediately. Excellent. A happy birth was just what she needed to pick up her spirits. She made it to the Rose Garden in record time only to discover that a happy birth could also be excessively depressing.

A pregnant shopgirl was married to a footman. They couldn't afford the lying-in hospital, so they arrived at the Rose Garden together. He carried her up the stairs, held her hand when she screamed, and refused to be thrown out of the room to boil water or fetch rags or whatever else was suggested. The girl held his hand, buried her face in his chest, then screamed loud enough that his whole body seemed to shake with the force of it.

"No more screaming," Janelle chided as she wiped the sweat from her eyes. Was that sweat or was the roof leaking? "Hold in the scream and put it into your push."

"That's the way," the footman said as he settled his wife against his chest. "I'll hold you up. You just push." And he did hold her in every way she needed—holding her up behind her back and gripping her hands. If it were possible for a couple to birth a child together, this would be the way to do it.

"Push now!" Janelle commanded as the contraction began.

"Baby's head is visible!"

And that was definitely not sweat dripping down her face. The roof was leaking, but it was too late to adjust position, so Janelle shifted so that the drips fell upon her and not the child.

"Once more. Big push."

And then it was done. A baby girl slid out, already wailing at the indignity. She was perfectly shaped, had a smattering of hair, and a set of lungs that would serve her well.

"A girl," Janelle cried. "A strong, healthy girl."

The mother and father laughed as if with one breath. Together they reached for the child, though Janelle was too busy to fully see it. She cut the cord, wiped the worst of the mess away, then wrapped the babe in a towel. Only then did she carefully pass the child over.

Then she sat back on her stool and watched. Love flowed everywhere in the room. Normally the connection was between mother and child. Janelle usually focused on the amazement and adoration on the mother's face. But in this, the mother and father were one. They both held the child, they both gazed with awe, and though the babe did nothing but blink in confusion, the two were united in their absolute devotion to their child and to one another.

Love.

It made her heart ache with longing.

Even worse, when she looked away, she saw the major with his coat off, his forehead slicked with sweat (it really was hot in this room), and a wet rag held above her head as he caught the drips that would have landed on her shoulder.

Good God, how long had he been there? He caught her surprised look and his expression challenged her to deny him. This was not a place for men, and yet two were here, fitting in seamlessly.

It put her off her game to have him standing there, so solid, so adamant as he caught raindrops before they landed on her head. It was the first she'd seen him in more than a week, and her heart swelled at the sight. It took everything in her to not leap into his arms. But she forced herself to sit still while she drank in his rugged, handsome face.

"You needn't do that," she finally managed, referring to the rag he held above her head. "I've experienced worse."

"Won't be much longer," he returned. "Rain stopped twenty minutes ago. This is just the runoff."

"And a leaky roof."

"That as well."

It wasn't scintillating conversation, but it showed an ease she had with no one else. He would stand above her, protecting her from everything including the rain. And she would allow it because she valued his help in all ways.

Her throat dried as she looked at his face. His left shoulder was catching the drips from another leak, and his back no doubt caught even more. Such was his size that she was completely dry. She wanted to say something, voice her thanks, laugh at the silliness of a man trying to catch raindrops, or simply smile in welcome. She never got the chance as Madame Florina stuck her face in.

"Almost done 'ere? You got another, jes' coming up the stairs."

The major turned his head. "A lower room, Madame. Your roof is more like a sieve."

"Them rooms are for the customers. Don't want drips on their backside."

"I don't care. There's payment here, too. Put the next mother in a dry room."

Mothers gave Madame Florina a shilling whenever they delivered here. They deserved a good room, too. The problem was that the whorehouse customers didn't like to hear the screaming, and frankly, she couldn't blame them.

Madame Florina and the major commenced a stare down. Janelle didn't watch. Contractions were beginning for the afterbirth. Besides, she already knew Gabriel would win. Indeed, a few moments later, she heard Madame Florina flounce away with a huff.

"The lower rooms have windows, too," Gabriel said beside her ear. "You need a room where the air moves, even when it's raining."

Amen to that.

She focused on the task at hand, doing the work she felt blessed to do. And when the worst of the mess was over, she received another surprise.

"I found you a helper," Gabriel said.

She frowned as she turned to him. "What?" He was all the helper she needed right now. Then she saw Polta grin at her from the door.

"'Ello, mum," the girl said with a quick curtsey. "The next mother's got a few minutes yet afore she needs you. I can finish up here if you like, then join you when it's done."

"Polta, have you come to take me up on my offer then?"

"The major and me have come to an arrangement. I'm here to be yer regular girl."

"You have, have you?"

Gabriel nodded solemnly. "She drives a hard bargain, but yes. She's to be your apprentice, if you want her."

She did. She'd already seen the child's worth. The girl had a look in her eye that reminded Janelle of herself at that age. "Go with the major to see that the other mother is settled right." She looked back at the new family before her, her heart squeezing again at the sight. "I'll finish up here."

"I'm not leaving you," Gabriel said. "We've got things to discuss."

A shiver slid down her spine at his low tone. It had nothing to do with his words and everything to do with the sound of his voice, the intimacy of his nearness, and the sight of a husband and wife cuddled together with their child. What would she give to have that with Gabriel?

"I'm fine—"

"I'm not leaving," he repeated. Fortunately, Polta had it well in hand.

"I'll see that it's done right," she said as headed back down the corridor.

Janelle nodded, her attention split between the work she was doing and Gabriel at her back. "This is not the place for you. I'm perfectly safe."

"I'm not worried about your safety," he said. "I'm worried you'll disappear again." There was a growl in his voice that betrayed his annoyance. "Just how many babies have you delivered in the last week?"

She tightened, unsure whether to be pleased or disappointed that he thought she'd been running around working after she'd already said she'd keep him apprised.

"You found me tonight," she said, her tone neutral.

"Because I've paid and threatened Madame Florina if she didn't tell me. Do I want to know what you've been doing?"

"No." Easiest question to answer. "Now be quiet. I'm busy."

He remained silent, helping when asked and catching drips when he wasn't. In time, she finished with this couple and went on to the next. Sadly, the next mother was not in the same loving situation. A maid with no husband. Her eyes were haunted even as she moaned. She wanted nothing to do with having Gabriel there, and so he was banished to the hallway. Janelle heard him asking Madame Florina about the girl's particulars. He'd find out if there was any way she could be helped. But in meantime, Janelle's attention was all on the coming birth.

She relaxed into that work, fully satisfied that Gabriel would manage everything else.

She was almost right.

Chapter Twenty-Eight

THE HOURS SLID by. Gabriel kept his ear peeled to the sound of Janelle's calm voice over the cries of pain. He watched the men who bumbled their way into nearby rooms, making sure that none came close. And he thought about the way Janelle had looked as she held the newborn babe. Satisfaction filled her expression and a tenderness that pulled at his gut.

He'd also caught that she didn't press into her spine as usual when she stood up. Instead, her hands hovered near her low back but didn't connect. He'd seen her wince a few times as well, and her movements weren't as fluid as normal.

She was hurt.

He boiled with fury at the realization. Not only had she been hurt, but he hadn't been there to protect her, and that was a dereliction of duty that cut down to his soul.

There was nothing he could do about it as she worked. He knew that nothing short of being knocked unconscious would take her away from delivering that baby. So he waited, worried, and plotted. He had an idea, but there were several million details to sort out first.

The child was born three hours later. It was another hour to finish up and a bit more to check on the happy family on the third floor. They didn't even care that the roof still dripped on their heads. Then finally, Janelle dismissed Polta, which gave him a chance to catch her hand and pull her away.

"I've got something to discuss with you," he said.

"Not tonight," she said, her expression filled with real regret. "I ache."

His gut tightened. He knew she'd routinely delivered two babies in a night, sometimes three. Her pain came from something else, and he was determined to find out what.

"I've got a bath set up for you."

She looked at him, momentarily still. "No," she finally said. "I'll do it at home."

"Because you're hiding bruises? What happened?"

Her eyes widened and she took a step back. He let her go but would not allow her to run away. He should have known better. She was not a runner. She lifted her chin and faced him eye to eye.

"Would you marry me?" She blurted the words out, and then she gasped and pressed her palms to her mouth. Clearly, she hadn't thought the question through, but then a moment later, her hands slid away. Her chin remained firm and her gaze steady. "If I cried off from Lord Benedict, would you…could we wed?"

His breath was frozen in his chest. The calm of absolute terror held him in place, and he couldn't react, couldn't speak. It was as though a goddess stood before him and offered him everything he'd ever dreamed of. A good wife, a family built on love, all the things that made life worthwhile.

He needed to say something, do something, but every part of him was trapped between yearning and fear, desire and despair. And with every second that passed, the sparkle in her eyes dimmed.

She thought he didn't want her. He saw her eyes darken with pain, but he didn't know how to explain. Never in his life had he been offered something so precious. But never in his life had his gains come free. Or even cheap.

Finally, he choked out words. They were the least of his thoughts, but all he could manage.

"You are not mine."

"I can see that."

This time he did touch her. He caught her fingers and tried to entwine his with hers. "You know I want you."

"Do I? Do you?"

Good God, was she blind? Even now he burned for her. He sighed and tugged her down the hall. "Your usual room is ready and the water for a bath is hot. Please let us talk there."

"It's not love then," she said, her voice so raspy he knew she fought tears.

"It is love," he returned, unable to lie. "I cannot give you what you want most."

"And what's that?"

"This," he said, gesturing to the room behind them. "The work, the babies. There is a way to do this, but only with Lord Benedict's money."

"What if I want babies of my own—"

"You can—"

"—and a man who holds my hand when I birth them?"

"I will."

She looked at him. "You won't. You've just said as much." There was accusation in her tone, a betrayal that he understood, and yet it still infuriated him.

"Do you think this is easy for me? You offer me everything I want. You, a woman of merit beyond compare."

"Merit?" she mocked. "Beyond compare? You sound like you're quoting a gothic novel."

"And you are being a child who believes fairy tales," he shot back. He grasped her face. He tilted her head with one hand and pressed his mouth to hers. There was little room in this narrow corridor, and he took up all the space as he captured her with his kiss. She softened into him, her hand wrapping around his waist as she pulled him closer. She opened, and he plundered her mouth, owning this part of her in the only way he knew how.

Her body fell into him, and then abruptly stiffened. He heard her whimper in pain, a quiet sound she clearly tried to silence. He pulled back, his eyes wide and his breath rasping in his throat.

"What happened, Janelle? How are you hurt?"

She sighed, looking weary to the point of breaking. "It doesn't matter," she said, her voice dull. "It won't ever happen again."

That was not an acceptable answer, but he had no power to force an explanation. So he focused on this moment and what he could do now.

"Do I carry you? Or do you walk?"

Her chin lifted in defiance, but it didn't last. Soon, her expression fell into despair. Tears welled up and she closed her eyes while he brushed them away with his thumbs.

"I am not the man you want," he said.

"No," she agreed. "You're an idiot."

He chuckled. "I am that, too. Come."

He drew her down the hall to her bath. It was a back room on the third floor, but one that was serviced by an outside stair. He'd made sure the fire was lit and the water hot. And as he locked the door behind them, he cupped her face again.

"Let me take care of you tonight."

"And what of you? Who will ever have you if you run every time a woman loves you?"

He sniffed, insulted. "I never run."

"Do I believe your words or how you kiss me? Do I hear the sounds from your mouth or see the adoration in your eyes?" She jerked her head at the bath. "The things you do for me?"

He didn't answer except to pull at the buttons of her gown. She had already given her leather apron to Polta. "Let me see what happened," he coaxed.

"Not until you tell me the truth." She gripped his jaw and pulled his gaze up to her face. "Do you love me?"

How fierce she was! He loved the strength of her, the determination to fight for what she wanted, no matter the reality of the world. She was a woman who lived two completely different lives, and she did them both with grace. Never could he imagine a woman he'd adore more. He wanted to shelter her, ease her, support her...spend his life in service to her.

"Gabriel!" she snapped. "You will answer."

"Yes," he said. "A thousand times yes."

"Then marry me. We can find a way—"

He stopped her words with a kiss. He stroked away every impossible thought before it was uttered. Because he already knew that they were unreachable dreams. After all, he'd spent the last week mulling over possibilities that could not come to pass.

"Gabriel," she gasped as she pushed back from him. "Listen."

"Will you give up midwifing for me?"

She frowned. "What?"

"Do you give up your work to be with me?"

"We will need coin somehow. I can help with that. Midwives are usually paid."

"But would you give up your work for me?"

She shook her head. "Why would you ask that of me?"

"Because I would have to give up my employment with Lord Benedict to marry you." He swallowed. "Do you think I serve him for no reason? Do you think the war against Napoleon means nothing to me?"

She frowned. "Of course, your work is important. As is mine. But he will not dismiss you. You are too good at what you do for him."

Possibly, but not likely. "The embarrassment would be severe. And though he might forgive us, the world would not. He cannot appear strong before kings while his manservant whisks away his fiancée right under his nose."

She frowned. She hadn't considered that, but he had. He had worked and worried the thought in his mind until he saw no way out.

"It's not just the money," he said. "Benedict is an earl and a diplomat. I would find no other work after I betrayed him. No one would risk favoring me over him."

"Babies are born everywhere. We could go—"

"Away from your family? Your aunt loves you. Your brother adores you. I know you have feelings for them."

She winced. "They could come see us."

"They would damn us as fools, and I wouldn't blame them." He stepped forward, knowing he had to end this discussion the same way he had ended all his tortured fantasies. "What do you think of this building?"

"What?"

"I think we can buy it."

"What!"

"I have found a better building to house the Rose Garden. My mother will sell. She hates how much work this place needs. The new place is better suited for a whorehouse anyway."

"And what would I do with this?"

"Repair it. It used to be a foundling home anyway. Already women come here to find you. The gypsies sell potions here. There's a storefront on the east side."

"I know it. It used to sell ribbons and ropes."

Ropes were the least of the items. There was a man who made toys of all sorts for use upstairs, but he was too old to work now. His hands cramped and lacked strength, and so he would sell the shop to them. Gabriel knew because he'd already talked with the man.

"You could set up an apothecary there. It will work much better than your kitchen stillroom."

He saw the idea take hold. Her eyes widened and her gaze grew abstract as she sorted through possibilities. Then she shook her head. "Your mother will not sell."

"What? Of course—"

"I met her yesterday. Do you know the apothecary shop to the west?"

"The place the Chinese princess owns."

"Your mother owns it. The princess rents it. Indeed, I think she has acquired the whole block."

"What!"

"She offered to give Betty a place there—"

"She never gives anything away."

Janelle nodded. "All on the condition that I throw over Benedict, become Betty entirely, and never speak to you again." Her expression darkened. "Why does she hate you so?"

So many reasons and none at all. "Because I don't dote on her."

"She's your mother. Shouldn't she dote on you?"

He wrapped her in his arms, holding her close while emotions rolled through him. "You will make a wonderful mother."

She settled against him, but a second later, she shoved him back. "I told her no."

"Of course, you did. You have more resources as Benedict's wife."

"No, you idiot! Because of you." She gave a self-mocking shrug. "I found something I want more than Betty's dreams." She pressed a hand to his heart. "You."

What could he say to that? How could he deny a woman whose heart was in her eyes as she gave herself to him? Not in body, but in soul. He wanted to give her everything.

"You don't need her to get your dreams." He lifted her hand to his lips and pressed a kiss there. "You don't need to choose between Betty and Janelle. You don't have to compromise anything ever again."

He waited a moment while she absorbed that. He held his breath while her lips curved into a tentative smile. He saw her growing excitement as she pressed her fingers to her mouth.

"You really think it is possible." A statement, not a question.

"Not if you marry me."

She jolted as if slapped. "Gabriel—"

"Only if you marry Lord Benedict. His money can get you that, not mine. His resources would allow you to build what you want and to hell with my mother. No one would ask twice. Many wealthy women have favorite charities. You could be the patroness of—"

"A place for women."

"Yes." But not with him. At least not as his wife.

He saw the knowledge sink into her body. As much as she trembled with excitement, a weight pulled at her shoulders and drained the strength from her knees. He saw it coming and was there to support her, but she didn't reach for him. Instead, she crumpled slowly to the floor, sinking down until tears slid down her cheeks.

He met her there, knee to knee. "You can have that," he said. "I can see it done. But only if I give you up."

"No," she murmured.

"Yes. But this—" He pressed his mouth to hers. He kissed her quickly, then slowly, until neither of them could breathe. "This must stop. I will not dishonor you or Lord Benedict." Or himself. His honor was all that he had left, and he would not forswear it even for her. Especially for her, because he would not give Lord Benedict any reason to toss her aside.

"I don't need all this," she said. "Not really. I haven't had it before. I don't need—"

"You would destroy your own dreams, and for what?"

"You. Haven't I just said that to your mother?" She looked into his eyes. "I would give it all up for you."

He could see she meant it. He could see the love in her eyes and feel the promise in her touch. She would give it all up for him. How she humbled him. He was so unworthy of her.

"We cannot," he said. "You will lose too much."

"I will gain more," she said. It was a lie. She would gain nothing, and so he ended it in the clearest way he could.

"I will not do it." He pulled her hands from his face. "I will not marry you, Janelle. I swear it. You will never be my wife."

Chapter Twenty-Nine

THE LAST OF her strength left her. Janelle had never failed at anything she worked for. She might have to sneak around to accomplish it. She had hidden books and studied in the dark. She had taught herself to lie and found people who would help her deceive her family. And she had, bit by bit, created a life in two worlds.

It was hard, this dual existence. She'd appeared at parties right after delivering a baby. She'd spoken polite nonsense while her heart was still aching from a stillborn birth. And she'd been pleased as punch at never losing a mother to childbed fever, and yet she'd never told a soul about the accomplishment.

Then she'd met Major Vance, and her life began to unravel. Because of him, she had to choose what she wanted when she was so used to having it all.

With him, she could be Betty alone. No need to live up to some society image of an aristocrat. She could be with him as his wife. He would keep her safe as she worked. Together, they could provide for the mothers of London because she knew he shared her vision.

Or she thought he did. Just as she thought he loved her.

I will not marry you.

Never had she thought she would be the one to propose. Never had she imagined she would lay her heart bare to a man only to have him refuse her. And yet she had done it, and he had said no. Indeed, he had refused her while her bodice lay half undone by his hands. He had said it after demanding he see the bruises on her body and kissing her until she lay willing in his arms.

I will not marry you.

He didn't say anything more, for which she was grateful. He seemed to understand that another word from him would break her, and she was already trembling with the struggle to suppress her sobs. Instead, he knelt on the floor beside her. He was across from her, his hands gentle on her arms and his temple pressed against hers. They were so close that they breathed as one. She might even think he wept, though she could not see for certain.

She stayed there on the floor, and he with her, while exhaustion overwhelmed her. Too tired to fight, too weary to feel. She sat there and breathed because it was all she could do. And he waited in silence with her.

Eventually, the silence ended. In time, she grew tired of her own anguish. She was not one to remain defeated, even in love, but she also needed to hear it one last time.

"You want me to marry Lord Benedict?"

"Yes."

"And what of my love for you?"

A pause, then words spoken firmly though his voice broke in the middle. "I am grateful," he said. "It will sustain me for the rest of my days."

"Even if I hate you tomorrow? Even if I curse you with every breath I take?"

"Even so."

She let his words sink in. She understood that even if he did love her, he would not admit it. He had weighed the options of their future, marked what was and wasn't possible for them, and decided on the best course.

She lifted her gaze to look at him. Her next words came out without conscious thought. "Will you be my lover?" If she couldn't have him for life, perhaps she could have a piece of him now. Something.

Desire sparked in his eyes. "I ache for you, Janelle. I have thought of little else since the day we met."

She heard the refusal in his tone, so she voiced his objection before he could. "But your honor will not allow it."

Hurt flashed in his eyes. "You are another man's wife."

"Not yet."

"Soon enough."

"There is no love between me and him."

"But there is between me and him. Would you have me throw away all my self-respect?"

Her heart squeezed as she tumbled even further into love. "No," she whispered. "I love your honor. I love your strength. You have far more than I."

"Not true," he said as she pushed herself upright. He matched her movements, his gaze searching her face. "You are—"

"Shut up," she rasped. "Just shut up. I don't want to talk anymore." She closed her eyes as she pulled out the pins in her hair. "I need a bath."

He stood up and threw more coals on the fire. The heat would be welcome. There was a screen behind which she could remove her clothes. She made her way to that now. Easy enough to strip off her dress, stays, and shift. These were Betty's clothes and would be cleaned by Madame Florina. And here, she saw that Gabriel had thought of everything. Folded in a neat pile atop a travel bag were Janelle's clothing for afterwards.

But for right now, she was neither Betty nor Janelle. Neither married nor single. She was simply herself seeking a hot bath after a long day.

She knew he was in the room and part of her wanted to hurt him. Let him see the woman he refused. Let the sight of her naked body fill his lonely nights the way she dreamt of him.

But in this she erred. She was so used to her bruises that she had forgotten they were even there. Certainly, her body ached, but it often ached and the pain from her beating had passed. All that was left were the black and green marks on her back because she had curled tight to protect her face and belly.

So she forgot, and he saw when she stepped into her bath.

She heard his gasp and felt a flash of embarrassment. She was not an immodest person, but she regularly saw women's bodies at the extreme of endurance. She thought of her own form as functional more than an object of beauty or titillation. But now she hunched, thinking she had been too bold.

But then he was at her side, his large hand skimming the edge of her back.

"Who did this?" he rasped.

God, she was an idiot. How could she forget? "It's over," she said as she pulled away from him and sank into the bath. "Go away."

The water felt good. It was hot and cleansing. She wanted nothing more than to relax back into the peace of it. But even as he let her sink into the bath, his eyes scoured her body, no doubt seeing every blemish, ripple, and scar.

She closed her arms down tight and let her head drop forward to hide behind her hair. "Go away Gabriel. I am fine."

"Who did it?" he demanded.

"My father." No reason to protect the man. It was a parent's right to beat his children.

"I will kill him."

She lifted her chin, flicking back her hair to stare at him. "He will not touch me again so long as I marry Lord Benedict."

She saw his face strain under violent emotions. His hands were fists planted on the side of the tub. "You tried to end the engagement?"

She shrugged. She hadn't gotten far enough to suggest it before her father had turned his rage on her, but that had been her intention.

"He has beaten you before?"

She shot him a wry expression. "Not often. Certainly not to excess, by most men's standards."

"Not mine," he said, and the violence in his tone soothed her.

She didn't want him to beat her father. Not really. But the idea that he wanted to made her smile.

"Thank you," she said softly.

"Only the weakest kind of man beats a woman."

She didn't argue.

"He will never touch you again. I vow it!"

She forced herself to uncurl. She allowed herself to rest back against the side of the tub knowing that he could see her breasts and belly, her mons and every curve of her body. Because of the light, it would be in shadow, but if he looked, he would see.

"I told you," she said. "He won't touch me again now that you have refused me. I will marry Lord Benedict as arranged. I will honor my marriage vows, and I will use his money to build a place for women." She closed her eyes as she envisioned it. "I will be a countess," she murmured. "People will call me, my lady. And my house for women shall be called My Lady's Birthing Place or My Lady's Hospital." She grimaced. "That doesn't sound right. Too grandiose. It needs to be something quiet, so no one will notice it. Something the women know but the men will ignore. My Lady's…"

"Apothecary."

She opened her eyes. "That is her place. I will not meet your mother's terms. She will not dictate to me who I will and will not have in my life."

He nodded, and yet she saw determination in his eyes. He would find a way to give it to her. She should tell him to forget it. She had no desire for either of them to say one more word to his mother. But she was also angry with him, and so she held her tongue.

She looked at him, her body relaxing in the water, her mind steadfastly refusing to give in to the emotions churning between them. She would not acknowledge the violence of her father's beating. It was a thing of the past. She would not address Gabriel's rejection. He had given his answer, and she would not beg him to change his mind. Her mind was fixed upon the future, and what she wanted to build.

"You really think I can have it. A place to treat all women with respect. A place for good medicines and healthy births."

He tried twice before he answered. On the third try, he nodded. "I will see it done."

Of course, he would. Logistics weren't exciting, but they were the hallmark of any successful endeavor. And Gabriel managed those better than anyone. Hadn't her fiancé said as much?

"Thank you," she said.

He broke at that. He gasped as his body convulsed. He gripped her hands and pulled them to his mouth.

"Gabriel?"

"Do not thank me," he said. "Do. Not."

It was then she realized that as much pain as she was in, he experienced an equal share. He wanted her. She knew that. And he was denying himself. The reasons didn't matter anymore. The decision had been made, and he grieved as much as she.

She curled her arms around him, wetting his shirt, and letting their tears mingle cheek to cheek. "Come into the bath with me," she murmured. "I will not ask for love. I do not even ask for more than your flesh against mine. For a little bit."

He shook his head. "I will not risk it. You do not know how much you tempt me."

"As much as you tempt me," she said. "But in this, we will both be strong. And weak." She didn't know what she was saying. It was all jumbled about in her head.

"Let me bathe you," he begged as he lifted his eyes to hers. "Let me…please."

She smiled, though the effort brought tears to her eyes. "Of course." Then she kissed him. She put all her love, all her wishes, and even her most precious dreams into that kiss. As their lips touched, her mind's eye handed him everything she wanted, knowing he would keep her desires safe.

She gave him the image of his strength behind her as she

strained, and their child held between them in the aftermath. She poured into him the whisper of their children grown and the sight of him walking their daughter down the aisle or meeting their son on equal ground as adults. And when she broke the kiss, she knew their tears had mingled. He'd felt what she passed to him. And he'd accepted it while his eyes dripped with loss.

"Gabriel," she began, but he shook his head.

"Shh. Just let me soothe you."

She nodded, and at his urging, she leaned back in the bath. He gathered a washcloth and stroked it over her body. Such attention to every inch of her, peppered with kisses, infused with caresses, and finished with a climax that had her crying out while the water sloshed around her.

Then before she could object, he scooped her out of the water. He set her on a rug before the fire and kissed her as he had the time before. His mouth between her thighs, his shoulders so wide as he braced her legs apart. He gave her such pleasure that she could not contain it and her cries echoed in the room.

But then it was her turn. Completely naked, she sat before him and demanded his clothing. "We will share this now, Gabriel. Or I will never speak with you again. I swear it."

She already knew the pulse and thrust of his organ. It lay thick and hot beneath his clothes. He removed his shirt first while her gaze roved hungrily over his torso. She noted every bulge of muscle and ripple of scar.

"I am going to kiss you everywhere, Gabriel," she said. "And what my mouth touches, I stake claim. For this night, you are mine."

"For always," he said, but she shook her head.

"Do not say such things. You have already refused that."

He pressed his lips together and said no more. Instead, he held her gaze as he stripped out of the last of his clothing. And then he knelt before her, a man naked with his cock sprung up between them. He spread his arms wide and gave himself to her so long as she did not ask for the loss of her maidenhead.

What a man, she thought. Strong with sculpted muscles and hardened bone. But that was the least of his appeal. His honor pulsed through him with his blood, and his devotion remained in the way he waited upon his knees for her tiniest whim.

She lay him back as he had done for her. She took her time, washing his body with a wet cloth, bathing him with her kisses, and then teasing him with her teeth. She learned the ripple of his stomach when she bit his nipple. She kneaded the strength of his muscles when she blew kisses across his belly. And she gloried in the power in his thighs when he thrust into her mouth like a man unleashed.

He gave her everything he had to give, and she took it with pleasure. Until he collapsed in exhaustion, and she curled into his side. They held each other that night. And they whispered to one another such thoughts. They didn't talk about her woman's place or his role for Lord Benedict. Nothing of their future and not a whisper of their dreams.

Instead, they spoke of childhood things and lessons taught to the young. She told a tale about escaped pigs, and he confessed to stealing sweets from angry vendors. They shared everything they could of the people they were. And then, well before dawn, he roused them both.

While she checked one last time on the new mothers, he called a hackney. Then he wrapped a dark cloak about her and escorted her down the outside stairs. They said nothing in the dark carriage but held hands while pressed hip to hip.

One last kiss. One last desperate, wishful, anguished press of lips and tongue. Then she ripped herself away and ran to the servants' entrance at the back of her house.

Two days later, her father appeared for tea with a hideously swollen black eye. He glared at her over his drink, his mouth tight with pain and hatred. If there were other marks on him, she didn't see them, though he moved with the care of an injured man.

"You will marry Lord Benedict," he growled at her.

She bowed her head.

"Yes, Father," she said. "I will."

Chapter Thirty

GABRIEL WALKED INTO his mother's home with such hatred in his heart that he feared for his soul. It could not be moral for him to despise any one as much as he did his own mother. He'd spent his childhood trying to cater to her whims, satisfy her needs, and do anything—everything—to earn the love that Janelle gave so easily.

It never worked. But rather than cut her from his life, he parsed his time and his patience as best he could. He answered her demands when his work allowed, he bartered with her when he needed to, and he did his best to give her the respect due a parent despite his complete disgust of everything she valued.

How dare she try to pull Janelle into her clutches? How dare she touch the one pure thing in his life and try to destroy it? And now it was time for a well-earned reckoning. He would have her out of his life once and for all. And he would get Janelle the apothecary shop, too, and never speak to the bitch again.

Such was the force of his fury that when he appeared on her doorstep at nearly noon, he was tempted to kick the portal down. Instead, he used the knocker with excessive force, knowing he was waking her from her sleep.

A maid answered the door. A true maid this time. Or perhaps he should call her a housekeeper for her gaze was hard, her age somewhere in the middle years, and a scar ran from temple down the side of her face into her jaw. He knew her immediately.

"Mrs. Jimenez," he said, dipping his chin. "I've come to speak with my mother."

"It's too early. You know that." Her response was short and to the point, as usual. Mrs. Jimenez had come to his mother's home when he was a teenager. Her wound had been a livid red then. Her mood as well. She been cross with him then and, obviously, nothing had changed except the color of her scar.

He pushed into the house. "I don't care. I'll speak to her in her bed if need be, and to hell with whomever is in there with her."

He did not put his hands on Mrs. Jimenez. He had some control of his temper, but that did not stop the woman from stepping directly into his path, her jaw firm and her eyes flashing in fury. "It's not about what you want," she all but hissed. "This is her house, and you'll mind your manners."

"She has not minded hers," he countered. "And I am done forgiving it."

Mrs. Jimenez had a hard right cross. He'd had occasion to experience it. He saw her fist tighten the moment he set a foot on the stairs.

"I can best you," he said, his voice low. "I do not wish to, but I will."

"I would get my licks in," she countered.

"You might," he agreed. Then he turned his cold eyes on her. He allowed all his rage to show then. Not just for how his mother had ignored him throughout the years, but how she allowed others like Mrs. Jimenez to take out their grievances upon him. He'd been the only male who was not a customer, and some of her servants had focused all their fury on him. "But I would win in the end."

Her face contorted then in a slow, evil smile. "That's what all you men think, but not with her." Her chin jerked upward to where he saw his mother standing as if she were Venus stepped from the sea. Golden curls, pouty lips, and eyes that widened as if in surprised innocence. "In her house, she wins. Every time."

"Not today." He looked up to his mother. "I have things to

say, Mama, and you will hear them."

"Oh, la di dah," the woman returned with an airy wave of her hand. "So important, so manly. I would be impressed if you weren't acting like a brute." She looked to the housekeeper. "I'll have tea in the parlor. He can say his *little things* there."

Gabriel ground his teeth together. It never worked to approach his mother with anything but a cool head. Any show of emotion gave her the upper hand. He knew that, and yet he was not a man of stone. By interfering with Janelle, she had gone too far.

He walked with measured fury into the parlor. He had no desire to sit in any of those chairs. God knew what kind of mess had been on them. But he did not want to stand at attention while his mother lounged before him, so he perched on the edge of the cleanest-looking chair. And if she felt insulted for his lack of manners, then all the better.

His mother didn't comment except with a raised brow. Mrs. Jimenez gave him her back as she brought tea in a single cup on a beautiful tray. She set it before his mother, then casually kicked him as she walked past him.

He was prepared for it. Indeed, he remembered countless such blows from when the woman had first come to serve his mother. At the last second, he twisted his foot so that hers caught the hard point of his boot. She howled in reaction.

"You kicked me!" she screeched. "You filthy brute!" She raised her arm to strike him, but he stopped her with a hard stare.

"I am not a child anymore," he said. The tone of his voice was all that was needed. Her eyes blazed fury, but her blow did not land. Instead, she flounced out of the room.

"Is that what you've come to?" his mother drawled as she sipped her tea. "Quarreling with the servants? This is the paragon of virtue I have raised?"

She didn't raise him at all. She'd used him as her whims required. And his heart held only disdain for her now. God, he wanted out of this house. He'd thought arriving here before the usual crowd descended would make things easier. It had not.

Best get to the point.

"Why would you try to cut Miss Caddick from Lord Benedict? What do you care who she marries?"

His mother sipped her tea, saying nothing. She didn't even look up. Eventually, he sighed.

"Mother? How long do you intend to ignore me? I can write some of Lord Benedict's correspondence while I wait."

She fluttered her eyes as she looked up from her tea. "Oh? Are we to talk then? I thought you were saying things."

Bantering with her was a losing game. He drew a set of documents out of his pocket and dropped them on the table between them. She didn't move, but her gaze landed on the neat rows of words. True to form, though, she said nothing. She wasn't one to show her hand early.

"That is the deed to an excellent building a mile west of where the Rose Garden currently stands. It's well constructed, the roof is new, and it's perfect for use as a whorehouse. Even better, it's got a side room for gambling and a beautifully appointed suite above stairs, perfect for Madame Florina. I've seen to every detail. Even fixed several holes in the walls. You should be rat-free now. I would get all new furnishings if I were you, but that is your choice. You can spend the extra thousand pounds how you choose."

"A thousand pounds and a building. My goodness, what brings me such good fortune?"

He met her gaze with an icy stare of his own. "You will deed me the Rose Garden and the building that houses My Lady's Apothecary."

Her laughter was high-pitched and hard. Over the years, he had heard all her different laughs from the faked casual to the sultry seductress. This one held true humor which was why it came out hard. It meant he'd surprised her, and she did not like to be surprised.

He waited until she quieted.

"The price is fair, I made sure of that. Both of your buildings are falling to ruin. It will cost more than you can imagine to have them fixed. But with the new building, you will have everything you need with absolutely no effort." His lips curled. "And I know how you prefer making no effort whatsoever."

"What do you know about my efforts?" she asked, sneering.

"Only what I heard grunting every night of my childhood."

She threw her cup of tea at his face. It was a quick flick of her wrist, a show of temper when she preferred to be the cool one. She was not so calm then, and he was pleased that he had scored a hit in their game of hatred. It didn't save his face or his clothes from the brew, but it was something.

She'd missed the papers, so that was good.

"Call your man of affairs." No woman could officially sign papers herself, but her man of affairs could. "Sign the papers, so that we can be done with this." He didn't mean done with this conversation. He meant they were done forever. He would never step a foot in her house or her whorehouse again.

She sat back in her chair, her arms going out to the side like a queen on her throne. Once, he'd thought the pose impressive. Now it was all he could do not to roll his eyes. When she spoke, it was with ponderous weight and pretended power. He had heard kings and queens with less strength in their voice.

"You have no power over me. I will not agree, and you are a fool to think I would."

"The Rose Garden is falling to ruins. The Apothecary, too, for all that there is a garden in the center. You have no interest in repairing it, so in a few year's time, it will be rubble about your ankles and worth a fraction of what it is now."

"It is mine. And I can hire roofers and rat catchers as well as anyone else."

"You can, but you don't. It's a bother you hate."

"You'd be surprised what I will make an effort to do."

Perhaps. If she were well motivated. "I have never interfered with your affairs before, Mother. Never once spoken about your petulance, your tempers, or your…illness." She had no illness that he knew of, but that never stopped rumors from spreading. "I can see to it that you never have another protector again."

"As if I need that."

"You would, if the roof fell in at the Rose Garden. And that is nothing to say of the disease that runs rampant there. I know your customers, Mother. It would be easy enough to direct them elsewhere."

"And then I shall end up on your doorstep, my doting son. I shall sit in Lord Benedict's office and wail at how you have abused me."

It wouldn't work. She would be expelled within minutes. But he would never live down the shame of it, especially since she would come back day after day until he killed her out of frustration.

He stood up, making sure his movements were slow. At his full height, he intimidated most people, including his mother. Or so he hoped. "You will sell me your buildings, Mother. Or I will see you ruined."

She spread her hands wide. "Then do it. Destroy me." She leaned forward. "I know how your piety works. That holy soul of yours would forbid you to cast your mother out in the street, no matter how much you loathe her."

It was true, but such was his fury at this moment, that he didn't care. "Agree, Mother. Now. Or I will do that and so much worse to you. I know how. I know what you value, I know the ways of the *ton*. There is no love left in me for anyone, least of all you."

She looked at him a long time. She must have seen how implacable his will was, how dark the hatred that painted his soul. And so she switched tactics. Instead of arrogant royalty, she crumpled into a wounded bird.

"How has this happened?" she cried. "You are my son! How could you threaten me—"

"Call your man of affairs." He pulled out a quill and set out an inkpot. He turned the pages to where she and her man would place her mark. If she would not take the feather from his hand, he would set it between her fingers and force her signature.

But before he could, she folded her arms across her chest and leaned back.

"No."

What? Good God, he was giving her a fair deal. Better than fair, truth be told because of the repairs required to her buildings. If nothing else, he thought she would see reason. When all the artifice was boiled away, she had always acted according to her own best self-interest. And this offer gave her what she most cared about.

Or so he thought.

"No, Gabriel, I will not sign."

"Then I will destroy you."

"Perhaps." She shrugged. "Probably. But that will take time, won't it? And you want this finished now, don't you? Why else would you appear at my door with papers in hand?"

Because he wanted to be rid of her. The sooner the better. "Because I have other tasks this day. Do you think England runs on its own? Do you think Napoleon was defeated without—"

"Yes, yes. You're *soooo* important." She rolled her eyes, and he felt a push toward violence. How dare she—his own mother—make fun of his life's work? To think he had once wanted her to be proud of him. He'd even come to see her after returning from Spain. He'd shown her his medals and tried to talk about the people who came to him for advice. Earls, dukes, even the Regent himself wanted his opinion.

She'd wandered away the moment she'd consumed his sausages.

He shook his head, hating his next words even though he meant every single one. "Ruination, then. Very well." But damn it, it would take so much time! He knew he could afford to be patient. Janelle had waited this long for her dreams, she would abide a while longer. Years even. But he wanted to give it to her now. He wanted to work night and day to make the place what it could be. For her. *With* her. And he couldn't do that as long as his mother stood in the way.

He gathered the papers, the quill, and the inkpot and turned to leave. She waited until he was nearly at the door before calling him back. But she didn't speak with fear in her voice. Her words came as a silky kind of enticement. And damn him for pausing at the tone.

"I will give you what you want," she said. "But I have conditions."

He knew she would. He had funds in reserve to offer. A few other minor ways to sweeten the pot.

"Yes?" he said, satisfaction coloring his tone.

"You may have the Rose Garden, but not the Apothecary."

"No. It must be both."

"But I shall allow your Miss Caddick to run the upstairs rooms how she wishes. I shall even give her a portion of the profits."

"There will be no profits when that building falls down."

"That will take some time yet, I should think."

Years. Decades most like, because the bones were good. He crossed his arms. "It must be both places or none."

She quirked a brow. "If it must be both, then I shall tell you my conditions."

He grunted. "Then get on with it."

"Do you know how hard it is to have your own son despise you? You're a bastard, my boy, and yet you curl your lip at the way I fed and clothed you."

What boy wanted to hear his mother spreading her legs for coin? He knew more about his mother's activities than any boy ought. And he'd seen more than any child should.

"Your father wanted nothing to do with you. I gave you everything. You are nothing without me."

"I am what I have made of myself despite you. I am a man of honor. I am respected and employed in honest work."

"Yes, I know about the honest work of war. Killing, destroying. How many did you rape? What did you pillage?"

"None. Nothing." His voice was cutting because in his heart of hearts, he knew he lied. He'd never raped a soul, but he hadn't been able to stop everyone under his command. The perpetrators were thrown out in disgrace, but it had happened under his watch. That, perhaps, wasn't his fault, but the pillaging? An army required supplies, and sometimes they had to get them in less than honorable ways. He'd paid if he could. But sometimes he'd taken when there was no way to repay the debt. He'd done what he could, but his first duty was to England and his men.

Guilt must have shown on his face because she saw it. She knew it.

"A man of honor," she spat. "You come from me, Gabriel. You are mine."

He shook his head. There was no point in speaking the denial, especially since he fought night and day to be the opposite of his manipulative whore of a mother.

"Here are my conditions," she said. "You may have the Rose Garden and the Apothecary, but I own the land. You will pay me rent."

He could work with that. "How much?"

"Not a single coin," she said, her expression shifting to a smirk. "We will move the Rose Garden to your building, but we will call it Gabriel's House. You will run it with Florina."

"The hell I will."

"I want everyone to know where you come from." She tapped her chest. "Me. You grew from me, and you are just like me."

"No."

"You will run my whorehouse for me. You will care for my girls, cater to the vices that fill those rooms, and everyone will know that it comes from you."

"I do not have time. I cannot—"

"You can hire whomever you want, manage it however you

will, but your name will be on the door. Your face will be seen inside it. And if you do not run it to my satisfaction, then I will burn the apothecary to the ground. I will see the Rose Garden destroyed. I will tear down the walls just to spite you."

"That would see you hung in Tyburn. No one can commit such a crime and escape justice." That was a lie. Most crimes were never punished.

"It would be worth it," she countered.

She meant it. She would do whatever it took to see him humiliated, even if it killed her. He had spent his entire life showing himself to be a man of esteem despite his parentage. A man who could be trusted, who had no vice, who would protect the innocent as a knight of old. That was what he called himself in his secret thoughts, Sir Gabriel, Knight of the Round Table. He was not Gabriel, owner of a whorehouse. Nor Gabriel, the man who saw every vice fulfilled.

"What is she worth to you, this Miss Caddick?" his mother taunted. "I offered her everything she could want, if only she would give you up."

"You asked her to abandon her family, her marriage."

"That's not what she wanted. She turned me down because of you." His mother curled her lips. "I know what you did in the bath at the Rose Garden."

"Nothing. Miss Caddick is still pure."

She grinned. "She's a virgin, of course. Your honor would demand as much. But pure?" She scoffed. "Decidedly not." She rose to her feet. "I could ruin her too, you know. I could see that Betty Gill never worked again."

"There will always be poor, pregnant women who need help. You cannot stop that or her."

"But I can make it hard. I can fight her in ways you cannot even imagine." She laughed cruelly. "You knew nothing of what went on in the Rose Garden, of the women who help each other, of the medicines or the priests who are there when a kind hand is needed."

"You were not the one to create that." He would stake his life on that.

"But I know of it. I know how it works. And I know how to make things hard."

"You would destroy a good woman out of spite? Are you really that depraved?"

She shrugged. "I would destroy a son who has forgotten who he is."

"And what is that?"

"My son."

How could he argue that? She was right. For all that he had built himself up, for all that he cast himself as a man of honor, he had debauched his best friend's fiancée. That was not his mother's doing. It was his own.

He almost laughed. It made sense that lust would take him down. He was, after all, a whoreson.

And seeing him silent, his mother pressed her advantage. "Do you agree? Say yes and I will go to the solicitor with you now. I will sign the papers, and you will abide by them." She chuckled. "Your *honor* will see to it."

To do this would mean the end of his diplomatic career. Though the men of government frequented whorehouses, they would never interact with one who owned it. Not when his name was emblazoned upon the walls and his mother shouted his parentage to any soul who would listen. To agree would destroy his career, but it would give Janelle what she wanted. She could have the rooms above the apothecary shop and the building next door. She could build whatever she dreamed for the benefit of all.

"Get dressed," he snapped. "I will have this finished today."

Four hours later, it was done. He was enslaved to his mother.

Chapter Thirty-One

BENEDICT REFILLED HIS glass before staring back at the fire in his gloomy London bedroom. It was the night before his wedding, and he despised everything about the room, including himself. He focused instead on his drink.

Brandy was not his libation of choice, especially tonight. It was too rarified a thing when what he wanted was something coarse and cruel. The swill they'd consumed in the peninsula came to mind, as did the men who'd been with him.

Gabriel.

The man was everything Benedict wished he could be—capable, intelligent, and ruthless if the situation called for it. It was ridiculous that because of a quirk of parentage, Benedict was considered the better man. Gabriel had taught him everything, from how to start a fire to how laundry was managed. And while Benedict could see battle strategy in landscapes and the formation of men, Gabriel had taught him about morale and the way food and medicine got from one place to the next.

A battle was not a chess game. It was people and provisions in weather and terrain. Gabriel had taught him that, and Benedict would have failed without him.

He let his head drop against the side of his wingback chair. How odd that he missed the rough living of those days, especially the mornings. How many times had he been awake to see the dawn? He loved watching the men rouse with rough grumbles and crude talk. Gabriel especially would stand outside in nothing but his breeches as he shaved his face. Such a simple thing, but Benedict had been mesmerized by the fluid motion of his fingers, the flex of his chest, and the shifting planes of his face.

He'd always thought Gabriel had a gentleman's hands despite the blunt tips and broken nails. His writing was precise, his fingers capable of tenderness as well as wicked thrust. He wasn't greatly skilled with a rapier, though he had the finesse to manage it. His best talent was with a knife. Penknife, dagger, dirk, or stiletto, Gabriel had mastered them all. And Benedict had spent many nights dreaming of Gabriel using his skills in ways that were best left unexamined. Fever dreams, he called them, when there was no fever except in his very unnatural mind.

A knock sounded at his door. Two clipped raps that always shivered a thrill through Benedict's body. Normally he contained it. Tonight, after almost a bottle of brandy, he let the feel of it slide through his soul before he spoke.

"Come in, Gabe."

"Gabe, is it?" the man said as he stepped through the room. "You only call me that when you're foxed."

"Don't insult that divine creature. I'm stinking drunk." He gestured languidly at the chair facing him. "Join me. Finish this off before it kills me."

Gabriel tensed. It was a subtle movement, but one that never failed to depress Benedict. Gabriel was his closest friend and would be the best man at his wedding. That his natural instinct was to flinch away when invited to a cozy drink in Benedict's bedroom said clearly that Gabriel understood far too much of what had never been spoken between them.

Thankfully, the man covered well and settled easily into the opposite chair. He poured himself a glass—a large enough measure to finish the bottle—then sipped it slowly as Benedict had taught him.

"Ah," Gabriel said, pleasure infusing his tone. "That's a fine brew. Where'd you get it?"

"Wedding gift from Castlereagh."

"Good man."

He agreed in silence, sipping his drink in long, slow pauses while he let his gaze rove over his best friend.

Gabriel returned the look and his expression deepened into a frown. "You're going to have a sore head for your wedding."

He knew it.

"Ben, I've had to do something I didn't want to."

A distraction. Excellent. "I'm listening."

"I manage a whorehouse now."

Not at all what he'd expected to hear. "Your mother's?"

"Yes."

"Is this some kind of filial duty?"

"A bargain I was required to make."

Gabe's mother had always been a manipulative bitch. It stood to reason that she would find a way to trap her son.

He looked down at his hands. "It means I must resign."

"What? Why?"

Gabriel didn't answer. He simply waited for Benedict's sloshed brain to catch up.

"Well, I suppose you can't work at the Foreign Office, exactly. But you know, it could make some things much easier with men like LeFauvre."

Gabe shuddered, a distinct movement that might have spilled his drink if he hadn't had the steadiest hand with knife or drink.

"Good God, you hate the very idea, don't you?"

"Yes."

"Do you want to talk about how it happened?"

"No."

"But you're going through with it."

Silence, then a clear and definite response. "Yes."

Very well. Actually, that fit quite well into his plans. "Don't worry," he said as he drained the rest of his glass. "It will all work out all right."

"Benedict?"

He didn't answer except to wave a negligent hand. If Gabriel wouldn't share details, then why should he?

"Benny, what are you planning?"

His gaze slid back to the fire. Gabe knew he was always thinking something, seeing months and years into the future. Except tonight, his thoughts always slid back to the morrow. "I want to go back to the castle tomorrow, right after the wedding breakfast. We'll spend the next month in Cornwall."

"What?"

Benedict slumped in his chair and let his head tilt toward the ceiling. He always preferred looking up there when he lied. "I can't stay here in London. You know how it is. I'll be called upon by every dignitary and conman in London, offering congratulations in one second and trying to pick at me in the next. I won't do it."

Gabriel frowned. "But the house is set up for her. There are flowers in the bedroom, her housekeeper is already installed. You want to transfer all of them to Cornwall by tomorrow evening?"

He shuddered. "Heavens, no. I can't have them dashing about Cornwall. Good lord, someone will break their neck." His gaze slid languidly over to Gabriel. "Just you and her. There's staff there—"

"There's no one but an ancient groundskeeper."

And an elderly couple who served as caretakers plus tenants, none of whom went to the castle except when explicitly invited. It was heaven.

"We'll manage," he said. "We did in the Peninsula."

"She's a lady, not a soldier."

Was there something in Gabe's tone? Admiration perhaps? "You like her now."

"I liked her before."

"No, you didn't." He smiled. "You see her merit."

Gabe stared into his drink, his expression maudlin. "She's a worthy woman."

High praise from his rigidly moral best man. "I can't do it, Gabe," he blurted. "Not in London with everyone staring."

"What?"

"I can't father a child here. I…" He shook his head. "Not in London."

"It's not done in London. It's done in the dark in a bed. You could be in Antarctica, for all that you'll know."

"I'll know." He blew out a breath. "She should be Arthur's wife. He should be at the altar tomorrow. He'd have her tupped and brimming with child in an hour." Arthur had been his older brother, the man who should have become the earl. The one who had lived to swive and would have populated his nursery with a dozen strapping boys to carry on the name.

"Maybe so, but you're the better man. Miss Caddick will be better served by you."

If he could manage to serve her at all. "I never wanted the earldom. I wanted to stay in the military." But he'd been forced to sell out the minute he became the heir, no longer the spare. "Tomorrow should be Arthur's day."

Gabriel set down his glass—drained clean when he was usually a modest drinker—and dropped his elbows on his knees. "What's this about, Benny? Is it really about Arthur?"

No. "I've been thinking about our campaigning days. About drinking swill and pretending we were in the royal palace giving the king what for."

"Nah," Gabe drawled. "I wanted to kick the general's ass, not the king's. And you were the one who played pretend."

He did. He'd pretended so many things back then. Surrounded by men who lived on a razor's edge, knowing they could be dead in the morning. There'd been times when they'd been so drunk that boundaries were crossed, needs were expressed, and…

And he'd had quarters all his own.

One man had remained close enough to touch, but far enough away to maintain discipline. Gabriel was not steeped in self-loathing. His only sin was being a bastard by birth. In every other aspect, he was as regulated as a nun. He didn't pray morn and night, but he did keep himself in order. And he kept everyone else—including Benedict—in order as well.

How he had dreamed of breaking Gabriel to his will. Of finally bending the man over or, more accurately, dropping to his knees in surrender to the dominant male.

Benedict closed his eyes, letting that fantasy wash over him. Tears sprang to his eyes, the maudlin whine of a drunk in his mind.

"This should be Arthur's night. I should be drinking to his wedded bliss."

"Benny, what can I do to help?"

Don't ask that question. Don't ever, ever ask that question. But it was too late. The words were in the air.

He opened his eyes and looked at his closest friend. Gabriel had seen him through the war. He'd fought by his side in battle and again amidst the delicate manipulations of diplomacy. He was his truest friend, most steadfast soul, and his one true love after Michael's death. Gabriel was the one who held him in his grief, who had nursed him when he was sick, and who now stood before him like a warrior angel of old.

Tonight, Benedict was drunk enough to say it. Not out loud, but in his mind, in his heart, and in the way his eyes burned when he looked across the room.

"Gabe," he whispered. Then his gaze slid steadily, desperately, to his bed.

Need throbbed in his blood. Desire and dark fantasies thickened his groin. Shame washed through him, a self-loathing he could not release, and yet it didn't stop the wish. How he wished.

Gabriel stood up, his movement hasty. "I'll see everything changed for tomorrow," he said. "I'll make sure Miss Caddick is comfortable in your castle."

Yes. Make sure his wife had everything she needed.

Benedict closed his eyes in defeat. "I had the east tower fixed up for you. Two rooms. One for your correspondence and one for your bed." He'd taken special care with the bedroom. It had every luxury that could be created in a crumbling castle turret.

And the bed was large enough to support two brawny souls, intimately and enthusiastically engaged.

Unfortunately, Gabriel's interests had never tilted toward "brawny."

Gabriel reached out, his fingers quick as he snatched Benedict's glass straight out of his hand. "You've had enough, my lord," he said. His shoulders had gone back, his chin was lifted, and he was acting the servant, even as he disciplined the raw recruit. Did he know how attractive that was? How handsome he appeared when he took charge?

Benedict looked back at the bed. "She'll be a wonderful mother," he said. Then he turned back to the fire, the sight of his bed now sickening him.

"You'll have good sons, my lord."

"If you 'my lord' me one more time, I will brain you with the nearest bottle." There was force in his words. Well, some anyway. And bitter frustration. Whatever was in his tone, he knew it was the response Gabe had been looking for. His voice softened even as he backed toward the door.

"Get to bed, Benny," he said. "I'll come for you in the morning."

Take me to bed, Gabriel, so I can face the morning.

He didn't say the words out loud. He never said them out loud, for fear of ending their relationship forever. So he said nothing as the man who knew him best backed out of the room and shut the door. Gabe would be up for hours now, changing the plans, seeing to the logistics of moving everything to Cornwall.

It was a petty cruelty, a jab at Gabriel's competence and his own utter wretchedness. Make the subordinate work through the night because he could not—would not—do what Benedict really wanted.

With a growl of fury, Benedict curled away from the bed, glared at the fire, then fumbled as he pulled out a silver flask. Forget brandy. He would drink what he wanted.

Rot gut, hot and cruel, slid down his throat.

Chapter Thirty-Two

JANELLE SPENT THE night before her wedding with her brother Alexander. He'd arrived mid-afternoon from Cambridge, his tawny hair curling wildly around his unshaven face, with a smile of warmth that heated a very, very cold place around her heart.

"Hullo, cow girl." It was a reference to the first time she'd met Mrs. Sundy and the very first baby she'd help birth—a calf that had come largely all on its own.

"Hullo, ignoramus," she returned, squeezing her brother with all her strength. He didn't even flinch, which meant he'd grown stronger. "I'm so glad you're here."

"I made it in time for tea."

"And I'm grateful for that."

With a last doting look at one another, the two siblings entered the library for tea, just as they had as children. It was the three of them today. Not even Aunt Esmee or Uncle Jonathan were allowed. Thankfully Lord Benedict was working, but there was a quiet kind of insult to Lord Benedict's parents who were left to find their own entertainment on the day before the nuptials.

Either way, her father didn't seem to care as he glowered at them, his black eye swollen and his jowls quivering with fury. Both she and Alexander had been trained to say nothing until spoken to, and so Janelle served tea while Alexander silently defied their father by sprawling in his seat. His eyes were deceptively languid, and Janelle thanked God that no matter what happened in her future, as of tomorrow morning, she would be out from under her father's thumb.

That thought hit her broadside.

In the morning, she would be free of her father. And though it gratified her that Gabriel had taken a fist to her father's face, it nevertheless changed nothing in the dynamic between herself and her parent. If anything, it entrenched his animosity even further. The only one who could make a change to that was her.

And to that end, she set down the teapot and refused to pour.

"Father," she began, her tone clear. "In the morning, I will be quit of you—"

"I'm leaving school," her brother abruptly declared. It was a rush of words, meant to forestall whatever Janelle was about to say. Her little brother was protecting her by diverting the discussion, but she couldn't let him take the heat for her. He still required her father's money to survive.

"Alex, you don't need to—"

"Actually," he said, his jaw firming. "I left it months ago. I'm working on steam engines for the navy. Brilliant work, very exciting." He pulled what looked like two metal cogs out of his pocket. "This is a bolt and a nut made out of metal. Look at the precision of the thing! Every one perfectly made, exactly the same. Tiny pieces of metal can be cut now by a machine, and when a piece goes soft or breaks, a new identical one can be popped in. No fuss. Can you imagine it?" His eyes sparkled with delight. "You don't have to hand cut a new engine. Just pop in another gear, and you're back to work. It's marvelous!"

She'd never seen such enthusiasm in her brother's face. She leaned forward to see the strange metal lump. "Alex, that's—"

"You will stand and explain yourself!" her father bellowed.

Odd how even the greatest noise had no effect if one is already braced for it. This was her father's usual command when he was out of sorts. He would force them both to stand before him, their hands rigidly at their sides while Alexander was forced to repeated Latin phrases or stammer through philosophical treatises, whatever her father determined was appropriate for a gentleman's education. And indeed, it was exactly the kind of brutal instruction that had gotten Alex into Cambridge to study despite his apparent interest in games of chance and women of loose morals.

Except this time, Janelle had no intention of standing to attention, and neither apparently, did Alex.

"I am explaining," her brother drawled. "There is no need to bellow." And though his posture appeared insolently relaxed, Janelle saw the tension in his jaw and the fury in his eyes. "But since you interrupted my discourse, Father, perhaps you could explain how you got that black eye." He leaned forward slowly. "Did Janelle finally have enough and pop you one proper?"

Her father's response was quick and brutal. His favorite attack was a lightning-fast punch to the jaw, followed by a heavy blow to the belly. She'd seen it often enough to know it was coming, but she'd never been able to stop it. Her brother did.

He leapt out of his chair with a cat-like grace. While their father's punch was extended, he gripped the man's arm and wrenched it around. The momentum of the second punch had already begun, and somehow Alex used it to spin their father around.

And then, Alex landed a heavy uppercut that sent their father flying, straight back into his chair. It was only by quick reflex that Janelle managed to get the hot teapot off the tray. Otherwise, the thing would have overset and spilled everywhere.

"Good catch," her brother said, not even winded.

"Where did you learn that?"

He winked at her. "There's lots that I've been doing lately." His tone was light, but she heard the fury underneath. But unlike the explosive moody boy she remembered, this man was calm, even as he moved to tower over their father. "Move and I'll only knock you back again," he said in a flat voice.

"This is how you treat your father, you fecking bastard!"

"If only I was," he said grimly. "That would make things so

much easier."

"Don't say that, Alex!" Janelle said as she set the teapot down. "You're his heir. There's money and a title—"

"I've money enough, Sister." He swallowed. "I'm only sorry that I didn't come back earlier." His gaze roved over her face and body. "Did he hurt you badly? I should have protected you. I should have—"

"I wanted you to go." She flashed him a smile. "I got my revenge, and I'm gone tomorrow."

"Yes, you are." He held out his hand to hers. "May I take you out to tea, Janelle? So we can talk without him?"

"Yes," she exclaimed, amazed by the mature man she saw before her. When had her baby brother grown up? She was still adjusting her thoughts when her father attacked again. But again, Alex was ready for it.

He blocked their father's fists easily, throwing the man to the floor this time. "Stop it, Father, or I will leave you too injured to walk her down the aisle tomorrow."

"You filthy..." Curse words poured from her father's mouth, but Alex turned his back on them. He held out his hand to her, and she stared in awe. He'd turned his back on their father!

"Quickly now," Alex said. "He isn't fast enough to catch me, but I don't want him to grab you—"

"He won't," she said as she rushed toward the door, her brother's long legs easily keeping pace.

"I'll disown you!" her father bellowed.

"I don't care!" Alex called back over his shoulder before he grabbed his hat from the hall table with one hand while hauling open the door with the other. They were outside in a trice and down the street a moment later.

Free!

My God, she had never felt so free. And yet even as she took full joyous breaths, she couldn't help but worry about her brother. Her father would disinherit him. He'd let the title pass on to Alex—there was little choice in that. But he could see that

Alex never received a penny of their considerable wealth.

"Alex—"

"Don't worry," he said as he patted her hand. "I can handle him."

"But—"

"I don't need his money. And he doesn't scare me anymore." His gaze dropped back to her as his brows tightened. "I'm so sorry it took me so long."

"I have been fine. I *am* fine," she said, investing all her strength into those words. Her heart was broken, her marriage a mystery, but she would be all right. Especially now that she saw what a fine man her brother had become. "Tell me everything," she said.

"If you tell me first about Lord Benedict. Do you want to marry him? Shall I rescue you from him as well?"

The idea had its appeal. Like him, she wanted to be able to throw off everything of her old life and become Betty Gill completely. But that would mean giving up her dream of a place for women to get medicines and deliver their babies safely. It would mean never seeing Gabriel again, if only as a friend. It would mean losing so much of what she wanted.

"I respect Lord Benedict," she said. "A very great deal."

"That's not love. It isn't even joy."

"No," she admitted. "But he is giving Betty everything she could possibly want." Except love.

"Betty is still around, then." His voice indicated worry, not disgust. That had always been his way. He never cared what she did. He only wanted her safe.

"Absolutely. And she has big plans."

"Tell me everything."

She laughed. They had so much to say to one another. "Buy me a Gunter ice, and I will."

They talked late into the night. Indeed, she didn't even spend the night at her home for fear of her father's fury, but slept in her brother's tiny flat while he curled up on the floor. He escorted her home when the dawn was just breaking, and he waited outside her door as she bathed and dressed for her wedding.

She would have preferred that he walk her down the aisle, but in this, her father's determination to uphold his image prevailed. It seemed he had also spent the night elsewhere but appeared at the church door dressed and moderately sober. He spoke not one word to her or her brother, and she said not one thing to him.

What was there to say? He was as unimportant to her now as an old pair of shoes. She kissed her brother and waited for the music to begin. Her true friends were Betty's companions—Nanny, Mrs. Sundy, and Madame Florina. But they could not serve as her attendants, so Aunt Esmee walked ahead of her as bridesmaid, and Janelle waited for her new life to begin.

But in that moment before she walked down the aisle, her father had one last thing to growl at her.

"You'll be a countess because of me. Remember that, girl. I did this for you."

"You've never done anything *for me*," she said. "Only *to me* for your own purpose. And I shall make sure that you never do such a thing to my children. And if you disown Alex, I'll disown you. Everyone will know that you are banished from the Earl and Countess of Atterbury's estate like bad meat." She paused a moment so her next words could really sink in. "Remember that, Father."

Then she began their walk down the aisle.

Chapter Thirty-Three

FATIGUE PULLED AT Gabriel as he stood beside Lord Benedict before the altar. He had worked through the night, he had seen to every detail of the nation's work, wedding work, and honeymoon that had been laid at his feet. And he now stood at the top of the church aisle and felt every cell in his body tremble with awe.

Stunning was too tame a word for Janelle as she strode beside her father. Her chin was lifted, her shoulders back. She walked with the fierce expression of a warrior goddess. Her gown flowed about her in silk and lace. It framed her body, glorified her beauty, and trailed behind her like blessings in her wake.

The music swelled as she approached, and he caught her gaze as a man might catch a sunrise. God's manifest glory, untamed and untouched, brought before him not to be claimed, but to be adored.

Such were his thoughts. Grandiose and sublime. They had to be because if he thought of her as anything less than a goddess, then nothing would stop him from claiming her as his own. He would fight every battle, wage every war, if only she would be his when the victory came.

It was all he could do to stand frozen in place when Lord Benedict took her hand and led her to the altar.

He clenched his hands into fists rather than pull her into his arms. He locked his jaw tight when she spoke her vows to someone else. And he kept the misery from his face when she at last looked at him.

It happened at the end. When her veil was lifted and the groom kissed his bride, Gabriel stood without breath because to allow air into his lungs would invite him to release a howl of rage and despair. Husband and wife pressed together for a kiss, but when she straightened, her gaze was not on Lord Benedict but on him. And in that moment, they both looked and said nothing. They touched gaze to gaze and did nothing.

He broke first. His gaze fell to the floor in shame. He had failed her and now...

She was Lord Benedict's wife.

Chapter Thirty-Four

JANELLE KNEW NOTHING of her new husband's plans. The wedding breakfast was finished and their guests departed before the man mentioned travel to Cornwall. He wanted to leave within the hour, and Janelle could do no more than gape at him in shock.

"I do apologize," he said. "I thought you'd been informed. The major should have it all arranged."

He turned to look at Gabriel who was across the room in close conversation with a mustachioed man. Who was that gentleman? Servant or guest? Good lord, her head was addled. She and Alex had consumed way too much wine the night before, and now her head pounded enough to make everything a little irritating.

Of course, her own discomfort was nothing compared to the red-rimmed eyes of her new husband. Naturally, he covered better than she. He smiled often and spoke warmly with every soul who came to congratulate him. She did her best, but there were moments when she felt completely unequal to the task.

And now Lord Benedict expected her to embark upon a many hour trip to a ramshackle castle as if it were as easy as changing one's shoes.

"We cannot rely on Major Vance to communicate between us," she said, her tone verging on peevish. "We must speak to one another or our marriage is over before it has even begun."

His face tightened in frustration, and she tensed in fear.

Sometimes her father looked like that, and it was a prelude to something very ugly. Had she just joined her life to a man with a violent side? A moment later, his expression turned into one of genuine regret.

"You are completely right, Janelle. I have been much too distant with you and that is not how I wish our marriage to begin. We shall make a point, perhaps, to breakfast together every morning. No matter what my duties, I shall endeavor to have that single private meal with you. And then, in time, we shall bring the children into it, yes? So that they can share in our private delights."

Not every private delight, she thought. Then she felt like an immoral tart for the very idea. Obviously, he was not thinking of their marriage bed, and it was only her anxiety that kept the concept at the forefront of her mind. That and all the bawdy innuendoes that were inevitable at a wedding breakfast. She'd mistakenly believed that those in political or diplomatic careers were of a refined mindset. That was decidedly not true for at least a third of the guests.

In any event, she needed to focus on her current situation. "You want us to leave in an hour?"

"If possible."

"I haven't packed—"

"Excuse me, my lady, my lord," interrupted the mustachioed man. "Forgive me for interrupting, but Major Vance asked me to relay certain particulars regarding this day's travel. He apologizes for his abrupt departure, but he has gone to acquire my lady's portmanteau."

"What?" she said as she scanned the nearly empty room. Gabriel had indeed departed. The damned man hadn't dared look her in the eye since the ceremony itself. He certainly hadn't said a word to her, and...

And she didn't know how to feel about that. Angry or grateful? Heartbroken or relieved? Good God, she wished her head didn't ache.

"My lady, your maid was informed this morning to pack a portmanteau for you. My lord, I understand your luggage is already in the carriage."

"Thank you, Doyle. We shall depart immediately for my lady's former home."

Janelle had trouble sorting through all the "my lady" and "my lord" references. She was not used to being addressed as such. Then her husband referred to her "former home" and Janelle gave up all attempts to control her life. At least until her head stopped aching.

Lord Benedict extended his arm to her. She obliged by setting her fingers upon it, then smiled benignly at the servants cleaning up the mess from their breakfast. And that was yet another oddity. She'd thought they would be shown to a bedroom as happened after most country weddings, but that was not the case here. They'd stayed until the last guests had departed and now were set to travel to Cornwall.

"Please lead the way, my lord," she murmured.

"There is time for you to say your goodbyes."

Good. Her father had left nearly an hour ago, but her brother, aunt, and uncle were there to wish her well. She promised to visit them as soon as she returned to London, then hugged them each tightly. She held Alex for an extra-long measure and when they separated, he winked at her with a sloppy kind of grin.

Then she was in a carriage, finally private with her husband, and all she wanted to do was close her eyes and wait for the throbbing to go away. Apparently, Benedict did, too, because he immediately dropped his head back and closed his eyes.

Very well. She mimicked the gesture all the way to her father's London home. Once there, she pasted on a warm smile, received all the teary well-wishes of her servants—former servants—and then watched as the footmen settled a very large trunk onto the boot of their carriage.

Everything happened so fast because of Gabriel, who directed everyone with efficient commands. She'd thought him stunningly handsome in his uniform as he stood at the altar. He now wore a travel outfit as befit a man who planned to ride postillion all the way to Cornwall.

"That can't be wise," she murmured. "He cannot have had much sleep last night."

"None whatsoever," Lord Benedict commented grimly. She hadn't even realized he was beside her, but she heard him clearly despite the noise.

"Surely we can manage without him." She didn't actually think that was possible, but she had no desire to see Gabriel collapse from exhaustion.

"We cannot."

"But—"

"We *cannot*." Those were the sharpest words she'd ever heard Lord Benedict utter, and she turned to him in surprise. Then she watched as his cheeks turned ruddy. "I will switch places with him once we get out of London. He can rest in the carriage."

Herself and Gabriel alone in a carriage? Absolutely not.

"How sore is your head?" she asked.

He shrugged by way of dismissal, and she realized that of the three of them—Gabriel, Benedict, and herself—she likely felt the best. Her throbbing head had less to do with the wine from last night and more to do with her broken heart.

Suddenly resolved, she turned to her husband. "My lord, you realize that you have married a practical woman, do you not?"

He frowned at her. "Of course, but—"

"I see no reason to put on missish airs just because it's my wedding day."

"I never thought you were."

"Good. Because I'm not." She waved over her maid. "Please put a riding habit in a small bag for me. I shall change at the first posting inn."

Lord Benedict touched her elbow. "Miss Cad—Janelle. Don't be silly. We're on our honeymoon. You can't—"

"What? Enjoy the air on a beautiful spring day? Of course, I can. And if you are about to fuss that I shall ride astride, I refer you to my first statement."

His lips quirked. "About being a practical woman?"

"Sidesaddles are the most impractical things in the world."

"You are steady on a man's saddle?"

"And on a sidesaddle, a donkey cart, a draft horse, and every manner of gig." She wouldn't win any races or look stylish doing it, but she was competent enough with all of it.

"Because of your hobby?"

"Yes." She lifted her chin. "And because of that hobby, I am fully aware of how much pain you are in. Was it all drink or do you have another aliment?"

The man's eyes widened as his lips twisted into a self-mocking smile. "I am indeed fortunate in my chosen wife. I find I like 'practical' very much."

"Good." Because she had no intention of changing. She noted that he did not answer regarding his ailment, but she knew the look of a man with a sore head. And if there was some other difficulty, then she would discover it soon enough. After all, by all accounts, they were about to become very private for an extended period of time.

NEVER IN HER wildest imagination could she imagine a more awkward trek across England. They each took a turn riding postillion. It was the only way, she learned, that Lord Benedict could get his favorite horse to the castle. Meanwhile, Gabriel insisted on maintaining every appearance of being a servant rather than a best friend to Lord Benedict. He would not insult his employer by riding inside the carriage, so he sat up top with the coachman and nearly killed himself when he toppled in his sleep.

Fortunately, their coachman had quick hands, and Gabriel

woke as he was being jerked back into his seat.

She was never more grateful to arrive at a crumbling old castle with massive overgrowth and dangerous ruins. She didn't care if the bedding was moldy or threadbare. She would sleep in her clothes and curse anyone who disturbed her. And unless she missed her guess, Lord Benedict felt the same. What Gabriel thought was beyond her, as he'd ridden ahead to ready things for their arrival.

So it was that when she finally stepped onto the rutted court-yard, she was greeted by an elderly couple of retainers, Mr. and Mrs. Carr, a very young maid Mary and her equally slight brother Bob. Gabriel stood half hidden in the doorway. Lord Benedict clearly knew them. After all, he'd been here less than a week ago, and everyone indicated their surprise and delight that he had returned with his new countess.

She greeted them as best she could and then was led directly into a master bedroom with excellent apportionment. She had just received her trunk, thanks to Gabriel's vast shoulders when her husband sent message to her via Bob.

A packet of missives has arrived, and I shall be working on them until the late hours. Please rest and we can regroup in the morning.

—B

So they were to communicate via missive. Or at least, he was. She soon learned from Mrs. Carr that his lordship had food and wine and was already at work at his desk in a lower solar. Indeed, over the past few weeks, he had slept there on a well-apportioned couch more times than he had rested in his bedroom which was attached to the solar.

The major had also been given food and drink. His bedroom was at the top of the east tower—the only one still habitable— and it attached to both the great hall on the main floor, the rooms taken by Lord Benedict for work and rest on the second floor, and hers on the highest floor. The rest of the edifice was a ramshackle mess, but Mrs. Carr would be pleased to give her a tour in the morning.

It would seem that all three of them had gone to their own corners to regroup. She didn't know why her marriage had turned into a triangle of awkwardness, but she hadn't the strength to fight it. So with a smile of gratitude, she dismissed Mrs. Carr and young Mary, then fell into bed.

Chapter Thirty-Five

JANELLE SPENT THE next day alone. Mrs. Carr and Mary did their best, but neither even lived on the grounds. Lord Benedict slept in the room next to his solar and closeted himself with Gabriel. And so she explored, walking carefully over the ruins and finding the quiet surprisingly helpful. By late afternoon, she had come to three decisions.

First, she had married Lord Benedict and would therefore learn to be a proper wife to him.

Second, she loved Gabriel but had chosen another. Therefore, she would treat him with as much friendship as was possible for as little time as possible.

Third, it was time to prepare for her wedding night.

That last one had her insides quaking, but she gained nothing by quivering in maidenly fear. Indeed, she was more knowledgeable than most brides of her station and therefore, would face it with calm.

She was able to bathe in a nearby stream and found the cold water bracing. She applied an herbed oil she'd been given from her aunt to soften her skin and dressed in a flowing gown for the evening meal. Not too formal, not too casual.

And completely wasted.

Lord Benedict arrived late, pressed a kiss to her forehead, then apologized as he showed her a messenger bag that apparently contained several documents that required his immediate attention. His expression was pale, his manner excruciatingly awkward, and his gaze tracked to the bottle of wine. He didn't touch it but asked Mrs. Carr to bring him food and drink in his solar. Then he headed for the door while she stared at him in shock.

"My lord," she called. "This will not do."

He froze before leaving the room. "I know," he said, in a tone low enough that she barely heard him. Then he straightened his shoulders and turned back to her. "I shall call upon you tonight. Everything will settle after that."

"I hope…" Her voice trailed away. Whatever she hoped was left unvoiced as he rushed away.

She slumped in her chair, losing all her carefully constructed poise. She'd always seen Lord Benedict as a larger-than-life person. He'd seemed important in the diplomatic circles. Several at her wedding breakfast had called him exceedingly intelligent, saying he had a strategic mind and a biting wit. He'd been kind and unfailingly generous when dealing with her. But the man who jerked toward wine bottles and waved messenger bags at her was nothing like the person she'd known before.

Her husband seemed anxious, even graceless. And how could she blame him? She felt exactly the same anxiety. As each minute ticked by, she thought more and more about the intimacy to come. She knew it wouldn't be the passionate encounter that she'd experienced with Gabriel, and the less she thought about that, the better. But would the act with Benedict hurt? Would he be aggressive? Perfunctory? She hoped he was kind, but she had no idea what to expect from this new version of him and she was too nervous to confront him.

She waited, which was not at all in her nature.

He arrived well after dark. She'd kept the fire well-tended, so the room was pleasantly warm even though she stood near the open window. She turned as he approached. Her aunt had told her to allow the moonlight to land upon her body in such a way that she seemed to glow in profile. And as the night was warm, she had discarded all but a thin chemise.

"It never fails," Aunt Esmee had said. But she hadn't said what would fail or what would work. The implication, however, wasn't that her husband would blanche and freeze one step inside the door.

He did not wear a night shirt but loose trousers and a tied robe on top. He wore no shirt and when he braced himself on the wall, the tie released, and she saw his naked chest beneath. His body was lean and trim with little fat on him, and she approached him with a trembling smile.

"My lord—" she began but stopped when he held up a hand to stop her. He stood before her in the most casual pose, but his skin was pale, and she noted that awkwardness still dogged his movements.

"I apologize, my dear, but this cannot go in the usual way."

"I'm sorry?"

He fidgeted before her. Not in any obvious way, but she was learning his movements, and he was definitely anxious.

"I thought it might be possible. Weeks ago, when I proposed, I thought myself able. But then I saw the way you looked at one another. We had just spoken our vows. We had kissed. And your eyes went to him."

A cold shiver went down her back. Shock and horror that he knew. He *knew!* "Benedict, I would never betray you. I... He..."

He stepped up to her and pressed a finger to her lips. "Now is not the time for lies, Janelle."

"It is not a lie!" she cried, but he had already left her. He crossed to the bedroom door, his heavy tread thumping in a steady rhythm. In her head, it sounded like the death knell of her marriage. They hadn't even had a wedding night, and now...

He knew.

Then he opened the bedroom door and called up the stairs. "Gabriel!" It was a command that rang louder than any trumpet. An order across the battlefield. A demand from superior to subordinate, and Janelle shrank into herself at the sound.

What had she done?

Gabriel appeared a bare moment later. He moved as if at attention for all that he was in his shirtsleeves. He came to the door and his gaze hopped quickly to where she stood, her arms wrapped protectively across her chest. He had seen every inch of her before, but now she hid herself from everyone. The confusion of the moment made her feel so small.

He took a step toward her, then abruptly froze. "My lord?"

Benedict shook his head. "Go to her," he said gently.

If he'd spoken harshly, Janelle would have run, though she had no idea where. She knew a man's fury and would not stand still for it as she had with her father. But Benedict's words were neither slurred with drink nor cold with fury. Indeed, his very gentleness brought her head up and gave her the strength to speak.

"This is not his place," she said, though the words cut her as she spoke. "This is our marriage bed, Benedict. He—"

"He will have to stand in my stead."

The words made no sense to her. It was as though her mind stopped the sound from any meaning. Not so, apparently, for Gabriel. He rocked back as if punched, and the horror in his expression cut her to the quick.

"Benedict, no!"

Her husband nodded. "It must be. I cannot do it."

"The hell—" Gabrial said, the words strangled.

Benedict shook his head, his expression tortured but no less firm. "I had it in the back of my mind from the beginning," he said to Gabrial. "You are the man I love most in this world, and she is the perfect woman for you. All I need do is step away and allow nature to take its course."

"Do not blame this on nature," Gabriel snapped. "You cannot have meant… Even you would not…"

Benedict shrugged. "Maybe not. But here we are."

Janelle looked between the two of them, her mind twisting and her breath choked. She didn't understand all the words, but one thing was clear. This was her wedding night, and her husband had just refused her. But why? What had she done wrong?

Chapter Thirty-Six

GABRIEL HAD NEVER witnessed a more tragic sight. A beautiful, fierce woman standing in confused humiliation while her husband turned from her on their wedding night. He couldn't even hate Benedict for the situation because he knew the man felt a despair deeper than anything Gabriel would wish on anyone. It was there in his eyes, for all that he stood as composed as if he addressed royalty.

It was horrible, and Gabriel was in the middle of it.

He went to Janelle. How could he not? She wore a silk chemise of ethereal white. With the moonlight touching her, she glowed like a fairy or a goddess come to earth. Yet he knew she was a flesh and blood woman, one who turned to him now. How he wanted to wrap her in his arms and hold her safe, but that was not his place. And it took all his discipline to keep his hands to himself.

"Hand me my wrap please," she said, her voice low.

He saw it folded on her trunk at the base of the bed, and though he didn't want to, he left her side to retrieve it, then watched as she pulled it on. It was not a seductive movement. Indeed, it was the opposite of one, and yet he saw the flush to her skin, the rise of her full breasts, and the tempting cradle of her hips.

His blood surged. It shouldn't. He couldn't. And yet, the way her hair tumbled around her bowed shoulders made his hands itch to stroke her. He would ease his hand down her spine as she settled herself. Her back would straighten, her shoulders lower, and her chin would lift as she faced whatever came.

But he didn't touch her, and so he was left watching as she pulled herself together enough to speak in a ragged voice.

"One of you two needs to start talking now."

He glanced at Benedict and saw that the man would not explain. In all the years that he had known Benedict, the man had never had once uttered his needs aloud. The shame was too great, and so he locked the words inside. Which meant it was left to Gabriel.

"My lady—" he began, but at her flash of irritation, he amended his words. "Janelle. As much as your husband values you, I'm afraid he does not find you attractive—"

"So I gathered," she said, her fingers going to her face.

"No, no!" he said, immediately catching her fingers. "It's not you. You're gorgeous. Any man would say that."

She frowned, her gaze going to where Benedict leaned stiffly against the mantel. "But—"

"Benedict is one of those men who finds beauty in the male form, not the female."

Her gaze turned back to him. He could see her mind working, but in this she had been too sheltered to quickly grasp the truth. "You mean, like Greek statues?"

"And living, male bodies." He could see she didn't understand. "For a man to have children, he must use his cock."

She turned back to him. "I do know how children are made."

Of course, she did. "But sometimes a man cannot make his cock stiffen no matter how much he tries. Especially if, for example, he is attracted to men and feels a distaste for women."

She gaped at him, clearly struggling to understand. And when it finally sunk in, she turned to Benedict. Her next words weren't angry. That was still to come. But they held a bite even though it was phrased as a question.

"But you married me. You *married* me, even though you have a distaste of me?"

Benedict straightened off the wall, though he did not meet her eyes. "You are a good woman. You will be an excellent mother."

"No, I won't!" she cried. "Not if..." She pressed her hands to her face, her body tightening until he feared she would shatter.

"Sit down, Janelle." Gabriel touched her arm, guiding her gently to the bed. She didn't sit so much as lose strength in her legs. He was there to see that she didn't fall.

"Why did you marry me?" she asked, the words half whisper, half plea. "Why—"

"I thought I could," Benedict said. "I was not supposed to be the heir. My brother—"

"Has nothing to do with this!" she cried out. "He has been dead for years. You've had years to figure out what to do. Years to—"

"He thought he could," Gabriel interrupted. Janelle turned to him, her eyes wide, and he spoke to soothe her. "He still might," he offered. "It's a matter of tricking the mind."

"Tricking the mind?" she gasped. "How? I cannot be a man."

"But..." He tried to be dispassionate. He tried to solve the problem and not look at her and feel everything that was written on her face. "If you presented him with your back, perhaps. So as to hide your breasts."

It wouldn't work. He knew it even as he said it. Even with her magnificent breasts hidden away, her curves were all female. Her hips, her narrow waist, her soft skin and musky scent. All woman. All her.

"It won't work," Benedict stated, misery in every word.

Good God. "Perhaps, Benny, you could prepare yourself ahead of time. You—"

"What do you think I have spent the whole day doing? I have tried everything." Finally, he looked at Gabriel, putting extra weight into his next words. "Everything. Pictures, scents, dreams. Everything."

"Nothing?"

Benedict shook his head. "I cannot do it."

The finality in those words hit all three of them. He saw the anguish in his friend's eyes. He felt Janelle's flinch as she understood the problem. And he knew a misery that railed at God or fate or whatever had created this mess.

There was no part of Janelle that didn't draw him, no aspect of her that he didn't desire. Even now, in this miserable disaster of a situation, his cock lay heavy against his thigh. She was beautiful, and he wanted her. She was another man's wife, and yet he loved her. If only he had been born the earl and Benedict, the bastard. He could have the woman of his dreams, and Benedict would have an excuse for his desires. Society believed all manner of perversion afflicted those born illegitimate. But it was Benedict who needed an heir and Gabriel who was cursed to long for another man's wife.

Gabriel sighed. "Maybe in time…" His voice trailed away as Benedict shook his head. Then anger burst through him, pulling out the commander in him for all that he was the subordinate. "Damn it, Benny! Don't shake your head at me. You created this mess. It is upon you to find the solution."

Normally when he used that tone, Benedict snapped to attention. It was the one sure-fire way of breaking his friend out of the turmoil in his head. But this time, Benedict didn't stiffen. His chin did not go up and he did not pull up to his full height. If anything, he relaxed.

"I have," Benedict said, his voice low. "You need only embrace it."

Janelle noticed the change in his tone. Her head came up as her hands clenched the fabric of her gown. "What?"

There was a chair nearby, one set at an angle to the fire which still allowed a full view of the bed. Benedict crossed to that and sunk down.

The man had changed tactics. Gabriel had seen the shift often enough to know that Benedict had given up on one plan and had moved seamlessly to the next. His tone confirmed it because there was a note of command in it.

"Take off your clothes, Gabriel. Janelle, please do so as well."

"What?" she gasped.

Gabriel did not make a sound. He couldn't. Every part of his body had locked down tight.

"Surely you have heard of this, Janelle. I know Gabriel has. Three people in a bedroom, and all entertained."

"Not like this!" Gabriel choked out. "Benedict, I…I…"

His friend's eyes cut to him. "You what, Gabriel? Do you think I haven't seen it? We have faced battles together, I have watched you with tarts, and I know that your body and mind are caught." He gestured at Janelle. "Have you had her yet?"

"No!"

"But did you want to?"

Yes. A thousand times yes. He felt his cheeks flame with heat, and he saw Janelle's gaze drop to her hands.

"I am pure, my lord," she said, her voice clear. "I did not betray you. I would not."

"I could not," Gabriel said.

"I think you could," Benedict said. "If I allowed it. If I begged you to do it." He looked at his wife. "Look at him, Janelle, and tell me that you don't want this, too."

She shook her head, her mind clearly struggling. And while her gaze hopped between the two of them, Benedict pushed it even further.

"Didn't you just tell me you are a practical woman?"

"Riding postillion is not the same as… as…"

"Riding my best man?" Gallows humor filled Benedict's tone. It was the way he covered his own self-hatred. But as much as Gabriel understood what drove the man, he could not allow this to continue.

"Don't be cruel," he snapped. "This isn't the time to jest."

"It is exactly the time," Benedict returned. Then he stood up, his movements languid again and assured, though there was a manic gleam in his eyes. "Very well," he drawled. "I will state practicalities. I need an heir, but I cannot do the deed. You and I have a similar look, Gabriel. Same jaw, similar hair. Even our eyes are near enough."

"You cannot have planned this!" Janelle cried.

Gabriel knew better. Benedict could absolutely have planned this. He'd known it was a possibility. "Is that why you left for the last three weeks? Is this why you threw us together?"

The man shrugged. "I allowed for various possibilities." He quirked his brows. "This, I think, is the happiest one."

"Happy!" Janelle exclaimed.

"Yes," Benedict said, his tone growing harder. "Your children, Gabriel, your flesh and blood will inherit my title, my fortune. Your daughters will be ladies, your son an earl. Isn't that the fondest wish of your bastard heart? Isn't that a dream come true for you?"

"Not like this."

"There is no other way." He came close enough to murmur into Gabriel's ear. "This is the only way to have her."

His every thought rebelled at the idea. But his body, oh God, his body was already burning with the idea. Especially when Benedict pulled Janelle to her feet. He didn't jerk her upright, but took her hand and slowly, inevitably drew her upright until she faced him.

The moonlight outlined her every curve. He saw the uncertainty on her face, but he also saw understanding. Then she turned to her husband.

"You cannot truly wish this?" It was phrased as a statement but spoken as a question.

Benedict touched his knuckles to her face. "I love him as I love no other. I chose you as I have chosen no other."

"But—"

"Do you love him?"

She winced and looked away. She would not confess to loving someone other than her husband. But Benedict would not let her hide.

"Tell him you want him."

"Stop torturing her," Gabriel said before she could speak. He already knew her desires. She had told them to her, whispered them into his ears, kissed them into his skin. And he had wanted to make every one come true.

Benedict sighed and took his wife's face in his hands. He was gentle as he drew her face up to his, but he didn't lower himself to kiss her as Gabriel would. Instead, he spoke clearly and allowed no modesty to color her answer.

"Do you understand what I am asking?"

Her body strengthened as she faced her husband. "You need an heir. And you would like your wife and your…" She swallowed. "And your best friend to give you that heir. Because you cannot."

"Yes." He stroked her cheek. "Do you agree?"

The pause was long enough that Gabriel nearly went mad from waiting. But when it came, it hit him like a blow.

"Yes."

The word jolted through Gabriel's body like lightning. Then she continued, her voice low but no less clear.

"But I do not think he can. I…" She sighed. "I asked him, Benedict. I asked him before the wedding, and he—"

"He refused. Yes, I had guessed as much. He has always been loyal and more godly than the priests themselves."

Janelle jerked out his hands. "Do not mock him!" she snapped. "You are putting him in an impossible situation!"

Him? It was no hardship to tup a beautiful woman. It was not impossible to cuckold his superior officer and his best friend. It was merely…

Benedict shook his head. "Honor has always meant more to Gabe that his life. But I think you underestimate your allure, Janelle."

Benedict's hand was quick where it flattened Gabriel's trousers. A single stroke, both infinitely pleasurable and immediately repulsive. It was a clash of physical and mental response that left him stiff and awkward. And it was exactly what was needed to show that he was already hard at the thought of having Janelle.

"He wants you," Benedict said as he took a step back. "You want him. And I want an heir." The man smiled as if this were the most natural situation in the world. "There is the solution, my dearest friends. Now it is up to you to execute it."

Chapter Thirty-Seven

"STOP IT!" JANELLE snapped at Benedict. "Let me think!" At that moment, she couldn't possibly hate her husband more. It was one thing to keep her ignorant of his…difficulty…until after their wedding. It was another thing entirely to bring Gabriel into this disaster.

And yet if there were anyone she would want with her tonight, anyone who could hold her hand while she made sense of this, well, it would be Gabriel. Indeed, she believed it would always be him. She turned away from her husband and stepped up to the man she loved.

"I won't do it," she said, "if you don't want to." She reached out and grabbed his near hand. It was clenched tight at his side, a hard fist that was part of a body gone rigid. "It doesn't have to be you."

She winced when she said that, but it was nothing compared to the reaction he gave. He gripped her arms and his eyes blazed into her. "You will not go elsewhere!"

"I won't," she swore. "I…" Her heart wrenched in her chest. "I don't know what to do. I don't want to hurt you."

His gaze softened at that, and his expression shifted as if it were torn. She saw anguish and pain, but also desire. And a wrenching whisper of hope.

"Do you want this?" she whispered.

"Yes." His word was barely audible.

"Then why do you hesitate?" She guessed at the answer.

Honor. Loyalty. Pride. Any of those words would fit, and she could argue every one. "When the husband and wife both allow it, there is no sin," she said. He understood practicalities, and Benedict was right. This was a solution.

But a moment's thought told her Gabriel's refusal wasn't about practicality or logic. If it were, he'd already be in her bed.

"This is about love, isn't it?" she asked. "You love him and have pledged to serve him however he asks. You love me, you have said as much. So what is the thing that love cannot conquer?" She touched his face, stroking along the harsh cut of his jaw.

He closed his eyes, and his body shook. His hands tightened on her arms as his breath heaved. "I want this," he finally rasped. "I want you, but it cannot be right."

And there it was. The rule of right and wrong, honored or sinful. She had long since decided that the church's laws were not meant for everyone. She had tended good women who the church damned through no fault of their own. She guessed that Lord Benedict had felt cursed the first time he felt his unnatural urges, and yet he served his country nobly and was accounted a great man.

But what of Gabriel? He was a bastard, tainted the moment he was born, surrounded by sin throughout his childhood. He had built his life in another direction, serving his country and acting with a warrior's honor. And now she was asking him to bend the one thing he valued over all other things—his morality.

"I'm sorry," she whispered, her heart breaking. "We are asking you to break—"

"Not break!" Benedict pressed, taking a step forward. "Bend, Gabriel. A little bend."

Gabriel turned to her husband, his eyes flashing and his voice grating like stone on stone. "You want this, Benny? Truly?"

Benedict didn't hesitate. "I do."

"Then leave. Get out of this room. Hell, get out of the castle. The rest is between her and me."

Her husband's eyes narrowed. He looked to Janelle, and she nodded, telling him that she agreed. More than that, she wanted him out of the discussion.

"Go," she ordered.

Benedict nodded, but he didn't leave yet. Instead, he spoke, his voice gentle but no less clear. "I have thought of other options," he said. "There are babes to adopt quietly. She could pretend to be pregnant."

Janelle blinked. The depth of his thoughts unnerved her. Her mind hadn't even gone to such places, but apparently he had already contemplated it.

"It could be done," Benedict continued, "but I prefer this."

"To be cuckolded?" Gabriel asked, the words spoken like an accusation. Benedict shook his head.

"If I cannot sire the child, then I would have a child from the two people I care for the most." He swallowed. "Gabriel, how many times have I said you are the better man? A thousand times out loud. A million more in my thoughts."

"You are a good man."

"As are you."

They looked at each other long and hard. What passed between them, she did not know, except that a measure of tension left Gabriel's body. And when it drained away, Benedict nodded. Then he gave her a half smile, one of apology and respect before quietly leaving the room.

Which left the two of them now. She said nothing. It was enough to stand near him, to feel his hand—now gentle—upon her arm. And to wait for what he chose.

Rather than speak, he pulled her into his arms. He tucked her close and set his cheek against her forehead. He was not a man to speak his pain, and yet she heard it in the rasp of his breath and the slow stroke of his hand up and down her back.

"Why would you agree to this?" he whispered against her forehead.

"Because I love you."

Only now when she was pressed against him did she feel the way those words struck him. He tensed almost imperceptibly. Then he trembled as if shaking them away.

"You don't believe that," she abruptly realized. "You don't think I can love you." She jerked backwards, staring into his eyes as she struggled to understand. "I wanted to throw everything away for you. I asked you to marry me! Do you think I would do that for anything except love?"

He shook his head, his mouth pressed tight. And in that one gesture she finally understood.

"You don't believe you deserve love. Somehow, somewhere, you decided you cannot receive what is freely given." She pressed her palm to his chest above her heart. "You cannot believe it in here."

His head bowed until she could not see his face. But she did not need to see to know that his eyes were wet with tears. He shuddered in her arms, and she knew that finally she had come to the core of it.

"I cannot force you to believe, Gabriel. You must open yourself to the idea that I love you. That Benedict loves you as truly as if you were brothers. I have said it. He has said it." She cupped his face in her palm and stroked her thumb across his cheek. "But you must love yourself before you can feel anything from us."

She waited for her words to sink in. She had known people who could not accept their own value, no matter what was said. But in this, he proved stronger than those others. He lifted his gaze to hers.

"Help me," he whispered. "I cannot believe it without you."

She smiled. That was the easiest thing to do. She lifted her face to his and she began to whisper words between kisses. She began with the easiest. "I love you." Then she pressed her mouth to his. The kiss was short, barely a press of flesh, because she wanted to say more. "I think you are the best man I know." Another kiss, this time to his cheek. "You're honest—" Kiss. "—smart—" Kiss. "—kind—" Kiss. "True—"

She would have said more. She felt every word she uttered sink into his body as if pushing open a stuck door. At first, he flinched or stiffened, but with every word, he moved more with her than against her. His hands stopped tightening and began to stroke more than clench. And where his breath seemed trapped with catches and jerks, he now inhaled as if waking from a long sleep. Deeper and stronger as his mouth opened against her cheek.

And then he abruptly scooped her up into his arms. She gasped in surprise as she flung her arms around his shoulders. He carried her quickly to the bed, laying her down before stroking his knuckles across her cheeks.

"You are so beautiful," he said as his gaze roved over her face and then down her body. "I cannot believe you are m—" His voice cut off before he said the word "mine."

"I am yours," she said as she smiled at him. "My marriage wasn't formed from love. We both know that. My heart and my body are yours." She trailed her fingers across his cheeks. "My children, too."

His eyes flashed fire at that, a burst of joy that lit up his whole face. Then he kissed her. The press of his mouth was fierce, the thrust of his tongue possessive. She opened herself to him, loving the feel of him taking her. He left no part of her mouth untouched.

His hands coiled across her jaw and neck, then stroked down her body. His hands were unsteady, but the strength in them was real. And though he stroked a fire in her skin, she grew frustrated with how careful he was with the fabric.

She brought his face up to hers. "The silk was for Benedict. Tear it away."

The sound he released was half groan, half growl. His fists bunched against her chest as he ripped the fabric from breast to stern. And when the seam caught and held, he used his teeth to break the thread. He didn't let any part of it pull on her body as he removed it.

When she lay completely naked before him, he sat back. He looked at her with such hunger as his fingers traced the moonlight across her skin. Such reverence in his caress. It made her skin tingle and her heart swell.

"My turn," she said. She wasn't gentle as she pulled off his clothing. She felt a strange savageness as she stripped him naked. She was claiming him as surely as he wanted her. And while she pulled every scrap of fabric off his body, he stroked his hands through her hair, and he kissed whatever he could reach of her body until they tumbled about the bed in a wild abandon. It was maddening getting all those clothes off him. And it was made more difficult as his fingers found her breasts and her thighs.

She was on her knees when she finally managed to pull off his falls. His organ sprang free, thick and ruddy. She smelled his scent, felt his heat, and bent to taste it because it was right there. Because she wanted him inside her body. And because she knew it would pleasure him.

It did. His body went tight, and his hips flexed. He went deep into her mouth while a shudder of delight slid through his frame.

She thought she had the upper hand. She knew how this put him at her mercy. But in that, she erred because his fingers found her cleft. He stroked her deftly, quickly, and the urgency built in her so fast that she writhed.

He toppled her easily. And while she gasped on the bed, he kissed her breasts. He knew just how to tease them. He knew she liked it when he sucked on her nipples and teased the tight buds with his teeth. Her whole body felt so alive. Every cell reached for him. Every breath felt shared with him.

She wriggled, loving the feel of the hot length of his cock. He growled as he pressed against her, but it wasn't enough, and it wasn't in the right place.

She wrapped her arms around him, trying to pull him upwards, but he refused to budge. "Not yet," he murmured against her ear while his fingers pushed into her body. One at first, hard and calloused. Then a second with steady pressure.

"Not yet?" she gasped. "Gabriel, please!" She was bursting for waiting, but he nibbled at her jaw while his fingers kept up their work.

"Such a sight," he said. He lifted up to watch her while a third finger joined the second.

He stretched her as he did that, and her eyes fluttered at the marvelous feel. Her legs were spread open, and her buttocks kept tightening, pushing him deeper.

Her stomach coiled tight. She knew what was coming, she knew the feel of pleasure as it burst across her skin, but this time she wanted more. This time was for them together. So she gripped his shoulders and pulled him forward. She grabbed his face and impressed her words upon him.

"I want you now."

He grinned as he moved, and she finally felt the weight of him atop her. He settled between her thighs, and she moaned as he slid his cock along her cleft. Twice he did that while she tried to drive herself down on him. Twice he held back, using his knees to press her thighs apart.

"This is love," he said as his cock finally slid to her opening.

"Yes," she said, not understanding why he was waiting.

"Janelle," he said, his words urgent enough to catch her attention. "It's not for him or for children. It's for you," he said. "For love."

So many words when she wanted action. So much thought when she was all but bursting for need of him. But his seriousness settled into her mind. His intensity brought her heart to match where he was.

This wasn't just penetration or propagation. This was love shared between them. Love felt and returned.

"I love you," she said.

"I love you," he said.

And then he thrust home.

A flash of sensation—bright pain, quickly fading. Then pleasure grew inside her.

He was so big, so hard. She was shocked by how much she wanted it. "More," she whispered as he thrust over and over.

She gripped him with arms and legs, loving the ride. She was impaled and exploding with sensation.

Until she shattered. Pleasure filled her. Ecstasy infused her.

He met her there, his body pulsing with hers.

And they held on to each other.

Riding the love.

As one.

Chapter Thirty-Eight

B ENEDICT WOKE THEM in the morning. He had spent much of the night just outside their door. He was punishing himself, he knew. He thought that sitting on hard stone while another man tupped his wife would be fitting punishment for his failure.

But a strange thing happened as the night wore on. Instead of growing angry with every rough exclamation, instead of feeling pain with the moans of pleasure or sighs of delight, he found himself feeling a sweet joy. His best friend and his wife were finding happiness together, and that made him…well, not quite happy. He was sure that given his perversion, he would never taste that emotion without shame. But at least he was content in their joy, and that was more than he had dared hope for.

So soon after dawn, he roused himself from his solitary punishment to feel a new hope inside. He performed his toilette as per usual, and then he gathered the breakfast Mrs. Carr had left for them, carrying it to the master bedroom.

He knocked quietly then entered, setting the tray down on the nearby table. Gabriel woke at once, his eyes popping open as he tightened his arm protectively around Janelle. She was sleeping, curled sweetly against Gabriel's side, but she woke and blinked, clearly trying to dash the sleep from her eyes.

"Good morning," Benedict said, his tone kind. That was not his usual way. He was refined in his diction, and often brusque. But this morning, he looked down on his closest friends and smiled, though a part of him damned himself for looking not at the beautiful woman but at the chiseled body of the man.

"Benny," Gabriel said, his tone tight.

"I've come to talk to you both about how the next few months shall go."

Gabriel pushed upright in the bed, using the sheet to cover her, not himself. Honestly, it would be less distracting if he'd done the opposite. Nevertheless, Benedict grabbed his wife's wrap, absently noting the shredded negligee on the floor, and handed it to her. She donned it quickly, her cheeks red with embarrassment while Gabriel thankfully, managed to pull on a shirt.

"I should like to stay here for a month," Benedict said, doing his best not to let his gaze linger on the tuft of chest hair peeking out through the V in Gabriel's shirt. "We shall rise not so very early and go riding, all three of us."

"All of us?" Janelle asked.

"All of us. I want the villagers to get used to the three of us together. I also want us to be easy companions, and that can only happen with time."

Gabriel was already thinking, his agile mind no doubt figuring out what Benedict planned. He would be able to guess a great deal, but not all. And Benedict looked forward to seeing Gabriel's face when he heard the rest. Or at least all that Benedict planned to share right then.

"The daytime will be left to our own pursuits, though I expect I shall need Gabriel's help." He sighed. "There is already a great deal of correspondence to manage."

"Of course, my lord."

"And you will always call me Benny, now. I think becoming the father of my children deserves at least that much."

Both Gabriel and Janelle stilled at that, but then they looked at one another with a kind of wide-eyed delight. Love had grown between them last night. It was now a palpable thing in the room. Odd that he didn't feel excluded by it. At best, he felt a whisper of a wish. No one would ever look at him like that, though the look they gave him now was close.

Very, very close.

"There is more," Gabriel said, his head tilting as he studied Benedict. "You have more than morning exercise in mind."

"I do," he confirmed. "The locals shall know you both. Janelle, there are even a few pregnant ladies I would like you to help."

She straightened up. "Really? Betty will be happy to—"

"Good God, not Betty!" He rolled his eyes at her. "You will help them as my wife and the lady of the castle."

She gaped at him. "But I thought... Isn't it unseemly for a lady to work?"

"If you had studied history rather than medicine, you would know that most ladies worked extremely hard and were often the midwives to the area. Furthermore, you will find that a countess is allowed a great deal more than a baron's daughter."

He watched as the realization rolled through her. Her mouth opened in surprise, but then steadily shifted to happiness. "I can be a midwife here? Without hiding?"

"Only a fool would stop a woman—wife or otherwise—from helping his people. So long as you are safe, I shall do everything I can to support your endeavors."

Gabriel took her hand in his. "I will see to her safety."

"You bloody well will. At least for now, I want you with her whenever she goes visiting and within earshot whenever she works."

"Done," Gabriel said, though Janelle rolled her eyes.

"I have been delivering babies for years without either of you hovering over me."

Benedict drew breath to explain that he would brook no argument, but he needn't have bothered. Gabriel was there before him, speaking reason to the stubborn woman.

"I can haul water and carry your bag. You know I will not interfere unless you need help. And it is dangerous for a countess to travel around at night without protection."

His voice allowed no argument, and she didn't give any. He didn't know if she saw reason or if she simply wanted Gabriel near. Either way made no difference. The decision was made.

"There is something else," Benedict continued. "When I was last here, I fired my steward. He was making a right hash of things and couldn't even bother to hide it. He's gone, and I want you to manage the land in his stead."

Gabriel gaped at him. "You what?"

Ah, there was that look that he adored. Total shock. It wasn't often that he surprised Gabriel. They had spent too much time in each other's company for that. But right now, he had shocked the man down to his toes.

"You've always wanted to own land, Gabriel. You've dreamed of it."

Gabriel shook his head. "I… No."

"You never thought it possible. You never thought you'd have the money to buy anything."

"I don't."

"And you still don't. But now you can try your hand at it. You've left the military. You cannot be a diplomat now given your agreement with your mother. This is something to learn." He gestured outside to the extensive land around them.

"I have to be in London."

"Part of the time. Perhaps most of the time. But you'll need a place to escape to, somewhere to clear your head of London." Then before Gabriel could argue more, he shrugged. "In any event, you've got a month to figure it out. Maybe more." He flashed a smile at Janelle. "Long enough to get you with child. I want no questions if I have to hurry off to Vienna."

Janelle's cheeks colored at that, but she nodded.

"I've told Mr. and Mrs. Carr and those children to stay away while we honeymoon. You can hire workmen if you like, Gabriel. Fix up whatever you think necessary. Just be sure they are gone by evening meal which we will share together. And then," he grinned as he gestured to the bed. "Then I shall retire to my den and you two shall make me a son, yes? I shall love a daughter equally well, of course, but a son will carry my title."

Gabriel leaned back against the bedboard. "You've got this all figured out then, don't you?"

"I do," he answered, trying—and failing—to not appear smug. "Do you know Gabriel purchased the Rose Garden and My Lady's Apothecary for you."

"What?" Janelle gasped. "How?"

"You should ask Gabriel that. It was a heavy price." He winked at Janelle. "In any event, it's your wedding present from him. And mine is that I shall pay for the repairs to the property." He grunted as he drank his tea. "He'll manage the repairs though because I haven't the least interest in that."

Janelle pressed her hands to her mouth, her eyes wet with tears. She started to say something, but appeared too overcome to speak. As usual, Gabriel was already working the logistics.

"We can split our time between here and London," he said. "There's a great deal to do in both places, but we can manage it." He looked to Janelle. "If you want it."

"Of course, I want it!" she exclaimed. "It's everything I've ever wanted!"

Such a wonder to give to a woman who knew the value of what she was offered, who appreciated the gift even as she planned to expand and grow things that he had merely started. And then she surprised him by setting her hand atop his. She curled her fingers around until he had no choice but to entwine their fingers together.

"What about you, Benedict? What of your happiness?"

"Don't you understand?" he asked. "Give me children, Janelle. Lots of them. Give them your intelligence and his strength. Let me teach them what it means to carry a title and let Gabriel show them how to thrive when everything is stacked against them. That will be the secret joy of my days."

It wasn't a lie, but it also wasn't the full truth. She was still too innocent to realize that he would never feel the happiness that she did. He was too twisted around with shame to ever stand fully in the light as she did, as Gabriel would one day soon.

But for the moment, he had forged a good foundation. Even if he could not fully participate in happiness, he could feel satisfaction in what they built. And he would be content with that.

His gaze turned to Gabriel who watched him with steady eyes. Gabriel knew what Janelle did not yet comprehend—that Gabriel was the bridge between Benedict's darkness and Janelle's light. He was the one who would forge all three of their lives into perfection through sheer force of will. He was the brick and the mortar on which all things were built.

And for that, Benedict was eternally grateful.

"Thank you," Gabriel said.

"It is my absolute pleasure," he answered. And then he pushed up to his feet. "Now eat up," he said as he pointed to the tray. "We're all staying in this morning. I shall be busy sorting out a way to satisfy those damned Italians. Napoleon has fired them up, and now they want blood. They are a lovely people in general, but stubborn when they have a mind to be."

"I shall be down immediately," Gabriel said and began to climb out of bed. Benedict stopped him.

"You will not move a muscle this day except in the pursuit of rest and what pleasure you desire. My lady, he has done the work of ten men these last few weeks. I will be very cross if he exerts himself today in anything but the most restorative of ways."

"Restorative?" Janelle said, her tone laced with humor. "I've heard it called worse things."

"Excellent," Benedict said as he headed for the door. "I shall leave his care in your expert hands." He had his hand on the doorknob when his wife called out his name. Her tone was sweet, but no less firm.

"Lord Benedict!"

He paused, twisting around enough to see the earnestness on her face. "Yes?"

"There is love here," she said. Then she grimaced at her awkward phrasing. "I mean, I have love for you, too. We both do." And though Gabriel didn't speak, he nodded his agreement.

The wall around Benedict's heart softened and warmth spilled through the cracks. Odd how a woman's smile could do that for him when he usually had no use for them. But Janelle was different. He had known it from the beginning.

He smiled. "You once spoke to me about finding a secret elixir. A magic potion of some sort to ease the pain of childbirth."

She nodded. "I'm hoping for something to prevent childbed fever as well, but—"

"There is no elixir, I think, to keep pain away. No life can avoid it, but I think you have found your magic potion to get us through it."

Janelle shook her head, not understanding him, and no wonder. She did not have the history with him that Gabriel did.

"Benny is talking philosophy," Gabe said. "He does that when he is happy."

And now his wife appeared even more confused. "Philosophy?"

"Love, my dear," Benedict continued. "That is the secret. Gabriel is the bridge between us and a glorious future. But you, my dear, you carry the magic."

She snorted. "I am not—"

"You are," Gabriel interrupted as he pressed a kiss to her palm. "You are the magic elixir, the special potion, the love that will cement us together."

She looked at the two of them, her expression amused. "It appears you both speak nonsense when happy. Very well, I am the magic elixir. You are the bridge. What are you, my lord?"

"Happy," he said with complete honesty. "Very, very happy."

Then he left them to their amusements while he sought his own. And if God was kind, his heir would appear in good time. Then life would become very exciting indeed.

Epilogue

TWO WEEKS OF bliss later, Janelle stepped into the castle great room, only to pull up short. She had flowers in her arms and a vague plan about setting up a display in the dining room. She'd never spent time on such things but had become enamored of the idea when seeing a young girl gathering blooms that morning. The little girl planned on giving them to her brand-new baby sister who had been born just that morning, thanks to Janelle's help.

And now, Janelle wanted to try her hand at flower decor, only to see that Gabriel had beaten her to it. He stood at the front of the great room by the huge fireplace. He'd set greens down on the floor and put vases of flowers on the mantel. And he smiled as he looked up at her, though his expression held chagrin. "I thought you were resting!" he said.

"I was. But then I thought about flowers," she said, feeling stupid. He was dressed in his military uniform, as exquisitely handsome a sight as she could ever imagine, especially as the late afternoon sunlight dappled his hair. "What is all this?" she asked.

"I wanted to ask you something," he said as he came to stand in front of her. "Something for just us, while Ben's in London."

Despite her husband's determination to stay with them for the entire month, Lord Benedict had been called away. He was due back this evening, but for the moment, the castle held just her and Gabriel.

"Do you know anything about my father?" he asked.

Janelle frowned. "I…um, no. Nothing much except that he's the Duke of Torbay."

Gabriel nodded. "He's Scottish on his mother's side, though he tries to hide it. And if there were any soul I wished to claim from my bloodline, it would be her." He lifted the flowers from Janelle's arms and sprinkled them amid the greenery. "She was a kind woman, worthy of being cherished. She would have loved you."

"Did you spend much time with her?"

"Not enough. She found me in the last year of her life. She brought me to live with her in Scotland for one summer. It was the best summer of my life." He grinned. "Until now."

Warmth spread through Janelle. She was pleased that Gabriel had had some love in his boyhood. "I want to hear all about it."

"Soon. But first, there is a thing that they do in Scotland that I'd like to try. It's not approved of by the Crown, but some traditions are stubborn. It's called a handfast ceremony."

Janelle had never heard of such a thing, but she could tell it was important to him. And so she listened, even as he sank down on one knee before her.

"Gabe?"

"It's a marriage, Janelle, but it has no legal power in England."

She flushed, looking down at his upturned face. How handsome he was there on one knee before her. How much she adored him.

"Janelle, will you handfast to me? Will you love and honor me as a wife would her husband? As I swear to do the same with you?"

Her breath caught in her throat, her heart beating triple time. "Yes," she whispered. "Yes."

She sank down to her knees before him, before the fireplace and the array of flowers, and in a pool of sunlight. He matched her pose, holding right hands. She wanted to kiss him right then and there, but it wasn't the moment. Instead, she spoke clearly.

"I will love and honor you as a wife does her husband, for you are my heart and my soul."

His eyes shone, and his hand tightened with hers. Then he used his left hand to pull a cord of braided colors out of his pocket. He wrapped it around their wrists.

"These cords are binds between us. Red for love, blue for devotion, black for strength, and green…" He flashed her a grin.

"For fertility?"

"Yes."

She smiled as she took one end of the cord and wrapped another loop around their wrists. "Devotion, strength, fertility," she said, "and love. So much love."

"My heart and soul," he said.

"Until death do us part."

"We are wed."

Then he kissed her, lightly at first, then with increasing strength. And though she was not a fanciful person, she felt the promise in that kiss solidify into a vow, as surely as if his heart and hers were magically linked forever.

It was love, of course. Love that bound them, strengthened them, and overflowed into everything they touched.

Their kiss would have continued. Right there in a bed of flowers, they would have consummated what they had just promised. But they were interrupted.

At some point, Benedict had slipped into the room. He clapped his hands in happiness, startling them and admonishing them in the way that was purely his.

"In order to be legal," he said, "the vows must be witnessed. Glad I made it home in time."

Gabriel groaned as he pressed his forehead to Janelle's. "Ben, must you interrupt?"

"I must!" he said cheerfully as he stepped up to them. And before Janelle could say anything, he dropped another piece of paper in front of them. It landed on the flowers, like an offering to them.

"What's that?" Gabriel asked as he peered at the sheets of linen.

"That's really why I had to go to London. Consider it a hand-fast present."

Janelle reached for the papers. "What have you done?"

"I bought the brothel."

"What?" Gabriel cried.

"Well, I can't very well have my steward's name all over a brothel, now can I?"

"But Benedict," Gabriel continued, "you can't own one either!"

"No, I can't. But I can sell it to Madame Florina for a tidy profit. On the condition that neither your name nor mine ever be associated with her business again."

Gabriel stared at Benedict, his mind clearly spinning. Janelle's was, too, but she recovered quickly. "So he's free?" she asked. "He's free of his mother?"

"Completely."

She grinned as she turned back to Gabriel. "You're free, my love. She has no hold on you."

"Free," he whispered. Then he scooped her up, rising to his feet before spinning them around. "Free!" Then he stopped, setting her gently back down. "And happily bound to you, my love."

How she loved this man. "I love you, too," she whispered.

"And I," Benedict said as he headed to the kitchen, "think I'll go celebrate my good fortune. You two...carry on."

About the Author

Flirty, dirty and fun! That's how Katherine Lyons likes her love stories. One would think that would lead her to contemporary romance, but she's always loved the witty dialogue and hot, sexy humor of regency romance. She's a big fan of *The Bridgertons, Big Bang Theory* (even though it's over), and her favorite movie is *The Avengers* because she loves the MCU. Stop by her website to sign up for her newsletter, special contests, and geeky giveaways!

www.katherine-lyons.com

www.ingramcontent.com/pod-product-compliance
Lightning Source LLC
Chambersburg PA
CBHW061306030726
47595CB00001B/226